One White Lie

LEAH KONEN

PENGUIN BOOKS

PENGUIN BOOKS

UK | USA | Canada | Ireland | Australia
India | New Zealand | South Africa

Penguin Books is part of the Penguin Random House group of companies
whose addresses can be found at global.penguinrandomhouse.com.

First published by Michael Joseph 2020
This edition published by Penguin Books 2020
001

Copyright © Leah Konen, 2020

The moral right of the author has been asserted

Printed and bound in Great Britain by Clays Ltd, Elcograf S.p.A.

A CIP catalogue record for this book is available from the British Library

ISBN: 978–1–405–94487–8

PENGUIN BOOKS

One White Lie

Leah Konen is an author of young adult fiction, and *One White Lie* is her debut psychological thriller. As a journalist, her work has been published in *Elle Decor*, *Metropolitan Home*, *The Fiscal Times*, *Parenting*, *Good Housekeeping's Quick and Simple*, and *The Huffington Post*, among others. She lives in Brooklyn and Saugerties, NY, with her husband and their dog, Farley.

For Eleanor

One

People have all sorts of ideas about what they'd do if it happened to them.

They'd tell their friends. They'd make that call. They'd leave. They certainly wouldn't continue on like normal, banging out personal essays or temping at whatever online mag needed a freelance editor for the day. They'd tell their family (assuming they still had family in their lives to tell), they'd keep themselves busy (pottery class! political campaigns! yoga!). They'd heal, and they'd move on, and they'd *rebuild their lives*.

That's what I'd always thought, too.

The exit for Woodstock, New York, came into view, my eyes flitting nervously to the rearview mirror as I quickly pulled off the ramp. Suddenly, I was in the country, pastures and horses, rundown schoolhouses, abandoned barns, and bucolic churches sprinkled over the landscape: *Rural Mad Libs*. I found Shadow Creek Road at the end of a particularly snakelike stretch. I turned, so eager to get out of the car and get to step two of this plan that I hardly slowed at all . . .

I slammed on the brakes as the deer froze, staring me down.

My body lurched forward; Dusty yelped as he thunked against the side of his crate. My blood pumped heavy and fast, flushing me with heat. I struggled to catch my breath as the doe's eyes flashed at mine. *What are you doing? What in God's name do you think you're doing?* She pranced away, the heft of her body disappearing into the tall grasses of the meadow, as quickly as she'd come.

My throat burned hot, acid rising, and I rammed the car into park. I jumped out and rushed to the passenger side, whipping open the back door. 'You okay, buddy?' I asked. Dusty licked my hand, my erratic driving apparently not doing him too much harm. 'I'm sorry,' I said, attempting to swallow the bitterness in the back of my mouth, nauseated at the realization that I was unable to prevent my own dog from getting hurt. I couldn't bear to lose him, too.

A car pulled up behind me, an old butter-yellow Mercedes. In the air, the smell of fried food – Davis and I had once dreamed of converting a diesel Mercedes to run on biodiesel, used cooking oil, free from restaurants. A woman climbed out of the driver's side, graceful and lithe. Her golden hair shimmered in the sunlight, falling down her back, stick straight. Her cheekbones were high, her boobs perky, and her arms annoyingly taut. She wore black spandex pants and a loose black tank over a hot-pink sports bra – the kind of woman for whom 'athleisure' was invented. What did she want?

'You okay?' she asked, eyes scrunching up with concern. 'Do you need help?'

Her words made tears prick my eyes. I needed more help than she could possibly know. Quickly, I shut the door as Dusty whined. 'It was just a deer,' I managed. 'It surprised me, but I'm fine.' Before she could say anything else, I was back in my car, shifting into drive.

In the rearview mirror, I saw her, eyes locked straight ahead – watching to make sure I was okay, or watching me? She was still following when I reached the farmhouse, the one the agent had told me to look out for. It was gorgeously decrepit, with red siding,

2

peeling white trim, and a sloping roof whose edges sharpened to a point. I passed it, watching as the woman turned into the driveway – my new neighbor.

I inched down the road but didn't see another house, only a meadow on one side and fat-leaved trees on the other. I pulled over, checking the rearview once again. I grabbed my phone. Its SIM card had been replaced yesterday, but the screen was shattered – it would take at least a hundred dollars to fix it. I opened my new email, keying in my password and finding the response from the agent, Jennifer Moon, whose email signature featured two colors and a swirling font.

> Hi Lucy! Thanks for your quick reply. I'm so thrilled you'll
> be renting the cottage, and yes, cash payment is just fine!
> Your little blue house is JUST AFTER the red farmhouse,
> with a small porch facing the driveway. This is your new
> HOME! The key is in the lockbox, code 3321. Welcome!

Gravel ground beneath the wheels as I jerked back onto the road. My dad would have freaked that I'd bought the Accord from a guy on Craigslist, handing over a precious three thousand in cash for a key on a 'Miami, Florida' key ring. He'd panic at this whole plan of mine. Of course, if he were around, I wouldn't need one. He and my mom would be my plan.

Finally, I saw it. It was quaint, royal blue, with a tiny wooden porch surrounded by uncut grass. Hell, it even had a porch swing, something I'd always wanted, back when I'd imagined Davis and me, far away from the city, a little girl with my eyes and his mouth playing with blocks at our feet. The possibilities seemed endless then, our future stretching out like dominoes, one day triggering the next.

I parked and quickly freed Dusty from his prison. He peed on the first bush he could find, then followed me onto the porch. I entered the code on the lockbox, and a silver key fell into my hand. The front door opened easily, almost too easily, and once inside, I checked the dead bolt three times.

The place was furnished. The last tenant had been a single woman, too, but the house was owned by an older couple who'd relocated to Phoenix a few years ago to be near their grandson – all info Jennifer Moon had offered before I had a chance to ask.

Dusty did a perimeter check, just as he'd done at the shitty Days Inn in Queens where we'd been holed up for the last two days, his tiny white body fluttering around like a giant cotton ball. I surveyed the room: two small navy sofas in front of a wood-burning stove with logs sitting next to it; bookshelves filled with Catskills hiking books, a Buddhism paperback, and a set of encyclopedias; a wooden rocking chair in one corner and double windows on either side.

The bedroom was a sardine can, with a wrought-iron bed my mom would have loved and a gaudy floral quilt she would have hated, a desk too small to be useful, and a closet in the corner. I grabbed my tote bag and emptied the contents onto the bed:

- Birth certificate
- Social Security card
- Passport and IDs
- Debit and credit cards
- Mom's scarf
- Dad's hammer
- Envelope of cash

Arranging them on the bed, I touched each item, as if it might disappear in front of me if I didn't keep tabs. Dusty scrambled across the papers, but I shooed him away. This was my life. Plastic and paper, cash and silk. I grabbed the envelope, counting the money once again – just over ten grand – then placed the hammer on the nightstand for protection. I fingered the scarf, creamy white and bordered with a stripe of royal blue and flower buds. Lifting it closer, I inspected the marred, murky brown corner. I would never forgive Davis for that. I let it fall to the bed, then stared at the rest of my things, trying to figure out what to do with it all.

Outside, a twig snapped, sharp as a firecracker.

Dusty barked and I bolted up. I grabbed the hammer and ran to the window, pulling back the drapes, heart like a drum.

A rabbit, long-footed and gray. It hopped off.

I took a deep yoga breath. I was like a scared animal sometimes, worse than Dusty with his tail between his legs.

I set the hammer down and pushed the bed aside, metal screeching against the floorboards. I knelt, knees leaving prints in the blanket of dust, and carefully pressed each plank. After five minutes, I found one that felt loose, a few inches off the baseboard. I pried it up with the claw of the hammer, creating a space about ten inches long, four inches wide, then tucked away each item, everything but money for rent and my mother's scarf, and pressed the board back into place. I ran my hands from side to side, scattering the dust, before repositioning the bed.

I needed a drink. I'd forced myself to abstain since I left, knowing I had to keep a clear head. It was almost three, earlier than I'd start in regular life, but it seemed okay, considering. This was my new reality: I lived in a sweet little cottage, woodland creatures romped about, and I stored my possessions under the floorboards – who's to say I had to wait till six?

'What do you think?' I asked Dusty. 'Has Mommy earned a drink?'

From my suitcase, I retrieved Davis's last good bottle of whiskey, the one I'd stolen two days ago, and headed to the kitchen. I glanced around the room, and my eyes caught on a doggie door, something I'd have to train Dusty to use properly. I poured a couple fingers of whiskey into a small juice glass and took a sip. I peered outside – the fenced-in postage stamp of yard was surrounded by an expanse of woods. This was the perfect place for us. It had to be.

Back in the bedroom, I situated myself on the bed, opened my laptop, and logged in to the VPN I'd signed up for, the one that would scramble my IP address, keeping my connection untraceable, just in case. I loaded my old email, fearing the worst, but there were no new messages, nothing more than retail spam and nonprofit solicitations, stoking fear in a bid for more donations.

I read over the draft I'd written last night, chest constricting at the thought of what my best friend, Ellie, might already know.

> Hey girl!
>
> Sorry for the last-minute notice, but I'm going to miss dinner tonight! I've decided to go back to Seattle for a few months. I'm going to finally go through my parents' storage unit and try to actually make progress on my freelance career somewhere that's slightly less expensive than Brooklyn. In addition to thinking, WTF, you're probably wondering about what happened with Davis. I'm sad to say we're going our separate ways. I wanted to tell you in person, but I just couldn't bear it. I'm sorry.
>
> Love you dearly, and I hate to bail without saying bye, but it all came together really fast. When I'm settled, let's plan a West Coast reunion, pretty please?
>
> .Xxoo
> L

Before I could doubt myself, I hit Send.

Two

You'd think it would be easy to cut ties with a man like Davis, a natural reaction for a forward-thinking woman like me. But it wasn't. Instead, he was like any other addiction, far easier to return to, to rationalize, than to give up completely. Just. One. More. Little. Sip. If only there were an AA for shitty boyfriends, for the women who found them impossible to leave.

It was nearing four, and my first glass had been drained, before I got up the nerve to email Davis.

> I went back to Seattle. You can't control us anymore.

Then I attached the photo, my insurance against any future punishment. The only one I had.

Inside me, I could feel it, the hatch opening up, just a crack, anger brewing at all that had happened between us, but I shut it tight, as I knew I had to, took a deep breath, and hit Send.

For a split second, I imagined him reading it, his knuckles turning white against the edges of his phone. Then I imagined the alternative, and I prayed he was okay, my stomach tying itself in knots as my heart beat mercilessly.

Pushing the fear aside, I logged out of my old email and back into my new one, lucykingwriter92@gmail.com, filled with only

7

the back-and-forth about the cottage, a 'Welcome to Gmail' message, and a few errant pieces of spam.

Then I did what I'd been doing for more months than I'd like to admit, to cope – I drank.

When I'd run out of internet black holes to fall into, when the second glass had become the third, when Dusty whined for food and I realized it was almost nine, I opened a can of dog food and ordered a pizza for myself, from one of the only places in town that delivered. Then I drank some more.

Dusty pawed at my face.

My eyes sprang open. It was morning, light surrounding the edges of the drapes like a halo. I had all my clothes on, and I was on top of the quilt, hair smushed, like a doll tossed aside after playtime was over. My jaw was tight. I'd been grinding my teeth, something I did when I was scared, a habit from childhood that was impossible to break.

I still hadn't gotten used to waking up without Davis. It was hard not to imagine him in his spot, legs tangled among the sheets, the nook of his shoulders ready for me to nestle into. His blond hair unkempt, his cowlick untamed, his thick glasses, ones we'd picked out together, sitting on the nightstand, waiting. His eyes fluttering open – *Morning, babe.*

Now his place in bed was occupied by a grease-stained box of Cicero's pizza. The smell of sausage turned my stomach.

For better or worse, Davis had become an integral part of my life very quickly. There to accompany me to a friend's birthday party. There to see the latest indie movie, try a recipe I'd found online, listen to the new LCD Soundsystem album and have an hour-long debate about whether it was any good. There to crack a nerdy joke about the incest vibes in *Star Wars*. To hold me when the grief of missing my parents made me, occasionally, inconsolable. Eventually, there to welcome me fully into his apartment, his world. To warm the bed, to be my partner in dog ownership, our shared responsibility making Dusty, my everything, a possibility . . .

There to toss all those possibilities straight to hell. To reveal his true self to me, little by little. To redefine my understanding of the concept of surprise.

Dusty jumped up, sniffing at the leftover pizza.

'Down,' I said, tasting a gummy bitterness in the back of my throat. 'We'll go in a minute.' My phone sat on top of the box, ominous. I tapped it to life. It was after eleven. No calls or texts, but it's not like there would be. Davis didn't have my new number, my SIM card made sure of that.

I pulled myself out of bed, then peeked through the drapes just as a car drove slowly past. I forced myself to take a deep breath. I would have to let go of this, this feeling of being watched. I let the drapes fall shut, careful that not even an inch of window was exposed, then approached the mirror hanging on one side of the door. There, framed by my unruly brown curls and impossible to miss, was the bruise. Angry and white in the middle, purple and blue, watercolor splotches, at the edges. Circling my cheekbone like a bull's-eye, about three inches across.

I grabbed my purse from where I'd tossed it on the nightstand and dug for the Dermablend, which my mom had gotten me hooked on when acne was my biggest nemesis. As I dabbed it on, my cheek burned hot, skin vellum-delicate, and for a second, I was back in our apartment on Wednesday night, the room going off-kilter and beginning to spin as pain seared the side of my face . . .

Dusty whimpered, almost like he was sympathizing, but I knew he only wanted to go out. I surveyed my masterpiece – the bruise, scratch, and my light smattering of freckles disappearing behind the makeup, blurry as a generous Instagram filter, hazy and unblighted as the *Mona Lisa*. Beauty magazines never covered tips like these. Stuff like this, you had to figure out on your own.

I heard a crash, and jumped. Next to me, Dusty had pulled his leash from where I'd tossed it on the nightstand, and the metal hook had clanged against the hardwood floor. I inhaled deeply and knelt to scratch behind his ears. The warmth of his skin, the cotton-softness of his fur, calmed my pulse, my breaths coming slower – then my eyes landed on the floorboards, lit by the sun.

Quickly, I pushed the bed aside. The floorboard in question was propped up ever so slightly, as if it had been opened. I racked my brain. Had I, after a whiskey or three, lifted it to check? No. I would remember something like that. Had Dusty crawled underneath and scratched around, like he always used to do in Brooklyn? Most likely. Still, I checked the contents anyway, pulling everything out, running through my list again. All there. My stomach flip-flopped, but this time not from anything I'd had to drink.

I re-hammered the floorboard, repositioned the bed, and quickly searched the cottage. No sign of anyone here but me.

It wasn't possible, I reassured myself as we headed out for our walk, and I locked the door behind us, checking several times to be sure. This time, I'd made damn sure he couldn't find me.

After all, I'd learned a lot in the last few months.

This wasn't going to be like before.

Light dappled the side of the road, and a breeze wove through the uneven grass of the meadow. Dusty hopped along, equally intrigued by the lack of dogs and the abundance of green. No park in Brooklyn could compare to the *Walden*-esque utopia before us.

We walked slowly, Dusty wanting to pee on every stick and flower, the harsh light of day making it all feel more real. Made-for-TV movies flashed to mind, the ones I used to watch in the musty basement with my mom. The heroine's escape from the bad guy was the climax, the triumph. You didn't see this part, when she didn't know how to begin again, when she wondered if Thoreau got bored, alone in the woods.

We reached the farmhouse, the picturesque Mercedes parked next to a pickup spattered with mud. Up close, it looked as idyllic as it had yesterday, though it needed a good bit of work. A window was cracked, and the exterior begged for a fresh coat of paint. I tugged the leash, but Dusty was obstinate – he stopped in front of the mailbox to do his business.

I heard yelling. I couldn't make out the words, only raised voices, a screech that could be the scraping of a chair against hardwoods, a definitive stomp.

I stiffened, rapt. Old walls were thin, I knew that. Davis and I used to exchange terse whispers in the kitchen at night. Early on, he'd laughed about it, said that in Brooklyn, you didn't have the luxury of having a good fight. It had been funny because it had been true. Our arguments were lovely and indulgent then, full of banter, like two people reading a script for a sitcom.

That had changed. Davis had found plenty of methods for getting his way without ever attracting the attention of the neighbors. I still don't think the lady upstairs ever knew anything was going on.

The front door burst open, and I heard the woman's voice – 'Don't ever do that again!' – and I swear, I expected to see me walk out – eyes glistening, hands shaking, trying to make sense of what had happened but knowing there was no way to make sense of things like that.

Inexplicably, Ms Butter-Yellow Mercedes only shook her head, grinning, as if she even knew how to argue with grace. She wore her hair in a smooth ponytail this time, and her clothes were, again, all black, tight, and stretchy, sneakers on her feet. Her eyes locked on mine. 'It's you.'

Her words caught me off guard, and I felt naked and exposed, a kid in the cafeteria not knowing where to sit. I needed to do something, so I reached for the doggie bags, but there weren't any in the holder. Shit.

'The woman from yesterday, right? Can I help you?'

'My dog,' I said, finding my voice and nodding to Dusty. He pulled on the leash, wanting to say hi. 'Sorry, he kind of – well – on your lawn, and I forgot the bags. I shouldn't have let him go in your yard at all . . .'

She marched down the path, her ponytail a pendulum. She was even more stunning up close, her smile wide and white, all teeth and gums, like the grin of a child. Her eyes were gray, her brows blond but thick, and she was probably older than me, five or ten years, maybe; it was hard to say.

'Don't jump, Dusty,' I said.

'Oh, it's okay.' She looked from Dusty to me. She was a couple of inches taller than me, and she smelled of warm earth with a note of something biting. Dirt stamped her knees, and there was a crunchy green plastic basket sitting in front of the overgrown flower beds behind her. Before she'd been arguing, she'd been gardening. 'You must be renting the cottage?' she asked. 'The place that Jennifer –' She paused abruptly. 'The Clarks' place, the ones who went to Phoenix.'

I nodded. 'That's the one.'

'I'm Vera.' She stuck out her hand. Her fingers were short and a little stubby, probably the one thing she worried about when she made a mental list of her flaws. Unlike my acne scars, stubby fingers were a decadent flaw to have. 'Nice to properly meet you.'

I hesitated only a second, suddenly nervous, before I said, 'Lucy.'

'And who's this?' she asked.

'Dusty.' I smiled. It was hard not to smile when talking about Dusty, even now.

Vera's voice morphed into full baby-talk mode. 'Aren't you just da cutest with your fluffy wittle head and wet wittle nose.' She looked up. 'Boy or girl?'

'Boy.'

'Who's a good boy?' Vera asked, as Dusty tried his best to lick her chin. 'Dusty's a good boy, that's who.' She stood, her pants now covered in Dusty's white fur. 'How long are you staying?'

It was strange. Only minutes ago, she'd been fighting with whoever was in that house. Now she was carrying on like nothing was the matter. My cheekbone lit up, not with pain so much as awareness of all that had transpired. Could it be so simple; could you argue and yell and walk out and meet your new neighbor?

I raised my hand, blocking my cheek. The sun was too bright; the kind of day that uncovered secrets, melted away snow hiding a dead body, penetrated the dermatologist-approved concealer and revealed something nasty. 'I'm not sure,' I said. 'It's just month to month right now.'

Vera's expression went sour. Was she trying to avoid looking at the bruise, or had she not noticed? Her face brightened again, a light on a dimmer, turning up and down at will. 'Well, hi, neighbor,' she said. 'Welcome to Woodstock. You from the city?'

Reluctantly, I nodded.

She smiled matter-of-factly, then looked down at Dusty. 'Oh, and you don't really have to use the bags around here. No one does. Between the deer shit and the bear shit, it's not a big deal.'

I nodded, skin prickling at the thought of bears casually waltzing by. She stared, as if waiting for me to say something next. 'We should probably get going,' I said, tugging on Dusty's leash.

'You should come over for dinner,' she said suddenly, her smile turning on again. 'You just got in, and I know you don't have groceries in the house. Unless you're the kind of person who does that first thing, and in that case, I hate you. Please share your secrets to perfection with the rest of us.'

The sound of my laugh surprised me – it had been a long time since I'd heard it. In another time and place, the answer would have been easy. I'd have suggested we get a drink, and we'd have met at some cocktail bar with exposed brick and bartenders who read Bukowski, ordered concoctions made with ridiculous things like absinthe rinses and egg whites. By the end of the night, we'd have been great friends, having exchanged everything from the number of nights per week we slept with our partners to the unbearable pain of a UTI. In this world, however, the thought was unnerving. What if she posted something about me to Facebook or Instagram? What if it had been so long since I made a new friend, since I expanded my circle beyond Davis and Ellie and the world we'd created together, that I forgot how? What if my internal compass was so fucked, I'd completely lost any sense of who I could trust?

'I didn't go shopping yet, but I really –'

Vera cut me off. 'Good. Then I don't have to hate you. Come over. Eight thirty. You're not vegetarian or gluten-free or allergic to any other wonderful things, are you?'

'I don't know –'

'You don't know if you're allergic or you don't know if you want to come?'

I laughed again.

'Look,' she said, 'I'm the kind of person who cooks way more than I need to. If you find yourself in need of a hot meal, come over. You can meet John, my husband, and I promise we won't be screaming about the laundry.'

It shocked me, the way she casually admitted she'd been fighting with her husband. It made me feel like I was the messed-up one, not her.

14

Vera shrugged. 'And if you don't, no big deal. We'll just eat too much and drink too much and it will be all your fault.' She nodded down the road. 'I'm going for a run. Don't give me your answer now. I'll hopefully see you at eight thirty.' She turned and headed off, and I watched as her walk quickly broke into a jog. She was captivating, that's for sure, an enigma of a woman. Still, I shouldn't get too friendly with anyone right now. I didn't know who I could trust anymore.

Dusty pulled, trying to go after her, but there were things I wanted to do today, things that needed checking, arranging. I tugged at the leash and turned on my heel.

I jumped. A gray-haired woman stood there, lines etched at the corners of her mouth, eyes deep-set and deep brown, eyes that had most certainly been considered beautiful once. 'Sorry,' I said. 'You startled me.'

She wore a maroon sweater that had to be too hot for this weather, and faded jeans – she looked to be in her late sixties. A medium-size dog, about twice the size of Dusty, was tethered to her; he bounded toward us and sniffed at Dusty's nose.

'This is Dusty,' I said, the usual protocol.

'Did she bother you?' She pursed her lips, like she'd tasted something bitter.

'Huh?'

She pointed up the road to where Vera was still in sight, running, her pace quick, purposeful. 'About the dog. I saw that he went on her lawn and all. She really doesn't like dogs. She's never been friendly to Pepper, at least.'

'Oh,' I stammered, pulling Dusty a little closer to me. 'She didn't seem to –'

'If she bothers you, you just let me know,' the woman said. 'I'm Maggie, I live down the road. Next door to you, I believe. Neighbors have to look out for each other, you know.'

'Lucy,' I managed. I took her hand in mine; it was clammy and cold. She smiled, and I noticed one of her teeth was gray – dead.

'You should watch out for them,' Maggie said suddenly.

I pulled my hand away and took a quick step back. 'What?'

'Vera and John can be very charming,' Maggie said. 'But they only really care about themselves.'

Three

At first, only the tiniest things seemed to go missing.

An invoice for one of my freelance clients. The leftovers of an expensive meal I'd wanted to reheat. A favorite pair of socks. My bright blue Sharpie. The scarf of my mother's. Gone, or so I thought. In a different place altogether. The invoice, tucked underneath a stack of books. The leftovers, turning moldy in the cabinet instead of in the fridge. The socks, in the bottom of Dusty's bin of toys. The Sharpie, inexplicably dropped into my hamper and put through the wash. My mom's vintage silk scarf – tucked away in the drawer next to threadbare dish towels, one corner having been used to sop up a mess in the kitchen, permanently stained.

Things so small, so insignificant, I half thought I was going crazy. Maybe I was just forgetful, flighty, as Davis was always implying.

Except things had never been misplaced when I was on my own – only after I moved in with him.

Now, afternoon bleeding quickly into evening, rain tapping lightly on the roof of my new cottage, I moved from room to room, noting what was what and where, writing it down in my composition notebook.

Living room: trail map and *History of the Catskills* (on coffee table), encyclopedia set missing the letter *H* (in bookshelf), and on and on. Kitchen: tea tin (four packets of Earl Grey, two of mint), scratch pad (opened to a shopping list: bananas, black beans, coffee), utensil drawer (surprisingly, a complete set), knife drawer (six knives, red Lucite handles).

Perhaps these behaviors had always been there, brewing, but it wasn't until Davis that they rose to the forefront – an attempt to control the uncontrollable. I'd started writing things down to preserve my sanity, to help me understand.

And when I had, it had slowly become clear, a Polaroid sharpening into focus. I wasn't flighty. My brain was not a sieve.

These were punishments. Tiny ones, sure. Suited to my own tiny crimes. For not laughing at one of Davis's jokes when we were at a party together. For asking him to do the dishes more. For writing that note to him – yes, in bright blue Sharpie – about the faucet that was always dripping.

The rain had stopped, and it was after seven by the time I got to the bedroom, which I'd saved for last. It was clear of any paraphernalia, nothing there besides furniture. I tossed the notebook onto the bed and dragged my bag into the closet. A small dresser hugged the wall inside. I filled the drawers with black tees and denim shirts, light sweaters and layers. The smaller underwear drawer sat on top. When I tried to pull it open, it stuck, creaking, but I tugged harder and it gave. A dusty furniture brochure sat within the drawer, had probably been in there since the piece was made – the fifties, the sixties – who knew.

As I grabbed the brochure, a stack of photos fell from it, five of them, glossy, 'Catskills Photo' printed on the back. Every picture showed the same man. All were extremely close-up, so close they almost seemed intimate, snatches of brown hair and a salt-and-pepper beard catching the light. He was rugged, with deep-set eyes and a strong chin, the kind of guy who made you think, *They don't make men like this anymore.*

I shoved them back into the brochure and tossed it back in the drawer. I added my bras and underwear and the scarf of my mother's, then slammed the drawer shut. The photos were nothing, the odds and ends of a life left behind. Probably the boyfriend of the last tenant. Grabbing my notebook, I marked them down anyway. Bedroom closet: five photos in top drawer of dresser (all of one man). Then, with my phone, I took a photo of the list I'd made for each room, just in case.

Situating myself on the bed, I took a deep breath, trying to reassure myself that there was no way Davis could find me. I had a fresh SIM card, which meant a new number, my social media accounts were deleted, and my old email would only be accessed when I was logged in to the VPN, a necessary risk for work. Even my new home was like a fresh start – filled with perfectly impersonal items, things that weren't even mine, as if here, I could become someone else altogether.

If I were Ellie, I would have been freaking out. My best friend couldn't go even a day without posting something to Instagram. But Ellie would probably have found a way to handle all of this differently. She was always good at difficult things, a friend who'd understood so clearly how to be there for me, never bringing up my parents unless I wanted to talk, inviting me over on Mother's Day and Father's Day to ply me with plotless buddy comedies and wine, take my mind away from it all.

Still, I can't say how she would have handled this. This was different from my parents; no one knew what was happening except Davis and me. Basic logic, therefore, made him my only ally. Even now, I half wanted to call him, all, *Babe, isn't this crazy? Can you actually believe this is happening to us?* I wondered if he would answer or if the phone would just . . . ring.

I opened Instagram instead.

I typed Davis's handle into the search bar, and he instantly popped up. His account was public, but he hadn't added anything in three days. The thought of him, plotting ways to fuck with me, made my skin crawl. The thought of him, wasting away in our apartment, *alone*, did, too.

I scanned through his posts: Us at the dog park. Hiking in the Poconos with Ellie, sweat on our foreheads. Sunbathing in South Beach. Laughing at some sort of inside joke. In the beginning, I was always laughing when I was with him. Always. I hovered over the Message button – there was so much I wanted to say.

I won, fucker!
You didn't think I could, but I did.
I miss you, and I hate myself for it.
I'm scared, terrified.
You'll never see me or Dusty again.
Are you okay?

On cue, Dusty nuzzled me, staring at me with his big puppy eyes. *It's not worth it,* he seemed to say. *It's not worth the risk.*

Quickly, I closed the window. It was only seven forty-five now, and the hours before me seemed suddenly endless. I grabbed my notebook and began another list, one of to-dos.

- *Figure out money/bank*
- *Fix phone*
- *Buy real food*
- *Get food and treats for Dusty*
- *Pitch new articles*
- *Write ones already assigned*

I let the pen drop and checked the time on my phone again. Only a couple of minutes had passed. There was a *shush* of wind outside, and my skin pricked, my downy hairs standing straight up. My eyes flitted to the window – I had that sensation again of being watched – and I peered around the drapes, but there was no one there. I breathed deeply. I was simply being paranoid; after all, being alone wasn't a skill I'd had to cultivate in Brooklyn. There was always a press party or a dive bar trivia night with Ellie. Before Davis, there'd been the endless barrage of dates. Good and bad, funny and excruciating. OkCupid in the old days and Tinder and Bumble just before Davis had come along. So many ways to fill your time with other humans. Brunch the next day to trade bad-date stories.

And then Davis, a relief from all that. Davis, who stopped the endless loop of profiles and photos, like a stack of résumés for the job of Boyfriend.

I looked at the clock. Not even another minute had passed.

Have a drink wasn't on the to-do list, but it should be.

Go to dinner with potentially cool new neighbors wasn't, either.

I headed to the kitchen, poured a finger or so of whiskey, and eyed Dusty, daring him to judge. Then I retrieved the pizza from the fridge and stared at it. Whatever Vera was cooking seemed infinitely more appetizing. Dusty eyed me – not judging, just begging.

Screw it, I thought. I grabbed a piece of crust and tossed it to him. He didn't usually get people food, but it was okay. Tonight we were both breaking the rules.

Four

Watch out for them.

Maggie's words echoed in my head as I stepped onto Vera's porch, the planks creaking beneath my weight. The porch lights were muted, one of the bulbs was cracked, and mouse droppings surrounded the front door. I knocked, but nothing happened; after a minute or so, I knocked again. Silence. I peered inside, but it was mostly dark, like no one was home. Squinting, I spotted a chair turned on its side.

What the hell?

I knocked for the third time, waiting, and was about to turn around when the door flew open.

'Hope you weren't waiting too long,' Vera said, looping a bony arm around my shoulders and leading me into a barely lit foyer. 'I stepped out back to sneak a cigarette. Nasty habit, I know. Then I looked at my phone and realized the time. I'm so sorry. I'm an awful host, aren't I?'

Without waiting for an answer, she flipped on the lights and released me from her grasp. 'The electric bills are stupid in an old house, so we try to keep the lights off when we're not in the room. I like to pretend we're being old-fashioned and not just cheap.' She said nothing about the turned-over chair, only knelt down and set it right side up. Then she took my bag and hooked it over a rung, shutting the door behind her without bothering to lock it, a decision that made my insides twist. 'Anyway, you're just in time. The lasagna is about to come out of the oven. I hope you're hungry!'

In the light, I took in the house, large and spacious in all the ways that my cottage was not. A beautiful staircase dominated the foyer, with a living room on one side and a dining room on the other. The smell was strong. Basil and warmth. My mom always made a casserole when it was cold out or I was sick – turkey tetrazzini, my favorite – like her mother had before her and her mother before hers. A whole line of women taking care of each other. A line that had been cut short, the umbilical cord slashed, in an instant – just like that.

I took in Vera, too. She wore a black leotard and a silky charcoal skirt that came down almost to her ankles, an evening take on the athleisure I'd seen earlier. Her feet were sandaled, toenails painted navy blue and slightly chipped. Her ponytail snaked down her back.

I glanced into the living room, where a tufted leather ottoman sat in front of an overstuffed sofa, surrounded by antique furniture, the kind you picked up at estate sales. Dark brown wooden beams stood out from the ceiling, and below me, the hardwood floors were banged up but beautiful. Her home had plenty to be jealous of but little to hate. It was imperfect, far from museumlike, with dust on the baseboards and clutter on every surface: junk mail, water glasses marked with lipstick, shoes tossed into the corner.

And books, books everywhere. Stacked in the hallway, lining the inset shelves in the living room. Art and philosophy (Warhol, Kant); high and low (*White Teeth*, *Twilight*); Ta-Nehisi Coates on top of Daphne du Maurier. Books always made me feel safe. Suddenly, I wished I'd taken more from my childhood, could read myself the ones my mother had once read to me.

'John,' Vera yelled up the stairs. 'Lucy is here!' Not 'Lucy, the neighbor.' Or 'Lucy, the woman I told you about.' Just Lucy. She didn't wait for anyone to bound down the stairs, but led me through the living room, where I detected the faint scent of weed, and into the kitchen in back. Unlike the rest of the house, it was small and cramped, as if whoever had designed the formal rooms in front had forgotten that people actually had to, you know, *cook* and tacked it on haphazardly. White tiles were everywhere – on the floor, on the backsplash – caked with grout and pasta sauce, one of them cracked all the way across, and a small kitchen island was piled on one side with even more junk mail and on the other with containers of spices and an empty tub of ricotta.

'I brought this over,' I said, retrieving Davis's good whiskey from my oversize purse and handing it to her. 'It's already opened, which I know is a little gauche, but it's good – promise.'

Vera's eyes lit up. 'Oh, screw gauche,' she said. 'I love gauche, in fact. This is wonderful. Now I'm going to be gauche myself and insist we drink it right now.' Without waiting for my reaction, she pushed the junk mail aside and set the bottle on the island, pulled three glasses out of a weathered cabinet, and grabbed ice from the freezer with her bare hands. When she shut the fridge, I saw a whiteboard on the front, with a to-do list so different from mine, it was nuts. Only one item: *Rachel*.

Vera pushed a glass at me, poured tall, and I took it gratefully; I tried not to sip too fast.

'John!' she called again. Footsteps thudded from down the hall.

He walked in, and I coughed, choking as a bit of whiskey slipped down the wrong pipe.

Brown hair. Gray-flecked beard. A strong, chiseled jaw. Red plaid short-sleeved shirt, phone tucked inside the chest pocket. And that feeling, the one I'd had when I saw the displaced floor-board. That weight in my gut, telling me things aren't what they

24

seem. Whether nefarious or benign, I'd become a pro at knowing when there was more to the story. Not from journalism but from Davis.

I was staring at the man from the photos, without question.

'Hi there,' he said, wrapping me in a hug. It caught me so off guard, I spilled whiskey down the back of his shirt.

'Christ.' I pulled away and wiped the edge of the glass with my sleeve. 'I didn't mean to.'

Vera grabbed a linen dish towel and blotted John's shirt, almost as if on cue. 'John's a hugger,' she said. 'I should have warned you.' She leaned in to kiss her husband, but she just barely missed, her lips landing on his cheek instead.

'Guilty as charged,' John said with a laugh. The sound was big and guttural, taking up the scarce space in the tiny room, and it vaguely reminded me of my dad's. 'Is a handshake any better?'

I nodded as I took his hand, which was warm, rough, and flecked with what looked like paint. 'I'm usually a hugger, too, it's just that you caught me by surprise.'

It's just that five photos of you are tucked away in my underwear drawer.

I gestured to the whiskey. 'Please have some before I go any deeper into my hugging history.'

They both laughed. A sugary feeling, one I hadn't had in a long time, of being appreciated by someone new.

Vera pushed the third glass into John's hand. 'To neighbors!' she cried.

'And new friends,' John said, raising an eyebrow. 'Especially ones who bring us good whiskey.'

I lifted the glass to my mouth, and we all drank at once.

The lasagna was delicious, with layers of meat and ricotta and sauce and noodles, like my mom used to make. They didn't even serve a salad, didn't pretend to be doing anything but eating pasta.

Vera shoved a huge forkful into her mouth as we told her how wonderful the meal was, sauce spreading over her lips. Maybe that was the chink in her perfect-girl armor: She'd never been taught how to eat properly.

Unlike Vera, John was eating his carefully, slicing each noodle into neat little squares. 'So Vera said you were from the city?' he said, setting his fork down momentarily. 'Let me guess – Brooklyn?'

'Yeah,' I said. 'How could you tell?'

'Your hair,' Vera interrupted. 'All chic but unmanageable. A total Brooklyn do.' She scooped another forkful of lasagna into her mouth and chewed it fiercely, swallowing fast.

John leaned back in his chair, turning to Vera. 'So let me get this straight: There's a difference between Manhattan hair and Brooklyn hair?'

She rolled her eyes. 'Oh, you wouldn't know.'

I smiled to myself. 'Let's just say one normally involves a flat iron.'

'Isn't that the truth?' Vera asked, laughing. 'And you can pry mine from my cold, dead hands. We're from the city, too, actually. Only we were never cool enough to live in Brooklyn. We were old fuddies, in the East Village.' She beamed. 'So why did you move? Do you have family up here?'

I shook my head, eyes on my plate.

'Where are you from originally?' she asked.

I took a sip of the wine John had opened as soon as we'd sat down. Despite my fears, there was no real reason to lie. 'The Pacific Northwest, but I don't get back there much.'

'That's where your family is?' Vera pressed.

I swallowed, my throat tightening ever so slightly.

John laid his hand over Vera's, as if to stop her.

'What?' she asked.

'Don't be so pushy, V,' he said, giving her hand a squeeze. His voice was kind, unlike Davis's when he used to correct me. His eyes flitted to mine, crinkling at the corners; somehow, he got it.

Vera wriggled her hand out from beneath his. 'I'm not being pushy,' she said. Her fork clanged against the plate. 'Wait. Am I?'

'No, no, of course not,' I said instinctively. I trailed my finger along the edge of my plate, then took a deep breath, like I had so many times before. Better to spit it out, one fell swoop. 'There was a bad accident my junior year of college,' I said. 'I lost both my parents. I'm an only child, so . . .'

Her hand landed on mine, warm and baby-soft, but I flinched at her touch, and she pulled away. 'Oh god, how awful,' she said. 'I didn't mean to make you upset.'

For a second, the hole inside me where my parents should have been grew so much, it was like I was made of nothing, as empty as a tossed-aside bottle of wine: hard on the outside, tough to crack, but filled with little more than air, dirty dregs. I dabbed my eyes with my napkin, careful not to disturb the Dermablend, then forced a laugh. 'Sorry. I don't even know why I'm crying.'

I expected to hear the usual half-hearted response – *oh, so sorry for bringing it up, I didn't mean to pry* – but to my surprise, John's eyes clouded. His face sagged, looked suddenly older. Vera bit her lip.

'It doesn't get any easier, does it?' he asked, once more taking Vera's hand.

I widened my eyes, willing him to go on.

He cleared his throat. 'My parents died a year apart. Lung cancer,' he said. 'Mom when I was twenty-six. Dad when I was twenty-seven.'

I shook my head, but didn't say anything, because I knew there wasn't a single word in the English language that would suffice. Words were made to describe, to explain, not to console.

'I'm not an only child, but my brother was only nineteen.' John's eyes penetrated deep. 'He's got schizophrenia, been in a home for years.'

'Christ,' I said for the second time that night.

Vera forced a laugh. 'Welcome to the neighborhood! We sure do know how to keep things light.'

John's head swiveled toward her. 'Seriously, though, if I hadn't met Vera, I don't know what I would have done.' He turned his hand over, lacing his fingers through hers.

My insides ached; I'd thought the same thing, not so long ago. From the beginning, Davis had felt almost like a healer, my very own emotional balm. He was the family I'd lost, the unconditional love I craved.

Or I'd thought he was, at least.

Vera unlaced her fingers and fiddled with her napkin. 'We're so glad you moved in,' she said, changing the subject. 'The woman who lived in your place before, well, she and I were quite close – I guess we all were.' Her eyes briefly caught John's. 'She moved to a place right in town, but even before then . . .' Vera folded her napkin into a tight little square, then shook it, undoing her work. 'Anyway, I was afraid the new tenant wouldn't be cool, but look.' She smiled. 'Here you are.' I felt myself blush.

'Should we go out to the gazebo in back?' John asked, clearing his throat and pushing his plate forward. 'We've still got half a bottle of wine to at least attempt to drink away all our sorrows, and it's not too hot out.'

'Let's do,' Vera said, voice light. 'And I promise not to ask any more serious questions.'

'I'm going to hold you to that, V,' John said.

When I didn't object, John scooted his chair back and stood, tossing his napkin onto his plate.

'So were you friends with the previous tenant, too?' I asked him as we squeezed through the doorway to the living room.

'Rachel?' he asked, the name on the whiteboard clinking into place like ice in whiskey. 'Of course we were friends,' he said. 'She was my neighbor, just like you.'

Five

The two of them came to life beneath the string lights of the gazebo.

John looked almost painfully striking, his jaw strong, eyes bright. Nestled beside him, Vera was a siren. A goddess-witch, her hair now free, cascading past her shoulders.

It wasn't just that they were beautiful. They were the kind of people who made you feel like you were in high school all over again, who took everything you'd been forcing down your throat about body positivity and loving yourself since you were sixteen years old and shot it straight to hell. You could be as beautiful as you told yourself you were, but you would never be them. Cheerful, easy, in love. The kind of people who made you want, desperately, to be liked.

Vera and John can be very charming. But they only really care about themselves.

Vera patted the space beside her, and I sat down as directed, clinging to my glass.

'So what brought you guys up here?' I asked.

Vera smiled, and the two shared a brief conspiratorial look, as if they delighted in telling their story, one chapter in the history of them. 'We wanted to open an art gallery forever,' Vera said. 'But we could never afford the space in the city, so one day, we decided, let's do it! I run the day-to-day – I was trained in arts management at Pratt – and John paints in his cabin-slash-studio in the woods. I show his pieces, as well as others'.'

'Wow,' I said. 'That sounds so idyllic. It's one of those things people always talk about doing but never do.'

Vera's smile faltered, just the tiniest bit, and I wondered if I'd misstepped.

'I'm sure it's hard leaving the city, though,' I added. 'Starting fresh and everything.'

They exchanged a glance, and John took a rather large sip of his wine.

Vera sighed. 'It is, yeah. It can be hard to meet people. You've got weekenders who do the city and the country, and you've got people who were born and raised here. The in-betweeners, like us, we don't always quite fit in. It's a little easier if you're right in the heart of downtown Woodstock, but even a few miles out, it's different. When we moved here, we were the only people who didn't grow up on this block. The neighbors didn't really warm up to us,' she said.

Maggie flashed to mind. It wasn't that far-fetched to imagine a local woman set in her ways finding a pair of Manhattanites self-centered. Perhaps that's all there was to it.

I took a sip of wine, desperate to get us back on comfortable ground. 'Are there any spots I should know about? Good restaurants? Bars?'

'Bars!' Vera said, laughing. 'I hate to break it to you, but the bar scene around here is severely lacking. Nothing like you'd get in the city. Hardly anything's even open late in Woodstock.'

'There's Platform,' John offered.

'Platform?'

He nodded. 'It's pretty interesting, actually. Quaint. In an old converted train station, right downtown. Open till two and everything, unlike the other spots, which are pretty much just

31

extensions of restaurants, so it's kind of the catchall for people in this area.'

I made a mental note. 'Do you guys go there a lot?'

Vera laughed, but for a second, it sounded almost bitter, and her eyes caught John's.

'We used to,' he said cautiously. 'But, you know, we're getting older. Not as tapped into the scene.'

I laughed. 'You guys aren't old.'

Vera bit her lip. 'I'm thirty-nine.'

'And I just turned forty,' John added.

'Oh, come on, that's not old,' I said.

Vera nudged her husband. 'Says the girl in her mid-twenties!'

'I'm twenty-eight,' I said, feeling myself blush. Perhaps Vera saw it in the haze of the lights.

'No, no,' she said. 'Don't misunderstand me. You don't seem overly young or naive or anything, just, I don't know . . . *lovely*.' She shrugged. 'I know we're not *that* old, but it can feel that way sometimes. Anyway, the main reason we don't go out so much anymore is because we're trying to watch our finances. John hasn't Van Gogh'd yet, so his paintings only bring us so much. And we recently had to lay off our gallery assistant and cut our hours.'

'"Van Gogh'd"?'

John grinned rakishly, turning to Vera. 'I thought we agreed to stop sharing our plans for my impending demise with our dinner guests. My god, she's only just met us.' He arched an eyebrow. 'So here's the thing: After my inclusion in the Whitney Biennial didn't pan out exactly as I'd hoped, we started joking about how I could *disappear*, you know, wander off somewhere and get on the map.'

I leaned slightly forward. I knew a thing or two about wanting to disappear. To seep into nothingness, where Davis could never find me. To leave behind not even so much as a record of my pres-

32

ence. No failed relationship. No loss of my parents. Nothing for anyone to pity.

'I read a book about it once,' John went on, leaning back, shoulders relaxing as he took another sip of wine. 'This Swedish artist faked his death to give his work more value. And, believe it or not, it worked – for like a decade or something. We started calling it Van Gogh-ing. He wasn't popular in life, but after his death – you get the idea. Though I have no interest in cutting my ear off.'

'Well, it would certainly make *my* life a lot easier,' Vera said, beaming. 'I'd have a star in my portfolio.'

John squeezed her knee. 'That Porsche isn't going to buy itself, right, V?'

She turned to me with a devilish smirk. 'We love art, but we love money more.'

I laughed, her words refreshing. An honest, callous love of money, not the WASPy bullshit that forces us to pretend like it doesn't make the world go round.

Mom would cringe. Like a slap across the face, the weight of missing my mother. I imagined her subtle indignation: *Your new neighbors said* what? *Out loud?*

Vera seemed to pick up on my change in demeanor. 'You know we're just joking, right?'

'I'm not dying anytime soon,' John added. 'Porsche or no Porsche.'

'Of course,' I said. And then, humoring them, 'If I were an artist, I might Van Gogh, too!'

As we made our way through the wine, they explained how they first met, nearly fifteen years ago, when John was in art school in the city and Vera was an assistant at a gallery. It was as close as possible to love at first sight, even though they didn't believe in that, not really.

I filled in the pieces of my history, too.

Vera asked about college, and I told them I'd majored in journalism and minored in computer science at the University of Washington. I neglected to mention the video, the one blasted across every social network: me drunk and dancing, taking off my top in a dive bar, giving a lap dance to anyone who wanted one, letting one guy suck on my nipples for an electric-blue kamikaze shot. In my experience, pity or misplaced anger was worse than any ding to my reputation; plus, in the digital age, I figured we all had less-than-stellar moments living somewhere in the cloud.

And then, reeling from the loss of my parents, New York. Moving here to be a journalist, unaware that 'journalism' would turn into something else between the time I set out to do it and now – writing indulgent personal essays and asinine listicles it was hard to have the heart for but that paid the bills anyway, everything from 'What I Learned from Dating Nerds in My Early Twenties' to '16 Apps to Get Your Personal Finances in Order.' I explained how I wondered sometimes if I would one day run out of topics to mine for a few hundred bucks, if I should just write a book already, like I'd always imagined I would . . .

Our faces softened as the solar string lights waned, and maybe there was nothing better in the entire world than sitting outside in the Catskills in the middle of September with new friends and a good bottle of wine.

'It's amazing,' Vera said as she pulled a little black vaporizer out of the pocket of her skirt. 'After things with . . . well, with Rachel' – her eyes, again, flashed to John – 'I was so eager to meet someone new, someone like-minded, you know. I joined this god-awful book club in Woodstock. I even signed up for Meetup. It was horrible. But now you're here. An awesome Brooklyn woman – plop – right next to me. Do you mind?' she asked, clicking the vaporizer to life.

I shook my head, taking another sip of wine, hardly able to quell my curiosity. 'So I guess you're not friends with her anymore?'

'Huh?' Vera looked up.

'Your neighbor,' I said. 'Rachel. You guys had a falling-out or something?'

'Oh,' Vera said as John glanced down at his hands. 'I don't walk to the other side of the street if I pass her in Woodstock,' she said. 'But friendships change, you know. People disappoint you.' She dug again in her pocket, quickly looking away. 'Shit,' she said. 'I forgot to grab the weed.'

I jumped up, eager to make up for prying. 'I can get it. I have to go to the bathroom anyway.'

John stood, too. 'I'll come with. You'll never find it in the catastrophe that is our junk drawer.'

Vera held up her glass so the wine sloshed inside it. 'Bring back some more – there's another bottle on the counter.'

John and I walked off together, and as the crickets buzzed, my body did, too.

Six

I swear, my wife is obsessed with you,' John said as he shut the door behind us.

The wine went to my head, and I reached for the wall, my hackles instantly rising. 'What?'

John only grinned like a schoolboy, bashful, and I immediately felt foolish. 'Oh, I only mean she likes you a lot,' he said. 'I can tell already.'

I steadied myself on the chair rail, then forced a smirk, trying to lighten the mood. 'You said "obsessed" a second ago. Why'd you have to downgrade me so quickly?'

There was that deep laugh again. 'Fine. I will adjust it back to obsession level. But only because you asked.'

I ambled to the counter, strewn with unrinsed dishes. The chaos made me feel like I didn't have to be so perfect, like we were all good and messed up. I looked at John, who I just knew would never spend his time coming up with creative ways to screw with me, who knew loss as well as I did, and the thought struck me quick and foolish and entirely inappropriate – *What if all this were ours?*

I felt my cheeks redden. I had given up on properly judging men long ago, and besides, he was married. 'I have to go to the bathroom,' I managed. Avoiding his eyes, I stumbled down the hallway and into the first door on the right.

In the scalloped mirror, I took myself in. My hair was a wreck, the curls sticking up straight, and my lips were dyed purple from the wine, but my bruise remained covered. I teetered over to the toilet. I had the feeling I used to have before Davis, that *anything can happen* feeling. Brooklyn magic, bars open till four a.m., later if you tipped the bartenders well, people bouncing from street to avenue, all thrumming with possibility. It was a feeling I hadn't had in a long, long time, one I certainly shouldn't have with my new, married neighbors, one I shouldn't have with anyone, really, not in my current state. The sort of feeling that got you in trouble, that led to drunken moments recorded for posterity, but it lured me all the same. Fish, meet hook. I washed my hands, then used a little of the water to scrub the wine off my lips and tame my curls. A knock on the door made me jump.

'You okay in there?' John asked.

'Fine,' I called. 'Be out in a sec.'

He was there when I opened the door, big and strong in his button-down, a Brawny man or Mr Clean with more hair, or one of the myriad grocery-item mascots that told us what we should look for in a man. I felt myself wobble, and John reached out to steady me, grabbing my elbow. 'You really sure you're okay?' he asked.

I nodded, shrinking away from his grasp – no man had touched me since Davis.

Besides, I shouldn't have let myself get so drunk, not when I was just beginning my new life, when I still didn't know who in the world I could trust.

'You know,' John said, weight shifting from foot to foot, obviously picking up on the change in my demeanor, 'I didn't mean to freak you out or anything, saying my wife is *obsessed* with you. I guess it sounds a little nuts . . . but like she said, she's been eager to meet someone new. She's been really upset since everything changed.'

37

Rachel. The photos flashed into my mind, pushing my other thoughts aside. They'd seemed so intimate, I'd thought the guy in the pictures must have been the boyfriend of the woman who'd lived in the cottage before me. What's more, Vera's eyes had turned to John almost every time she'd spoken about her former friend.

It couldn't be, I thought. Even in one night, I could see that John and Vera were in love with each other. It practically oozed off of them.

'Did something . . . *happen* between them?' I asked. 'I mean, between all of you?'

John sighed. 'You know, Vera can be very black-and-white in the way she sees the world.'

'What do you mean?'

He opened what must've been the junk drawer, rifling through spare keys, Ziplocs full of screws, and loose batteries until his hands grasped a baggie of weed. He answered without looking at me: 'I mean that she thinks there are good people and bad people. Period.'

So something *had* happened, I realized, the thought sobering me up. Something that perhaps was more forgivable to him than it was to her. I found myself hating this Rachel woman, for whatever she had done.

But it couldn't be *that*, I told myself. If these two – both of them gorgeous, smart, and downright enchanting – couldn't find a way to make it work, who could?

I raised an eyebrow. 'And you don't?'

'I think people are products of their circumstances. We react to what life throws our way. Know what I mean?'

I held his gaze. I knew what he meant, better than he could ever imagine.

'What I'm saying is, I'm a bit quicker to forgive than V. It's the Midwest in me.' He paused, reaching for a fresh bottle of wine.

'Anyway,' he went on, steering us back to safe territory. 'My wife is my everything,' John said. 'I only want to see her happy. I'm always on her side.'

By the time we got back to the gazebo, I'd mostly regained my composure. John topped off our glasses as Vera crumbled the weed into the vaporizer. When it was ready, she sucked deep, then paused, finally blowing out a huge plume of misty smoke like she was Gandalf. 'Have some?' she asked.

Against my better judgment, I took the vaporizer from her. I was being paranoid, I realized, and I couldn't let myself live like this. Afraid of every single person I met. This was my new life, after all. I was allowed to have some goddamn weed.

I took a draw, coughing a few times, then leaned forward, passing it to John. By the time I leaned back, I was tingly all over, my body itching with awareness – every hair, every inch of skin. When Davis and I got edibles, we had such good sex. Crazy good, where time slowed down and it's all there around you and inside you, so lovely you don't want it ever to stop.

'It's good, huh?' John asked. 'Vera knows how to find the best everything.'

'Super good,' I said, smelling all the scents of the woods – musty earth, sunbaked grass, and something sweet like spun candy. I brushed the hair out of my face and shrugged out of my cardigan, the wind gone again and the air ripe and present, like it was giving me a hug.

I thought of whatever had happened with Rachel, and I realized something – Vera craved my friendship as much as I did hers. If I could only hang on to the two of them, to nights like this, to my fresh start, I felt that it would somehow all be okay . . .

'Oh my god, Lucy, what happened to your cheek?'

'Huh?' I froze, hand dropping to my side.

My fingers were printed with beige-orange Dermablend. 'Oh, I –'

'It's purple. Did that just happen?' Vera asked.

John's eyebrows knit together in concern.

'No . . . I . . .' I stammered. 'I mean, I don't know exactly *what* happened, like exactly how I got it . . .'

She understood before he did. Because she was a woman, just like me. And if you had a huge-ass bruise on your face, and you didn't deliver a believable excuse right away, it could only mean one thing.

'I know that sounds bad,' I said. 'Shit, I've had too much weed. It's not like it sounds. *Really.*'

John leaned forward. I think that's when he got it, too.

Vera put her hand on my leg. This was my moment to shrug her off. *Oh my god, you didn't think . . . did you? Jesus Christ, don't be so dramatic. I was actually drunk in a bar, ran right into the table, if you can believe it. Brooklyn nights, am I right?* But I had a feeling I was already a beat behind. As if all the wine and the weed were messing with my story.

'It's not like that,' I managed, but in their faces, I could already see it: my pain, my shame reflected.

'I should go,' I said, pushing away my wine and quickly standing, then grasping the post of the gazebo as the world began to spin.

'Are you okay?' Vera asked.

'Yes, it's just, it's getting late,' I said, trying to find my balance, to steady the quavering of my voice.

Against my protests, Vera insisted on walking me home – just to be safe – and back at my cottage, Dusty pawed at her ankles, desperate for affection, as I stumbled to the kitchen, opening the door to let him out.

Vera poured me a tall glass of water. 'Drink it,' she said.

I shook my head weakly. 'All this, it's not what you think.'

'Okay,' Vera said, though I could tell she didn't believe me. 'Fine. But you still need to drink some water.'

When the glass was finished and Dusty was back, she led me to my bedroom and turned the quilt down.

'I just had too much,' I said as I slid out of my jeans and crawled into bed. Vera disappeared, returning with my glass, re-filled. My water fairy.

'Thank you,' I said. And then, 'Sorry.'

Vera set it on the nightstand and sat on the edge of my bed, as if she were actually going to tuck me in. 'You have nothing to be sorry about.'

If she sat there any longer, I knew I would cry. 'You should get back home,' I said.

Vera nodded, stroking my arm. 'Just know that you're safe here, with us,' she said. 'You don't have to worry anymore.'

Seven

Light streamed too bright around the edges of the drapes, and images from last night flooded my brain. The three of us sitting in the gazebo. Vera's eyes as she'd discovered my bruise, even though I'd done my best to brush her off.

Dusty nuzzled against me, and I forced myself out of bed, letting him out the back door while I guzzled water. Back in the bedroom, I steeled myself and chanced a look at my old email. Sure enough, a reply from Ellie.

> What was that email about? Seattle? What happened?
> And I tried to call you. It says your phone's been
> disconnected? Holy shit, are you okay? Call me, please.

My insides knotted as I stared at her words. No mention of Davis – I wondered if she'd spoken to him, or even seen him.

How could I explain to her that disconnecting my phone wasn't about her – it was about him? His moves and counter-moves. His need for control. Even if I told her everything, I feared Davis would find a way to explain it, just as he had with me.

He'd made it seem so innocent, the first time he tracked me, just six months into our relationship. After a late Friday night with a friend, I'd awoken to three missed texts from the night before.

Where are you?

When are you coming home?

I know you're doing your thing tonight but I'm worried.

I'd found him in the kitchen, my subtle hangover already ex-acerbating my guilt. He was at the counter, scrambling eggs. 'I'm so sorry,' I said. 'I had too much to drink, and I stopped checking my phone.'

Davis's hand stopped stirring. He stared at me for maybe a beat longer than he should have. But then, a smile. 'It's fine, babe, really,' he said. 'I logged in to your Apple account and used Find My iPhone to see where you were. That okay?'

We'd been living together a couple of weeks by then, and we were up-front about our passwords, like many couples were. Besides, I hadn't had anyone to keep tabs on me in years. Ellie was my emergency contact, but I was never hers. Of *course* it was okay.

It was the second time he mentioned it that truly gave me pause. A week later, another night out with friends, only I hadn't missed any texts this time – he'd just gone in and checked where I was. I considered changing my password, not sharing it with him this time, but it seemed silly – paranoid.

And then, a few months after that, the Nest camera, propped on the table by the door. Wi-Fi enabled, hooked up to his phone. He'd had his apartment robbed before, and we were living in Bushwick, which had its fair share of crime. It was just a precau-tion, just a fun new gadget, got him a renter's insurance discount and everything. I told myself I was worrying for nothing, that Davis's reasons were benign, but I also knew, from that point on, that he was watching me – or at least he *could* watch me if he wanted to – every time I came in or out.

It was only later that I understood just how closely he'd been keeping tabs, just how deeply we were entwined.

Now my hands hovered over the keyboard, wanting to explain what I'd never been able to before.

For so long, I'd been dying to tell Ellie the truth. There was this brunch, just a few months ago, when I'd been so close. She and I had ordered grapefruit mimosas and huevos rancheros, and I'd promised myself that morning, hopeful as a pack-a-day smoker: *This is the day I'm going to quit. This is the day I'm going to tell Ellie.* But one sip of mimosa, and Ellie had gone straight into updates on her overbearing mother and her douchebag dad. 'Thank god for Davis,' she'd said before I'd had a moment to start. I couldn't say a word.

I knew about the Gutman family long before I met Davis. Nervous mom who spent her life trying to control her children. An endless stream of classes and extracurriculars when they were younger, dictatorial rules when they were older: No eating after eight p.m. Social events must be approved three days in advance. Their dad, who pretended not to care about the rules, was the reason for them. He got physical when he got mad. The abuse stopped inexplicably when they were in middle school, but the effect on their mom never wore off. She couldn't control her husband, so she controlled her kids. It was half of why it was so easy to connect with Ellie when we ended up sharing a booth in that bar, my first week in New York. Her parents were in her life, sure, but she hated them. Her world had been shattered long before mine had.

Davis was my boyfriend for three years, but he'd been Ellie's brother for her whole life.

It was a few years after we became friends that she told me her brother was moving to New York. I'd never met him, despite how close Ellie and I were – New York is strange like that. You can know everything about someone and never meet their family.

Our apartments are too damn small. The first time Davis and I kissed, two months after his move, on the linen sofa in Ellie's apartment, I thought, *How lucky am I?* I was in awe of this man, who'd grown up like that but treated me like this.

When I had no choice but to admit to myself that he'd become abusive, I half wanted to laugh. Such clichés, the two of us. He had become his father. And I, desperate to find a new family, had dived headfirst into a romance that was chock-full of red flags, even early on. It never failed to amaze me how he and Ellie had turned out so differently. She drowned the fire of her childhood, with yoga, talk therapy, wine. Davis, on the other hand . . .

Davis always had the embers going, ready to stoke with a little kindling – suspicion, jealousy, *me*.

I headed out before noon, stopping at the grocery store to stock up on things that were easy to cook for one, then followed a winding road past wooded stretches and an old church with stained-glass windows into downtown Woodstock.

I parked on a side street, in front of a run-down house and a trickling creek. The place was verdant, fertile. I followed the road to the main strip, and an open square filled with a circle of silver-haired ladies banging on drums. The smooth stone sidewalks were packed with people; I spotted Brooklynites up for the weekend, a roaming pack of high school kids and a sweet older couple strolling hand in hand. I walked on, past peace signs nodding to the town's eponymous festival, clothing shops selling comfort shoes, and street vendors hawking moonstone rings. Mountains loomed behind brightly colored storefronts, and an artsy flag hung over a thrift shop. The place was idyllic. A dream.

I stopped in a pet shop to get some chew sticks for Dusty, then ducked into Schoolhouse, a restaurant down the block. I took a seat at the counter, and while I waited for a menu, I surveyed the spot. Reclaimed wood, antique lighting, craft beer – one of those places you always find in quaint small towns.

Behind the counter, a chalkboard menu listed the offerings, and a bulletin board held the usual fliers. Advertisements for guitar lessons, information on upcoming town halls, and a PSA on bright orange paper.

PRACTICE SAFE HIKING!

Always go with a buddy.
Pack plenty of food and water, flashlights, and extra batteries.
Remember to sign in and sign out EVERY TIME.

I half wanted to laugh. When Ellie, Davis, and I had gone hiking in the Poconos, we'd never signed in or out, and we definitely didn't have a flashlight, let alone one with extra batteries – but I suppose there were plenty of things I had yet to adjust to in my new life.

A girl pushed a brunch menu at me, printed on brown craft paper and warped from overuse. She was young, must have been in college, but even at a glance, she was striking. Copper hair, smooth as corn silk, skin creamy and freckled, dark eyeliner rimming her eyes, and stud earrings crawling up her ears. She looked as if she'd stepped off a boat from early twentieth-century Ireland and immediately stopped at the mall for accessories. 'We're out of the kale bake,' she said, voice huskier than I'd expected. 'And the vegan sausage. But we have chicken apple links instead. I know it's not the same, but –' She shrugged. 'You want something to drink?'

'Coffee, please.' I glanced over the menu. 'And I can go ahead and order. I'll take the eggs Benedict – and a side of sausage,' I added, suddenly hungry.

'Great.' She tore off a sheet of paper and walked to the kitchen,

46

pinning it among the line of orders. She returned with a coffee and handed it to me, then leaned against the bar. 'Food will be out in fifteen or so.'

'Thanks,' I said, taking a sip of coffee. It was extra-hot and smooth, just like I liked it. I glanced around. She was the only waitress here, but almost all the tables were empty – she must not've been too busy. 'Do you know, is there a gallery in town?'

'The JV Gallery?' she asked.

JV. John and Vera. I nodded.

'Sure, it's just a few blocks down, across from the bank.' She crossed her arms, tilted her head slightly. 'Not sure if it's open, though. They cut their hours pretty drastically.'

'Oh yeah?'

She wiped down the counter with a dingy rag, then looked up at me, as if sussing out the situation. 'Why do you ask?'

I ran my finger along the handle of the coffee cup. 'I heard about it, thought about checking it out.'

The girl raised an eyebrow. 'You must be up for the weekend, then?'

I hesitated, briefly considered lying, just in case. But if I liked this spot, I'd be back – there were only so many restaurants in town – and lying would only draw attention to me. Besides, this was my fresh start. There was no reason to think Davis would figure out I was here. None at all.

I shook my head. 'No, actually, I just moved to town.'

'So how did you hear about the gallery?' she asked. 'Only because most people who live here – they don't really go to that place.'

I took a quick breath and the girl seemed to sense my hesitation. 'I mean, it doesn't really matter if you don't want to say.'

I exhaled, feeling silly. She was just a kid, and here I was, being cagey. 'My new neighbors mentioned they owned it, actually. Just wanted to see it in the flesh.'

'Really?' she asked. 'John and Vera, huh?'

'You know them?'

She sighed. 'If you actually live in town full-time, just about everybody knows everybody.' She wiped the counter again, then arched an eyebrow. 'You should probably check it out. They need the business, especially now.'

'What do you mean?'

She smirked. 'This town isn't as artsy and progressive as it likes to think it is. They haven't had great luck here. Locals won't touch the place, honestly.'

'Oh,' I said, remembering how Vera and John had described Woodstock last night. 'Why's that?'

Her lips formed a thin line. 'They just won't. Anyway,' she said, changing the subject, 'what do you do? Not too many jobs up here.'

Again, a spot of hesitation – I didn't want to give too much away. 'I freelance. I can work from anywhere, really.'

'Graphic design?' she asked.

'No, I –'

'Photography?'

'I'm a writer.' I practically blurted it out, then took another sip of coffee. This was getting ridiculous. How could it possibly hurt to tell her?

The girl's face lit up. 'No *way*,' she said. 'I've been wanting to meet a writer. That's what I want to do, too. I'm trying to decide between novels and screenwriting. Or maybe a memoir – I know I'm too young for that, but I think young people have more to say than people think.' She reached out her hand. 'I'm Al, by the way.'

'Al,' I repeated, marveling at the progressiveness of the younger generations, with their gender-neutral nicknames. Not Alice or Allison, not even Allie. Just Al.

I took her hand in mine, realizing she was waiting for me to introduce myself, too. 'Lucy.'

She pulled her hand back and tugged on the end of her hair. 'Anyway, what do you write?'

'Magazine articles, mostly,' I said, keeping it vague. 'Some personal essays.'

'That's so cool,' she said, without a trace of irony. A bell dinged, and she floated over to the kitchen and returned with my plate. It smelled like oil and salt and roasted garlic, and in a flash, I was back at this restaurant I used to go to with my mom and dad in Seattle.

'Thanks,' I said, pushing the memory away and pulling my plate forward.

'So where do you write for?'

I hesitated, not wanting to divulge too much. 'All kinds of places. Whoever wants to pay me.'

She grinned. 'Maybe I'll come across something of yours one day.'

I forced a smile. I knew she wouldn't.

'So how'd you get into it?' she asked.

By the time I was done eating, we'd discussed all the safe things, things that could not be tied directly to me: my early obsession with Jane Austen; Al's preference for the Brontë sisters, particularly *Wuthering Heights*; and the importance of reading *The Elements of Style*.

I tipped generously, despite my limited funds, remembering what it was like to be just starting out.

Outside, I breathed in the restorative mountain air, feeling better than I had in a long time. There was something about Al, the way she could look at her future with such hope and possibility – the world of writing her proverbial oyster – that gave me hope, too. Maybe she wouldn't make the same mistakes I had; maybe at least one of us would wind up with a different sort of fate.

The sidewalks were still teeming with people, and as I walked down the block, toward the real estate office, where Jennifer Moon had told me to drop off my rent payment, I found myself trying to separate the locals from those just visiting.

Tattooed couple with a French bulldog and tattered jeans: *definitely* up for the weekend.

Older woman dressed almost exactly like my neighbor Maggie, in a nubby sweater that was oversize, cozy, and probably a little too warm. Likely a local.

Ms Moon's office was closed. I tucked the sealed envelope into the locked letterbox, per her instructions, then gazed at the fliers taped in the window. All the lives you wished you could live, like Sylvia Plath's figs: a Frank Lloyd Wright–style ranch, nestled against a creek; an 1820s mansion, six bedrooms and desperate for a renovation; a one-bedroom cottage on Overlook Mountain. Once, I had dreamed of all this with Davis. We'd stalked Trulia, looking at places all over – in the Berkshires, the Catskills, the Shawangunks, the Poconos. 'The mountains are calling, and we must go.' We never got up to Woodstock, though. Too hippie, too artsy, he'd argued. Too full of itself. I never told him that Ellie and I had been once, years before he moved to Brooklyn, that I'd secretly loved it. Would he figure it out?

I briefly imagined him reading my email, grabbing the coatrack, bashing it into the walls. Finally losing it on someone – *something* – other than me. Then I imagined the alternative, and I rubbed at the back of my neck, turned to keep going.

As I did, my body slammed into something. I caught my breath and looked up to see a man, hair long and silver. He reeked of cigarettes. 'Sorry,' I said quickly, as his eyes bored into me. 'I didn't mean to –'

'Watch where you're going,' he scoffed. And then, as he passed me, under his breath but loud enough for me to hear: 'Fucking weekenders.'

My heart began to race at the prospect of confrontation. I

took a deep breath, but already the man was around the corner, out of sight.

He doesn't matter, I told myself as I walked on. Besides, I wasn't a weekender. I lived here now. This was my fresh start.

A couple of blocks more, and the crowd of people had thinned. Across the street, I saw Platform, the bar John had mentioned. It was, indeed, as quaint as he'd promised, painted bright red with a green metal roof.

Another half a block, and there it was: the JV Gallery.

I didn't care if no one went there, like Al said, or if locals hated it. It still felt like a beacon, reminding me of them, of what Vera had said – *you're safe here, with us.*

Through the floor-to-ceiling glass storefront, I gazed upon white walls, gleaming wooden floors, canvases, photographs, and sculptures. The sign read CLOSED.

I took a deep, calming breath. I was okay. It would all be okay. I had Vera and John, at least, and the next time I saw them, I'd have some story at the ready, explaining my bruise away. I would save face, and we'd have more wine, and everything would be fine.

I backed up. I should get home – I didn't want my groceries to spoil.

But flecks of faded paint on the bottom of the windows captured my eye. I knelt to look closer. Most of the paint had been scratched off, but I could just barely make out the words.

My blood ran cold.

YOU FUCKING PERVERT

Eight

I was still reassuring myself as I turned onto my street.

The graffiti was probably nothing – just kids, rebellious teen-agers, someone playing a prank.

This town was my new start. Vera and John were the first friends I'd made. And I wasn't going to let anything cast a shadow over that.

But as I approached my house, my chest seized up and my foot slammed on the brakes, bringing everything to a halt.

A car idled in front of my cottage.

My heart raced.

Was it Davis? Could he really have found me already?

Part of me wanted to gun it, drive far away and forget about everything – screw the money I'd just dropped at the office. Run. *Again*. Only I couldn't. My life was in there, things I needed.

More important, Dusty was in there, too. Helpless and on his own.

I forced myself to lift my foot, to let the car inch slowly forward.

As I crawled, I scanned the vehicle for a Zipcar sticker, a Hertz plate cover, anything that would give it away as a rental, because Davis didn't own a car. There was nothing. It was just a navy-blue Subaru with normal plates.

Please don't be Davis please don't be Davis.

My foot hovered over the accelerator, ready to hit the gas if necessary, as I drove past the car . . .

I exhaled. Through the window, I saw a woman.

It wasn't him. I hadn't been found. Not yet.

Slowly, I pulled into my driveway and got out.

I squinted as I watched the woman emerge from the car, my headache from this morning still lingering, joined now by a sick feeling in the pit of my stomach.

'You're home!' the woman said cheerfully, walking quickly toward me. 'Don't worry, I only just got here.' Her body was round and soft, and she was draped in one of those loose-fitting earth-toned dresses that obscured your curves, the kind you had to be at least forty to pull off; all the shops in town sold them. In the sunlight, a cluster of gray hairs stood at attention on the crown of her head, popping against the rest of her deep-auburn hair. Her eyes were pale blue and piercing – same color as the sky.

'Sorry, but do I know you?'

She laughed as she tugged at the neckline of her dress. 'Of course you don't. I've started this off all wrong.' She stuck out her hand. 'I used to live here,' she said, taking mine in hers. 'I'm Rachel.'

'Oh,' I managed, quickly pulling my hand back. In person, she was nothing like the woman I'd imagined. Older, for one thing, definitely mid-forties, but it was more than that. By the way John and Vera had talked about her, I'd pictured some sort of vixen, a femme fatale. This woman was attractive, sure, maybe once she'd even stopped whole rooms with her bottomless eyes and Titian hair, but not now. Now she'd blend right in with the rest of the Woodstock ladies of a certain age, clad in amethyst rings and Birkenstocks. I stole a quick look at her feet, confirming.

'I'm sorry to bother you, er . . .' She paused, an eyebrow raised.

I had no choice. 'Lucy.'

'Lucy,' she repeated. 'It's just, I have a freelance client who sent one of my checks here. I had the mail forwarding turned on at the post office when I left at the end of July, but it only lasts a month. I put my new address huge on the top of my invoices, but this man apparently can't be bothered to read that even when it's printed in bright red ink. I could ask him to reissue it, but I've already been waiting for over a month, and I kind of need the check. I didn't want to bust into your mailbox while you weren't here. That would be creepy,' she said.

'And a felony,' I added.

'Right,' she said, grinning. 'I just thought, maybe you wouldn't mind checking for me? It's awfully rude to ask, but I'm a bit desperate. I was going to ask John or Vera to ask you, but it seemed easier to go straight to the source.'

Quickly, I shook myself out of my trance. 'Of course,' I said. I walked over to the mailbox and opened it. Sure enough, there was loads of junk mail addressed to her, and a slim white envelope that looked decidedly like a check. I handed it over.

Her eyes lit up, sparkling, as we walked back to our cars. 'Oh god, I'm so relieved. I was about to ask my ex-husband for a loan, which is just as horrible as it sounds.'

'No worries,' I said.

'I'm a photographer,' Rachel went on. 'So it's not like the money is coming from some endlessly running faucet. More like a drip drip drip, you know what I mean?'

I nodded as it dawned on me – that explained the photos.

'Glad you got your check,' I said as I popped open the trunk. 'I should probably get my stuff inside. Groceries.'

'Oh,' she said. 'You have lots of bags. Let me help you.'

I paused. I wasn't sure if I should be inviting strangers into my home . . .

'Least I can do after you helped me,' she added.

'Sure,' I said, my curiosity quickly getting the better of me. It's not like she was some sort of criminal or anything. 'I mean, if you really want.'

We grabbed the bags, and she followed me inside.

Dusty ran to greet us, pawing at Rachel's legs. 'Down, Dusty!' I said as I walked in. 'He loves people.'

'And I love dogs.' She set the bags down and swiftly scooped him up, holding him to her chest.

'Wow,' I said as he nuzzled her neck. 'He doesn't usually let people do that – not besides me.'

'I grew up with dogs. No less than three at a time. On a farm up in Rochester. I swear to god they all think I'm one of them. That's what my ex used to say, anyway.' As if on cue, Dusty licked furiously at her chin. She allowed it for a moment, then set him down and grabbed the bags again as her head swiveled back and forth. 'Love what you've done with the place,' she said.

I smirked. 'Did you try to make it your own?'

Rachel laughed. 'Not really. Just embraced the woodland hippie chic,' she said. 'Right down to the Buddhist tomes. I lived here while I was knee-deep in a divorce, so it felt easier than arguing with my husband about who was going to get the Eames chair that we never should have spent so much on anyway.'

A chuckle escaped my throat. She was warm, cheerful, and impossibly down-to-earth, the last person you'd expect to get into any sort of feud with anyone. I walked to the kitchen. 'You can just set the bags on the counter.'

Dutifully, she did, and I followed her back out to the main room.

She spun on her heel. 'Watson, I think I've spotted something I left behind.' She walked toward the bedroom, and I pictured her opening the dresser drawer, pulling out the photos, tucking them into one of her dress's oversize pockets.

She stopped at the doorway instead. 'The quilt,' she said,

turning back to me. 'Please don't tell Maggie I abandoned it. Not sure if you've met her yet – older woman who lives next door. She gave it to me for Christmas. Got it at some antiques fair or something.'

'I met her yesterday, actually,' I said. 'Er, do you want it back?'

She grimaced. 'Not really. I'm going for a minimalist thing in my new place – turns out, I got the Eames chair after all – and that quilt looks much better here. I'm afraid it's your cross to bear now.'

I stifled a laugh, then took a deep breath. *I should tell her about the photos, hand them over,* I thought. I had the perfect opening. Only something stopped me. The way Vera kept looking to John every time she said Rachel's name, practically poisoning the air between them . . .

'Mind if we trade numbers?' Rachel asked. 'Just in case any more of my important mail comes here? Not the junk, of course.'

'Sure,' I said, pulling out my phone. She rattled off her digits, and as I keyed them in, a text from Vera popped up on my screen.

So much fun last night, I hope you're feeling okay today!

I swiped it away quickly, like a child caught doing something naughty, then saved Rachel into my contacts.

When I looked up, her face was momentarily unreadable, but quickly broke into a grin. 'I should get out of your hair,' she said, walking briskly back to the living room. 'Thank you so much.'

'Anytime,' I said, turning to follow her. A thought occurred to me then, quick as a flash. 'Oh, and Rachel?'

She flipped around. 'Yeah?'

'This is kind of weird to ask, but I was just in town, and I went by the gallery, the one that John and Vera own. There was this awful graffiti on the window – kind of, well, calling one of them a pervert – do you know what that's about?'

Rachel's eyes widened, then returned to normal so quickly I half thought I hadn't seen a thing.

'Sorry, I –'

'No, it's fine,' she said, shaking her head. 'It's just teenagers, I'm sure.'

'Okay,' I said, forcing a grin to ease the tension. 'That's what I thought, but I just wanted to ask.'

She nodded again, and in a few quick steps, she was gone, Dusty whining as I closed the door behind her.

Once her car was out of sight, I returned to the bedroom and carefully slid the top dresser drawer open. Beneath my underwear and my mother's scarf, John was still there, tucked neatly away.

I stared at the photos, all sorts of imaginings entering my head: clandestine portrait sessions, exchanged love letters . . . *Something* had happened to throw their friendship off balance, that much was clear. Was it your run-of-the-mill affair? Had it not been teenagers after all? Had someone found out, painted those words on their gallery? Had Vera done it herself, in a moment of wifely rage?

No, I thought. It didn't make sense. It was probably just a portrait session. I was getting ahead of myself.

I nestled the photos back into the furniture brochure, then froze.

One, two, three, four.

I flinched. There had been five yesterday. *I swear to god, there were five photos.*

Pain seared my chest as I rushed from the closet, practically pouncing on my notebook. I'd written the words clearly: *Bedroom closet: Five photos in top drawer of dresser (all of one man).*

What the ever-loving hell?

You won't leave, Lucy, you don't have the guts.

Returning to the closet, I counted them again. I checked the other drawers, finding nothing. A feeling so real and physical, it was etched into my brain. Of knowing it had been one way, knowing the invoice had been right there on my desk, the scarf tied around my side of the headboard, but staring at a reality turned ever so slightly off-kilter.

I sank onto the bed and stared at the wallpaper – it looked like the pattern in my childhood bedroom in Seattle.

I didn't need Ellie or even Vera. I needed my mom. My body ached for her, the phantom limb that was my mother once again making itself known. The one you needed when shit hit the fan, when you had the flu, when you didn't get that promotion, when you ran out on your boyfriend and felt like you were losing your mind.

The one you'd never stop craving, no matter how often you told yourself to stop.

My phone rang, and I jumped, the sound still foreign, intrusive. It was Vera.

'Hi,' I managed.

'Hey, neighbor.' Her voice was bright. 'I was going to text you again but I thought it would be easier to call. We're going on a hike in twenty minutes or so, want to come? I've filled the Camel-Bak and we've got granola bars and dark chocolate. All you have to bring is your lovely self.'

In the background, I heard John's voice. 'Tell her it's a relaxed hike. Not too hard. No need for gear.'

'I don't know,' I said, hands shaking. I couldn't leave before finding that photo. What if Davis had somehow, inexplicably, figured out where I was already? My stomach twisted, and I imagined the gelatinous hollandaise coating my stomach as my headache reminded me that it had never fully gone away.

Vera laughed. 'That's what you said yesterday about dinner, and don't tell me you didn't have fun.' She seemed to have written off the discovery of my bruise completely. I was grateful for that, but I still needed to figure out what was going on. 'Besides, it's the most gorgeous hike. I know you'll love it.'

I was about to mutter an excuse – rain check, work to do, over-indulged at brunch – when my eyes caught a slice of something glossy, peeking out from beneath the dresser. I rushed into the closet and grabbed it. The fifth photo.

'Lucy?' I heard on the other end. 'You still there?'

Relief flooded me so wildly, I almost wanted to cry.

Nine

We made our way to the trailhead in John's truck.

It was dirty, dust caked on its silver exterior, likely from driving out to his studio in the woods. Through the back window, I saw two-by-fours, bits of plywood, and a huge roll of fabric wrapped in plastic, jostling every time John stepped on the gas. He'd told me that he made his own canvases – so much more affordable, so much more control. As I sat there, smelling stale coffee from tossed-aside to-go cups and the naked stink of weed, I tried to imagine Davis in a pickup – he'd always wanted a VW, *that* was his dream car – or him with two-by-fours, or a circular saw.

No question, Davis knew how to work with his hands, but not to make things – to break them instead.

As we rode along, Vera switched songs like a DJ in one of the clubs Ellie and I used to go to in Bushwick, moving on after forty-five seconds or so, taking only the verses she wanted – croony Dinah Washington, bouncy Katy Perry – and leaving the rest. She sang loud and slightly flat, John's head turning toward her as frequently as safety allowed, his fingers always twisted through hers, the two of them knit so tightly together.

'Slow down,' Vera said, as a turnoff came into view. 'I want to go by the cabin. My hiking boots are there.'

John nodded, making the turn, and we found our way to a dead-end road.

'This is John's studio,' Vera said as we pulled up in front of a small cabin, even tinier than what I'd imagined. Wooden siding painted dark gray, faded and eaten through by weather or bugs or who knows what. A roof that looked like it was barely holding up. Trees everywhere. Bushes and vines. The ends of summer's growth.

Vera flipped around in her seat. 'I'll just run in and get my shoes. Back in a sec.'

I watched as she flitted across the dirt and into the cabin, not even stopping to unlock the door.

'You don't lock it?' I asked, hardly able to contain my surprise. I couldn't imagine leaving anything unlocked – no matter how remote.

'Not out here,' John said, matter-of-factly. 'We used to, but then we got out of the habit. I was teaching these art classes, and it got easier for us to leave it open, in case students beat me here. There's nothing valuable inside, just canvas and paints. I keep all my finished work back at the gallery anyway.'

He retrieved his phone from his pocket, scrolling through news feeds as he tapped his fingers on the steering wheel. I found myself suddenly wondering what he'd say if I showed him that video from college, whether he'd pity me or judge me or accept it as one of those things. Then I remembered how Davis had reacted, despite my trying to convince him that it wasn't that big a deal – *You're telling me these assholes have seen my girlfriend like that?* – and I pushed the thought away.

'So do you still do the classes?' I asked.

John looked up, catching my eyes in the rearview, and shook his head. 'Not really.'

'Got tired of it?'

The wrinkles in his forehead deepened. 'No, but like with the gallery, the market ebbs and flows. There's not as much interest in them anymore. Haven't done them since the spring.'

I thought of that girl in the café – Al – *locals won't touch the place*. And the graffiti – *you fucking pervert*. What had happened to turn their business upside down? Could an affair with a neighbor have had that much of an effect? Wasn't Woodstock supposed to be progressive?

Vera burst in then, a pair of muddy hiking boots in her hands. 'Let's go.'

We wound back the way we'd come, made another turn, and I imagined John inside the studio, teaching classes, when people had still wanted to take them. Painting, drawing, what have you. It sounded lovely. Indulgent. The kind of life one was meant to live. The kind I'd dreamed of, after all was lost.

Then, for the briefest of moments, I imagined Rachel in there with him.

He eased onto the brake and made another turn. The road crumbled to gravel as gangly trees arched their arms around us, luring us into a bare parking lot, not a car in sight.

'There's no one here.'

Vera turned around. 'That's why we love this trail,' she said. 'We have it all to ourselves.'

We unloaded the car, Vera looping the CamelBak over her shoulders, me grasping a metal water bottle they'd loaned me. John pulled on an old pack and retied his laces, then checked his phone, swiped away notifications.

'This one's always ultra-prepared,' Vera said, eyeing his screen.

He tucked it into the back pocket of his jeans. 'I *may* have downloaded the entire area to my off-line Google Maps. It only uses your GPS coordinates, so we can't get lost when the service goes out.'

'We've done this plenty,' Vera said. 'There's no way to get lost.'

John rocked back on his heels, looked at me. 'My dad always

told me it was better to be overprepared than under. It's a hard habit to shake.' He was right. Your parents never left you; their little pieces of wisdom followed you wherever you went, like a cloud casting a shadow. I loved and hated that he knew that as well as I did.

We paused at the marker for the trailhead, and Vera lifted the lid to a metal box marked PLEASE REGISTER. She retrieved a clipboard from inside, its papers ruffled like tulle. She signed her name on it, as well as John's, and then handed it to me. 'You should sign in.'

My limbs tightened as I remembered the notice at the restaurant. It was silly, but the idea of signing my name, physical proof of my whereabouts, was terrifying. Only it didn't matter, I reminded myself. I'd been careful this time. I'd taken all the necessary precautions. Hell, I'd gone above and beyond.

Vera narrowed her eyes. 'Is that a problem?'

'See, now this is what I meant about being pushy,' John ventured, nudging her with his elbow.

Vera rolled her eyes and I found myself wishing I'd known what it was like to bicker without fear.

'Gimme,' I said, taking the clipboard and glancing over the sheet. Vera Abernathy and John Nolan. She hadn't taken his name – I loved that. Quickly, I scribbled *Lucy King* on the clipboard in elaborate script. I added the date and time, just as Vera had done above. 'I've seen these before,' I added as Vera looked at me, trying to read me like a book. 'I just didn't think anyone actually filled them out.'

'We didn't used to,' Vera said, a hand on the strap of her Camel-Bak.

John took two big steps ahead, eager to get going, and she followed.

'What changed?'

Ahead of me, I saw Vera shrug.

'A girl disappeared here last year,' she said, without bothering to turn around. 'They didn't find her body until weeks later, half-way down the river.'

I was winded by mile two. It wasn't the distance so much as the climbing, so steady and constant I could hardly appreciate the change from birch groves to ferns, storybook oaks to running brooks.

Vera and John had told me this was a fairly easy climb, but I wasn't exactly in the habit of hiking, and besides, my head still ached from the night before, the exercise only exacerbating it. They walked ahead easily, pointing out butterflies and chipmunks and other wildlife to each other, and to me.

'You okay?' Vera turned, perching a hand on her hip. She had a light sheen of sweat on her forehead, whereas I was covered in it. 'Want some water?'

I nodded. The bottle she'd loaned me had long ago been emp-tied. She held the spout up to me, and I leaned down, drinking, as if she were the momma dog and I was the suckling puppy.

John knelt to tighten his laces, then stood. 'I hope we aren't tiring you out,' he said. 'We're used to hiking now, and Vera here's a runner, but I guess you probably don't get much of that in the city. Apart from those goddamned subway stairs.'

I was too tired to laugh. I finished drinking, and Vera offered the spout to John, but he shook his head. 'Okay, big, strong man,' she said. Then, turning to me: 'It's the Wisconsin in him.' She laughed and he did, too, and I remembered how he'd used a sim-ilar line only last night. They were perfect for each other – weren't they?

Water sloshed in my stomach; my insides felt like jelly. 'You guys should go ahead,' I said. 'I don't want to slow you down.'

'You're not,' John said, though we all knew it was a lie.

A prick of heat in my chest. I didn't like the thought of them waiting; it would only add to the pressure to pick up the pace, and I hated feeling rushed. 'Go. Just wait up at the summit, and we can hike down together.' My voice rose the slightest bit. 'I'd rather be able to go at my own pace.'

They exchanged a look.

'*Seriously.*'

Vera bit her lip, but her determination waned. 'Take the Camel-Bak, at least.' She shimmied out of it and handed it to me, then linked her hand in John's. Quickly, they disappeared out of sight.

I'm not sure how much farther it was to the summit, but it felt like it took me ages to get there. Wet leaves and mossy rocks tripped me, my calves ached, and my breath came in short, angry bursts. My stomach seemed ready to empty itself at any moment, and my soul craved the safety my mother had once offered: protection from the dangers of hikes, the fear of being found, angry men swearing at me for daring not to be a local, the ache of loneliness I'd come to know too well.

I found them at a clearing, standing close, talking among themselves like no one else existed. Vera's lips were drawn into a thin, flat line as John said something I couldn't hear.

Her eyes caught mine, and her expression instantly brightened. 'There you are,' she said, tightening her ponytail and grinning almost too wide. 'We were getting worried!'

I stumbled up the rest of the hill and sucked hard on the water from the CamelBak. 'Sorry,' I said, practically wheezing. 'Did I take that long?' My stomach twisted again.

'Not at all,' John said, eyes flashing briefly to his wife. 'We're just used to this one. Old pros.'

I stepped forward and took in the views. Mountains rolled on all around us, every shade of green, clouds skimming the horizon like a painting. I gazed down at a rushing river below. My throat felt thick and coated with mucus. It was so far down to the bottom. 'Is this the summit?' I asked.

Vera shook her head. 'It's about a half mile more, but this is the, well, the spot.'

'What spot?' I asked.

She scratched at the strap of her tank, exposing her sports bra – neon green, this time. 'Where that poor girl fell. They say she stepped out to take a photo, and the rocks just crumbled. The river's just below.'

'That's why I like to be careful,' John said. 'With my GPS and all that. It's easy to disappear on a hike. You read stories in the news all the time. Someone takes a photo, heads off the trail, and then that's it.'

I was too afraid to go closer to the edge, but I could hear the water rumbling over the riverbed. Leaves rustled behind me, and I jumped, gasping.

Before I could stop myself, I imagined Davis, standing there, ready to push me off the ledge, end it all, give me the punishment I'm sure he thought I deserved.

Vera stepped closer, reaching out a hand toward me. 'What's wrong, Lucy?'

Instinctively, I took a step away from her.

'Are you okay?' John asked, but I backed up even more, shaking my head –

'God,' she said. 'You look green.'

I bent over, hands on my knees.

The river rushed in my periphery, and I retched – one, two, three times.

I'm so scared, I thought as tears filled my eyes and spilled down my cheeks, and I continued to heave.

John stepped forward, pressing a napkin into my hand, and when there was nothing left to spit out, he helped me stand up straight, his hand, strong and steadying, resting on my elbow, bathing it in heat. Electricity. 'Whatever happened to you,' John said. 'Whatever *he* –' His voice deepened with anger, protectiveness, but he took a breath, calming down. 'Whatever it is, it's going to be okay now.' He squeezed my elbow gently. 'We'll make sure of that.'

Vera sidled up, too, wrapping an arm around my shoulders, nowhere near as strong as John's but comforting all the same. 'John's right,' she said in my ear as more tears came. 'Like I said last night, you're safe with us.'

Something crazy happened in that moment, something I hadn't expected, pushing every intrusive thought away.

I believed them. What's more, I decided to tell them the truth.

Ten

Perhaps things wouldn't have gotten so bad if I had better learned to prevent Davis's triggers.

Maybe then I wouldn't be standing in the middle of the woods upstate, bile sour in my mouth as I tried to explain the details of a failed, abusive relationship to my new friends.

But it was a lost cause from the beginning – there were simply too many things that could piss Davis off.

He didn't like criticism – no one did, but he really hated it – especially in public.

He didn't like me flirting, or anything that could be construed as flirting, which included wearing sexy clothes outside of our apartment, spending too much time on my makeup, smiling too long at waiters or bartenders he deemed attractive, or engaging in banter with male coworkers, even if it was only about work.

He didn't like me talking about my exes. Not even stupid, insignificant ones. Not even as a joke.

He didn't like any openness about our sex life. Though it was always good between us, one of the ways we were undeniably in sync, it was his and his alone to enjoy. No sharing even the smallest details with others.

He didn't like me trying to control him, no matter how tiny the ask. He was an adult, he said. He'd do it all in his own time.

He didn't like me going places without telling him. Hours that couldn't be accounted for. He was like a nosy client that way, needing to know how I spent every minute of time he had decided was his.

I know it sounds terrible, like some sort of prison sentence, but really, it wasn't. I would have left far sooner if it were. As with any person you spend all your time with, you learn what gets under their skin. You do your best to avoid it. You grow as a person, as a couple. You communicate your needs.

And the good, it was so good. The sex, the emotional support, the excitement of us. Once, we took a road trip to Niagara Falls, spur of the moment, upon learning that neither of us had been. We kissed slowly as the water sprayed around us.

But I was human. And no matter how hard I tried, I couldn't completely avoid setting him off. And as time went on, as our second year together blended into our third, his punishments began to escalate, began to get physical.

A loosening of the screws that held the mirror over my side of the bed in place – the antique one that had been given to me by my mother. He'd been so convincing, helping to bandage up my head, looking up places on Yelp that could replace cracked glass. I found the screwdriver two days later, sitting between pairs of socks, out of place, almost like he wanted me to discover it.

And then, waking up in the middle of the night. An intense shooting pain in my arm, Davis beside me, breathing deeply, sleeping, or so I thought. A bruise appearing, pale purple, the next morning. His face, blank, when I'd asked him if he knew how I'd gotten it. *It's your bruise,* he'd said, laughing. *Not mine.*

Davis's cruelty was never random, was never something that just exploded. He swore far less than the average New Yorker – and never at me. And in our years together, he raised his voice only a handful of times. Instead, his anger simmered until he found a way to channel it. He was proud of his control. He looked down on those who didn't have it, people like me.

When I tried to leave last May, after the fourth time I'd woken with bruises on my body, I wasn't stupid. I knew by then how much he watched me. I changed my Apple password, and I disconnected that damn Nest camera. I didn't use my credit card, either. Still, I underestimated how tied together we'd become. At the only dog-friendly hotel I'd found in Brooklyn, where I'd been holed up for two days, I'd found a card advertising the hotel's app – *Download to get free high-speed internet,* it had promised. Apparently, Davis had set us up as a family in Apple, which meant that even with my new password, our app downloads were synched and shared.

When I went down to the lobby for Dusty's afternoon walk, which I always did right at three, he and Ellie were waiting for me, the sun streaking through the windows, a beautiful late-spring day. He came up to me and hugged me tight, asked me how my 'solo staycation' had been, told me he'd brought Ellie along for a surprise brunch at a nearby dog-friendly restaurant. I'd been too in shock to argue, to explain to him – and her – that I'd been considering leaving for good. Maybe a part of me wanted to buy his story, wanted it to be okay for us. His punishments were all so strange, so hard to pinpoint, that sometimes I told myself they'd never even happened. And waking up to bruises – could I even be totally sure they were from him? What if I'd started sleep-walking and didn't know it? What if? What if?

Besides, what he offered me, when things were good, was so much. He was my family, even if a completely dysfunctional one.

We're meant to be together, he'd said when I was back in the apartment, and then, later that night, much later, just as we were drifting off to sleep: *You can't leave me, babe. Ever.*

I'd woken that morning to a jolt, a smack, a red-hot pain across my face. To Davis turning around, walking from the room as if

70

nothing had happened. I half expected him to look back and smile – *Sorry, babe.*

And as if that wasn't enough: The next day, I was walking Dusty, my face coated in makeup, when his leash snapped in two, and he chased a squirrel across two lanes of traffic. I was able to catch him, thank god, nearly killing myself as I ran out in front of the oncoming cars, but when I examined the leash afterward, it looked like it had partially been cut. And when that night, I pulled the pocketknife that had been a gift from Davis's grandfather from his tossed-aside jeans, it became so clear.

It didn't matter that Davis always kept that knife on him, to open Amazon boxes and meal-prep subscriptions. I still knew it, deep down.

He had done this. He had put Dusty at risk to hurt me.

If I tried to go again, Davis would find a way to take away what I cared about most. Which meant that I couldn't *try* – I had to succeed.

I didn't tell Vera and John all this, standing there in the middle of the woods, sun beating down on the trail, my stomach still churning, the river careening below. I couldn't sum up three years of Davis and me in one conversation. I didn't tell them what had happened on Wednesday – it was still too raw, too fresh – though the images flashed in my mind anyway. The searing pain on my cheek. The way I'd struggled, hands shaking, to dial 911. Then the smash of my phone against the exposed brick wall of our apartment.

But I told them what mattered: that he'd controlled me, that he'd hurt me, that he'd made it clear I could never leave.

John stroked my back and Vera scooted closer, drawing us tighter together.

Most of all, I told them what I knew myself, so deeply:

No matter what happened, Davis could never, *ever* know I was here.

71

It was only when I was back, when they'd dropped me off – my legs already aching from the hike, my nauseated stomach begging for water, my heart both light and heavy with the relief and shame of someone finally knowing – that my world, momentarily pasted back together, tore open again.

I grabbed my computer, queued up my untraceable VPN connection, and logged in to my old email, needing to check. To know.

There it was, what I'd been fearing.

What, at the same time, I'd been praying for.

An email from Davis.

You won't get away like this. I will find you, I swear to god.

Eleven

Our dinner looked almost savage against Vera and John's big white ceramic bowls – coq au vin in an oxblood sauce. With my fork, I jabbed at a last bit of chicken. Succulent and rich, with just a hint of tartness.

Vera pushed her dish forward and leaned back in her chair. 'That was perhaps the best take-out we've had yet from the French place. Don't you think?'

I nodded, pulling my cardigan tighter, as a breeze snaked through one of the windows, cracked open a couple of inches. Over the past six weeks, Woodstock had changed almost as much as I had. The sky was darkening earlier now, the late-October air was crisp but not yet cold, and the leaves had lit up with color, splashing the landscape with watercolor hues.

'Almost makes the ten-dollar delivery charge worth it,' John said with a laugh. 'I can't stand to think how much we've racked up in charges lately.'

He was right. We did order a lot of take-out. If Vera was up to it, she'd make lasagna, her pièce de résistance, or John would whip up an elaborate meal, a recipe with a ton of steps and ingredients, using practically every pot in the house, roux and roasted eggplants caked onto cast iron. Occasionally, I cooked for them at my place, things that were simpler, like my mom's turkey tetrazzini. John would always know which recipes had come from my mother and which hadn't.

But too often, we'd order something. The steak house that wrapped baked potatoes in foil, the French restaurant whose sauces were like crack. Chinese to-go, paper bags printed with grease.

I never expected our relationship to blossom so quickly. But after the hike where I told all, they invited me to dinner the next night, and then I insisted on returning the favor, and before we knew it, more nights of the week than not, we were eating together.

We never went into town, despite my repeated asking. Not to that bar, Platform. Not to Schoolhouse for brunch. Once Al, the waitress there, had asked me why my neighbors never came, and I told her what they'd told me – that being so close to the gallery made it feel like work. From the look on her face, I don't think she quite believed it, and I can't say I did, either. There was the graffiti, for one thing, which still didn't sit right with me, even though I told myself it was just rebellious kids. And the fact that locals wouldn't go to the gallery. And then the way that Maggie, the older woman next door, who always managed to time her dog walks with mine, went quiet, her eyes ominous, if I ever mentioned my friendship with Vera and John.

What's more, I never saw a visitor at the farmhouse besides me – no one going in, no one coming out. Even for a couple of artsy introverts, it was strange. And Vera and John – they weren't exactly introverts anyway.

And then there was the day, last week, when I went over to find Vera and John staring at the tires on John's truck. 'Cheap, unreliable tires,' Vera said, when I asked her about it. But I wasn't stupid – they looked slashed.

There was something off about them, about their standing in this town, that much was clear. There were people who didn't like them, for whatever reason. But in spite of my curiosity, I didn't hound them for answers. They'd become too dear, too important to me already. I was too afraid of losing them to push.

Rachel's name had disappeared from their whiteboard – erased, just like that – and though her junk mail still collected in my mailbox, she never came by to retrieve it again. If it had been an affair, if she'd been the one to slash the tires, it was none of my business. And I wasn't willing to risk our nights together, tucked away at their place or mine, to find out.

Vera leaned back even farther in her chair, taking another sip of wine. She was sitting almost cross-legged, one knee hooked over the other, her hand on the table, barely grazing John's. He turned his hand over, and their fingers intertwined, like puzzle pieces – a perfect fit.

Life wasn't perfect. I won't pretend it was.

Though Davis hadn't emailed me again, his lack of contact didn't quell my fear. I knew he was planning, waiting for the best time to strike.

Many mornings, I woke up with a hangover, and my money was dwindling fast. Though I was still pitching articles and writing essays, my payments went directly from the publishing companies to my bank account, which I'd been too afraid to access since coming up here, in case Davis had found a way to keep track of where I made withdrawals. I was planning on making a trip to the city soon, emptying it all and then leaving right away, but even so, there was only so much in there. The wine and takeout could not go on forever.

As I took another sip of wine, I let myself glance at Vera and John's intertwined hands again, unable to help myself.

There was something else threatening the carefully balanced triangle we'd created – more than what the residents of Woodstock felt about a couple of Manhattan snobs. More, even, than Davis.

Me.

It was impossible to make it stop, though I had tried. Over the past six weeks, whenever John and I were alone, I couldn't help but fantasize, imagining him and me, together. Picturing a world where *I* would be the one he reached for after telling a joke, where *we* would retire upstairs in the farmhouse, not them.

Like last week, in my kitchen: Vera on the sofa a room over, John next to me at the counter where we couldn't be seen. Our hands had accidentally touched as he passed me the plates, and he'd laughed, jovial and deep, as he nudged me with his elbow: 'I'm pretty sure the cook's not allowed to do dishes.'

I turned, and he was right there, and all sorts of fantasies ran through my head.

It was a stupid crush, a schoolgirl one, really, one that had bloomed so quickly I found myself replaying Mr Darcy's words in my head – *I was in the middle before I knew that I had begun*. John was everything I'd ever been looking for in a man. Safe, but sexy all the same.

The feelings weren't mutual, and I was thankful they weren't. To him, nothing had transpired in that instant beyond run-of-the-mill helping with the dishes. His eyes were for Vera, not me. Whose wouldn't be?

But still, I'd thought of him, the closeness of him, the way he smelled like wood chips and orange oil, when I reached beneath the covers in bed that night.

Sometimes I wondered if maybe it hadn't even been an affair, if Rachel had simply fallen prey to his charms, too. If Vera and John's friend, that warm, cheerful, and seemingly harmless divorcée, had developed a crush on John, and if that's what had torn the trio apart. If, one night, I'd have too much wine, and my feelings would show – I'd give myself away.

I wouldn't, I told myself. My love for Vera, it was strong enough to prevent me from ever showing my cards. Vera, whose honesty was refreshing, whose demeanor was mothering without being controlling, encouraging without ever feeling fake. Vera, who – even more than John – had become my true protector, the one I could count on above all else. Vera's goodness like a magnet, an ionic tug. He was my crush, but she was my love, warmth deep in my insides, comforting as chicken soup, sweet and rich as dark chocolate. She was the mother I didn't have anymore, the friend I could be honest with – my missing pieces, all the women I needed but no longer had, rolled into one. Between the two of them, I felt like I had a family again. On our own, we were off-kilter – messed up by a combination of our histories and our proclivities – but together, we were different. Whole. They had promised to keep me safe, and so far they had kept their promise.

Now, if only I could figure out a way to spend time with them without burning through so much money. I took a last sip of wine, draining my glass.

Vera noticed immediately. She grabbed the bottle of pinot and topped me off.

'By the way,' I said, broaching the subject as delicately as I could, 'pretty soon I'm going to have to cut back on the take-out and fancy wine.'

John leaned back in his chair, the wood creaking. 'Fun fact: We should probably cut back, too.'

Vera's head tilted to the side. 'You don't like my delicious wine?'

I shrugged, forcing a laugh. Though Vera and John always said they needed money, it didn't stop them from spending it. 'Of course I do,' I said, scratching at the table. 'But you know, just the usual, trying to make ends meet.'

Vera bit her lip. 'Don't you have savings?'

I hesitated mid-scratch, stretching my fingers out. Her bluntness still managed to surprise me sometimes. John's face scrunched up, but it didn't stop her. 'Like a safety net, you know?'

'Not really,' I said quietly. 'And I don't have my parents to fall back on for help. We don't have to talk about it.'

John caught my eye. 'Sorry,' he said. 'We spend so much time together, we've forgotten what's appropriate.'

'Exactly,' Vera said, ignoring his point. 'We've been spending almost every day together. I'd think that by now we could be direct with each other.'

'It's not a big deal,' I said. 'I just can't go on like this for many more months.'

'You're our guest,' John cut in. 'Let's just call tonight our treat.'

I shook my head. 'You don't have to do that.'

'We want to,' he said. 'Really.'

Vera nodded, only there was something else there. A *but* in her expression. She and John exchanged a glance. He shook his head so slightly it was almost imperceptible, then scratched at one of his cuticles. Suddenly, there was a wall, invisible but impenetrable, them on one side, me on the other. Only this time, it wasn't about long-abandoned Rachel; this time, somehow, it was about me.

'We might as well,' Vera started.

'Oh, come on, V,' John sighed. 'Not right now. Not when we're –'

'She deserves to know,' she snapped.

Her words shook me, and I felt my pulse tick up.

John's smile deflated, but his eyes split me in two, imploring me to forgive whatever was about to be said. 'I'm sorry, Lucy, we didn't want to say anything just yet.' He cleared his throat. 'Everything's been so good. I know we've only known each other, what is it? Two months? It's just we've all gotten so close, and we don't want to screw that up.' He bit his lip. 'But since Vera's already begun . . .'

It was less than two months, actually, but those six weeks had seemingly changed everything.

John took Vera's hand in his, and they stared at me, and for a second, I know it sounds crazy, but I swear I thought they were going to ask me to have a threesome. The truth is, I can't say I hadn't thought about it. The truth is, I would absolutely say yes.

Vera took a deep breath. 'See, you don't have to worry about spending money for several more months – not with us, at least.'

'Huh?'

'John has to leave,' she said finally, her hand slipping from his.

I noticed the wine spilling first. I'd dropped my glass, and the liquid swam over their wide walnut table, where there were already many stains.

'Sorry,' I said, turning the glass right side up, but the wine was already a bull's-eye the size of a dinner plate.

'Don't worry about it,' Vera said, tossing one of her linen napkins on top. Ruining it, surely.

'I don't understand. What do you mean, leave? You guys are separating or something?' I asked, the words sharp, slicing at the security we'd established.

Vera laughed. 'No, of course not.'

'Far from it,' John said, as jealousy stabbed at me instead. They were as rock-solid as the table – stained, wine-soaked, but held together.

Vera cleared her throat. 'I suppose I didn't start off quite right. I'm leaving, too.' Her lips pressed together, as if that were somehow answer enough.

'What?' I asked, heart pounding brutally. She'd said she'd protect me, but was I disposable to them, a human takeout container? Toss it in the trash when you're done – no need to do the dishes.

They were like family to me. They were supposed to be, at least. My dream, finally realized, after so much pain and heartache.

They exchanged another glance, trading invisible secrets. They were married, a team; I, an extra cog. I shouldn't have been so naive. 'Should I?' she asked.

'Go ahead,' he said, but his shoulders slumped.

'John and I are *not* splitting up,' Vera said, taking his hand again, giving it a reassuring squeeze. 'But he is going to be heading up north.'

North? I figured we were far enough north already. 'What for? To paint?' The words sounded stupid as soon as they were out of my mouth. I scratched at my forehead, at baby hairs matted down, droplets of sweat.

'No, no,' Vera said. A smile stretched across her face, but it was too thin. Forced. I knew her well enough to tell the difference. 'He needs to get out of Woodstock for a while. Things' – she eyed him briefly – 'are escalating.'

'Escalating?'

'There are . . . well, I know this sounds dramatic, but there are people here who want to hurt me,' John added.

I stared at him. It did sound dramatic – of course it did – but at the same time, I'd been waiting for this, for some sort of explanation that tied it all together – the graffiti, Maggie's obvious dislike of them, their hesitancy to go into town, the slashed tires. Was it more than an affair? Something somehow worse? John was so good – so steady and strong – it was hard to imagine someone wanting to do him actual harm.

Vera took a deep breath. 'The details aren't important. The point is, John's going to disappear for a bit. It's for the best.'

My eyes ping-ponged back and forth, as the word *disappear* stuck to the sides of my brain. I was the disappearer, not John. Not her, too.

'Not really disappear,' she added, with a laugh. 'And I'm going to join him, once I settle up the gallery business and get the farmhouse set up as a rental. We were trying to think of the best way to tell you, but now that you mentioned money, it seems almost perfect, you know. We could actually *help* you. You could manage things for us, while we're gone. The gallery, the farmhouse. The money could help get you back on your feet, and you'd still have plenty of time to write.'

I stared at her – at my friend, my protector, my Vera. 'Just like that?' I asked, my voice already hitting an embarrassingly high pitch. 'You're leaving? And you want me to *work for you*? Christ. Way to let me know.'

'Not work *for us*,' Vera said. 'You just said money was tight. We've been meaning to tell you anyway, and we thought . . .'

'It's getting late.' I scooted my chair back quickly, and it caught the bottom of my stretchy skirt, one I'd borrowed from Vera. I walked briskly to the kitchen, plucked my keys from among the clutter of takeout containers, and made for the kitchen door.

'I'm sorry this is so messed up,' John said, rushing up behind me. 'We didn't mean for it to come out like that.' I turned. He stood only a foot from me, his forehead beaded with sweat. I had the most overwhelming desire to kiss him, turn my crush into something real, grab his face in my hands, feel the swaths of stubble on his cheeks, taste our dinner on his tongue. Run back to Vera, tell her what I'd done, remind her that if she could fuck with my security, I could fuck with hers, too. I could try, at least.

'I don't even know what to say,' I said. 'I'll see you later.'

In seconds I was out the back door. It had begun to rain, and a light drizzle kissed my forearms. I hastened down their driveway, making my way through the dark, ignoring the sounds of wind through grass, coyote howls and owl hoots, the smells of ozone and earth. In the distance, I heard a clatter of thunder as the wind picked up, pushing at me. By the time I got to my cottage, I was out of breath. I'd left the porch light on, hazy yellow, and drops of rain stood out on my shirt, speckled like blood spatter. Another clap of thunder; the rain picked up, crying.

The door.

It was ajar, a thin but unmistakable opening, a clean, laser-cut slice in the wood. Pulse pounding like a migraine, my throat unbearably tight, I shoved it open. 'Dusty,' I called. I flipped on the lights frantically. 'Dusty!'

An empty room. I strained to hear the pitter-patter of doggy paws, dreading the sound of a human's footsteps, of Davis's, instead. Nothing.

'Dusty,' I called louder. I rushed into the bedroom and scanned the room, grabbing my dad's hammer in the process. My sheets were ruffled as they had been when I left, and my computer was closed – hadn't I left it open?

'Dusty!' I cried, sprinting back to the living room.

In the kitchen, I fumbled for the lights.

Dusty sat upright, taking me in, his tail a metronome. I let out a deep sigh, lungs deflating. The doggie door swung behind him. I'd apparently trained him to use the thing right. Hot tears filled my eyes as I knelt to scratch beneath his chin.

'Did you miss me?' I asked him, and he licked my hand. 'Are we going to be okay?' He cocked his head to the side. He didn't know the answer, either.

I returned to the living room, locked the front door, and checked it twice. It didn't close properly unless you bolted it; I knew that, which is why I always did – no matter what.

Grabbing my notebook, I checked every item in the house against my ever-changing inventory, as I had every day since I'd gotten here, but nothing was out of place. I must have forgotten to lock the door; it was the only logical explanation.

Forcing myself to breathe, I brushed my teeth, topped off Dusty's food, drank more water, and sank into bed, but the thoughts were insistent: I couldn't do this alone; I couldn't be here without them. She'd told me I wouldn't have to. She'd told me they would protect me. I had promised myself I wasn't going to be stupid, I wasn't going to trust where I shouldn't, but they had convinced me to let my guard down, and now look how that had turned out.

They were my family, what I'd been seeking for so very long.

In a way, it felt like I'd already lost them.

Twelve

Vera came two days later, in the afternoon.

I ushered her in without exchanging any pleasantries, my relief at seeing her muddled with anger, deep in my chest, at what they'd said, the way they'd said it.

She took a seat on my sofa, looking downright bashful, her hands folded in her lap, her face flushed. Dusty jumped up, and she nuzzled him briefly. She cleared her throat, and I took the seat opposite her. 'I'll get right to it: I really am sorry,' she said. 'For springing all of that on you the other night.'

I picked at a loose thread on the knee of my jeans. 'It was strange not seeing you guys for a couple of days,' I said, without looking up. 'I didn't realize what a rut we'd gotten into.'

I'd meant to say *routine*, but *rut* had come out instead. I wanted to hurt her, I supposed, for tipping the scales we'd balanced so well, for reminding me I couldn't count on anyone.

She didn't take the bait. 'I wanted to give you space.'

I shrugged. 'Okay.'

Vera tugged at the sleeves of her top – all black, as usual, and nearly sheer. 'You didn't call me, either, you know. I figured you didn't want to talk after you ran out like that.'

'I didn't *run out*,' I said, averting my eyes as my voice cracked. 'It was late. I was tired.'

She abandoned her place on the sofa and sat next to me instead, hooking her arm around my shoulders. I didn't shrug her off; it felt so good to have her near me.

'I'm sorry,' I said, steadying my voice, feeling foolish. 'I don't have a lot of people in my life anymore. I don't have family, and I don't have a partner, and it's been nice spending time with you guys, and when you rip the rug out from under me like that, tell me people want to hurt John – which you've never even thought to hint at before – and don't even give me a chance to take it in, and then ask me about watching your house . . . it's like I mean nothing to you.'

She held me closer, tucking my head into the crook of her neck. She smelled like laundry. Her lips found the edge of my forehead, planting a kiss right where my hairline began, and she began to slowly rub my back. 'That couldn't be further from the truth, Lucy. The reason we told you is *because* we care about you so much. I should never have mentioned money. I can see now how insulting that sounded.'

I pulled away, disentangling myself. 'What exactly did John mean when he said people wanted to hurt him? And why didn't you tell me? Don't you think I, of all people, would understand something like that?'

She scooted away from me and stared at her hands. 'I didn't want to tell you because I was afraid you would judge us.'

'Judge you?' I asked. 'Wait, does this have something to do with Rachel?'

Vera looked up, her eyes cutting. 'No,' she snapped. 'It has nothing to do with her.'

She exhaled slowly, and her tone softened. 'I'm sorry. I might as well just tell you the truth. About a year ago, John started teaching art classes.'

'In the cabin,' I said.

She nodded. 'The first few sessions went really well. They were way better than the normal hippie-dippie offerings here. People loved them – locals, mostly, but sometimes a weekender would drop in, too. Anyway, in February, he got the idea to do one-on-one lessons. I guess one of his students was asking, this girl Claire – she was in high school, but she took her work very seriously. I encouraged it, it just seemed like a natural extension of what he was already doing. He took on other private lessons, too. Only after a few months' – she swallowed – 'there were rumors that he and Claire were . . .'

I narrowed my eyes, weight pressing at my chest. 'Were what?'

Vera tugged at the collar of her top, as if suddenly hot. 'I guess people thought, *why is he giving these lessons way out in this cabin in the woods? Why not in town?* Why not in our house, or at the gallery, where I was? Woodstock can be very progressive, but at the same time, it can be small-town, especially for the people who live here year-round. It's a tight-knit community. Insular. People talk. Sometimes, people talk a lot.'

My heart ticked faster. John wasn't like that. John *couldn't* be like that. 'There were rumors that they were *what*, Vera?'

She blinked slowly. 'I don't know, Lucy. It was all hearsay, but . . . well, you know.'

Vera, brutally honest Vera. She'd run up against something even she couldn't say out loud.

'Did she actually . . . *accuse* him?'

Vera shook her head quickly. 'No, but still . . .' She pressed her hands to her knees. 'I overheard someone talking about him at Platform, that bar we told you about – I used to go there for happy hour, after I closed up the gallery – maybe they didn't realize his wife was sitting right there, or maybe they did and just didn't care. Anyway, I went home, and I just *lost it*. I broke half the dishes in the cabinet. Good stuff, too. Stuff he'd gotten from his grandmother and all that. But when John got home, he swore up and down that nothing had ever happened. He seemed appalled that I'd even think it, with a teenager and everything. I asked him how the talk started, and he said he didn't know. Maybe some of her friends let their imaginations get the best of them. Half the people in that class had a crush on him – you've seen John, he's a good-looking guy.'

'But if the girl never even said he did anything . . .'

Vera sighed. 'Her dad was furious, came to our house scream-ing, saying he knew something happened. Afterward, I tried to talk to Claire, but she didn't want to talk to me. And then I guess people found out about that and thought I was harassing, well, a *survivor*, you know.' She lifted a hand, then let it drop. 'I wasn't harassing her. I was just trying to understand. I only ever tried to talk to her a couple of times, but people made it sound like I was stalking her or something, and then that got around, and it all just snowballed. People thought it didn't matter if Claire accused John or not – she was a child, and tons of crimes like this are never reported, which I obviously know. I'm a feminist, too. I just . . .' Her voice trailed off.

I knew the words running through my head were wrong. You believed these sorts of stories. You just did. That's what you did if you were a good woman, a good human. I remember read-ing about that film director, how the girl he raped didn't even want the government to go after him, not after so many years; I had told Ellie that it didn't matter – he still deserved his punish-ment, no matter what the victim thought, what the victim said.

Only this seemed different. This was John. I took a deep breath. 'Do you actually think it's true?'

Vera pressed her lips together. 'Call me awful, but I couldn't believe my husband had a relationship with a sixteen-year-old.'

Her eyes studied my face, searching for my reaction, and I knew it deep inside me: I believed in John's goodness.

In over a month of trying to quell my stupid crush, he'd never done anything even close to inappropriate with me. He loved

Vera; even more, he respected her. I knew vile, hollow men. Davis. All those awful guys in college. John wasn't one of them.

What's more, this explained it all. The graffiti. The way Maggie had told me to watch out for them. The tires, most definitely slashed by Claire's father. It wasn't an affair; it was a rumor.

'I don't believe it, either,' I said finally.

A smile crept across Vera's face.

'So you want to leave because of this gossip?' I asked.

She sighed. 'If it were only that, I would stay and try my best to hold my head high. It's the lawsuit that's got us scared.'

'Lawsuit?'

She sank into the cushions, as if begging them to swallow her whole, and Dusty nestled himself between us. 'Claire's father. He's a top contractor in the area – through his business, he's become friends with a bunch of lawyers, even a judge – and he's over here all the time, driving up and down the road. He says he's just helping out his wife with her work, but I know the truth. I know he wants to scare us. Sam Alby.' She paused, narrowing her eyes at me. 'You haven't seen him, have you? When you moved in or anything?'

'No,' I said. 'I don't see many people on this street.'

'Okay.' She sighed. 'At first he was going on about a criminal case, but nothing ever came of it; then he started talking about a lawsuit. He hasn't filed yet – from what I hear, his lawyer is still speaking to people in town, trying to get witnesses to assassinate John's character – but it's going to happen very soon. It has to. In New York, the statute of limitations for emotional distress is only one year.'

Vera bit at one of her nails, then stopped abruptly, lacing her hands together. 'I spoke to a lawyer. Since Claire hasn't reported a crime, the police can't charge John for statutory rape, but she – well, her father – can sue us for emotional distress, and the damages have a high ceiling. Even if he can't prove it, even if Claire won't testify, we could be tied up in it anyway, hemorrhaging money. He hates John, he believes his daughter has been violated, and he's not going to let it go,' she said. 'Any lawyer worth their salt starts at three hundred dollars an hour. We've only got twenty grand saved between the two of us. That's sixty-six hours of work, Lucy – I've calculated it more than once – not even two goddamn weeks. We would be *completely* wiped out by a lawsuit, and once the savings were gone, we would have to take out a second mortgage, dip into the little equity we have in the house. And if Sam Alby did win . . . the house, the cabin, the business, it's all in both of our names. He could take everything. It would destroy us.'

She tugged at the ends of her hair. 'John found this area an hour west of Lake George in the Adirondacks. It's really remote, all woods and state land. He wants to go there, not tell anyone where we're going. If we use our savings and rent out the house, if the gallery sells a bit more, if we had one big show that could kind of put it on the map, perhaps we could come back after the statute of limitations is up, once things have died down . . . Don't look at me like that.'

'Like what?' I asked.

'Like I'm foolish,' she said. 'The more I think about it, the more John and I talk about it, the more I know it's foolish. I know moving, even if John *calls* it disappearing, isn't going to stop a lawsuit from going through. If we go, we have to really go. We have to make damn sure Sam can't harass us anymore – and that his lawyers can't find us. Sometimes I think this asshole won't stop unless John is dead.'

Van Gogh. The name, the way they'd morbidly turned it into a verb, rang in my head. Their always joke.

Dusty jumped down, leaving white hairs all over Vera's black leggings.

'Look,' she said, lifting a hand before I could ask any more questions. 'I'm sorry to spring all this on you, it's not your problem to solve. I just hope you won't hold this against us.'

'Of course not,' I said. 'I would never hold anything against you. I just, I don't understand –'

Her hand found my knee, squeezed, almost a touch too hard. 'Let's not talk about it anymore, okay? Let's just try and go back to normal. We care about you, Lucy, we really do. Have dinner with us. We can even go somewhere nice. Screw Sam, we can even go somewhere *public*. There's a place just down the road in Kingston that's having a grand opening tonight. It's only fifteen minutes away, but hey, at least it's a different town. It could be our treat.'

'You don't have to do that.'

'I want to,' she said. 'Please.'

I hesitated, questions dancing in my mind. Questions I could tell she didn't want to answer. But did the details even matter right now? I had skeletons, too, plenty of them. We were linked, the three of us, by our torrid backstories. There was a reason we'd met, and I knew it maybe better than they did. They were the best thing that had ever happened to me, and I understood, deep down, that they were good. Our friendship couldn't just *end*, half-cocked plan or not. 'Okay.'

Vera stood up, brushing off Dusty's fur. 'Forget we said anything about this. I'll see you tonight.'

I nodded, but I knew as well as she did that I wouldn't forget. I couldn't.

The restaurant was dark, accented in rich wood and painted a shade of burgundy, like a scene out of *The Maltese Falcon*.

The waitress led us to a booth in the corner, John and Vera

piling into one side, me on the other. I hadn't seen John in days, and I noticed the changes in him like a lover would. His eyes were puffy, as if he hadn't been sleeping well. His beard was unkempt, needing a trim.

I glanced around, wondering if the gossip mill extended beyond the confines of Woodstock. My eyes caught a woman across the restaurant, her head turned toward us, her eyes fixed on John. Christ, I thought. Maybe it really was that bad.

I kept my gaze focused straight ahead as the waitress came and went, rattling off specials, bringing us wine, taking our orders, things that none of us could really afford – lobster fettuccine for John, rack of lamb for Vera, grilled branzino for me.

When the menus were gone, John looked up, his eyes quickly casing the room before landing on me. 'Vera said she told you everything.'

Vera set her wineglass down, nudging him. 'I told you we weren't going to talk about it tonight.'

'I know,' John said. 'I just – I want to thank you, Lucy, for believing me.'

I bit my lip, feeling suddenly awkward. I stole another glance around the restaurant, spotted another woman looking over, but it was hard to tell if I was being paranoid or not.

'It's nothing,' I said, turning back to John. 'I hope you'd believe *me* if it ever came down to it.'

'Obviously I would,' John said.

I took a deep breath, wanting to say more, wanting to say what I'd been thinking since Vera left my cottage . . .

'All right, enough already,' Vera said, lifting her glass. 'Cheers. To putting all this behind us.'

We lifted our glasses and clinked them together, quickly falling back into the comfortable familiarity of our little trio, leaving the bombshells of the last few days unspoken.

It wasn't until our dinners came out, smelling of rosemary and lemon and earthy roasted goodness, and I took a first bite of fish, that I again got up the guts to say what was on my mind. I swallowed. 'Whatever the plan is, I want to come with you.'

Vera froze, a forkful of bleeding lamb hovering in front of her mouth. John grasped at his wine.

I flaked off another bit of fish, summoning all the courage I had in me. 'I know that sounds wild, and I know you guys are still figuring out what you're doing, and we've only known each other a short time, but if you do go, I don't have ties here. My ties here are . . . *you*.'

Their hands intertwined, and Vera's mouth opened to deliver her verdict.

A crash, a wine bottle smashing onto her plate, breaking her glass, sending bones of lamb flying – onto the table, onto John's dish, into Vera's lap.

The wine was everywhere, droplets spattering the bottom of Vera's chin as if she'd been shot in the heart, covering my branzino, turning the white fish purple.

'Goddamn it,' Vera yelled.

'What the *hell*?' John looked up, became a statue.

The man responsible for the spill was large, with a thick neck and sausage-fingered hands. He looked to be in his mid-fifties, with receding gray-brown hair, and he wore a button-up denim shirt, Brillo-pad hairs crawling from beneath worn cuffs. His eyes were fixed on John.

'Oh my god, I'm so sorry!' our waitress cried, hurrying over.

'Sorry about that,' the man told her, his voice almost comically apologetic. 'I tripped on my way out, knocked their wine bottle right over.'

'It's okay, sir,' she said, surveying the damage as everyone around us stared. Vera blotted at the front of her shirt with a napkin, her gaze fixed on her lap. 'Let me go get someone to help.'

The man's eyes turned to slits once the waitress was out of sight. He looked disdainful, disgusted, but at the same time disturbingly calm. He didn't look at me or Vera, only at John.

'She was sixteen, you pervert,' he said, before walking away.

Thirteen

Come over,' Vera said as soon as we reached Shadow Creek Road. 'We can't let the night end like this.'

'Of course,' I said. John pulled into their driveway, and we all got out, still half in shock.

Once inside, Vera went upstairs to change and John headed to the kitchen to make us a much-needed drink.

I sat on the couch, caught the sound of glasses clinking, and leaned back, sinking deeper into the cushions.

They will definitely leave me now, I thought. *No question.*

I sat up straight, my body rigid, something digging into my back from the bowels of the overstuffed sofa. Turning, I lifted a throw to uncover the brass edges of a picture frame. I flipped it over. Vera grinned back, soft and sultry, like she'd taken some kind of course on maximizing her smile. John squinted, as if the flash had temporarily blinded him. And there she was, sandwiched between them, her auburn hair glossy.

Rachel.

Her smile was open and free, laugh lines etched into relief by the harsh lighting of the flash. She looked happy. They all did. Genuinely. What had changed? Had the rumors been too much for her? Or had something actually gone on between her and John?

'You can give that to me.'

I jumped. Vera stood over me, hand reaching for the frame. Her voice was unusually cold, her face blank. 'Stuff is always turning up in there,' she said, offering a weak smile. 'The cushions are too deep.'

'I wasn't trying to pry.'

'Oh, I wouldn't care if you did, you know me. I'm just shaken up from tonight.' She gripped the frame tight in her hands. 'That's our old neighbor, Rachel, the one we told you about.'

I know.

'Oh,' I said instead, clearing my throat.

Vera blinked rapidly, her hand still on the corner of the frame, and I wondered if I should tell her that Rachel had been to the cottage, that I'd given her her mail, swapped numbers with her.

Only, so much had happened tonight, it didn't seem like the right time. Or maybe I didn't want to risk hurting Vera – or, worse, hurting my own standing with her.

John came out then, glasses clinking. 'Sorry,' he said, forcing a laugh. 'Ice tray malfunction.'

Vera turned on her heel, strutting toward a cabinet in the corner of the room. She opened the top drawer, tossed the frame in, and shut it firmly, then opened another drawer and began to rifle through it.

John took a seat and swirled his glass, became suddenly enamored by the ice inside it.

After only a moment, Vera returned, tossing a sheet of paper and a blank, torn-open envelope on the coffee table. I leaned forward. The paper was standard size, with big words printed in the middle, typed in an ugly font, one only nominally better than Comic Sans, one my dad used to use on his letterhead. For a moment, I completely forgot about Rachel.

GO BACK TO BROOKLYN YOU PERVERTS

'Jesus,' I said, scooting back.

John didn't look up, but Vera cleared her throat. 'Sam Alby, who you had the pleasure of meeting tonight, sure has a way with words, doesn't he?'

'He left you that note,' I said. It wasn't exactly a question.

'Most likely,' she said. 'Or maybe it was one of his loser friends. Or his wife, for all I know, over here, checking on things. You've never met her, have you?'

'His wife? No, I don't even –'

'The notes started in April, just after the classes ended,' John said, cutting me off. 'They come pretty regularly now. Got this one just last week.'

The graffiti flashed to mind. It had to be the same guy. 'Have you told the police?'

Vera began ticking off her fingers. 'About the letters, yes. About the tires slashed on John's truck. The graffiti on our gallery. And about the dead rabbit that showed up on our doorstep, too.'

'A dead animal? God.'

Vera nodded. 'Just a few days ago, in fact. Thank god we don't have a dog or a cat or something, or else I'm pretty sure we wouldn't anymore.'

I closed my eyes. Suddenly, I wanted to be with Dusty, holding him as close as I could.

When I opened them again, Vera was scratching at the corner of her lip. John, for his part, had returned to staring at his drink. He looked almost green.

'The police don't care,' Vera said. 'Think it's just some drunk teenager. Or maybe a hunter, annoyed by the anti-gun bumper stickers we used to have on our cars.'

'I still wonder who down at the station came up with that creative line of reasoning,' John said, briefly looking up, his eyes catching Vera's.

'We know it's him,' Vera said firmly. Taking the note from the table, she folded it and meticulously slid it back into the envelope, as if she'd done it many times before, and returned it to the drawer. 'We're not even *from* Brooklyn. No offense,' she added with a small smile, returning to her place next to John, setting a hand protectively on his thigh. 'But I suppose it doesn't matter to him. The *Daily Freeman* does pieces on Brooklynites coming up here often enough, I think he lumps us all together.' She reached for her drink, took a cautious sip, and turned to John. On the floor, her foot tapped, impatient. 'Do you believe me now?'

He took a sip, but his mouth puckered, as if the whiskey had somehow gone rancid.

'Does he believe you about what?' I asked.

Vera sighed. 'Since the talk of the lawsuit, we've known we had to get out of here. If we stay, he'll destroy us financially. Or else' – her breath came shakily, her voice half-cracked – 'or else one of these days, he'll get tired of hurting us indirectly and actually do something to John. He's already slashed his tires. How hard would it be to cut the brake line? The cops would never be able to prove it was Sam, even if they did care enough to try and figure it out.'

Her eyes briefly caught her husband's, then turned back to mine. 'Where we disagree is, John hopes that it's all going to drop by us moving and not telling anyone where we go, waiting out the statute of limitations, but I think we need to . . . I don't know, I think we need to do something a bit more drastic.'

Abruptly, John set his glass down. He gulped, his Adam's apple bobbing up and down, then pressed his palms to his knees, as if willing his hands not to shake. He nodded to Vera, then turned to me, eyes steady on mine. 'You know that hike we went on, right when we first met?' he asked. 'Vera's idea is, well . . . I'm not sure if you remember, but a girl died there.'

'How could I forget?' I asked, feeling again that back-of-the-neck, hair-standing-up sensation, like Dusty with his hackles up. Knowing true safety couldn't be guaranteed anywhere.

Vera leaned ever so slightly forward. 'We want to be honest with you, Lucy.'

'I thought you *were* being honest with me,' I said. 'I can't handle any more secrets. It's like emotional whiplash.'

She nodded. 'What I'm trying to say is, can what we say not leave this room? Hell, not leave this coffee table?'

'You can trust me,' I said.

Vera's hands were folded neatly in her lap. 'I was thinking if John, you know, *actually disappeared*, maybe this would go away.'

'You already told me that,' I said.

'No, if it really looked like he was gone,' she went on. 'If he and I went to that spot, and he went off the trail – he's an experienced enough hiker to find his way – and if I told the police he fell, I think they'd believe me. Sam Alby would have no choice but to drop this.'

My gaze darted between them as I tried to understand.

'It's not as far-fetched as it sounds,' John said. 'They didn't find the girl for weeks. She was way down, past where the river feeds into the Hudson. It was awful, but Vera thinks, because of that, it would be believable if they didn't find me, that people would assume I'd drowned . . .'

'Wait,' I said, jaw agape. 'You're not actually serious. Faking your own death?'

It was ridiculous, something cribbed from a noir movie. People didn't do that in real life.

They do, though.

Vera's eyes caught mine, and silence hung between us, neither one of them trying to set me straight. 'Van Gogh,' I said finally.

Vera laughed. 'Yes, Van Gogh,' she said, blinking too fast. 'I didn't tell you before because I wasn't even sure John was on board.' Her eyes flashed to her husband's. 'Are you?'

John bit his lip. 'I don't think I really have a choice anymore.'

Vera turned back to me. 'Are you absolutely horrified?'

I paused. For the first time in ages, I held the power, not them. 'Why are you telling me now?'

Vera spoke first: 'You're like family to us. We owe you the truth.'

I pursed my lips. 'How would it even work?'

John scratched his chin. 'You saw it, that hike isn't far from my studio. Vera's idea is, I would go there, rest until dark, then leave in the middle of the night, head up to Lake George. It's not totally foolproof. Vera would have to get a car with plates that weren't tied to me . . .'

Vera cut in. 'I would manage it, don't worry. There's a guy, he's an artist, but he has other ways of making money, too.' She turned to me. 'John would drive up that night, but I would stay. I could mourn, keep the gallery going, and try to sell his works. Eventually, I'd put the farmhouse and the cabin on the market, get out the little equity we have, hire someone to manage the gallery, and join John when things were in good shape and his death was accepted as a finality.'

'And then?' I asked.

'I'm still me,' Vera said. 'I keep my contacts in Manhattan. I keep my career. John's paintings would sell – especially after such a tragic accident. Sam Alby won't have a damn thing left to do. He won't have anyone to sue or threaten. I could even come back occasionally. How could he stop me?'

John ran his hands through his hair. 'She's right. As drastic as the idea is, as hesitant as I've been to accept it, it would be a fresh start.'

'But what if someone recognizes you?' I asked. 'If your accident gets in the news?'

Vera's eyes caught mine. 'I thought of that, but more people die on hikes than you'd think. It's usually a quick news item. Maybe there's a photo, maybe not. Even when it is, it's a blurry one dug up on Facebook, unless the family releases a better one.

And up near Lake George, once you go west, even fifty miles, you're completely off the beaten path. It's not like this, there aren't people coming up from the city every second – it's practically Canada. There are places that are so removed from everything – places so insular and rural, I wouldn't worry about anyone recognizing him, especially if he shaves his beard, changes his hairstyle a little. John could build something new. Away from everyone.'

I felt a tug, deep inside, because she was right. People from Brooklyn came up here all the time. Davis had never had an interest in Woodstock, but there was no guarantee he wouldn't change his mind. The thought of being even harder to find was tempting. I bet there were places, up in the woods, where you didn't even run into cars, acres and acres of property where Dusty could just . . . run. Our little threesome could turn into a real family.

'There's this area, a protected wild forest. The towns in it are so small they're hardly a spot on the map. And they're so cheap. John could pay with cash. He'd have to use a different ID, but I think I could manage that, too,' Vera said as John nodded along. 'It sounds nuts, but I think it would actually work.'

'It would be better than living like this,' John added. 'Than not even being able to go out in public without causing a scene.'

A knife of a thought struck me, sharp and intrusive.

'It won't,' I said.

Vera sucked in a breath. 'What do you mean?'

'Everyone knows you guys are in trouble. Like you said, people talk.' I let the knife cut deeper, the thought slice further. 'Haven't you watched any old movies?' My mom and I used to watch them all, every noir we could get our hands on. 'You're his wife,' I said to Vera. 'If you tell people you watched your husband fall off a cliff, no one will believe you. They'd expect you, of all people, to be angry about . . . about everything.'

'I know that, but really. My record is clean. John and I have never had so much as a public disturbance. And besides, I love him,' Vera said, squeezing his hand. 'Anyone who knows us can see that.' Her eyes glistened. 'I stuck by him through all of this. Doesn't that count for anything?'

She had no idea the depths people went to hurt each other, the way love could turn so quickly into violence. 'You can't be the witness,' I said. 'You can't be the only one, at least.'

'What are you saying?' John's eyebrows furrowed.

'I'm saying, if you were actually going to fake your death, you'd need a witness who was unbiased, who wasn't married to someone being sued, who wasn't completely wrapped up personally and financially in all of this.'

They stared, waiting.

'You'd need me.'

Fourteen

I woke the next morning with a pounding headache, the previous night's discussion seeming far-fetched in the harsh light of day, a whiskey-fueled flight of imagination.

But as I made my way to the kitchen, brewed coffee, and urged Dusty out the doggie door and into the fenced bit of yard, the night replayed in my head: how a makeshift plan had bloomed between us, rising like steam on Manhattan's streets. Me, their witness. Me, involved. Me, with them.

I took a bitter sip of coffee, willing it to go straight to my head. Even if I wanted to help them, how could I risk it? I'd been so careful. I'd pulled the damn thing off. Davis didn't know where I was. Could I really chance blowing that all up for an idea so wild?

Around two, my hangover began to ease, and I left the cottage, Dusty leashed up for a proper walk. On the road, I turned left, away from Vera and John's.

Maggie's front door burst open as soon as I walked past. 'Lucy,' she called eagerly. 'You have perfect timing!'

'About to walk Pepper?' Her conveniently timed dog walks had become a bit of a habit, but as long as I didn't mention Vera or John, they always went fairly smoothly. Maggie was a little clingy, sure, but she was harmless, only wanted a friend.

'No,' she said, shaking her head but smiling, happy as a kid in a candy store. 'Come in for a second.' She motioned to Dusty. 'Bring him, too.' She turned before I could protest. Tugging on Dusty's leash, I followed.

Her house was small but quaint, all brick on the outside, all patterns and prints within. It was decorated just as you'd expect it – chintz pillows against rose-colored sofas, blue-and-white tea-cups and china on display, oriental rugs beneath carved wooden furnishings scraped up at the edges. As if someone had gotten lost at an antiques store, using nothing but a credit card to find their way out – the quilt she'd gotten for Rachel, the one that still sat on my bed, would fit right in.

And then, there she was, as if my very thought had summoned her – Rachel, standing in the entrance to Maggie's kitchen.

'Lucy, this is Rachel. Rachel, Lucy,' Maggie said. 'She's the woman who used to live in your place. I've been wanting you two to meet.'

Rachel was draped in diaphanous layers over dark purple leg-gings, her hair pulled back into a low knot at her neck. Dusty ran toward her eagerly, as if reuniting with a long-lost lover. We both smiled, and Maggie, head pivoting back and forth, placed a hand on her hip. 'Wait a second. You've already met.'

'Briefly,' Rachel said, kneeling to pet Dusty. 'When Lucy first moved in. I was missing a crucial piece of mail.'

'You could have asked me,' Maggie said, her voice suddenly hollow. 'I would have gone over and gotten it for you.'

Rachel lifted Dusty and nuzzled him again. 'I didn't want to bother you.'

'Oh,' Maggie said. 'Well, you know if you ever need anything . . . I mean, it's not like you're going to ask Vera. Not after every-thing.'

Rachel's lips pressed firmly together and her eyes found mine, only for a moment, as if checking for a reaction before she gingerly set Dusty down. 'I know I can always count on you, Maggie,' Rachel said.

Maggie turned to me, smiling, obviously proud of the fact that she and Rachel were friends. 'You want to join us for tea?'

'Thanks,' I said. 'But we really should finish our walk.'

'Well, next time.' Maggie glanced nervously between us, as if either one of us might disappear from her life at any moment. 'Rachel comes over on Thursdays. We'll make sure to invite you, since you know each other and all.'

'*Every* Thursday?' I asked.

'When I can,' Rachel said quickly. 'There's a miraculously not-yet-shuttered – pardon the pun – photography shop only a mile or so up the road. I get my film developed there, and sometimes I swing by on my way home.'

They followed me to the door, Dusty hesitant to leave.

'Next time,' Maggie said again.

'Yes,' I said, an echo. 'Next time. Nice to see you again, Rachel.'

Maggie shut the door behind me, and I urged Dusty back onto the road. At the end of her driveway, I heard my name. I turned to see Rachel walking toward me, her top flowing in the wind.

'Sorry,' she said. 'I told Maggie I had to ask you about another piece of mail.'

'Oh, I haven't seen anything else important. But there's loads of junk.'

'No, it's not that,' Rachel said. 'I just didn't want you to think, based on the way Maggie was talking, that Vera and I are huge enemies. Maggie likes to make it all sound way more dramatic than it is.'

I narrowed my eyes. 'What did happen between you two, then?'

She shifted from one foot to the other. 'Honestly, it was all a big misunderstanding.'

'Was it about –?'

'Look,' Rachel said, 'I don't need to go into all the details, but I just wanted you to know, I don't have any ill will toward Vera. I hope one day she and I can work everything out. So please don't tell her – as confident, as amazing as Vera is, she really does care about what people think about her. I hope you won't lead her to believe I'm over here gossiping about her. It isn't like that at all. You don't even really need to tell her I'm friendly with Maggie. I'm not sure she'd like it.'

I nodded, but Rachel stared, wanting further confirmation. 'Don't worry. I won't say anything.'

She grinned. 'Thank you. Thank you so much.' Then she turned, traipsing across the lawn and disappearing back into Maggie's house.

Dusty continued on, dragging me toward Rachel's navy Subaru, which I hadn't even noticed until now. I chastised myself for that – I should be more aware of my surroundings. Sure, Davis had been silent since that first email, but that didn't mean I was safe.

When Dusty stopped to do his business, on a stretch of woods that separated Maggie's property from the next one, I stole a glance back. I felt strongly that Rachel shouldn't be here – and weekly, no less. It was too close to Vera and John, to whatever had happened between them. What if I ran into her in the road? Or what if she decided to pop by and check her mail? What if Vera saw us? If she found out that I knew Rachel, even if ever so loosely, and that in all this time we'd spent together, I'd never thought to mention it, it would upset her – I knew it. And besides, now I'd agreed to keep a secret for Rachel. I didn't like that at all.

Vera saw the world in black-and-white, John had said. What if she thought that by even talking to Rachel, I'd somehow betrayed her? What if she cut me out, too?

I shook the thought away, tugging Dusty, turning around and

heading back toward the cottage. I was being silly. Vera and I were friends. And Rachel and I barely knew each other.

Besides, Vera and John were leaving.

Who knows – maybe I was, too.

I spent the rest of the afternoon in solitude, writing new pitches, finishing an article I'd been assigned weeks before that felt particularly apt – '13 Ways to Protect Your Info Without Breaking Up with Big Tech.' Vera called at four, but I ignored it. She called again at five, and that's when I decided I better head to town, lest she come over uninvited, as had become our way. I wasn't ready to talk to her, not yet: If she asked me if I'd meant what I said last night, I didn't know what in the world I was supposed to say.

Al greeted me with a smile as I walked into Schoolhouse and grabbed an open seat at the counter. The place was decorated for fall, accented with gourds and fake cobwebs. I glanced at my phone, checking the date – October 30. Halloween was tomorrow, and I hadn't given it so much as a thought. In another life, I would have planned a couples' costume for Davis and me – Princess Leia and C-3PO was our all-time personal best – but in this life, I wanted nothing to do with it. Fake fear was only fun when you had nothing to truly be scared of.

She wiped my place down and filled a glass of water. 'I finished the Stephen King book you gave me.'

'And?' I asked. *On Writing*, one of King's nonfiction books, had been an eye-opener for me, and I'd picked it up for her at the bookstore down the street last week. A sort of extra tip.

Al pushed a menu in front of me. 'Everything he says makes so much sense, but it's like, in creative writing class, they never go over any of that. They just tell you to "show, don't tell," or whatever.'

I glanced at the menu, remembering my creative writing

professor, sophomore year of college. The only real wisdom she'd imparted, as we workshopped our short stories and she tried not to fall asleep, was to 'write from the heart,' which was lovely in theory but useless as advice. 'I remember well,' I said. 'That's why it's good to read things like this on your own.'

Al leaned against the counter, crossing her arms. She wore a striped shirt in shades of burgundy and a berry lipstick my mother would have found trashy – complete with her copper hair, she was a perfect portrait of fall. 'I guess. Anyway, same as usual?'

'Please.'

Al snatched my menu away and posted the order in the kitchen. 'By the way, when are you going to bring your neighbors in?'

'They don't like coming into town,' I said.

'I know. But you'd think that John would want to show his face. Not be scared off by what people say about him and Vera.'

I raised an eyebrow. It was the first time she'd ever hinted at what had happened with Vera and John. 'So I guess that means you know about all of that?'

'*Everyone* knows about that,' Al said, rolling her eyes. 'Small town, you know.'

She flitted down the bar, off to take another order, and I was left staring at the cracks in the wooden countertop, realizing John and Vera were right – it was impossible for them to continue on like normal here.

I lifted the glass to my lips, wondering again if there was any way to make the plan work. But that's when I heard a familiar voice behind me.

When everything I'd built so carefully came crashing down.

Fifteen

Some things are instinctive:

Lifting your hands to block an incoming blow.

Averting your eyes at the sight of blood.

Turning when your best friend says your name.

In spite of the shock, her voice sounded bubbly, as it always did. The sound was baked into my bones.

Ellie stared at me. 'Holy shit.'

Al stared, too, her eyes narrowed, questioning, but she quickly averted her gaze.

'What are you doing here?' Ellie demanded. Her dirty-blond hair was tucked beneath a teal knit cap. Her cheekbones looked more prominent, as if the ten pounds she'd always been going on about losing had actually been lost over the last month and a half.

My eyes flitted around the restaurant, hunting for signs of Davis.

'Ellie,' I said, swallowing the name as soon as I said it, my tongue already thick in my mouth.

'What are you doing here?' she asked again.

Darkness crept at my periphery, blurring my vision. Around me, people continued with their lives, perusing menus, ordering craft beers.

'What are *you* doing here?' I asked, realizing too late that I should have gone to Seattle; I should never have attempted to hide in plain sight.

She blinked. 'We came up for a long weekend.'

'"*We*"?' I grabbed the counter, squeezing it so tight my knuckles turned white, imagining Davis hovering outside, ready to walk in at any moment. *Hey, babe.*

'Me and my boyfriend,' she said. 'The one I would have told you about if you'd answered a single one of my emails. If you hadn't *changed your number* and disappeared.'

I released my grasp on the counter, trying to understand. She had a boyfriend, so he was the other half of her terrifying *we*. Part of me wanted to throw my arms around her, ask her to tell me everything. She'd spent the last few years bouncing from one bad date to another, meticulously working through a string of guys who never wanted to commit, a devout Catholic praying over rosary beads. *You're so lucky*, she was always telling me. *You're so lucky you have Davis.*

'It's just you two?' I said instead, voice shrill. Al was wiping down the counter now, trying not to stare, but quite obviously listening to our every word.

'Yes, just us,' Ellie said. 'He's back at the Airbnb because he had to finish up some work, and I came into town to get a beer. The proper bar had awful Yelp reviews, so now I'm here.' Her eyes shot daggers at me. 'That's my story. Now what about you? Why aren't you in Seattle?'

Sweat pricked the corners of my forehead. I had to stay calm and *think*. 'Sit down,' I said, pulling out the chair next to mine. 'Have your beer. I'll explain.'

Ellie looked bewildered, like she'd just woken up from a strange dream, but she hung her coat on the back of the chair and motioned to Al. 'Two IPAs,' she said. 'Please.'

'You got it,' Al said, pretending this was normal, like she was not watching her pseudo-writing mentor being grilled about her whereabouts, being exposed as a liar, right before her eyes.

Ellie pressed both hands to the counter. 'I don't understand,' she said, her voice cracking. 'Do you hate me or something?'

'No,' I said. 'God, of course not. I love you.'

'Then why?' Ellie asked.

A bell dinged from the kitchen, and Al returned, delivering my eggs, a dish I'd had so many times. Now the smell made my stomach turn.

'I didn't know you had a boyfriend,' I said as my mind spun, trying to think of what I could possibly say to her, how to fix this. Al handed us two sweating beers, her eyes searching mine for answers.

Ellie took a gulp and set the glass down hard. 'Yeah,' she said. 'I have a boyfriend. His name's Andre, and we met on Tinder, and I thought it was just going to be a hookup, but look, here we are.' Her voice was suddenly cutting. 'And he's great, not that you give a shit.'

'I do give a shit, I swear. I'm sorry,' I said. 'I know I haven't been the best about –'

'You haven't been the best about *anything*,' Ellie said, her eyes turning glossy. 'I just, I don't understand. You and Davis broke up, I mean, it's weird and it's unexpected, but okay, it happens, but then you don't even want to talk to me? Why? Because I'm his sister? Not to mention, you change your *number*? God, I'm your best friend. I knew you long before he did. And now you're here, and I feel like, I don't know, like I'm going crazy.'

'You're not going crazy,' I managed. 'None of this is your fault. And you are my best friend,' I said, realizing even as I said it that it hardly was true; not anymore. My friendship with Ellie – something that had always been simple and good – was one of the many things Davis had taken from me, and I hated him for it. 'I just . . .' I took a sip of my drink, desperate to calm myself down.

The bubbles clung to the sides of the glass like soap, and the beer tasted bitter and flat.

'You live here now,' Ellie asked – or rather, stated. 'This is where you've been all along, isn't it? You were never in Seattle.'

I took another sip in lieu of answering.

'Where are you even staying?' she asked.

'Why?'

Her eyes widened. 'Jesus, what's wrong with you?'

'I'm sorry.' I scanned the room, my eyes landing on the exit. 'It doesn't matter where I'm staying, okay?'

Ellie tipped her glass back again, as if she were suddenly dying of thirst. 'Why did you lie to me?'

I tore at the corner of my napkin. 'Because it felt easier,' I said finally.

'Easier?' Ellie asked. 'What does that even mean?'

I took her in, my onetime best friend, her questions bouncing around my brain like lotto balls, and in that moment, as fear ballooned within me, I made a snap decision. It was the only way. It was the only chance that she would protect me, that she wouldn't go straight to him. 'I didn't want Davis coming up here, okay?'

'But why?' Ellie asked. 'People break up. I know that. Why did it have to be like this?'

I tore off another piece of the napkin, letting it fall to the counter. I didn't want to do it. Not here, not in front of Al, young and naive and maybe the one person on earth who seemed to actually think I had my life together. I didn't want her to see me this way, understand what I'd come to. But I didn't have a choice. This might be my only chance to stop Ellie from doing what I knew she'd immediately want to do. There was no turning back after this. But I'd been kidding myself if I ever thought there was a way to turn back. 'I was scared.'

Ellie's eyes narrowed. 'What do you mean, you were scared?'

Part of me felt for her. In a way, she was more naive even than my copper-haired waitress. Ellie wanted to believe the world was as she saw it. She didn't want to be surprised.

But the other part of me? It wanted to lift up the hatch and slap her – *hard* – across the face. Between Ellie's dad and her mom, she should know a thing or two about control. She should have seen it then; she should see it now. The writing was right there, on the wall, just waiting for her to take the time to read it.

'There's something I have to tell you,' I said. My fork tore at the eggs, the hollandaise sauce already congealing; it looked, suddenly, like yellowed pus, the color of the bruise that had taken up residence on my cheek for so long. A reminder of all that had happened. All I'd tried so hard to put behind me.

'What?' Ellie asked, not unkindly. 'Please, just tell me what's going on. I can't take it, this guessing, this trying to make sense of it.'

I took a sip of beer for courage. 'I was scared Davis would hurt me,' I said.

Her eyebrows flew up, and she paused a moment before opening her mouth. 'What do you mean, *hurt you*?'

I glanced to Al, willing her to move away, wipe the other end of the counter, take someone else's order, then lowered my voice. 'I . . .' I stammered. 'Listen, I tried to leave him, but I couldn't.'

'What are you talking about? What do you mean you *tried* to leave?'

'He tracked me,' I said. 'He's been tracking me since I moved in with him. On my phone. With that stupid Nest camera. That's why I changed my phone number. I didn't have a choice.'

Ellie shook her head. 'You can't be serious. Davis would never do something like that. The camera was for break-ins. Jesus. You must have misunderstood.'

'Listen to yourself,' I said. 'This is why I never told you.'

'It can't be,' Ellie said, catching her breath as her eyes filled with tears. 'If it was really like that, you would have . . . I would have . . .' Her voice trailed off, as if the rest of her sentence had gotten lost somewhere in a murky pool of misunderstanding and guilt.

I didn't want to use it; it was insurance, for his eyes only. But now I knew I had to, if I really wanted her to believe me. There were no words that could compare to the image – besides, I barely trusted myself to get all the details out. I retrieved my phone, began to flick through photos.

'What are you doing?' Ellie asked, voice shaking with fear.

I found it in seconds. The one I'd taken, just in case. The one that would shatter her, like he'd shattered me.

I turned it so she could see it, and her jaw dropped, taking in my face, half covered in a dark purple bruise, my expression haunted, my world torn apart. Then she scooted her chair back and stood, steadying herself on the bar. 'I – I'm sorry,' she stammered. 'I'm sorry. I don't, I just don't understand. I can't . . . I can't do this.'

'Please, Ellie. Don't tell Davis where I am. If you ever cared about me, if you still care about me, if our friendship means anything to you, keep this secret for me,' I said unsteadily. 'I'm begging you.'

She stared at me for another moment, then forced a nod, her face ashen, her cheeks slicked with tears.

'Okay,' she said. 'Jesus. Okay.'

Then she grabbed her things and left.

I looked back at the phone, at my bruise, at all the colors, and I was glad I had taken it. I was glad I would always have this to show.

'You okay?' Al asked, as soon as Ellie was gone.

I pushed a few bills her way, more than enough to cover the check, then stood before she could ask me any more questions.

'No,' I said. 'I'm not.'

. . .

I didn't notice the car behind me until I hit the windy ribbon of two-lane road, my second-to-last turn before I was home. I slowed down as I neared Shadow Creek Road, and the car slowed out of necessity. I paused at the stop sign a minute, as if checking my phone, but they didn't go around me.

Holding my breath, I pulled out and turned. The car did, too.

I approached the farmhouse, then made a sharp turn into Vera and John's driveway instead of going to mine. The car moved on without pause, and my breaths seemed to return, but now they came too fast.

I stumbled out, onto their driveway, making my way up to their porch as quickly as I possibly could.

John appeared at the door before Vera. 'What happened? You look terrified.' I followed him into the house, my breathing labored, my eyes already half-wet.

'Did someone hurt you?' he asked.

When I couldn't get a word out, he called up the stairs to Vera, then took my arm and led me to the living room. We sat together, his hand never leaving my elbow. His concern was like a salve, but it wouldn't fix this. Ellie had said she wouldn't tell Davis, but I knew that promise would only last so long. This news, it would break her. And eventually, she would reach out to her brother, ask him to explain. Maybe it was a matter of hours or days or maybe it was a matter of weeks, but it would come out; I was sure of it. And I was sure of another thing, too. Davis would find a way to manipulate the situation, get her to tell him exactly where I was. I couldn't sit around waiting for that to happen. I had to go – but I was afraid to go alone.

Vera was there in a matter of seconds, and she sat on my other side – they were my very own protective bookends. 'God, Lucy,' she said. 'Are you okay?'

My lips parted, but I couldn't find the words.

'What happened?' John asked again, leaning forward.

I swallowed, my throat tight. 'I told you about Ellie.'

'That's your ex's sister,' John said. 'Right?'

Vera interrupted. 'Yes, and her *best friend*.'

John nodded, releasing my arm from his grasp. 'Did she call you or email you or something?'

'I wish,' I said, shaking my head. 'I ran into her.'

'Here in town?' Vera asked, jaw dropping. 'Oh god, Lucy.'

John's eyes caught hers, then returned to mine. 'But he wasn't with her, was he?'

'No,' I said. 'At least, she said he wasn't. She was in Woodstock on her own, getting a drink while her boyfriend did some work back where they were staying.'

'Shit,' John said, his eyebrows knitting tightly together. 'Are you afraid she's going to tell him?'

'*Obviously* she's afraid of that,' Vera said.

He tugged at the cuff of the plaid shirt he always wore, not knowing what to say.

'It's going to be okay,' Vera said. 'It has to be okay. We'll find a way.'

John nodded. 'We'll keep you safe.'

I dabbed at my eyes. They must know how naive, how pathetic their words sounded. Sometimes things weren't okay. Life decided to ruin you. Or you were such a mess, you found a way to ruin yourself.

'What can we do, Lucy?' John asked. 'How can we help?'

'How serious were you last night?' I asked, forcing confidence into my voice.

They exchanged a glance. 'We were serious, Lucy,' Vera said, speaking for both of them. 'We talked about it after you left. John's come around. But we figured you weren't.'

John cleared his throat. 'I don't want to mess up your life, too. Not after you've already been through so much.'

I closed my eyes, then opened them again. This wasn't a joke. It wasn't some plot to toss about over drinks. It wasn't even Van Gogh-ing. This could save us all. 'We *need* to do this,' I said. 'We need to do this right away.'

'But what about you?' Vera asked. 'If the police interview you, and your name gets in the media – I know last night you said you'd try to avoid that, but what if you can't?'

I paused, wondering what would happen when the police took my name, but I shook my head, trying to focus only on what I had to do – get out. 'Davis will know soon enough,' I said. 'It doesn't matter anymore.'

In her eyes, understanding, but in John's, reluctance. 'That's really what you want?' he asked. His voice was warm and soft, a blanket of protection. He cared about me – truly. They both did. 'You're not just doing it for us? I couldn't handle it if you were only doing it for us.'

We're *the us now*, I wanted to say.

'I'm not,' I said instead. 'I'm doing it for me.'

'You're sure?' Vera said. 'You're positive?'

I hesitated, racking my brain, wondering if there was another way, but what I could hardly say to her, though I felt it, deep in my heart, was that it didn't much matter if there was another way. When I'd come up here, I'd only wanted protection, but then I'd found the two of them. Now I wanted both – safety and family – and even if we were a cobbled-together one at best, ours was a family I'd come to adore.

I wanted us like this, together, off the grid, away from Davis – a trio, however strange.

'I'm doing it for me,' I repeated. 'Believe me, I'm sure.'

Vera stood, began to pace. 'We'd need to go on a practice hike, you know, to get the lay of the land. This week.'

I shook my head. 'If we have to practice, it's got to be tomorrow. Davis could turn up any moment.'

'What?' Vera asked. 'We don't want to rush and mess it all up. I don't even have a car for John.'

'You said last night you knew where to get one.'

'Yeah . . . but . . .' Vera stammered.

'Then you'll have to do that tomorrow, too. You have to try, at least. I can't stay here, just waiting for Davis to find me. If he does, Christ, I don't know what he'll do.'

They stared at me in horror, and for a moment, I wondered if it all had been a joke. If they had never been serious about any of this. I felt it then, in the marrow of my bones, that I'd already lost them. That I was alone. Again.

Then they exchanged a look. Vera cleared her throat.

'Okay,' she said. 'We'll go tomorrow.'

Sixteen

We arrived at the trailhead for a dress rehearsal just after ten a.m.

It was Halloween, funny enough, a good day to cause mischief, to kick off the sort of macabre plan that really should be relegated to books and movies.

John found a spot in the back of the parking lot, which was fuller than it had been last time. *Must be people up from the city to see the leaves,* I thought. I imagined Ellie, somewhere nearby. I tried not to imagine Davis.

I zipped up my hoodie as we got out of the truck. The weather had changed in a matter of twenty-four hours. Our first real cold snap had arrived during the night, and the reprieve we'd had, the cricket-chorus nights in the gazebo, were like a faraway dream.

At the entrance, Vera grabbed the sign-in clipboard and immediately began riffling through it. Taking charge, even though John was disappearing, not her. Perhaps women were naturally better at planning how to disappear; perhaps they had more reasons.

'What are you looking for?' I asked, shoving my hands in my pockets to keep warm.

Her eyes flitted to me briefly before returning to the clipboard, glancing over names. 'We need to know what times are busiest,'

Vera said, without looking up. 'Run into someone hiking at the same pace as us, and the whole thing won't work. Mornings look pretty empty,' she added. 'At least during the week. It picks up around noon.' She flipped another page. 'We should go in the early evening, so there's not too long for John to wait before dark. On Fridays,' she continued, 'there seem to be a lot of people in early, but it drops off in the afternoon.'

'That's just the sign-in, though,' John said, his hand tracing down the sheet. 'This hike's out and back, so people will be coming down as we're going up.' He pointed to a cluster of names. 'Five people signed in an hour ago. We'll likely run into them.'

'Right,' Vera said. 'We want to run into, maybe, one person. So ideally, we need to arrive just as people are finishing up, but not so late that no one will be here.' She perused the sheets again. 'Practically no one goes on Wednesdays,' she said. 'But then no one will see us. Mondays are pretty dead, but there are still some hikers – long weekends and all. I don't see more than seven or eight people all day on the last two Mondays, in the afternoon.'

'So Monday,' John said.

Vera hesitated, mentally calculating whether she could get it all together by then. She looked to me. 'Is that okay with you?'

Two days. I could hold out two days. I prayed Ellie could, too. That she'd meant what she'd said when she weakly said okay to my pathetic plea.

I nodded. 'Monday it is.'

The hike was just as strenuous as the first time, and I was breathless when we reached the place where the girl had fallen. I peered over the edge, eyeing the water rushing beneath, and I imagined John, his body dashed against the rocks in the middle, wrenched away to who knew where. It was fantasy, fiction – something that would never actually happen, but I could see it playing out in front of me.

'It's okay to picture it,' Vera said, leaning in close.

I jumped.

'I know it's morbid,' she went on, 'but if we can see it in our mind's eye, we'll be so much more likely to believe it when we have to tell the police.'

'Hey,' John said. 'Please don't get *too* used to the idea of my death.'

Vera turned on her heel, her voice stern. 'I need you to take this seriously.'

'I am.'

She crossed her arms. 'I'm not kidding, John.'

He rocked back and forth on his heels, humbled as a child who'd misbehaved. 'I know. It just got a little real, I guess. But I promise, I am taking this seriously. I have to.'

'Yeah,' Vera said. 'You of all people should know that you do.'

The plan was to drop his camera off the edge, leave his backpack and water bottle behind (minus a small bag full of emergency items: protein bars, an extra layer, a long-life flashlight, a portable charger for his phone, a new SIM card so his phone couldn't be traced), and head off the trail. He'd make his way the four miles toward the cabin. There he'd shave his beard and grab a baseball cap, some money, a few items of clothing that the police would never realize were missing, and the car. Then, around midnight or sometime thereafter, he'd drive until he got far enough away to stop at a seedy motel that took cash. Once he was settled, once Vera and I had given our statements, he'd call and tell Vera exactly where he'd wound up. I would leave town as quietly as possible to join him. The police would have my number, in case they needed to ask me any follow-up questions, and if they asked me why I'd left, I could always tell them I had an ex who'd found me, much as I didn't want to. Most important, I would be away from Woodstock. Away from Davis.

Was it foolproof? Not exactly. But it was the only way for me to stay with them.

We walked on until we were clear of the trail, until we found a grove of trees and a bluestone slab where John could settle in, should he need to wait out any rain. It was completely covered, impossible to see from even a few feet away – John was confident he wouldn't be detected.

We retraced our steps back to the clearing, then choreographed every move, so as to limit the lies Vera and I would have to tell. John would hike in front, I would be second, with Vera lagging behind. Just before we reached the cliff, he would tell us he was going ahead to get some photos, and after a few minutes, I would follow.

It was crucial that I see him slip – it was the one lie that didn't contain even a shred of truth, one I'd have to deliver with conviction all the same: *Just after I got to the clearing, I heard him scream. I saw him slip and fall.*

'We'll try to call nine-one-one immediately,' Vera said. 'Only we probably won't have service until we get down to the bottom.'

I nodded. 'We should walk fast, maybe even run. It will help us when we call the police. Adrenaline, you know.'

'Yes,' Vera said. 'Good point.'

John paused, twisting at the strap of his backpack. He looked pale, almost ill. 'I hate this,' he said. 'I don't want to put you two in danger.' His voice was earnest, his eyes clouded with worry. 'If I got you in trouble, I couldn't live with that.'

'Well, you won't be alive, officially, so you don't have to worry about that,' Vera said, only the joke didn't land, for him or for me. She forced a smile. 'Don't worry. We won't get in any trouble,' she said. Then she stood on her tiptoes and kissed him on the lips.

I couldn't help but imagine standing on my tiptoes, doing the same.

Vera took the train to the city as soon as we were done with our hike. She was going to do her best to procure a car from her friend, for John to drive off in, one that couldn't be traced.

With her gone and me on my own, I made a low-key dinner and ate it while I caught up on Netflix and indulged in wine – binge-watching and nervous drinking were better than silence, better than waiting for Davis to suddenly appear.

The doorbell chimed as I was finishing my plate. Dusty barked wildly.

My pulse ratcheted up. I knew it was probably a trick-or-treater, though I'd kept the porch lights off in the hopes of keeping them at bay – but what if it was Davis, already here?

I sat stock-still, frozen, not wanting to make a sound. Praying whoever it was would just leave.

It chimed again, and just after, my phone buzzed: a text from John.

It's just me

My heartbeat slowed as I walked to the door and eased it open.

'I come bearing gifts,' John said, holding a bottle of whiskey. On his breath, I could already smell a bit of it.

'I'm glad it's just you,' I said.

He nodded, understanding the implication. 'Want company?' he asked, leaning casually against the doorjamb. Even his mannerisms had a way of putting me at ease. He straightened up. 'I mean, I can leave you alone if you're in the middle of dinner. Or if this is weird. Vera just thought, you know, that it would be good for me to be with you, in case your friend told your ex – not that we think she would. But in case you wanted company.'

'Not weird at all,' I said, the tightness in my chest loosening just the tiniest bit. 'Come in.'

I shut my laptop, then took my plate and wineglass to the kitchen, returning with two glasses for the whiskey and some ice. 'Do you think Vera was able to get a car?' I asked.

'I think so, probably. Her artist friend – I remember him – he was always kind of shady, knew how to sort out that kind of thing. She's staying the night, in any case – she might need to look again in the morning if she wasn't successful today.'

Our eyes caught, briefly, the logistics making it suddenly real.

'By the way,' John said, breaking the silence as he poured our glasses extra-tall, 'this is the good stuff. Vera suggested I bring it over, use it up before . . .'

'There will be whiskey in the Adirondacks, too.' For a moment, I let myself imagine it, us sitting in a cozy little cabin, quaint as John's little studio. Tucked up together in front of a fire, nature's bounty all around us, Vera there, too.

He shrugged. 'Will there?'

I laughed. 'Alcohol knows no borders.'

John smiled, eyes crinkling at the corners, and scratched at the scruff of his beard. 'I *guess.*' I had an awful intrusive thought, of running my fingers through his beard, pulling him toward me, waking up the next morning with scratches across my body.

'And you can paint more,' I said impulsively. John and I had never truly been alone together, and I needed to protect us with words. 'You can do nothing all day but draw and paint and make Ms Fancy Gallery Owner bring in the money.'

He cocked his head to the side. 'Yes, to be truly removed from it all. Perhaps I'll give up food and drink, too. Go all Marina Abramović on your ass.'

I laughed, and he did, too, but his was slightly less convincing. He sank back against the cushions, his body sagging.

'Are you nervous?' I asked.

He shrugged. 'No more than I should be.' His eyes turned down at the corners, his crow's-feet catching the light. Dusty hopped into his lap, and John scratched at his back, just above his tail. He knew exactly where Dusty liked to be scratched, just as I did. 'Maybe I'm just sad. I love it here,' he went on. 'I feel like it's home. I don't want to leave, but part of me is happy that I won't be looked at like this anymore, like I'm some sort of monster.'

I knew in my heart that he wasn't. He was only a man too naive to understand how certain things look. I didn't for a second believe that anything had happened between him and a sixteen-year-old, but at the same time, staying here and proclaiming his innocence wasn't possible, not after all the ways they'd been threatened. Maybe in some strange way, all of this was for the best, his death a relief, even, for the girl. After all, rumors were circling her, too.

'You're not a monster,' I said finally, letting myself look at him, really take him in. His worn sweater, jeans marred from wearing them while he worked. The way the skin roughened around his knuckles and the beds of his nails were never quite fully clean from paint. He was a man's man, wearing every one of his forty years with pride. He was old enough to be a sixteen-year-old's father – it wasn't possible.

I cleared my throat. 'Do you think you'll miss anything – or have any regrets – being dead, I mean?'

A smile crept up the side of his mouth. 'I'm sure I'll have some,' he said, and with the wildness of the whiskey already pumping through my veins, I let myself pretend he was talking about me, that he regretted not having a chance with me.

Another intrusive thought, crazy and wrong – of reaching for him, his roughened hands, his broad shoulders, instead of my whiskey.

The first glass drained easily, almost as if it were leaking, water through a sieve.

The second glass went quickly, too, both of us drinking too fast, painfully aware that this might be the last night of semi-normalcy for a very long time. For him – perhaps forever.

'What do you miss most about the city?' John asked, leaning forward to pour us a third glass.

Or was it *technically* a fourth?

I gazed into my drink, remembering. 'The way you passed so many people in a day, but you could still stay completely anonymous. You?'

'The smell of bread on our old block. I used to go out to get coffee and cigarettes, and all you could smell was yeast.'

'You smoked?' I asked. 'Even, you know, with your parents' cancer and all?'

'I know, it was reckless,' John said. 'But in the East Village in the early aughts, we all did.'

'Aughts.' I laughed, taking another sip. 'Such a stupid name for a decade.'

'Well, it was a hell of a decade anyway. And unlike you, I was old enough to truly appreciate it.'

'Practically an old man, really,' I said.

John raised an eyebrow. 'Well, I am quickly crawling toward death.'

I grinned. The air in the cottage, which had felt oppressive since I'd seen Ellie, was more pleasant with him in it. Our arms were only inches apart, and – another intrusive thought – if I let myself sink in a tiny bit closer, they would touch.

He set his glass down and turned to me. 'Do you want kids, you think?'

My eyes narrowed. 'That came out of nowhere.'

'Death, birth.' He shrugged, fooling with one of the cuffs of his sweater. 'Two sides of the same coin.'

I bought time with another sip. Truth was, I had wanted children, very badly. I'd once thought they were a possibility, even a certainty. 'I don't know,' I said, blinking back a sudden weight in my eyes. 'Do you?'

A change in our energy – his eyes looked awfully, unbearably sad. There was the slightest sheen to them, almost as if he was about to cry.

I forced a laugh. 'You started it!' The joke came out all wrong, poisoning the air like an acrid smell. 'Sorry.'

'It's okay. I did start it, didn't I? We wanted kids, yes. Then again, we didn't,' he said, studying the wall as if it would offer some sort of answer. 'It's complicated.'

He leaned forward again, pouring more into his glass, even though it wasn't empty.

'Should I put on some music?' I asked.

John shook his head, and I noticed dots of sweat on his upper lip. 'It's funny, when we first moved up here, I couldn't stand the quiet,' he said. 'Now I can't stand even a bit of noise. The crickets. A car passing by.' He leaned back, resting his head on the cushion, blinked a few times, glass still in hand.

Outside, the grumble of a car slowly passing by. Its lights splashed the room with shadows.

'Are you okay?' I asked, scooting a bit closer to him on the sofa.

He straightened, then blinked again, as if trying to focus. 'Yeah, it just got to me all at once,' he said.

I nodded. 'Me too.'

'I guess the good stuff is strong.' This didn't stop him from taking another sip. He stared at me. 'We had a miscarriage.'

'Oh.' I scooted back instinctively.

He gazed into his whiskey. 'Yeah.'

My brain felt like Swiss cheese, but I tried to focus on saying the right thing. 'Had you – er – had you been trying a long time?'

'We hadn't been trying at all. Our timing was never right. Vera wanted to have an abortion.' He took another sip. 'I couldn't do it,' he said, his voice cracking. 'I didn't want to do it, since it was ours.'

'But you guys didn't . . .'

'No, but she really wanted to. Maybe that's what I couldn't get over. I *am* a monster,' he said, scratching at his beard again. 'I should never have pressured her. I should have driven Vera to the clinic, held her hand, respected what she wanted. But then we lost the baby anyway.' He blinked once, twice, as if holding back tears. 'She's never gotten past it. It happened when she was eighteen weeks. She was only showing a little, but *we* knew. I think it was the first time I'd ever seen her gain weight. And she looked different. She was breaking out like a teenager, her hair was so damn thick. It was – *he* was – a boy. The internet said the size of an avocado. I came home right away and took her to the hospital – we were there for hours. And then the recovery. The procedure they make you have, to get all the tissue.' He clung tightly to his glass. 'I put her through all that. All for nothing. Sometimes, it feels like it only just happened.'

'Christ,' I said, forcing myself to speak, realizing that our faces couldn't be more than a foot apart. 'That's awful.'

'I wanted to try again, but she said no.'

'Like *never* no?' I asked.

'How can we now?' He looked down at his hands, then back up at me. 'It's so hard,' he said.

For a second, I lost the thread of conversation, found it difficult to remember what had been hard, the baby or losing it or not having one again? Or having to disappear, fake his own death? It was all jumbling, jigsaw pieces. Like the puzzles I used to do with my dad, back in Seattle.

'Before I met her, it was something I always imagined.'

It. I couldn't place what *it* was. God, I was drunk.

'A baby,' John reminded me. 'A family.'

'Yeah,' I said. 'A family.' It was like meeting people at a dinner party, their names floating away and bursting like bubbles. I blinked, trying to focus, my eyelids even heavier than before.

'I love Vera,' John said. I could hear a *but* in there, lodged in his whiskey-soaked words.

'But sometimes I think all we do is try to make each other people we're not. It's pathetic.'

I was suddenly so tired, but I had to stay awake. I had to tell him that I got it, tell him something so true, it could only come out when I was out of my mind like I was.

I would do anything for a family, too.

'Sometimes the smallest, tiniest part of me wants Davis to find me, just so I can see him again. He was the first person who really felt like family since I lost my parents in college. And as much as I hate him, I miss him, too.'

'That's so wrong,' John said. He stared, waiting for a reaction, but my body wanted only to shut down. Then he smiled, a grin that grew slowly, a grin that spelled broken rules.

'Sometimes,' he said, 'we want what we know is wrong.'

Breath caught in my throat. Something had changed. Something big.

John leaned forward, his breath warm, tickling my lips.

Seventeen

When I woke, I sensed it immediately, the difference.

The bed was warm. It smelled woodsy and aromatic, stale and salty, the distinct tang of male sweat. My eyes landed on Dusty, curled between us, and my first thought was of Davis. It was so natural, something I'd woken up to so many times. Then my mind woke up, too.

John lay, slack-jawed and fast asleep, in my bed.

I was in a bra and underwear and on top of the covers. He was fully clothed.

It hit me, a punch to the stomach, images running through my head like a sick, twisted film.

He'd leaned in, and I hadn't leaned away. Our lips had found each other's, hungry, and for a moment it was ecstatic, it was all I'd been wishing for, it was guilt, and I didn't pull away and he didn't, either, and then . . . nothing.

My head pounded and my stomach twisted. It was a kiss. It was only a kiss. Wasn't it?

I had that awful feeling, the one I'd had that morning in college, when I couldn't remember exactly what had happened but I knew I'd fucked up.

I'd fucked up bad.

There was no video this time, nothing to splash across every network, nothing to give everyone a reason to either judge me or pity me, but did it even matter? It had happened. I had betrayed her.

Jumping out of bed, I darted to the dresser and tugged at a drawer. I snatched a tank top and shorts. I let myself take him in for a moment, the way his mouth hung open as he slept, how his hair splayed out over my extra pillow . . . it was something I'd imagined so many times but hadn't ever wanted to really happen.

'John,' I said. 'John, wake up.'

His eyes cracked open, and it was only then that it sank in. The drapes in the bedroom were wide-open, as if waiting for Vera, or anyone, to come by and see him in my bed.

I ran to the window, wincing at the light streaming in, and pulled them shut, a brutal headache already raging behind my forehead.

'God. What am I . . .' He looked down at his clothes, then back at me, his eyes crinkling at the corners as he tried to make sense of it. 'Nothing happened, besides . . .' he said, leaving a blank, hanging there, taunting. 'Nothing *really* happened. It was a stupid mistake, just an impulsive . . . Shit. I'm sorry. We shouldn't have ever let it happen.'

He'd wanted it, he'd fantasized about it, too. The realization would have made me schoolgirl happy, only it was sharp, double-edged. I loved Vera. He supposedly did, too.

'Did you black out?' I asked.

His face was pale, his forehead covered in sweat, but he shook his head. 'I don't know, I don't think so? I just had a lot. Nothing happened. We kissed, and then somehow we got in here, and I – uh – well, we – must have taken your dress off, but I remember you snapping out of it and pushing me away, and then at some point, we both passed out.'

'So you did black out,' I said. 'You don't remember everything.'

'Maybe just a little,' he said, his face going red.

I looked at him. His sweater – even his shoes – were still on.

It was coming back in flashes – me, helping him lift my dress over my head and then seeing myself in the mirror over the dresser, remembering Vera, pushing him away. Then blackness again.

He was right. He had to be right.

Blood rushed in my ears, acid rose in my stomach – I ran to the bathroom and sank to my knees so hard it hurt, whipping the lid of the toilet up so it clanked against the tank. My vomit was brown and bitter. It came in three lurches, and I spit, trying to get it all out.

'Are you okay?'

I stood, wiping my mouth with the back of my hand. I couldn't bring myself to look him in the eye, my face burning with shame.

A crush, even a flirtation, was one thing. Betraying her was another.

'You should go,' I said softly. 'Vera will probably be back soon.'

'Of course,' John said. 'I'm so, so sorry.'

I looked up, finding his eyes then, and he didn't look away. For a second, in the haze of morning and the ripe smell of sweat, everything passed between us. Words unsaid. Feelings that couldn't – shouldn't – be expressed.

'It will never happen again,' John said solemnly. 'Never.'

He turned, walked out of my cottage, pulling the door shut softly behind him, Dusty chasing him, not wanting him to go.

It was only after that I realized it – John hadn't had to twist the dead bolt to get out.

My scalp prickled at what that must mean:

The whole night, the front door hadn't been locked.

I tried to go back to sleep, to close my eyes and forget about all that had and hadn't happened, but I couldn't. Eight thirty turned to nine, nine to nine thirty, thoughts stinging, head pounding, eyes locked on the ceiling.

At some point I did drift off, but awoke to a rap at the door. I checked my phone. It was nearly three o'clock.

I forced myself out of bed and made my way into the living room, peeked through the drapes. Vera.

Cheeks on fire, I desperately wanted to head back to bed, pull the covers up and disappear beneath them, but she'd already seen me. Slowly, I opened the door.

'Took you long enough,' she said. She had a perky smile on her face and was wearing a long-sleeved black dress, a silver scarf twisted around her neck.

'I was in the bathroom,' I managed.

Her hand landed on her hip. 'Are you going to invite me in?'

'Yes,' I said. 'Of course. You want coffee? Or tea or something?'

'I'm fine.' She sat on the sofa. 'Christ, you look awful.'

'Thanks,' I said, trying to act normal.

She threw her head back, laughing. 'John told me you two hit the sauce a little hard last night. So that's what happens when I encourage you guys to hang out? I hope I don't have anything to worry about.'

I forced a quick laugh, as if the suggestion were absurd, but my heart pounded anyway.

'So it was no easy feat,' Vera said, 'but I got a car this morning. A ninety-two Camry that somehow magically still works. Got back about an hour ago.'

I nodded along, trying to focus on the details, trying to push all thoughts of last night away.

Vera picked up on my discomfort anyway. 'You okay?' she asked. 'You didn't hear from Davis, did you? Or Ellie?'

'No,' I said smoothly, trying to gather myself. 'I'm fine. I'm just nervous, I guess . . . about tomorrow.'

Vera folded her hands in her lap. 'That's why I came over. I know you're as eager to do this as I am, but I wanted to make sure we were on the same page. With the car all set, things are officially in motion. We'll be heading out tomorrow around two, aiming to get to the trail no later than three. You're still good?'

Was I good? Far from it. I had betrayed her, even if we'd stopped. What we'd done was betrayal enough.

But the wave had already begun to build, growing taller and taller, and the only thing left was the violent crash against the beach.

'Of course,' I told her, delivering a smile. 'Of course. I'll be ready.'

Eighteen

Vera's handwriting was smooth as she signed her name on the sheet. The air was crisp and biting, turning her skin a paler shade of white. Her golden hair was pulled into an incredibly neat bun, as if she were off to a ballet performance after this.

Meanwhile, I was a mess. My curls had refused to be tamed, and my hands were quivering with nerves as I took the sheet from her, nerves I hadn't been able to shake since waking up yesterday with John in my bed, since Ellie had discovered me the afternoon before in what had turned into an awful adult game of hide-and-seek.

'You okay?' Vera asked, an eyebrow raised.

'Fine,' I lied, signing my name quickly. 'Good.'

I watched as John signed in, his scrawl of a signature shaky. His eyes connected with mine for a moment as he handed the clipboard back to Vera, his lips pressing firmly together, as if holding back words.

I looked down, his gaze too much. I wondered what he was thinking, or if I even wanted to know, as guilt clattered around inside my chest.

Vera surveyed the rest of the names, oblivious to the live wire linking John and me together. She told us that one person had come in at one thirty; we might pass them on the way up. If it worked out right, they could act as a witness, proof that John was there if anyone felt the need to check.

After that, I didn't get any more chances to read John's face, to search for feelings, for answers, for what we should do next. He took the lead, and though I was just behind him, Vera bringing up the rear, he didn't look back as we began our ascent through sheer carved rocks covered in moss. I wasn't sure if he was laser-focused on what he had to do or if he was avoiding catching my eyes again.

I tried to distract myself, taking in all the nature around us. The trees weren't fully bare yet, though it was deep enough into fall that there were plenty beneath our feet; the sounds of snapping twigs, crackling leaves, the pop of a branch, creating an afternoon cacophony. I kept my hands in the pockets of my hoodie, my water bottle hooked to my belt with a carabiner. I had to act normal. With Vera bringing up the rear, she could see us both, our every move, like actors in a play. I forced myself to take a deep breath, to focus on putting one foot in front of the other.

She would never know. She *couldn't* ever know. I loved her too much for that.

After more than an hour, we reached a small gap in the trees where you could just make out the river below. It was a force – movement and momentum, eddies and whitecaps – certainly going fast enough for a body to get lost. A frothing, crashing sound rose up and bounced around the valley, angry and forceful yet somehow melodic – white noise.

Around us, colors: burgundy and burnt orange, eggplant and goldenrod, the sort you normally only see in paint chips. Patchwork hills rolling out before us like the quilt that Maggie had given Rachel, the hues dark and brooding where the thick gray clouds blocked the sun, bright and vibrant where they didn't.

I flinched at a rustle behind me, a sound like someone was

following us. 'Don't worry, it's just an animal,' John said, turning for the first time to look back at me.

'Sorry, I'm just –'

He shook his head, as if he didn't need an explanation from me. And of course he didn't. His face looked as pained as mine was, nervousness crossed with shame, fear – desire? I wanted, suddenly, to touch him, to feel the warmth of his skin.

'Come on, Lucy,' Vera said, interrupting my thoughts. She pointed to the clouds overhead. 'It might rain soon, and we need to keep going.'

'Yes,' John said, the look of understanding disappearing from his face. 'We should keep on.'

It did begin to drizzle, droplets sneaking through the light cover of trees. We walked for another fifteen minutes or so before we passed the hiker who'd signed in ahead of us, an older man with a walking stick, a Vietnam veteran cap, and a bright orange vest. 'Happy trails, folks,' the man said, almost aggressively congenial, as his stick, made of some burly knotted wood, dug into the mossy, murky ground, softened by the light rain, penetrating the undergrowth.

We nodded back. 'You too.' 'Take care.' 'Careful in the rain.'

Remember the three of us if the police call. Remember it was slippery that day, that the man in front had a camera around his neck.

Another twenty minutes, and the trees had gathered thick and tangled around us. My hair was matted to my forehead from the wet, and there was a sound of tumbling rocks, a squirrel or raccoon crawling through the underbrush, and a smell of decay and rot. More than that, there was the blistering knowledge that John would disappear only a few turns up ahead. That everything that had happened would be left unaddressed.

And that sense, once again, that someone was behind us.

On cue, John paused, turning to us. 'I'm going to walk a bit faster,' he said. 'Get some photos while the light is diffused like this.' He tried to force a smile, but his chin shook, his beard full and thick. 'You guys are slowing me down,' he added. His script sounded strange and stilted, but Vera had insisted upon it, claiming that it would go better if we limited our lies, told the police things that had happened, had been said. Twisted truths were better than flat-out lies.

'Be careful,' I said, which wasn't necessarily part of the script, but it's what came out anyway.

'Have fun,' Vera said, a better actress than me. 'Get some good ones.'

John stepped forward then, approaching Vera, and my head swiveled back and forth, canvassing the area, making sure no one was about to approach.

His hands found her hips as he kissed her deeply. Her arms wrapped around him, and I looked away, giving them their moment, my insides twisting, fighting. They were so right together, and yet why had we kissed? Why had he spent the night in my bed? Was John his own kind of twisted truth?

'Jesus!' John's voice was shrill, incredulous. 'What the *hell* was that for?'

My head whipped up, trying to understand. Vera held a neon green box cutter in one hand. John cradled his forearm, a line of blood seeping from a slash just below the crook of his elbow.

He ripped his arm away. 'Are you fucking crazy?'

'I'm sorry, but you have to give them some sort of proof that you fell.'

She pulled out an extra-large bandage, unwrapped it, and slapped it against the wound, a temporary blockage. 'You'll be fine. This will tide you over for now, and when you're in the woods, you can bandage it up properly with the first-aid kit in your bag.'

'Why didn't you tell me?'

'Because you hate blood,' she said, matter-of-fact. 'You never would have agreed to it.'

I sucked in a breath, ready to yell at her, to protest, only, how could I? I'd seen John cut himself chopping vegetables once. He hadn't fainted or anything, but the blood had freaked him out – I remembered his reaction distinctly because it was such a contrast to the rest of his rough-and-tumble personality.

Besides, we did need proof – of course we did. Vera seemed to have thought of everything John and I hadn't.

'Are you okay?' I asked John instead.

He nodded, fingers pressing at the bandage. 'This is real now. Proof. No turning back.'

'No turning back,' she echoed. 'After you set your backpack and your water bottle down, you'll need to make sure some rocks and dirt fall from the ledge. Don't use your feet – it's too dangerous – use your camera. Just bang it on the edge a couple of times, enough so the scene looks disturbed, like you could have slipped. Then take your camera, cover it with blood, and drop it over the edge of the cliff. Make sure it falls straight down, so it hits the rocks on the bank of the river, not the actual water. We don't want it to get carried away. It's the only real indication you fell.'

He nodded, a dutiful pupil.

She slid the box cutter into her pocket. 'Go on,' Vera said.

John leaned in, gave her one final kiss, and then turned to me.

He approached me slowly, and my heart beat fast as I contemplated what he might do. He opened his arms wide, wrapped me in a hug. He felt so warm, so strong and so safe, and I remembered, once again, the sight of him in my bed, guilty as it made me feel.

'Don't bleed on her,' Vera said firmly.

John pulled away, but as he did, a whisper in my ear, so quiet I didn't think Vera heard: 'I'll see you soon.'

He turned around, hand holding the bandage tight, and we watched as he walked forward, around the bend, out of sight.

A flash of panic, of paranoia – what if I never saw him again?

I searched Vera's face for similar emotions but found none.

'Let's pause for water,' she said.

Nodding, I unhooked the bottle from my belt, then began to guzzle it. I wasn't even that thirsty, the cold preventing me, for once, from overheating, but I drank anyway, eager for something to do.

'Wait. Your backpack is open.' She zipped it shut, then out of nowhere, she pulled me toward her and grabbed my face in her hands, framing my cheeks, pressing. 'This is real, Lucy,' she said. 'We can't screw this up.'

My eyes caught hers, and I was as sure as I'd ever been. 'I won't.'

I went ahead on my own, making my way as planned. There were three turns exactly between me and the clearing, the sheer cliffs and rocks that would purport to take John away. I made the first one, and the grove seemed to close tighter around me, as if squeezing me just as Vera had done. I looked back. Already, I couldn't see her, though I knew she was just behind. I imagined John, alone and bleeding.

I made the second turn, the path opening up just slightly, the light peeking through the trees, dappling the ground, which had turned from stones to thick, fat roots, crawling beneath my feet like snakes. I walked the length of the path, and before the next turn, I paused, again rehearsing the script in my head. *Just after I got to the clearing, I heard him scream. I saw him slip and fall.*

I stilled my breath, listening for footsteps. None, nothing but the rolling of the river below, the chirp of a songbird.

Then I heard him scream.

Nineteen

It echoed through the woods, but I forced myself to count off beats in my head instead of running straight for the clearing. I imagined it all, him stepping away from the camouflage of the trees, the rocks slipping from beneath him, his camera in his hand as he fell to the bottom, his backpack and water bottle the only markers left behind. We'd all agreed it was better this way; if Vera and I watched John walk off the trail, we might get our stories messed up.

So I waited, twenty counts, and then, as if suddenly sensing danger, I ran.

The clearing was empty, not a soul in sight, but I spotted his backpack, about fifty feet up ahead. I bolted down the path, over rocks, around ivy, across fallen leaves, toward the spot, the light spatter of rain coating my face, letting myself pretend, for a moment, that my story was true, that I really had seen him. Letting myself feel those feelings just the tiniest bit: of being alone, of losing someone you love. Feelings I knew well, that the absence of my parents had printed on my heart.

Up close, the tableau was more frightening than I'd expected.

I shouted for Vera, as we'd agreed I would, then studied the scene before me. The backpack and bottle were upright and covered in water droplets – obedient pets waiting for their owner to return.

There was no blood – John must have been careful not to drip any – but the rocks and gravel on the cliff's edge were disturbed. It looked so real, so true to life. I stepped closer. The tiny bit of grass and mud just before the rocks was marked with . . . footprints. Had to be John's.

Vera had told him to be careful, but what if he'd gotten too into staging it?

What if . . .

I turned back, looking for John's footprints leading back off the trail, but the leaves were too thick to see any – there was nothing. It made sense, of course. He would have been careful to step only where the ground was covered as he walked off the trail, careful not to leave any tracks. My ears pricked, listening for the rustle of leaves, for John's movements, but I couldn't hear a thing.

I took one step closer, careful to stay out of the mud so as not to disturb his footprints, taking them in. They were thoughtfully placed, as if he'd stepped far too close to take a photo – an artist's work, his swan song. I reached out, wanting to run my fingers over them, these impressions of John, unsure when I'd see him again.

'What are you doing?'

I jumped up, my feet kicking at an errant bit of gravel, and I heard it bounce all the way down. I swallowed, throat tight. 'It just looks so real. If he really had fallen, we wouldn't even see him.'

'Exactly,' Vera said. 'That's the point.'

Her gaze was steely, like I'd disappointed her somehow.

'I don't hear anything,' I said. 'Do you think we should make sure he's okay? Before we . . .'

Vera shook her head firmly. 'We can't, Lucy,' she said. 'We have to stick to the plan.'

'Okay,' I said quietly, and then repeated myself, as if to prove the point: 'Okay.'

Her eyes softened, and the old Vera came back. 'He's fine, I promise, he knows exactly what he's doing out there –'

'But I hardly gave him any time to prepare.'

'It's okay, Lucy,' Vera said. 'He's good at this. He's doing his part – we need to do ours.' She retrieved her phone, rubbed it against her shirt to clear it of water, and made a show of keying in 911. 'No service,' she said robotically.

I nodded, wanting to look at the river again but knowing I shouldn't.

Vera stepped closer, and though her eyes were serious, there was kindness there, too. Coated in droplets, her hair practically shone. 'Can you do this, Lucy? If you can't, we can call it off. We can meet John in his cabin tonight. We can pretend that none of this ever happened. We can go back to –'

'I don't want to call it off.'

'You're absolutely sure?' Vera asked. 'Because there's no going back, once we do it. You understand that, don't you?'

'I understand.'

Vera took my hand in hers, cool and damp from the weather, and squeezed. 'Thank you,' she said. 'I love you. Now, let's get back to where we can make a call, before it gets dark.'

As agreed, we ran, retracing our steps, Vera, agile, leading the way; me, trying my best not to trip over roots and stones, matted leaves slick from the rain.

At a break in the woods, she stopped and checked her phone. 'I have service.'

'Me too.'

We stood, like statues, at the same place I'd paused to take in the colors, but now the sun was almost down, the hues hazy and fever-dreamy. There wouldn't be light much longer. We had flashlights, and so did John. Still, I couldn't shake the feeling, deep in my bones, that something had gone wrong. That John was in danger, that this wasn't going to work.

I heard a crackle up ahead, and my pulse quickened, but Vera didn't pay it any attention. She lifted the phone to her ear. 'Yes, hello, I think, Jesus, I think my husband –' Her voice cracked, her words turning into a wail. 'I think my husband just fell off a cliff. We're on a hike. God, he was just ahead, and he, and he must have stopped to take a photo, and –'

She paused, her eyes pinpointing a break in the trees that led to the next thicket of woods, her breath heaving from our quick run down. 'I don't know the address,' she said, voice strained. She was practically yelling now. 'We were on Platte River Trail, the trailhead by the parking lot just off of –' She looked at me.

'Chapel Road.'

'Chapel Road,' she said, and I didn't know if she'd truly forgotten or if it was all a part of her act. I briefly imagined her in athleisure, fresh from an afternoon run, standing in front of the mirror and practicing the 911 call like I used to practice the specials for the restaurant where I'd waited tables when I first moved to New York.

'No, we're not in the parking lot now . . . Please, I just . . . No, we can't see him . . . Yes, yes, I'll stay on. Hurry. Goddamn it, please hurry.'

Without getting off the phone, she gestured to me, and we continued down the path toward the parking lot, the trees enveloping us once again, darkening the ground around us. I fiddled in my backpack for my flashlight, already nervous about hiking in the oncoming dark, but my hands brushed against a bit of paper. Strange. I'd emptied the bag last night; there shouldn't be anything inside but my flashlight and an extra layer. Carefully, I unfolded the scrap in my hands.

My breath caught as water drops from the canopy of trees made spots on the paper. It was his handwriting, chicken scratch that I'd seen on the whiteboard that hung on their fridge, not elegant and swirling like hers. His letters were fat, short, and instantly recognizable.

> I'm sorry about the other night. Please don't tell Vera.
> I'll call you soon.

I folded it as quickly as I could, my hands beginning to tingle as sweat pricked the back of my neck. Vera was up ahead, still on the phone. I shoved the note into my pocket and hurried to keep up. After another five minutes, Vera got off the call. They were sending rangers from the New York State Department of Environmental Conservation, she said, as well as DEC police officers.

The rangers came first, in hunter-green uniforms and khaki hats, driving utility-terrain vehicles. They were going to do everything they could to find him, they said, as Vera continued to play distressed and I kept my mouth shut, not wanting to say anything wrong, wondering what would happen if the rangers found John as he was making his way toward the cabin, cash and supplies tucked away in his second backpack.

It was fully dark out by the time the officers arrived, in a cop car instead of a UTV, lights flashing, giving the parking lot an eerie clublike feel, turning the tall grasses and signposts into shadow people, dancing and gyrating as the glow flickered round and round.

Vera shifted her weight back and forth as a woman climbed out of the police car and approached. She was in a similar hunter-green uniform, but her weapons belt and wide-brimmed hat set her apart from the rangers. Against her large brown eyes and neat low bun, her hat and her gear looked too big for her, like they were weighing her down. Behind her, a short, stout man emerged from the passenger side and slowly headed our way.

'I'm DEC Officer Parker,' the woman said, her voice brusque but warm. 'And this is DEC Officer Roberts.'

'My husband,' Vera said, voice soggy and waterlogged. 'My husband, he –'

'Are you the one who placed the nine-one-one call, ma'am?' Parker asked.

Vera nodded. 'He just –' Her voice cracked, and she pointed to me. 'She saw. He just . . .'

Parker faced me. 'I know we've already got the rangers searching, but can you tell us what happened, ma'am?'

I felt my breath quicken and my pulse race, but we'd all agreed that would seem normal. We'd just experienced extreme stress. If my body showed no signs of it, *that* would be abnormal. I took a deep breath as I realized exactly what we were doing. This wasn't park rangers anymore, people asking you to stay on the trail and look out for your safety. This was a cop, and I was about to lie to her: 'John was hiking up ahead to get some photos, and just after I stepped into the clearing . . .' I paused to catch my breath, then stared down, as if transfixed by my own feet. 'I heard him scream. I saw him slip and fall off the edge.' Still staring down, I pulled everything I've ever felt, everyone I'd ever lost, my mom and my dad, Davis and Ellie, as close to me as possible. Then I wiped my eyes with the back of my hand and looked up.

'And when you looked over the ledge, could you see him, ma'am?'

Vera interrupted, 'No, because it's a goddamned river. It has to be at least a hundred feet down. We need to get down there, we need to –' She stopped abruptly, as if she didn't know *what* we needed to do.

Officer Parker stepped back, exchanged a whispered word with her partner, and I felt the hairs on the back of my neck stand straight up. I imagined them pulling out a polygraph machine right then and there, asking me all sorts of questions, Parker's once-kind face looking right at me: *I think you're lying, Lucy.*

Instead, her eyes flitted to the road, where yet another UTV had pulled in, driven by a ranger, a young guy whose shaggy hair peeked from beneath his cap. Parker turned back to me. 'Can you take us to where you saw him fall?'

The ride in the UTV was bumpy, air slapping at our faces. The ranger and Officer Parker rode in front, Vera and I in the back, though I kept my eyes focused on the woods and the trail, not daring to glance at Vera for fear that the wrong look would some-how give us away. I pictured John out there, waiting. Could he hear the sirens? The rumble of the UTV over stones and logs and roots? How far had he gone already? Could he really find his way four miles in the dark? Could the rangers have found him? This plan suddenly seemed insane.

And then there was the note, the one now tucked into my pocket. The note I was too afraid to open again and yet desper-ately wanted to: *Please don't tell Vera.*

Our happy new family, our much-needed escape, was starting off with a betrayal.

'Here,' Vera said at the clearing, and the UTV abruptly stopped, my knees smashing against the hard plastic seat in front of me.

'This way,' Vera said, Officer Parker's flashlight like a beacon.

There they were, the abandoned backpack and water bottle, just as we'd left them. Parker squatted down, then stood. From a duffel bag, she retrieved a camera, about the size of John's, and snapped a series of photos. Then she tucked it away and pulled out a large brown paper evidence bag and a pair of tongs like a giant tweezers. She expertly maneuvered John's water bottle into the sack, then folded the top and placed it inside her duffel.

Her flashlight found the footprints and the disturbed rocks – still there, the rain not strong enough to fully wash them away. She turned to me. 'This is where he fell?'

'From what I could see, yes.'

She retrieved her camera, knelt carefully, and took more photos, then stood. 'Can you tell me exactly what happened?'

Breath short, pulse elevated, I pointed to the edge of the clearing. 'I was a little bit behind John, and just as I stepped into the clearing, I heard him scream and saw him slip and fall off the edge here.'

A hit of nausea, a tickle in my throat. 'And then Vera found me, and we looked over the edge, but we didn't see him. We couldn't see him.'

'How long were you standing there before Ms Abernathy arrived?' Parker asked.

I shrugged. 'A minute or so,' I said. 'I called for her, but I'm not sure if she heard me. I don't know, it's hard to say.'

'Probably a few minutes,' Vera added. 'It took me a while to catch up to her. I didn't know – I heard yelling, but I couldn't make out what she was saying over the wind. God, I couldn't have imagined –' She looked away.

With her flashlight, Parker scanned the area, but when she didn't see anything else, she grabbed John's backpack and her duffel, her expression matter-of-fact. 'All right. Let's get down there.'

Vera and I piled back into the UTV. It revved to life, grumbling, and we made our way, not back toward the parking lot, but down a different path, toward the river.

Where both Vera and I knew John wouldn't be.

Twenty

I had made it. That's what I thought when I woke the next morning. I had made it another night in my little cottage, another night without Davis finding me. If all went according to plan, I only had one or two more nights to go.

I called Vera, but she didn't answer. So I walked over, only to find no one was home, and a horrible thought struck me – what if she had gone, too? What if the two of them were out there, in the wilderness somewhere? What if they'd used me and left me behind, tiring of my company before our family had a chance to start anew?

It wasn't possible, I told myself. Vera would come back from wherever she'd gone. John would call. And soon I would be gone, where Davis couldn't find me. Where Ellie couldn't, either.

By one o'clock, she still wasn't back. Meanwhile, it had begun to snow. I was sitting by the window, watching the flakes fall, tracing circles in the frosty glass and looking for any sign of Vera's car, when I saw a police cruiser coming down the road. It slowed, and as it did, my pulse sped up. It stopped in front of my house.

I whipped the drapes shut as my mind tried to make sense of it. It had to be routine, nothing more than a follow-up. Officer Parker had found the camera on the bank of the river last night, just before the rocks turned to water, smashed beyond repair and marred with John's blood. The rangers had searched the area, and there wasn't a single sign of John, and the working theory, just as we'd hoped, was that he'd been washed away, dying on impact or shortly thereafter. There was an all-points bulletin out for his body, but we both knew nothing would turn up.

A knock shook the door, and Dusty barked furiously.

I opened it to see Officer Parker and a man I didn't recognize. He was tall and wore a lightly crumpled suit, his round belly bulging behind the button-down shirt.

'Miss King,' Parker said.

'Hi,' I managed. My eyes flicked to the man and back to her. 'Is there news?'

Parker didn't answer my question, but her eyes were warm. 'This is Detective McKnight,' she said. 'Can we come in?'

Fingers tingling with nerves, I ushered them in and offered them coffee. Parker insisted she didn't want anything, but McKnight, after delivering a firm but sweaty handshake, took me up on it.

Standing in the kitchen, waiting for it to brew, my mind reeled. Again I told myself that this was all routine, that it was probably just a run-of-the-mill follow-up.

The machine finished, and I took two mugs from the cabinet, but one of them slipped, water through my fingers, and struck the floor, instantly shattering against hard ceramic tile. I imagined John's camera shattering. And John shattering, too.

'You okay in there?' the detective asked.

'Fine. Just one sec,' I called back, though if he only turned his balding head, he'd be able to see exactly what was going on. I shooed Dusty away, then swept the remnants of the mug into the dustpan and tossed it into the trash, as if it were evidence of my lies.

The mugs and the sugar bowl clattered slightly as I carried them into the living room, calling attention to my shaking hands.

I set one mug down in front of the detective, spilling a little of the coffee. He sopped it up with a napkin, then added four scoops of sugar. 'We're here because we have a few follow-up questions, and you're the only witness.'

Witness. The word sent chills up my spine, even though that's exactly what I was.

'Okay,' I said. 'However I can help.'

McKnight smiled, but it was a fake one. 'How close would you say you were to Mr Nolan and Ms Abernathy?'

The question threw me off balance. I'd expected him to have me run through last night's events again. I tugged at the sleeve of my shirt, then stopped abruptly. 'We're good friends,' I said.

'And how long have you known them?'

I folded my hands in my lap. 'Since September, when I moved here. We met right away, since we're neighbors.'

McKnight pulled out a notepad, nodding.

My mouth filled with saliva, and I took a sip of coffee.

Parker sat stock-still, hands on her knees.

'And where did you live before September?' he asked.

A deep breath. 'Brooklyn.'

'Right.' He didn't even serve me with a nod this time, as if that was the most obvious answer in the world. His eyes were beady – they didn't fit his round, doughy face at all. 'So what brought you to the area? Kind of a big change, no? Most people – people your age, at least – they come up for the weekends. What about your work?'

'I work from home,' I said.

'Doing?'

I hesitated only briefly. 'I'm a writer.'

He forced a smile. 'Have I read anything of yours?'

A lump rose in my throat, but I swallowed it back. 'Nothing big. I haven't written a book or anything. Mostly articles online.'

'Great,' he said, deadpan. 'So you just had a craving for some mountain air? And leaving all your friends in Brooklyn behind?'

'I had a bad breakup.'

He nodded, his shoulders loosening. 'Can you tell us again exactly what happened yesterday?'

At least I knew this one by heart. 'Yes,' I said, facing Parker. 'What I told you. We were hiking, on a hike we've been on before, and John went ahead to take some photos. I heard a scream – I mean, I stepped into the clearing, and then I heard him scream and saw him slip and fall.' My heart pounded, banging my chest raw over such a stupid flub.

McKnight took another sip of coffee and glanced, once again, at his notes, but he'd hardly written anything, just a few scribbles I couldn't make out. Parker was completely silent. McKnight looked to her and back to me. 'Yes, I know what you told Officer Parker and the DEC rangers,' he said. 'I've read the preliminary report. But I'd like to hear it all again, perhaps in a bit more detail.'

'Do you want me to describe the colors of the leaves or something?'

They both stared.

'Sorry,' I said. 'Yesterday was horrible, and now you're asking me to relive it. I just, I don't know what you want me to say.'

'It's okay,' Parker said. 'It's an awful thing, what happened. What you and Ms Abernathy had to go through.'

'It is,' McKnight picked up. He scratched at his chin, at an indentation that had probably been a cystic bit of acne when he was a teenager and was now a scar that would never go away. 'I guess what I'm trying to figure out is, you feel confident in what you saw?'

'Yes.'

'But you didn't see his body down in the river when you peered over.'

'No,' I said, confidence surging at our carefully made-up story. 'It's about fifty feet from the edge of the clearing. I ran, but still, by the time I got there, I couldn't see anything but the water. It was so drizzly, it was hard to see anyway.'

'I see,' McKnight said, making another note. Then his eyes caught mine. 'So why was Mr Nolan taking photos, if the visibility was so awful?'

I sighed. I was on solid ground – John had told me what to say for this bit. 'The diffused light is actually really good for photos. As long as you don't get water on the lens, light rain can be a great condition for shooting.'

McKnight smiled. 'Hey, I'm not a photographer – had to ask.'

I sagged against the sofa as I felt a lightness rise in my stomach. He believed me.

'So,' McKnight said. 'Just to be clear. Since it was drizzly and it was fifty feet away, like you said, you *definitely* saw Mr Nolan slip? There's no way you could have heard a scream but not seen anything, found the backpack and the water bottle and put two and two together?'

'No,' I said, without hesitation. 'I'm sure.'

He exchanged a look with Parker. Then he gave me a half smile, almost a smirk. 'I know you think I'm probably being a stickler about this, but I like to get the facts straight.'

'Of course.'

'And sometimes it's easy to get something mixed up. Especially since, like you said, it was raining. It was stressful. A lot was going on. It happened so fast. But you saw him? You actually saw him fall?'

'Yes.'

'Okay then.' McKnight tucked his notebook into his pocket. His eyes caught Parker's, long enough for her to grimace, then looked to me. 'Miss King, I hate to have to tell you this, but we have confirmation that Mr Nolan is dead.'

A flash of panic. 'What? How?'

McKnight stared at me, waiting, and when I didn't say anything else: 'We found his body this morning.'

No, I thought, shaking my head. *No, it can't be.*

'What?' I repeated, my face going hot, my eyes stinging with moisture, my words practically spilling out. 'Oh god. It's not . . . it can't.' I shook my head. 'Not John.'

Images bounced through my mind. John hurting himself on his hike through the dark, his body crushed, his bones damp and cold, the park rangers coming upon him in the night. He was supposed to be good at this. They had both said that, they had promised me he was.

The fall, the one we'd made up, what if it hadn't been made up at all? What if the scream I'd heard was real? What if he'd done such a good job pretending that he'd *actually* slipped, crashing into the river, being washed away?

Oh god, John. Oh god, no. He should never have. We should never have . . .

'Jesus,' I managed. 'He washed up somewhere?' Acid roiled in my stomach. Around me, the world began to spin.

McKnight raised his eyebrows, patting the notebook in his chest pocket. 'I could see how you would say that, since you *did* see him fall.' He paused, giving me an opening. 'But we didn't find him in the river. Or the woods. We didn't even find him in DEC territory, to be honest. I'm an Ulster County detective. DEC Officer Parker's really only here to hand off the investigation.'

Investigation. I sucked in breath. 'If it wasn't in the woods, it must not be John. It *can't* be John.'

McKnight's head tilted to the side, as if trying to make sense of a different language. 'Miss King . . .' His voice trailed off.

Tears leaked from my eyes. I couldn't get it out of my head, the image of his body dashing against the rocks. I'd told Vera we should check on him. I'd told her I was worried. It couldn't be. It just couldn't. It was all fake, something we made up. *It's not real,* I wanted to scream. *It's not goddamn real.*

None of this was ever supposed to be real.

McKnight cleared his throat.

'John Nolan was found in his art studio, up near Claverack Creek. Ms Abernathy discovered him there this morning.'

Twenty-One

There's no way,' I said, my voice cracking. 'It's not possible.'

'Well, I'm sorry to say, but it is possible,' McKnight said. 'That's *exactly* what happened.'

'It can't be,' I said desperately. 'No, you have to be wrong. It . . . it *can't* be him.'

McKnight opened the lapel of his suit, digging in the interior pocket. He came out with a crumpled packet of tissues and tossed it on the table, next to the sugar.

'It is him, Miss King. Ms Abernathy identified him herself.'

I shook my head harder, as if that could push his words away, as the hopes I'd been clinging to shuddered, their foundations cracking. 'Oh god, oh god, no. *How?*'

Parker stole a glance at McKnight, her face paling.

McKnight continued to study me, ignoring my question.

'No,' I said again as their silence stretched out, and before I could stop myself, more sobs were racking me, animal sounds. 'No, you're *wrong*.'

This couldn't be happening again.

I couldn't lose someone I cared about . . . again.

I'd lost too much already.

Besides, the plan was good: no way to mess it up; no way for John to die.

No no no no no.

McKnight tapped his foot against the floor. 'I'm surprised it's such a shock to you, given that you saw him fall off a cliff. Did you expect him to have survived such an accident?'

I had no words. I could only shake my head, feel the tears swim down my cheeks.

He pushed the tissues toward me, but I wouldn't touch them. He didn't care about me or John or Vera or any of us. He only cared about trapping me, making me feel small, tripping me up.

I searched Parker's face for answers, but she looked down at her hands.

'You don't have to answer that,' McKnight said, as if he were doing me some sort of favor. 'But the reason why I kept asking about what you saw . . .'

I paused, wiping at my eyes. Something else was coming, I could see it now. His trump card, the one he'd been holding, waiting to use, the whole time he'd been here. While I was making coffee, breaking a mug, handing him the sugar, he had had this in his head.

'The thing is, his body didn't show a single sign of a fall.' He blinked, once, twice. Parker looked up, her eyes filling with empathy, understanding. *You can tell us.* Good cop, bad cop.

'I'd like to know why you lied to us, Miss King.' McKnight said it so coolly, as if there were an answer I could deliver just like that. 'You can tell us. Really.' His head swiveled to Parker, then back to me. 'We can clear this up right now.'

My breath was suddenly short, my pulse merciless. I could feel myself reddening all over, warmth and guilt coating every inch of skin as my thoughts spun: *How?* We'd been rushed, but careful. And why was Vera over there this morning? The plan had been to wait for John to contact us. What changed?

Another thought struck me, pushing all thoughts of Vera aside: Ellie.

What if she'd told Davis right away, called him as soon as she left the restaurant? What if Davis *had* been up here with her, and she'd lied about it? What if he'd found us, me and John together, the drapes left open for anyone to see? The door unlocked, just begging someone to sneak in? I thought Davis would find *me*, hurt *me*, but what if he'd found another way to punish me? What if this was it, the ultimate blow? Someone I cared about. The man I had cared about after him.

'Explain what you saw,' McKnight said.

I shook my head.

'Miss King,' he pressed.

'I . . . I . . . It was raining.'

'And?'

'I guess I could have been mistaken.'

McKnight nodded, as if expecting this. 'So did you hear Mr Nolan scream, then?'

It was a relief not to have to lie. 'I did.'

'But you didn't see him?'

I shook my head. 'I heard the scream and then saw his backpack and, I don't know, I just assumed.'

Parker's gaze narrowed, her good-cop mask temporarily gone. *You lied to me. You lied straight to my face.*

McKnight crossed his arms and relaxed into the sofa like he owned the place. 'Glad we cleared that up. Now, this is important. Did Mr Nolan have any enemies?'

Enemies? Shit. What had Vera already told them? What if, when she'd found John's body, she'd completely sold me out? No, it couldn't be.

Only, if they were asking about enemies, that meant this was serious. This could be a murder investigation.

I pressed my hands to my knees. 'There were supposedly rumors about John,' I said. 'I don't know too much because I haven't been living here that long, but yeah, there were people who didn't like him.'

'Anyone specific?' McKnight asked.

Sam Alby flashed to mind, spilling wine all over Vera, threatening them with notes, dead animals, slashed tires. But if I told McKnight about him, would he put it together, deduce our plan? I couldn't risk it, not until I talked to Vera, got our stories straight. 'You'd have to ask Vera.'

McKnight stared at me a moment, then adjusted himself on the sofa, took one last sip of coffee. 'That's helpful,' he said, though we both knew it wasn't. 'Thanks for your time, Miss King.'

Parker followed his lead, shifting forward, as if to get up.

McKnight leaned across the coffee table and pressed a business card into my hand, creamy pale and old-school. 'If you think of anything else, let me know.'

'Wait,' I said, wheels suddenly turning. A sliver of hope, a tiny space in my chest, because I didn't want to believe it had been Davis, that I had selfishly brought my mess to them, delivered it to their doorstep, wrapped in brown paper and bruised skin. I didn't want to believe that I was the reason John had died. Maybe the question about enemies was just routine. Maybe they were still figuring out whether it was foul play or not.

'What?' McKnight asked. 'Think of something?'

'Are you definitely sure . . .' My voice faltered, trailing off.

'Are we sure of what, Miss King?'

'That someone hurt him intentionally?' I asked, more tears spilling out.

He stared at me; then he nodded. 'That is exactly what we believe. This is a homicide investigation.'

I shook my head, not wanting it to be true.

'Oh,' McKnight added, his notebook reappearing, as if it had only just occurred to him. 'What did you do last night?'

'Last night?'

'After you made the report to Officer Parker.'

I swallowed, my throat tightening. 'Vera dropped me off, and I stayed in. I went to bed early.'

'What time?' he asked.

'I don't know. Maybe nine o'clock.'

'Didn't see anyone else?'

'No, of course not – it was so stressful. I came home and watched TV and then I needed to sleep. I couldn't do much of anything after what happened.'

'Right,' McKnight said. 'Well, we're going to need you to come down to the station and make a proper statement, get your prints, in case they turn up on any evidence, run-of-the-mill stuff. How's tomorrow – eleven a.m.? That okay with you, Miss King?'

'Yes,' I said, nodding robotically. 'Yes, of course.'

'Great,' McKnight said, fake smile invading his face like a virus. 'We'll see you then.'

I followed them to the door. 'Hang on,' I said as Dusty watched them eagerly.

'Yes, Miss King?' McKnight said.

'How do you know?' I asked.

He raised an eyebrow. 'Know what?'

'That it was a homicide?'

Parker let out a breath. In the daylight streaming through the open door, her complexion looked almost green.

'Mr Nolan was stabbed,' McKnight said. 'Six times.'

Twenty-Two

Wretching, I heaved into the toilet, but nothing much came out, only spit and bile.

Porcelain cold against my skin, I remembered how John had been here, watching me do the same, only two days ago. It sickened me that that was one of the last times I'd seen him, ill with alcohol and guilt and shame.

I couldn't believe I'd never see him again.

I stood, washed my hands and splashed water on my face, then ambled to the bedroom. I opened the top drawer of the dresser, pushed aside my mother's scarf, and retrieved John's note, which I'd tucked away next to the photos last night. I traced my fingers along his handwriting.

Please don't tell Vera. I'll call you soon.

What had gone wrong?

I lay in bed all afternoon. I knew I should call Vera, should go over, hold her tight, but the guilt was too much, the sensation that I had done this, brought this tragedy to them.

Davis raced through my mind. His blond hair, his thick intellectual glasses, his body, nowhere near overweight, but softened from his graphic designer desk job. He wasn't the sort to live at the gym, and I'd liked that about him. He didn't seem the type to be able to kill, but he hadn't seemed the type to hurt me, either.

Could he really have done this?

I remembered a day, early on, sitting on the sofa in our underwear at Davis's place, before I'd moved in, our legs tangled like pretzels, a glass pipe on the coffee table, weedy ash scattered around like black snowfall. 'Would you ever forgive a partner for cheating?' he'd asked me.

'You got something to tell me?'

He grabbed the back of my calf and squeezed. 'Of course not. Just hypothetical.'

I pursed my lips. 'As long as you're not going to use this as your road map for cheating later . . .'

'I would *never* cheat on you,' he said. 'Scout's honor.'

I'd laughed, the gaping, guffawing type that only came out when you were deep in the chemicals of love. 'Then I probably could forgive, if it was a one-off and not a whole drawn-out affair, and if the person, not you, since you would never cheat, confessed to me on his own instead of leaving me to snoop. You?'

His hand stroked the back of my leg. 'I could forgive you,' he said. And then the stroking stopped. 'But I'd have to kill the guy.'

I'd laughed again. It had felt funny at the time.

Now my hands felt clammy, and my stomach twisted, tying itself up in knots. What if?

What if he'd found me, seen me, followed us to the hike, and then – *somehow* – tracked John?

It wasn't possible, it wasn't –

My stomach churned as I remembered the way Dusty's leash had been cut, the pocketknife Davis always kept on him.

What if that had been his weapon?

A crude tool, a blade so short, he'd had to stab John *six times* to kill him?

Fingers shaking, I dialed Ellie's number, praying I was wrong – but there was no answer.

I dialed her again. And again and again.

After who knows how many *Hi, you've reached Ellie*s, I tossed the phone onto my bed, shaking my head. It didn't matter. For a second, I didn't even care. John was gone. I would never hear from him. I would never meet him in our little hideaway in the Adirondacks. I would never kiss him or hug him or tear myself up about my feelings for him again. I would never be able to tell him everything I'd been thinking about these past two days. *I'm sorry, but I'm not. This can never happen again, but part of me is glad that it did. I've fallen for you, but I've fallen for her, too, and there's no good solution, but all that matters is that I don't want to lose either of you.*

Please don't tell Vera.

I heard a noise outside and jolted out of bed. I flipped on the lights frantically, wiped beneath my eyes, then approached the door. Maggie. Part of me wanted to turn around, hide under the covers, make everything – and everyone – go away, but she'd already seen me.

Slowly, I opened the door. 'Hi,' I said.

'Are you okay?' she asked, her eyes narrowed in concern. 'I saw the police come by.'

'I –' I couldn't even get a word out. Tears swam in my eyes.

'Oh my goodness,' Maggie said, rushing in without waiting for an invitation, wrapping me in a hug.

She led me to the sofa, and I found myself sinking down, spent. She took a seat next to me, Dusty jumping into her lap.

'Lucy, what happened?' she asked.

I stared at her, blinking back new tears.

John was dead. Stabbed. Fuck.

'Are you hurt?' she asked. 'Did someone, did someone attack you?'

'No,' I managed. 'It's just –' I took a deep breath. 'We went on a hike yesterday,' I said, voice wavering. 'Just a regular hike that John and Vera go on all the time, and John fell.'

'What?' Maggie asked, her jaw dropping. 'What do you mean, he fell?'

Already, I was messing this up. I needed to get my new story straight. 'I mean, he went up ahead to take some photos, and he disappeared. We couldn't find him, but we saw his backpack, and so we thought he fell and we called the police. His camera was at the bottom of the ridge, so we –'

'Oh, Lucy,' she said, eyes narrowing. 'Is he, was he all right?'

'No,' I said, scooting away from her, attempting to calm my breaths. 'The police think . . .' I bit my lip, wondering if I should tell her everything – only it hardly even mattered now. 'They think someone murdered him. They found his body this morning.'

She gasped, and Dusty, looking back and forth between us, began to whine.

'Murdered?' she asked. 'Here?'

I nodded weakly.

The implication in her words wasn't hard to read. That sort of thing didn't happen, not here, in this quaint little town hours away from the city.

Not here, where things were safe – not even to people like John.

'But why do they think – How do they – Is Vera okay?'

'Vera's fine,' I said, but even as I did, I knew it was a lie. Vera was alive, sure, but she was far from fine. Wouldn't be fine for a very long time. Maybe ever. And it was all my fault. 'I mean, she's safe, yes.'

'How do they know it was murder? Could it have been an accident?'

'I don't know,' I said, the lie coming easily. I couldn't bear to share the details. Stabbed. It was too intimate, too personal. Maggie hadn't even liked him. 'They wouldn't say.'

'Oh my goodness,' Maggie said. 'That's just, that's just awful.'

Her eyes focused on a point somewhere in the distance, and I could see it, suddenly: her wheels turning, piecing something together.

'What?' I asked. Her eyes were still locked ahead, avoiding mine, and I reached for her arm. 'Maggie, what is it?'

'Nothing,' she said, shrugging me off. 'Only, someone murdered. Someone from *our* street. It's horrible, isn't it?'

'Is there something else you know, something you need to tell me?'

The clouds in her eyes seemed to clear, and they found mine again.

'Just that I'm so sorry,' she said. 'I know how much you cared about him.'

I didn't go over to the farmhouse until after seven. The walk was awful, my flashlight casting shadows everywhere, turning every last twig into something tall and foreboding. I strode quickly, trying to tune out the nefarious sounds of night in the country.

Vera's car was in the driveway, and John's truck, too, but no lights were on inside. I knocked anyway, waited.

I was about to turn back when she opened the door. Her eyes were puffy, her cheeks sunken. She looked like a ghost, a specter of herself, and she smelled overwhelmingly of cigarettes.

I opened my arms and she fell into them, practically collapsing. She felt so small and bony, her body shaking, her head knocking into my shoulder.

'I'm so sorry,' I whispered. She shook harder.

I don't know how long we stayed like that, but eventually, Vera pulled away, her eyes avoiding mine. She ushered me in, and I followed her to the living room; she didn't offer me a drink, only sat on the couch. I took the space next to her, wondering if it was the first time we'd been together here without some sort of alcohol lubricating our interactions.

After a moment, she stared at me. 'Did John tell you anything?'

My pulse sped up. She knew. About that night, what we had and hadn't done.

'What do you mean?'

'Something had to have changed,' Vera said, scratching a patch of skin beneath her ear. Her breaths came ragged, and her hand continued to worry at the same spot, and when she pulled it away, there was a flash of blood beneath her nail; a tiny trickle of red crawled down her neck. I grabbed a tissue from the pack I'd shoved into my pocket and pressed it into her hand. Vera held it to her neck. I watched her, crumpled like that, cracking beneath her grief, and for a split second, I wondered: Why had she gone to the cabin this morning? Were there things she wasn't telling *me*? Things she knew but didn't trust me with?

Was there any way she could have . . .

The idea sickened me, but it came all the same.

Could she have seen John and me, gotten angry, changed her plan . . .

'Vera,' I said, as carefully as I could manage. 'Why were you over there? You were supposed to wait for him to contact you.'

She stiffened. 'He's my husband, Lucy, and I just knew – this morning, I woke up early, and, god, I just had this *feeling*,' she said. 'I had this awful, terrifying feeling. I don't know how, but I knew something was wrong, and I – I was right.'

Her shoulders sank, and sobs took her over.

Waves of nausea hit me, acid rising in my throat. I felt guilty for having asked the question, for doubting her even for a minute. She loved him, she was his wife, and now she'd lost him.

'I found him, just lying there,' Vera went on, her eyes clouding as she again began to scratch, this time at her throat. 'In a pool of blood. It was awful. But even worse than that, he was just . . . blue.'

Trying to push the images away, I took her hand in mine, laced my fingers through hers, and squeezed.

'You *really* don't know anything?' she asked.

I disentangled her hand from mine. 'No,' I said softly. 'No, of course not.'

Was that the truth? I knew Davis was angry, that he wanted to pay me back, that he could very well know where I was by now. That he kept a knife on him – always.

Careful, rigorous, perfectionist Davis. Murder was an escalation, but hardly an impossibility.

'I'm just as shocked as you are,' I said. 'You have to believe me.'

She nodded, tears leaking from her eyes. 'I do. I just . . .' She paused. 'I don't understand what happened. It was never supposed to be like this. It was supposed to be just us. It was . . .' She gasped. 'It was supposed to be a new start for us.'

Her body shook all over, and I held her again, pulling her close. Then, suddenly, she looked up. 'You're not going, are you?'

'What?'

'Davis,' she said. 'I know you were eager to leave, but you must see that you can't now. I'm lost without John. You have to stay.'

Panic flashed within me, stiffening my limbs. She couldn't think I could stay now, could she? Not with Davis out there, knowing or on his way to knowing where I was.

Not when I thought there was a chance he might have . . .

I blinked slowly, trying to figure out what I was supposed to do, to put together a plan when the one I'd had had been ripped to shreds.

'I'm here,' I said finally. 'I promised the police I'd go down to the station tomorrow and give a statement. Don't worry.'

Vera's sigh was so instinctual, so relieved, that I couldn't bear to go on. Of course I had to leave; she should know that. I had to stay one or two more nights, or else it would look suspicious and I'd have McKnight on my tail before I even left town. If I did anything cagey, anything to make myself even more of a suspect, who knew how long he'd ask me to stay?

But after that . . .

I'd push for a speedy memorial – true crime documentaries had taught me the body wouldn't be ready for who knew how long – then go. Back West, to L.A. – hell, maybe even to Seattle – back where I should have gone in the first place.

'I can keep you company,' I offered, too scared to be on my own.

Vera nodded. 'I was hoping you would. Stay with me tonight – please. I need you now more than ever.'

Twenty-Three

After going back to get Dusty – I couldn't bear to leave him on his own – the three of us huddled together in the bed she'd shared with John – a trio of a different sort.

Vera's spare bedroom was full of John's art supplies, so I'd offered to crash on the couch, but she'd asked me to sleep beside her, where he used to. Strange as it was, I'd said yes, and Dusty cuddled between us like this was our new family.

In the morning, I headed back to my cottage, holding my breath as I turned the key in the lock, inspecting all the entrances to make sure no one had been inside, looking under the floorboard beneath my bed to check that everything important was still there, heart pounding as I asked myself if I should just leave. Screw the police and their routines. Grab my dad's hammer and my mother's scarf and *go.*

But I showered and got ready instead, telling myself I could get through this. Be careful these next couple of days. Look over my shoulder. Examine every lock. Not give the police a single reason to suspect me.

Be smarter than Davis thought I was.

Just before eleven, I parked in front of the station, a one-story building a mile or so off the main strip.

It looked like it had been built in the fifties, and was nestled among a parking lot and woods. I parked near the back, hands trembling as I scanned the lot. Only one exit, the road I'd entered on. Again, I quelled the desire to escape, to drive off, become a shadow person, like John was supposed to be. Get the hell out of Dodge – and away from Davis. That would come soon, I told myself, only not just yet. I had to tread carefully. I knew this.

Grabbing my phone, I called Ellie again. But like each time I'd dialed her in the last twenty-four hours, the call went straight to voice mail. She wouldn't recognize my new number – she was probably screening – only I hoped to catch her anyway, hear her indignant tone, the words I craved: *No, I didn't tell him. I promised you, didn't I?* Prove to myself I was only being paranoid, that Davis had nothing to do with John's death, that it was someone else. Sam Alby, probably – or maybe even someone random, some crazed serial killer living deep in the woods like you always saw in movies, hiding away in John's unlocked cabin. Wrong place, wrong time.

One more unanswered call, and I shoved the phone into my bag and traipsed across the parking lot.

Inside, the station was dead, nothing like the station in Brooklyn where I'd once filed a police report over a stolen delivery of high-end linens. In that station, there'd been a cacophony of buzzers and radios, bells and whistles. Here, it was pin-drop still. A woman in uniform at the counter tapped away at a PC begging to be put out of its misery. Parker was nowhere in sight, but of course she wouldn't be. She was a DEC officer, concerned with business on state land, where the hike had been; not Ulster County, where John's cabin was, only a few miles away but an entirely different jurisdiction.

The officer looked up. 'Help you?'

'I'm Lucy King,' I managed. 'Detective McKnight asked me to come in at eleven?'

She kept tapping away; then, without looking up, 'You can have a seat, Miss King.'

It was fifteen minutes before he came out, giving me time to rehearse what I was about to say: *I heard a scream and I stepped out into the clearing. I didn't see John, but I saw his backpack and water bottle. That's why I thought he had fallen.* It wasn't what I'd initially told Parker yesterday, but I figured hammering down that narrative wasn't going to do me any good.

McKnight walked out. He nodded at me, then did a one-eighty. I waited a half second too long before I realized I was meant to follow him.

A dusty linoleum hallway. Then a room, glass windows and a table in the center, just like on TV. I forced myself to take a deep, calming breath. This was only a formality, like he'd said.

'Coffee?' he asked as I took a seat.

'Please.'

He returned a few minutes later with two steaming Styrofoam cups and tossed a couple of packets of sugar and creamer onto the table. He pointed to a camera in the corner. 'We're required to tape interviews.'

It was an announcement, not a question. He sat down. I did, too.

'All right,' McKnight said, getting straight to it. 'Why don't you tell me again exactly what happened on November second?' He glanced at his notes. 'Two days ago.'

I once watched this spy show where one of the spies told an informant that to lie properly, you only had to stare at the tip of the person's nose – it would look like you were looking them in the eye. So after going through the details – slowly, meticulously – when I got to the part in question, that's what I did. Eyes on the bulbous tip of McKnight's nose, I delivered my line as smoothly as I could, raising my volume slightly in an attempt to quell any quaking of my voice. 'I heard a scream, and I stepped out into the clearing. I didn't see John, but I saw his backpack and his water bottle. I assumed he had fallen.'

McKnight's fingers drummed on the table. 'So you *didn't* see him fall?'

'No.'

'Why did you say you did?'

Keep it simple, stupid. That's what my dad used to say.

'It all happened so fast. I got mixed up.'

'You're not mixed up now?'

'No.'

McKnight leaned back in his chair and crossed his arms over his paunch. He was pushing 250 pounds, I guessed, and he teetered on his chair, balancing on its back two legs – I swore it was going to slip right out from under him.

He let the chair fall forward, its front legs clattering against the linoleum, making me jump.

'Sorry,' he said, grabbing his cup. 'Refill. You want one?'

Mine had hardly been touched. 'I'm okay, I think.'

'Great. Just give me a second.'

That 'second' turned into five minutes. Ten. My hands became clammy; I wiped them against my jeans.

By the time he returned, I had partially calmed myself down. My story had been told, my portion complete. It was his job to look into the rest, the cobwebbed corners, the covered-up cracks. He took his seat and leaned back in the chair. He was the one who had to figure out if Davis – or Sam – or someone else entirely – had done this. I had to protect myself.

'Miss King, as far as you know, was Mr Nolan faithful to his wife?'

Fuck.

'I think so,' I said, our night together flickering through my mind like film through a projector. 'Why?'

McKnight leaned forward. 'We've been talking to people in

171

town. As I'm sure you know, Mr Nolan wasn't exactly next in line for Person of the Year.' He grinned slightly at his own joke.

I only nodded.

'There's talk of, well . . . extramarital activity. Any thoughts on that?'

I ran my tongue over my teeth. My mouth suddenly felt unbearably dry. 'I heard there were rumors about him,' I said. 'After the art classes and the private lessons and all that.'

McKnight nodded. 'Yes, I'm sure you've heard the rumors.' He folded his hands across his belly. 'If it's true about Claire Alby, well, that's a very troubling allegation. So young, you know.'

A pause stretched between us, and I felt the need to fill it. 'He and Vera, they were crazy about each other. He wouldn't . . . I don't believe that's true.'

McKnight's eyebrows shot up. 'Really? A woman like you. A feminist, right?'

'Yes,' I said, feeling instantly judged. His definition of feminism and mine were very different, I'd put money on that.

'You guys are supposed to believe each other,' he said. 'Right?'

'Has anyone actually accused John of anything? As far as I know, it's just small-town gossip.'

He cocked his head to the side. 'And some talk of harassment on the part of Ms Abernathy. As well as a potential lawsuit from Claire Alby's father.'

I bit the inside of my cheek. 'I don't know what you want me to say.'

McKnight held a hand up. 'Nothing. Maybe you're right. Maybe with him, it is all just gossip. But either way, it's got me thinking. Isn't it strange that stories like that would just pop up out of nowhere? Maybe, whether with her or someone else, Mr Nolan wasn't as devoted to his wife as you seem to think. Sound possible?'

He didn't. We didn't. Nothing happened. A vision of our lips connecting, pleasure and guilt intertwined as one.

'I don't know why you're asking me and not Vera,' I said. 'He was my friend, yes, but I can't pretend to know the ins and outs of someone else's marriage.'

McKnight leaned back in his chair. 'You're right about that. Marriage is long, with lots of ups and downs. You ever been married?'

I shook my head.

'Didn't think so.' He shot me a smile that I didn't trust in the slightest – his teeth were too long in the front, gums too red, like he was ready to devour me at any moment. He drummed his thick fingers against the table, waiting. 'Is there anything else you think I should know?'

Davis came to mind, but the thought of handing over his name on a silver platter, asking them to go poking around in my past, broadcasting my current whereabouts – it was too dangerous. What if Ellie hadn't told him after all? What if I was wrong? I couldn't risk it.

'What is it?' McKnight asked.

'Nothing.'

'You sure about that, Miss King?'

I clenched my jaw. 'I'm sure.'

'You and Mr Nolan,' McKnight said. 'You were just friends?'

Heat rose to my cheeks, giving me away. I should've been better at this, like Vera, able to turn on the grief in her voice at the drop of a hat, able to give the 911 performance of a lifetime, a performance that had become her reality.

'Miss King?'

'Yes,' I said. 'We were just friends. I'm friends with Vera, too, remember?'

McKnight pulled a pen from his pocket, clicked it three times.

'Yes, Ms Abernathy mentioned that. And we followed up with some of your neighbors, and they agree with how she portrayed it, that you all were quite close.'

My thoughts turned to Maggie, who'd comforted me only yesterday. Could she have said something like that, cast doubt on me so easily?

'Yes,' I said. 'We were. Are.'

He tucked his pen away. 'Most women I know, women Ms Abernathy's age, at least, not sure they'd be too happy with a woman like you around all the time.'

'A woman like me?'

He raised an eyebrow. 'Younger. You know.'

My eyes widened. Sometimes I swore that men were incapable of seeing women as anything but objects. To McKnight, I was evidence. A point-by-point analysis in his case. 'What do you even mean by that?'

He tossed his hands in the air. 'My point is, was Ms Abernathy okay with you constantly hanging around her husband?'

I felt as if I'd been slapped, and for a second I was back at college, watching that stupid video for the first time. Remembering how you could be judged – *snap*, like that – how, at the end of the day, it was always your fault. Not the guys goading you on, or the ones passing images of you around like porn. No, *you* were guilty until proven innocent; men, the opposite.

'Miss King?'

I practically spit out the words. 'I wasn't *hanging around* her husband. I was spending time with them. We were friends. That's all. I would never do anything to hurt Vera.'

It was true and untrue at the same time. I hated myself for it.

'Let me be even more direct,' McKnight said, letting his words hang in the air as my heart thumped murderously. 'Were you and Mr Nolan romantically involved?'

'No,' I said firmly. 'No, of course not. Like I said, we were friends. Good friends.'

There was that smile again – fake, disbelieving. I couldn't help it: I remembered the smell of John in my bed, the note in my backpack, all the times I'd woken up having dreamed of him.

McKnight scooted his chair back and turned off the camera. 'That's all for now, Miss King. Thank you for coming in. We really appreciate it. An officer will take your prints on your way out.'

I got up, steadying myself against the table, then moved for the door.

'Oh, and Miss King?'

'Yeah?'

'Get home safe, okay? They say it's supposed to rain, and I know you have trouble seeing clearly when the weather's acting up.'

Twenty-Four

Back in my house, after locking the door tight behind me, I headed straight to the bathroom, needing to scrub the fingerprint ink from my hands.

As I flipped on the light, I stopped short, the image searing itself into my brain.

The faucet was running, a tiny stream trickling into the sink.

Stomach twisting, I switched the water off, my mind flashing to the faucet in our prewar bathroom in Brooklyn. It used to stick, and Davis had a habit of not twisting it all the way off, leaving it dripping. It drove me nuts, and one day I playfully stuck a Post-it on the bathroom mirror with a message scribbled out in bright blue Sharpie – *Remember to twist the faucet all the way!*

Thanks, babe! he'd written on his own Post-it, and later I'd told Ellie and our friends about living with a dude, about our passive-aggressive but sweet notes to each other; we'd all laughed about it.

It was only that weekend, when I picked up my laundry from the wash-and-fold and the lady had yelled at me that I could have ruined her machine, that I realized that very same Sharpie had gotten into my hamper. My clothes were ruined. Permanent blue ink on every one of my whites. When I confronted him, Davis swore up and down that I must have left it in my pocket – *God,*

Lucy, what kind of maniac do you think I am? Who would do something like that?

After that, when Davis and I argued, I'd frequently discover the faucet running in the bathroom. A tiny little 'fuck you,' just for me. A reminder that should I criticize, should I make a request, I would pay. His signature.

Was this proof? Had he tracked me down? Had he killed John, left me this to let me know he was here, just in case I didn't put it together on my own?

Or was I actually being paranoid this time, like he always said I was? Had all the chaos and the grief and the fear and the shame of losing – and loving – John scrambled my brain?

I felt like I was coming undone, unable to tell up from down. Whether Davis was actually here, he'd succeeded in that, at least.

There was a sudden knock at the door, and I jumped instinctually, every muscle in my body going taut as blood rushed to my head.

Maybe it's Vera. God, let it be Vera. Please don't let it be Davis. Please let me be wrong.

I switched the faucet off and ran to the bedroom, grabbing my dad's hammer from the nightstand as the knock came again, more urgently this time.

I ran to the bedroom, pulled the drapes back, and peered through.

The relief was intense, my pulse instantly slowing, my body practically going limp.

I set the hammer down and opened the door. 'Rachel?' Her coat was a mossy green, and a multicolored tasseled pashmina snaked around her neck, dancing in the gusts of wind coming down from the meadow. In the misty, diffused light, her handful of gray hairs shimmered like fine silver. She held a clear vase full of yellow roses, tied with grosgrain ribbon and twine.

'Sorry. I hate to just show up at your door like this, but

Maggie told me about what happened to John, and –' She paused, then lifted the vase like some sort of offering. 'I brought flowers, but Vera's not home, and Maggie isn't, either, and I didn't want to leave them on her porch. It's supposed to rain, and then they'll be ruined, and I don't want to give her ruined flowers after, after . . .' She pushed the vase toward me, as if she couldn't bear to hold it anymore. She looked almost sick to her stomach.

As I took them from her, Dusty squeezed through my legs and pawed at Rachel's ankles, eager to see her again. 'Are you okay?' I asked.

She held on to the doorjamb, steadying herself. 'Yes,' she said, but her voice cracked. 'No. I don't even know.'

I reached for her arm, and she grabbed on so tight; I couldn't just leave her like this. 'Come in,' I said.

'No, I shouldn't. You've lost him, too. I shouldn't even be here –'

'Just come in,' I said. 'Sit down. Warm up.'

Reluctantly, she did, and, eager to relieve my own nerves, I made us both tea, using tea bags that had been left behind, that must have once been hers. Dusty curled into her lap as soon as she sat down, begging for pets.

I took a sip, but the tea was too hot, the tip of my tongue going numb.

'I'm sorry to just barge in,' she said. 'I know it's way too soon for flowers, I just, it was such a shock, when Maggie called me yesterday. Murdered . . . my god. Right here in Woodstock. I mean, I know that people were mad at him, after . . . but *god*, murder.' She fidgeted with a windswept curl before sinking her hand into Dusty's fur. 'I was friends with John, too, you know, and I couldn't just sit there, alone, wondering how Sam, how he –' Her voice broke. 'I just had to do *something*.'

'Sam Alby?' I asked.

Rachel shook her head. 'I don't even know. I just know Sam

was so mad, after what happened with Claire. I guess he was the first person I thought of.'

I nodded, and in a crazy way I hoped she was right. That it was Sam, that the police were questioning him – arresting him – right now. That Ellie had kept her promise and hadn't told Davis. That the awfulness of what had happened had not been caused by me.

'I'm sorry,' she said again. 'I'm not trying to play detective, I swear. I'm just in shock.'

'It's okay,' I said. 'Really. We all are.'

'Thank you.' She adjusted herself on the sofa, tugging at her pashmina. It was hard to imagine her and Vera being friends – they seemed so different: Vera precise, perfect, almost hard, everywhere that Rachel was soft and forgiving.

'You were with him, the day it, the day it happened?' Rachel asked, reaching for her tea. 'On a hike?'

I nodded. 'Yes, Vera too. Both of us were. John disappeared, and we thought he'd fallen.'

'God, it must have been awful. That hike. It's terrifying in that spot.'

My eyebrows knitted together, and Rachel immediately picked up on my confusion.

'Sorry,' she said. 'My ex always told me I had a sixth sense for these things. Was it *not* up on that hike they always went to? The one off Chapel Road? We must have gone, god, countless times. When Maggie said he disappeared on a hike, I mean, before he was found, I just assumed . . .'

I swallowed slowly, my eyes never leaving hers. 'Sorry, yes, that's where it was. I forgot you guys were so close.'

Rachel blinked back tears. 'We *were* close, and it's crazy how fast that can change. I wish I could be the sort of friend Vera needs right now.' Her eyes caught mine and she raised her cup to her lips, printing the rim with color. 'I'm glad she has you.'

Her words fell flat. She swallowed, took another sip of tea.

'You've probably wondered why we aren't friends anymore. Unless Vera already told you.'

'I did wonder,' I said. 'But Vera wouldn't tell me.'

Rachel swiped tears away with the back of her hand. 'Rumors were circling us, too, you know, as absurd as that sounds, me and John.' She laughed bitterly, and her eyes found her hands. 'He and I were working on this project together, and we were close, but I never – we *never* – if you ever thought that, if it so much as occurred to you, or if it ever occurred to Vera, I just want you to know that it's not true. John was like a brother to me, I swear to god. I would never, ever, *ever* have done anything to hurt her.'

She looked up, as if begging for some sort of mercy that wasn't even mine to give, and John's words, that first night, echoed in my head.

Vera can be very black-and-white in the way she sees the world.

'Then what happened?' I asked.

Rachel set her cup down. 'When people started talking, about him and Claire, I guess I didn't react to everything like Vera thought I should.'

'What do you mean?' I asked.

Her lips drew into a thin, even line. 'I mean that I believed what people were saying about John and Claire. Vera didn't.'

'Oh,' I said as my cup dropped from my hand, spilling tea all over the floor. Already, Rachel was jumping up, rushing to the kitchen, grabbing a towel. Before I could do anything, she was down on her knees, sopping up the spill, lifting the cup, which had split in two.

'Sorry,' I said quickly. 'You don't have to do that.'

She stood, shaking her head. 'Don't be sorry. It doesn't do anyone any good. What happened, happened. Shit,' she said, her eyes catching mine. 'I didn't mean to upset you. I just wanted you to know. And if Vera has any doubt, any doubt in the slightest, that something happened between me and John . . . if she ever asks you, I hope you'll tell her the truth. It was never like that.'

'Okay,' I said, brushing moisture from my eyes. I was the one who had betrayed Vera, not Rachel, and yet I was the one who was still in Vera's good graces. It wasn't fair. The realization stung.

'Why did you believe what people were saying about that girl, though? About Claire? You and John were friends. And there were rumors about you, too, which you clearly knew were false. Do you really think . . .'

Rachel swallowed, carefully taking a seat as she set the two halves of my teacup on the table between us. I spotted Dusty's white hairs on the knees of her jeans. 'At first I didn't. Like you said, John was already part of the gossip mill, and the whole thing just sounded *ludicrous*. Only later, I found out things about them that made me change my mind. And when I really thought about it, about how much he used to talk about her . . . "Claire's a *real* artist," he was always saying. Looking back, it was like he was almost, I don't know, obsessed with her. It was just strange.'

'But *what* did you find out?' I asked, heart beating quickly and Pandora's box tempting. 'What made you change your mind?'

Rachel stood abruptly. 'I'm truly sorry. I never meant to come over here and speak ill of John, especially now that he's gone. I know that's an awful thing to do.' She grabbed her bag, and I followed her to the front door.

'There had to be something,' I said. 'Something that changed your mind.'

She cleared her throat. 'It was always all talk, talk I don't need to be repeating to you. Not now that he's dead. Please give the flowers to Vera.'

Rachel opened the door and a gust of cold whooshed in, but before leaving, she turned back to me. 'The thing is, I always told myself I was going to believe these sorts of stories. No exceptions.'

'But Claire never even made that claim,' I said, suddenly defensive.

Rachel sighed, pulling her jacket tighter. 'Trust me, she didn't have to.'

'What do you mean?' I asked.

'It doesn't matter. All that matters is Vera couldn't handle it,' she said. 'Not when it came to her husband.'

I didn't keep the flowers.

After Rachel had gone, I broke every stem, thorns scratching the skin on my hands. Then I buried them deep in the trash, beneath expired milk and leftovers. I felt awful, but I couldn't have Vera knowing I'd met Rachel and never told her, not now, not when I was about to leave; it would hurt her too much. The flowers would only upset her anyway.

I called Ellie three more times, never leaving a message, but hoping she would answer, then went over all my outstanding freelance invoices, tallying up the money that would eventually reach my bank account, when I had a chance to get it. I was still too scared to go to the bank, even an ATM, just in case Ellie *hadn't* told Davis and he was somehow able to access my activity, but as soon as I left town, I would cut back through the city. The bank would be my first stop. There was a few thousand in there, and a couple of the invoices would be direct deposited soon. Not loads, but better than nothing. If Davis somehow saw the withdrawal, he still wouldn't know where I actually was.

When there was little left to do, when I'd checked the items beneath the bed again and made sure every window was locked tightly shut, I grabbed a change of clothes, leashed Dusty up, and headed to Vera's.

Her chimney was smoking, puffing along like an out-of-breath runner, a sure sign she was home, and I found myself wondering who would chop wood now when she ran out.

She looked even worse than she had yesterday, her hair limp and greasy, eyes ringed as if she hadn't slept in a decade. She led me into the living room and took a seat. 'You went to the police station today,' she said.

'Yes.'

A nervous quiet stretched between us, unusual and foreign, John's absence heavy, almost clinging to the scent of cigarette smoke in the air. 'What did they ask you?' Vera said.

'I don't want to upset you.'

Her back straightened. 'I'm already upset, Lucy. You don't need to protect me. What is it?'

I paused, picking at the cuticle of my thumb.

'God, just say it!'

She wasn't supposed to yell – not at me. But I shouldn't have been surprised. This was just one of those microscopic changes, like chopped wood, that seemed small but somehow meant everything.

'They asked about that girl – Claire?'

Vera nodded.

'They think it was true. Everything they asked was about whether John was unfaithful.'

Vera didn't say a word, only released a breath through her nose. After a beat, she let out a cold, mirthless laugh. 'So the police are chasing those rumors, too? *That's* what they wanted to talk to you about? It figures.'

'What do you mean?'

'Remember what you said to me?' Vera said, crossing her arms. 'You teased me about not having watched enough movies.'

I shook my head. 'I don't follow.'

'The *wife*,' she said. 'It's always the wife . . . right?'

'Yeah, but –'

'If they paint me as this woman scorned, that's motive, Lucy. That, and this lawsuit business. It all adds up to a hell of a lot. So yes, of course, it figures. It's the easy conclusion. It means they aren't doing their jobs.' Her voice wavered. 'It means no one is working to find out what actually happened to John. Find out who hurt him, who *killed* him.'

I stared at her then – at my protector, my friend. For a split second, I found myself wondering again. Could the rumors about Claire be true? Could Vera have somehow seen John and me together – and that was the last straw? Gone to the cabin that morning, pretending she only wanted to say goodbye one more time, and just – lost it?

No. If Vera wanted to leave John, she could have, so many times. She'd stuck by him through thick and thin, through a miscarriage she didn't even know I knew about, through his very public fall from grace – everything. I'd seen the way they nuzzled together. Yin and yang. She'd even stuck by him when her duty as a woman required her to believe a certain sort of rumor. When Rachel, his friend and colleague, hadn't. She loved him. I knew this deeply. Even if she was angry, she wouldn't have hurt him. Not like that.

Her eyes caught mine. 'Do you really believe John was unfaithful to me?'

A vision of him in my bed. Of John's lips pressed against mine. 'No,' I said, and it was only half a lie. 'No, of course I don't. But Vera,' I said, knowing I had to chance it, 'maybe you're looking at this all wrong.'

Her eyes narrowed – angry? – and for an awful second, I wondered if she suspected me. Then her gaze softened, and I knew it was okay. If the thought had entered her mind, it had left just as quickly. 'What do you mean?'

'They asked specifically about Claire Alby,' I said. 'Maybe

Sam is the main suspect. Wouldn't that make sense? I didn't tell the police anything about him, because I knew you already had and I didn't want to make it seem like I knew too much in case they put together what we were trying to do, but surely they know. You've made reports before.'

Vera nodded, like she only half believed me.

'Maybe this is actually a good thing,' I said, clinging to the hope that Davis hadn't done it, that it wasn't my fault. 'Maybe they're looking exactly where they need to be looking. Sam must've known where the studio was, since he was so concerned about his daughter being there alone with John. Maybe he heard about the accident, went there, found John, and –' I couldn't bear to finish the thought.

Vera paused, her eyes glistening. 'That makes sense, when you say it like that, and I should have thought of it before. I just – it's so hard, losing him, and then immediately having them dig into my marriage, spread it out for all to see. It's not fair, Lucy. It's not fair to us. To who we were.'

I shook my head. 'It's not.'

Tears dripped down her cheeks again, and I knew it then, deep in my heart.

She hadn't done this. She couldn't have. And I should never doubt her again.

We spent the afternoon making arrangements. She didn't resist when I suggested we hold a memorial soon, grieve John on our terms, not the police's, and together, we agreed to two days from now. We didn't go to the funeral parlor or anything, like they do on TV. We didn't look at a laminated book of flowers and caskets. We did it all online, like true modern women. I called a place I found on Yelp and helped her complete the obituary. It would be printed in the *Daily Freeman* tomorrow morning. She told me, again and again, 'Thank you so much for staying, I couldn't do any of this without you.'

When we were finished, we didn't talk about John or the police or anything that had transpired over the last few days. Instead, we parked ourselves on the couch in front of Netflix, devouring movies without much of a plot, without even a hint of romance or familial obligations. Noir wasn't fun anymore, when it felt like you were living it. Vera and I weren't ingenues in hazy lighting with finger curls and penciled lips. We were real humans, and our worlds were falling apart.

When we hit our second eighties comedy, I ordered pizza and made her eat a slice. We queued up *Airplane!*, and Dusty nuzzled between us, and it almost felt like we were a family again, even if I knew this family couldn't last.

When we began to get tired, we checked every lock in her house, more than once, and I followed her to her room, Dusty at our heels.

She fell asleep first, and as I listened to her breathe, I made my plans, tracing maps in my head, mentally packing away my things, and trying not to think of a killer out there – of Sam Alby contemplating his next move.

Or of Davis. Somewhere out there in the meadow, waiting. Watching me, watching us.

Deciding how best to complete his revenge.

Twenty-Five

The funeral parlor smelled like Pine-Sol.

Up front, the silver-haired minister had a rogue drop of sweat climbing down his forehead. It seemed rude and insubordinate, that kernel of body sweat, as if it didn't give a shit about John, it was only doing its thing.

'The Lord has a plan for all of us,' he said as Vera stifled a sob and I pressed a tissue into her hand. I hated when people said things like that, as if it were all part of some cosmic agenda; the only people saying that were the ones who'd won the cosmic lottery.

As he droned on, I focused on the photo of John sitting on an easel. We'd chosen it together, flipping through his pictures on Facebook until we came upon this one: him, laughing, eyes wide-open, in the plaid shirt he often wore around the house. Vera had selected a Keith Haring quote to open the ceremony.

The minister walked from the podium, and Vera stood, ready to speak. She took the tissue I'd given her, swiped beneath her eyes, and walked to the front. At the lectern, she paused, breathing deeply as she unfolded a sheet of paper with shaking hands. Her nails were a pale gray color, she'd pulled her hair into a perfect topknot, and she wore a charcoal-gray wool dress that nipped in at her waist, one I'd helped her pick out. Everything about her seemed more pronounced – her cheekbones standing out against her gaunt visage, her eyes puffy and wide, her blond hair pulled back tight against her scalp. Somehow, standing in front of us like this, she made even the most awful grief look beautiful – a modern Grace Kelly.

'I met John in New York City,' she said, eyes darting around the room. 'I know a lot of people say this, but for us, it was love at first sight.' Voice wavering, she bumbled through the story they'd told me together, of meeting in Chelsea, of feeling, immediately, that something had changed. She explained how she'd schooled him in the bar game of the evening and he'd loved her even more for it. She talked about seeing him grow through the years, and his strengths, from painting to wood-chopping to listening to her every single day. She talked about his grief, losing all the family he had so young. His family, who was absent, of course, his parents gone, his brother, who Vera had taken the time to call, not being able to make the trip without an escort.

As she spoke, I stole a look behind me. The showing was small, only twenty people or so, people I mostly didn't recognize, I imagined from their old Manhattan life.

McKnight sat in one of the back rows, his eyes locked ahead. He adjusted slightly, and as he did, I took a quick, shallow breath.

There, just behind him, in the very back, was Sam Alby. I stared at his thick neck, his gray-brown hair, brushed neatly for the occasion. Anger swelled in my chest – when had he come in? I couldn't believe he had had the nerve to come at all.

In the same back row, about a few feet down the pew, was the waitress from Schoolhouse restaurant.

I smiled, happy to see a familiar face, but her eyes didn't connect with mine.

Rachel was nowhere to be seen.

I turned back to the front. I had the strange feeling that no one here really knew John, not even close to the way Vera did, and she was simply telling us the story of his life as if he were a character in a book, or a quirky Manhattanite in a *New York Times* profile. That included me, too. I hadn't known that his favorite meal, despite his epicurean-leaning tendencies, was actually grilled cheese. Or that the two of them had differing opinions on the proper way to fold a T-shirt.

'That was the gift of being with him for fourteen years,' Vera said, her eyes finding the bottom of the sheet of notes in her hand. 'I knew him better than anyone.'

She folded the paper, then looked up, eyes suddenly focused. 'He wasn't perfect. No one is perfect,' she continued, her words cutting. I pressed my lips together, calm, stoic, as my insides roiled: I hadn't been good to her. I hadn't respected her marriage.

Vera cleared her throat. 'But whatever anyone might think about him, he didn't deserve this.'

Tears struck me viciously. As Vera walked back, squeezed past me, and took her seat, it lodged deep in my bones: She was right, so very right. I didn't care what Rachel had said, what doubts she'd tried to sow – John didn't deserve this, not in the slightest. John was good. Apart from that one stupid night with me, he was good.

When the service ended, Vera returned to the front to greet people paying their respects. I went the opposite direction, finding a place to stand against the back wall.

McKnight hovered on the left-hand side, watching us all, his chest pocket bulging from the width of his notebook. I knew he needed to find out what had happened, but still, it was cold, turning a memorial into work, something that required notes.

I leaned against the wall, watching a line of people I didn't know waiting to talk to Vera. The service itself was over, but she had the space until noon, giving people time to pay their respects. I wondered what they were saying to her, who they were to John . . .

'Shit, I'm late.'

I jumped, turning to see Rachel, sweat on her forehead, cheeks flushed. My eyes flashed to Vera up front. I didn't want her to see me with Rachel, who kept on talking, undisturbed. 'I didn't know if Vera wanted me to be here, and then I kept questioning myself, and I decided it didn't matter. *I* wanted to be here.' She adjusted the collar of her dress, loosely draped as usual but black for the occasion. 'I don't know the right thing to do with her, but I know I wanted to say goodbye to John. Did you bring the flowers over?'

I nodded instinctively, then stole another look at Vera, who thankfully seemed focused on the line of people.

'What did she say?' Rachel asked.

'She said thank you,' I lied. 'But she's getting a lot of flowers.' Another lie. 'They might all blend together for her.'

Rachel's eyes caught mine, as if wondering who else was bringing Vera flowers. But then she said, 'How are you holding up?'

'As good as I can be,' I said, wishing she'd stop talking to me.

'And Vera?' Rachel asked. 'Is she eating? Sleeping?'

It hit me then, just how much Rachel cared about her old friend. It wasn't all talk. In her eyes, I could see it, true concern. The way my mother used to look at me when I was younger. The way she looked at me before . . .

'Sleeping,' I said. 'Eating, not very much.'

'Well, I'm glad she's getting some rest, at least.'

I was, too, but I needed this conversation to end. I took a step to the side, trying to open up some space between us, but Rachel didn't seem to notice. I prayed for a distraction, something to pull Rachel from me, so Vera wouldn't see us standing here, carrying on as if we were old friends . . .

'Oh Christ,' Rachel said.

'What is it?' I asked.

'*Sam* came?'

'Oh,' I said. 'Yeah, I was surprised, too.' I took another step to the side.

'And his daughter,' Rachel went on, lips pressing together.

For a second, I forgot myself. 'His daughter? You mean, Claire?'

Rachel nodded. 'Over there in the front.'

My gaze followed Rachel's, but the only girl I saw was Al from the restaurant, standing in front of John's oversize photo, her copper hair catching the light. I shook my head. 'No. That's Al. I know her from Schoolhouse.'

Rachel's head swiveled toward mine. 'Al? Is that her nickname or something? Would make sense, wouldn't it? Al, like Alby? Either way, that's *definitely* Claire.' And then, as if to drive home the point: 'She's the girl who got caught up in all this.'

I could hardly focus.

Not on Rachel as she approached Vera, whose body straightened, rigid, when her former friend tried to give her a hug. Not on McKnight, leaning against a wall in the corner, eyeing us all, suspecting every single one of us. Not on Sam Alby, still in his seat, his presence its own sort of threat.

No matter where I looked, my eyes quickly returned to the girl I knew as Al, frozen in front of John's photo, captivated as if seeing a Monet in Paris for the first time. Or perhaps, I thought bitterly, a Van Gogh.

She had lied to me. Purposely given me a nickname that would throw me off. Left out any details of her relationship to John or Vera. She *had* asked about my neighbors – and more than once – only I'd never put it together. Why would I?

Sam stood, brushing his hands against his sides, then quickly walked toward her. Grabbing her by the shoulder, he whispered something in her ear. Her head twisted away, and she shrugged him off.

He turned, walking briskly down the center aisle.

It was another minute or so before she abandoned John's photo and headed down the aisle herself.

'Claire,' I said as I followed her out, down the stone sidewalk, toward the parking lot. It was morning still, not even eleven, but the sky was a blur of white, as if gauze had been carefully laid over the whole thing, obscuring any sun. Moisture clung to the air, weightless and ready to drop on us any moment. She walked quicker, and I ran to catch up with her. '*Claire*.'

She kept walking.

'Al?'

'What?' She spun on her heel, facing me.

'Which is it?' I asked. 'Claire or Al?'

In the haze, she looked ethereal, a Brontë heroine wandering about the moor, mooning for the older man she maybe thought she loved. 'Does it even matter?'

'That's your dad? You're . . .' My words dissipated like water droplets into the air. 'You, you knew John . . . Why didn't you tell me your real name?'

'People call me both, okay?' she said. 'Have since I was younger. Maybe it's a little easier to introduce myself to new people as Al now.'

'Okay,' I said. 'I'm sorry. I just, I don't understand.'

Claire popped a hand on her hip. 'What don't you get?' For a moment, she sounded just like a teenager, headstrong and hormone-stupid, who thought she knew better than anyone else. Like I had at her age.

'You could have told me. God, I thought you were in college. I had no idea.'

She pressed her lips together. 'Maybe I wanted to talk about writing with you, and not talk about all that bullshit. Maybe I didn't want you to ask me if I was okay, like everyone feels compelled to, even though they know nothing about me. Nothing.'

'Okay,' I said. 'I get it. But you asked why they never came – John and Vera – you asked me, even though you knew.'

She shrugged. 'I wanted to see if *you* knew.'

'You could have asked me outright. I would have been honest.'

She took a deep breath. 'I'm tired of all the gossip, okay? So when I have a chance to get away from it, I do. It doesn't matter if you knew John or if he was your friend or whatever. Everything that happened was none of your business,' she said. She glanced at the funeral parlor, where more people were filing out. 'And it wasn't my dad's business, either. Or my mom's. Or Vera's. Or anyone in this town's, okay?'

'I know, it's just –'

She began to back away.

'Wait,' I said.

Claire crossed her arms and sighed, as if all this had exhausted her. Her eyes caught mine, imploring me to understand. 'It's just like your business, with your friend coming into the restaurant – what she said and what you told her, that isn't anyone's business but yours.'

Twenty-Six

Back in my cottage, door locked tight behind me, I headed immediately to my bedroom and squirmed out of my dress and tights.

I still couldn't believe that Al was Claire.

She had seemed so guileless, but I shouldn't have been so surprised. When it came right down to it, we were all full of lies, every single one of us. The truth lay somewhere deep down in our hearts. But with each passing year, we added another layer of protection, like an onion growing. To get to the truth, you could peel back each layer, one by one. Or you could grab a knife and slice, crying as the chemicals hit your eyes. Claire was young and naive – she had fewer layers than I did – but that didn't mean she hadn't already begun to build them, hadn't learned that grand lesson of adulthood: that no one would protect you but yourself.

I tossed the dress onto my bed, pushing Claire – Al – out of my mind.

Time to pack. Time to get the hell out of here.

It was only as I pulled a sweater over my head that I realized – there had been no pitter-patter, no panting run. No Dusty.

Trying to stay calm, I slid into jeans and walked through the kitchen, calling his name. He'd probably only gone out back to pee. I twisted the doorknob, and a rush of cold burst in as I stepped onto the back patio, the stone chilling my bare feet. He wasn't in the yard.

'Dusty,' I called louder, heartbeat quickening as I returned to the bedroom, dropping to my knees, looking under the bed. Nothing.

'Dusty,' I called again. In the living room, I searched beneath the sofas, under blankets.

'Dusty,' I cried, more frantically this time. I ran into the back-yard and double-checked. My eyes welled as I repeated his name – nothing.

I slipped into shoes and pulled the door shut, made my way down the driveway. 'Dusty!'

Running down the road, the remaining bits of ice and frost licking my ankles, I headed toward Maggie's house – maybe she'd seen him, or maybe – god – she'd seen Davis. I was out of breath by the time I got to her porch, and I knocked three times, loudly.

Within seconds, Maggie opened the door. 'Lucy,' she said. 'I was –'

'Dusty!'

His furry little body rushed forward, his paws scratching my ankles, and I knelt, scooping him into my arms as I burst into tears.

'Oh dear,' Maggie said.

'You had him?' I asked as Dusty licked the salt from my cheeks. 'Why?'

'I spotted him running down the road,' she said. 'Luckily, I was able to rush out and call him in.'

'Why didn't you come over?' I snapped. 'Or leave a note?'

She stiffened, taking a step back, hand reaching for the door.

'I'm sorry,' I said. 'I just got home, and Dusty wasn't there, and –'

'I did. I went over right away, but you weren't there. Then I realized the memorial was still going. The *Daily Freeman* said it lasted until noon,' Maggie said. 'I didn't know you'd returned early.'

Dusty squirmed, but I only held him tighter.

'And it's not my fault he got out,' she said, lips pursed. 'Set up like it is, it's no wonder he did. You have to be careful.'

'What do you mean?'

She slipped her feet into a pair of Crocs, then pulled on her coat. 'Come on,' she said. 'I'll show you.'

She led me back to my cottage, but when we reached the property, she headed to the fence at the back. She hunched over and pointed to a spot where the ground sloped downward, creating a slim gap at the bottom of the fencing. 'I noticed it when I came over with him to find you.'

'You think Dusty got through *that*?' I asked.

'Oh, absolutely,' she said, eyes widening. 'Little dogs like him, their rib cages compress. They can scurry into tight spaces. It's the way they're bred. It looks like the ground has eroded a bit in this spot, maybe from the snow or rain creating mud. He could have seen a squirrel and chased it out.'

My eyes scanned the opening, my breath catching in my throat, my body going numb.

Davis was subtle. If he really wanted to mess with me, he would do something like this, something so nuanced, so seemingly benign, it would drive me crazy – just like the damn faucet. If Dusty had gotten hurt – god, if he'd died – not only would I have lost him, I'd be racked with guilt, half thinking it was my fault.

'You have to check that your fence is secure if you're going to leave a dog alone like that, with access to the yard. Especially if he doesn't have good recall.'

'Thank you,' I said, clinging to his little body. 'I should get back in. He's had quite a morning.'

I reached for the door, but she cleared her throat.

'By the way,' she added. 'Was Rachel there? At the memorial service, I mean.'

I nodded.

'Good,' she said. 'I worried that she wasn't going to get up the guts to go, but I know it was important to her.'

'Thanks again, Maggie,' I said quickly, eager for her to leave so I could pack my bags, get on the road.

'And if you need anything else,' Maggie said.

'I know where to find you.'

As soon as she was gone, I made for the closet, pulled my suitcase off the shelf. I began opening drawers, grabbing stacks of sweaters and jeans and throwing them inside.

When I reached the top drawer, I whipped it open and started to pack my underwear.

I froze, my mind beginning to spin.

My mother's scarf, which I'd kept in this very drawer since the day I'd arrived. Edged with a blue stripe, with rosebuds, with the stain Davis had created . . .

It was gone.

I ripped the drawer out, pulling so hard it chipped a bit of the wood, and flipped it over. Panties and bras and the vintage furniture brochure fluttered down like confetti.

The scarf wasn't there.

I tossed the drawer to the ground, and it clattered awfully, terrifying Dusty. My fingers began to tremble and my heart banged brutally as I picked up the brochure.

It was empty. John's photos, gone.

And even scarier: The note he'd left me, it was gone, too.

I wasn't crazy, and I wasn't paranoid. Something was happening. As much as I didn't want it to be, it was. This was more than a running faucet, more than a gap under the fence. This was real, tangible. Proof.

John was dead, for fuck's sake. Maybe it had been Sam Alby. Maybe none of it was on me. But maybe, maybe . . .

I could forgive you . . . but I'd have to kill the guy.

Who else but Davis would know what that scarf meant to me? To anyone else, it was nothing more than an old stained thing. What if Davis had killed John, stabbed him with the knife he kept in his pocket, then snuck back into the cottage, put Dusty in danger, and taken my mother's scarf so I'd get the message? Taken the photos and the note, too, just to fuck with me?

I grabbed my phone, trying Ellie one more time, desperate to know.

After five rings, she answered. 'Can you *stop* calling me? Put me on whatever Do Not Call list and leave me alone.'

'Ellie,' I said. 'It's me.'

A quick, sharp breath.

'This is you? Jesus Christ, I didn't know. Are you okay?'

I swallowed, my lips trembling as I struggled to ask the question. 'Did you tell him?' I asked, the words tumbling forth. 'Did you tell Davis where I was?'

The line went quiet, taut between us. A tightrope.

'Ellie, tell me. Please.'

'What do you want me to say?' she asked.

'You promised,' I said, my voice pleading. 'You promised you wouldn't.'

'He's my brother,' she said.

'Ellie.'

'He's my brother, I had to.'

Without another word, I hung up the phone.

Davis was here, he had found me, and I didn't have another second to spare.

It was time to go.

Twenty-Seven

I pried up the floorboard, a splinter digging sharp beneath my skin, then stared at my things – my life, all that made me who I was, in a handful of items. Easy to travel with, at least.

I checked everything twice, then packed it all into my tote, the same one I'd taken up here, back in September, and set it next to my suitcase, already filled to the brim with my clothes.

My mother's missing scarf tugged at me – I hated to leave here without it – but there was nothing to do about it now.

'What do you think, baby?' I asked Dusty, trying to force some levity into my voice so as not to freak him out too much. 'Want to go on another adventure?'

I checked the time on my phone. It was just past noon. Vera was probably still wrapping everything up with the guys at the funeral parlor. If I left now, she wouldn't even see me go. I had two missed calls, spaced five minutes apart, from a local 845 number. Part of me wanted to answer, just to see who it was, but another part feared it was Davis, having gotten my new number somehow, calling me from a local bar – or a pay phone, even, if any of those still existed.

I was too scared to take the chance, so I ignored the calls, slipped my phone in my pocket, and took my suitcase and Dusty's crate out to the car. I turned the car on to warm up and popped the trunk, tossing the suitcase in, then put the crate in the back seat.

Back inside, I walked through the cottage again. I was nervous, my anxiety kicking up, and I felt the need to check burners, make sure I hadn't left anything important in a drawer. Nostalgia hit, sharp and bitter, deep in my gut.

I was leaving again, just when this place had begun to feel like home.

My phone rang, buzzing in my pocket. The same number. Hands shaking, imagining Davis on the other end of the line, I hit Ignore. I closed my laptop and put it in its case, then unpacked the tote, ran through all the items again, and repacked them. My pulse raced as I did a final once-over. Then I leashed up Dusty and shrugged into my coat.

Outside, I locked the door twice, then tucked the keys into my purse and headed to the car, exhaust spilling from the muffler like a plume of smoke. I shut the trunk and eased Dusty into his crate. He whined, pure anxiety. *Me too,* I thought. *Me too.*

'Going somewhere?'

I startled, banging my head against the frame of the car. Rubbing it, I inched out, turned.

'You're not leaving town, are you?' McKnight asked.

Dusty began to bark, the sound of a man's voice setting him off. He pawed at his crate furiously.

'Only for a couple of days.'

'Where?'

'To see a friend . . . in Brooklyn,' I said, spitballing.

He crossed his arms. 'I called you three times.'

'I didn't recognize the number,' I said. 'I thought it might have been my ex.'

'I'd hoped to catch you at the memorial, but you left before I got the chance.'

I could only shrug.

McKnight tilted his head to the side, like Dusty did, as if trying to read me. 'I was hoping you could come down to the station. Any way you could push your trip back?'

'I really don't think I can.' I swallowed thickly, a lump already forming in my throat.

He squinted. 'We *really* need to talk to you today.'

'So I have to come?' I asked. 'I have to drop everything for this? Are you going to arrest me or something if I don't?'

Again, McKnight cocked his head to the side. 'Is there a reason I should arrest you, Miss King?'

Fuck.

He shoved his hands into his pockets. 'I think it'll be better for both of us if you follow me down to the station. Fleeing to Brooklyn wouldn't look very good for you right about now.'

Rage swam through me, through my belly, through my bones, and I wished I could charge, knock him over, get in the car, and floor it as I reversed, but he stood stock-still, stoic, daring me to challenge him.

'Let me just get Dusty all settled,' I said weakly.

McKnight crossed his arms. 'I'll wait.'

I grabbed Dusty's crate and my tote, then returned to the cottage, dropping the tote on the coffee table and letting Dusty out. He ran around happily, as if being offered some sort of reprieve. I looked out the window to where McKnight still stood, waiting, like a statue. Quickly, I opened the junk drawer, grabbed a roll of duct tape, knelt beside the doggie door.

This had to be routine, I told myself as I ripped off swaths of tape, made an X so Dusty couldn't get out again. I hadn't killed John, and I had no reason – no motive – to want to. With Sam Alby in the picture, there was no way I was a legitimate suspect. I would go with McKnight, do his damn interview, then come back, grab Dusty, and get the hell out of here. The whole thing shouldn't take more than a couple of hours. Vera would see me going, but I would make her understand. Maybe we could even reconnect, once I was safe somewhere. Maybe we could still be family – she and I – only, a long-distance family now.

The tote caught my eye. Could I risk it? I decided I couldn't. I stole into the bedroom, pushed the bed aside, and loaded the items back into my hiding spot, hammering the board down tighter than ever.

Then I locked the door behind me, got in the car, and followed McKnight down the road.

The station was just as dead as it had been before, but the woman at the front desk seemed to recognize me as I walked in behind McKnight, breathing deep, as furious as I was scared. Every path seemed to lead to more skeletons, more dangers, when all I wanted was to finally feel safe. I pictured Dusty, alone in that cottage, while Davis lurked somewhere nearby, close enough to hurt us.

In the interview room, McKnight didn't offer me coffee, only cued up the camera, took the seat opposite me, and leaned back. 'Do you have anything additional to tell me, Miss King?'

'About what?' I asked, trying not to snap.

He rested his hands calmly against the cheap plastic table. 'About anything. Ms Abernathy. Mr Nolan. The art studio.'

In a flash, a lightbulb went off, something that could possibly help him, something I'd forgotten to mention before because I'd been so defensive about my lies; something to show that I was on the right side of this. 'The cabin,' I said. 'I mean John's art studio. Where he was found?'

McKnight's eyebrows shot up. 'Yes?'

'They never kept it locked. John told me himself they didn't even use the key.'

His face fell – disappointment. 'We know that, Miss King. Ms Abernathy said as much in her initial interview. It's very common in that area, with a hunter's shack like that.'

Hunter's shack. I'd never thought about it that way, but I suppose at the end of the day, it was. Only, nothing had been hunted there. That is, nothing before John.

'Anything else, Miss King?'

'No,' I said. 'That's it.'

He sat still, stoic, waiting for me to say more. I didn't know what he was getting at, and the room felt suddenly hot, but a dry heat, one that makes your pits sweat and your skin split. They probably turned the thermostat up just for situations like this, probably watched *Law & Order* and took notes. Ellie and I used to consume every dark detective drama we could get our hands on, laughing when the actors overdid it. Only, it wasn't funny now. 'Why am I here?' I asked finally.

McKnight sighed. 'I was hoping, Miss King, that you'd be more forthcoming.' He reached beneath the table and pulled out a manila folder, then pushed it toward me. I could only imagine what was in it. Photos of John, dead, supine in his studio, six gaping stab wounds scattered across his torso. Acid rose in my chest, and I pressed my lips together; they were chapped, cracked. 'Would you like to open the folder, Miss King?'

I held my breath, then whipped it open. At first, I felt relief – a stillness in my bones; my balance, restored – it wasn't John.

Then my jaw dropped.

The photo in front of me showed a woman, stretched out on a bed, on her side, facing away from the camera, curves undulating like the tops of the East Catskills. Lacy underwear on top and bottom. Curly brown hair.

It wasn't John; it was me.

In my bed, in my cottage. Spread out, printed, for all to see.

My mind flashed to college, the morning after the stupid video was taken. To waking up, puke rancid on my jeans, and my room-mate, on Facebook: *Holy shit, girl, you've got to see this.*

Were the guys on the police squad the same as the guys in college? Probably.

Had every officer laughed in the break room about this? Had they called me a whore? Had they formulated this theory, that I'd killed John for not agreeing to leave Vera, over beers in a pub before going home to their sad, small little lives?

I pushed back my chair almost instinctively and shook my head.

'Didn't think we'd find this, Miss King?'

I bit the flaking skin off my lip. 'I don't know how you got this or what this is, but –'

'It was on Mr Nolan's phone,' McKnight said. 'Taken October thirty-first, two nights before your hike.'

I had to say the right thing, to not screw this up, too. 'I don't,' I managed, cursing myself for how flustered I'd gotten. 'I mean, it wasn't like that.'

'Like what, Miss King?'

A sour taste in the back of my mouth. I imagined old radiators, caked with dust and mold. Spores, seeping into my lungs like poison. 'Like it looks.'

'So you *don't* deny that Mr Nolan was in your bedroom that night?'

'No . . . I just mean . . . nothing ever happened,' I said. 'He had too much to drink. He stayed over. That's all. I don't know why he took that photo. I don't know –'

'And you *never* thought fit to mention,' he went on, 'that Mr Nolan spent the night with you two nights before he was mur-dered?'

'He didn't *spend the night with me*. It wasn't like that. It was nothing.'

'Does Ms Abernathy know about this little bit of nothing?'

My cheeks burned with shame. 'No,' I said. 'No, of course not. But –'

'But what, Miss King?'

'We didn't *do* anything. We had too much to drink, and he passed out in my cottage, but he woke up fully clothed. That's it. I had no idea he took this photo, or why he took it,' I said, as betrayal surged through me. 'But it's not my fault that he did.'

It was the truth, and I hoped McKnight could see it in my eyes. I couldn't imagine John doing something like that, while I was sleeping, no less – without my consent. Was he no better than those guys in college? Had I mistaken him completely?

McKnight leaned forward and adjusted the printout, as if he wanted it to be perfectly straight. 'I don't know if you and John were sleeping together, and I don't really care. Seems there was a lot of . . . activity . . . with people he wasn't married to. What I care about is why you lied about seeing him fall. And this, to me, is a reason.'

Blood rushed in my ears.

'Whether you slept together or not, you obviously were more than just friends. Sometimes, when those feelings start, people want to, you know, be with each other. Sometimes they make plans to leave their wives. Disappear on a hike and have their girlfriend *swear* up and down that they fell off a cliff. Even toss their camera down toward the river to make it look like they fell, to make sure their wife never guesses . . .'

He was so wrong, and yet he was so right at the same time. So close. 'You don't understand,' I said. 'That's not what happened.'

He scratched at his chin. I could see, on the edge of his cheek, the tiniest of cuts, probably from shaving. I remembered what he'd said to me about marriage, and I wondered if his wife had kissed that cheek this morning, if he had kids and a dog to go home to after he spent the day skulking around a memorial service and harassing me – an American dream. I glanced at his hand. There wasn't a ring. Maybe he was divorced, I thought, drank too much and smoked too much, like detectives did on TV, tried to numb himself to the overdoses and domestic violence disputes a mountain town would bring you. Maybe he was just as lonely as I was, could smell it on me.

'The truth is,' McKnight went on, 'neither of you saw him fall, and yet *you* were so sure he had.'

'I already told you this. It was raining,' I said. 'It happened so fast. I know I heard the scream, though. And then I saw his backpack and the water bottle, and I just thought . . .'

He held up a hand. 'Yes, it sounds like you know this part well. But why would your mind ever go to a fall in the first place? Why land on that story, exactly? Especially before Officer Parker took you down to the riverbank and you all found the camera. There are other options. He could have gone off trail. He could have been calling for help.'

I gripped the edge of the table, as if I could stop my head from spinning if I pressed hard enough. 'Then why would his stuff be right there on the edge?' I asked. 'What was I supposed to think?'

McKnight grunted, adjusting in his seat. 'Have you ever been to the cabin Mr Nolan used as his studio, the one where we found him? People in town say that he used to bring women there.'

'No,' I said. And then, correcting, 'Vera and John drove me by, but I never went inside.'

'Never?' he asked.

'I never went there,' I said, my voice stiff. 'I swear.'

He leaned back, his stomach resting against the edge of the table, spilling over just slightly. 'Here's what I'm thinking, Miss King, and granted, it's just a theory. I think maybe you and Mr Nolan came up with a plan in tandem. Maybe you guys agreed he would *disappear* on this hike, and you'd run off together. Then

206

he starts to get cold feet, he maybe feels bad about leaving his wife, he changes his mind – who knows, maybe he even reconnects with his old friend Rachel – and you don't like that.'

'No,' I said.

He wasn't as stupid as I'd pegged him – that scared me.

Could I tell him the truth?

Using my untraceable internet connection, I'd let myself google our situation the other morning and found a name for it: conspiracy to commit fraud. It didn't even matter if it hadn't worked. It was still illegal, still a crime. Besides . . .

'It's not like that at all,' I said.

His eyebrows rose. 'Then tell me what it *is* like. Because there's a reason you lied about seeing him fall, and I will figure it out. Believe me.'

The secret rose in my throat like vomit. 'I have nothing else to say to you.'

McKnight stared, waiting for me to change my mind.

Inside, I felt the hatch lift up, and my eyes sharpened as they met McKnight's. 'Do I need a lawyer?' I asked. 'Are you going to charge me with anything?'

He smiled ever so slightly, as if he appreciated my gumption just the tiniest bit. Then he made a show of checking his notes before looking back up at me. 'Not yet, no.'

'Then can I go?' I scooted my chair back.

He reached into his pocket and pulled out a card. 'You already have one of these, but here it is again, just in case you do decide to tell us the truth.'

'I *am* telling you the truth.' I stood and grabbed my purse from the back of the plastic chair. I reached for the door, eager to get out of the claustrophobic room.

'Oh, and Miss King –'

I turned back.

'In case you were still thinking about it, don't leave the area.'

I took a quick breath, my heart already racing.

No, I thought. *No no no.*

'That's not a request, that's an order. As long as the investigation is still in its early stages, we need you to stay right where you are.'

Twenty-Eight

Outside, I sucked air into my lungs, breathing deep as I tried to slow my pulse, puzzle a way out of this clusterfuck. I walked to the car, shut the door, and stared through the windshield, hazy. My hands hovered over the wheel, and I felt it, that need – in my gut – to run. It was all-encompassing, overwhelming, as much a part of me as my fingers and toes.

I had to get out of here, that much had been clear since the day I ran into Ellie. How different would things be now if I hadn't gone to Schoolhouse when I had, if I hadn't grabbed a seat at the bar the very same hour that Ellie had wandered into town for a beer? Would we have gone on that hike at all? We certainly wouldn't have pulled the plan together so quickly. Vera and John would have had time to dot their i's, cross their t's. Make it foolproof. Christ, would John even be dead?

I blinked slowly, trying to sort my thoughts.

It didn't matter. He *was* dead, and I was trapped.

I turned the key in the ignition, the car revving to life. It was one o'clock – Vera must be home by now. I began to drive. As I pulled out of the parking lot, a cruiser followed. I squeezed the wheel tighter to keep my hands from shaking.

The police car tailed me the entire way through town. When I couldn't stand it anymore, I made a split-second decision and turned onto Tinker Street, pulled into a parking lot, my breaths calming ever so slightly as the officer drove on. Fingers fumbling, I fastened my coat, tumbled out of the car and into the cool air, thin and crisp.

On the main street, I turned left, shoving my hands deep into my pockets as I walked aimlessly, trying to figure out my next step. I had screwed it all up royally, maybe even worse than I ever had before. I had chosen my escape incorrectly. I'd wanted to find a way to cling to the life I'd created in my twenties. I hadn't been willing to pull off the Band-Aid – I still wanted one foot in New York. After the night it all went to shit with Davis, I should have just driven out of town, gone west. Made that first email to Ellie a truth and not a lie.

Suddenly, I hated Woodstock. I hated its stone sidewalks, its overly forced progressiveness. Its hippie shops and its fresh fucking mountain air. I hated it all.

'Oh.' The word spilled from my mouth as I turned a corner.

There she was, in the alley next to Schoolhouse. She was leaning against the brick wall, scrolling through her phone with a fingerless-gloved hand.

'Claire,' I said, as if testing the name on my lips. 'You're here.'

It was a stupid thing to say – she worked here, after all – only I thought maybe she would have taken the day off.

Her head whipped up. 'What, do you have more questions or something?'

'No, I didn't even know you'd be here, I thought –'

'I don't get the day off just because I have a funeral in the morning,' she said. 'Plus, if I called out, they'd only use it as one more reason to gossip.' Her steely expression wavered just the tiniest bit, and under it, I could see how it hurt her, being the center of a story she'd never wanted to be part of.

'I'm sorry I chased you down this morning,' I said. 'I was

just . . . shocked. I didn't know you knew him. I mean, I didn't know you were Claire.'

For a moment, her expression was unreadable, but then her eyes narrowed. 'Well, *I* didn't know you still had a boyfriend.'

A constricted feeling in my chest, as if my windpipe had shrunk three sizes.

'What are you talking about?'

She shrugged. 'Your secret boyfriend. It's like, you want me to tell you things, even though you never asked, but here you are, chatting with me, and the whole time you forget to mention you've got some guy in the city. He was cute, too, with those nerdy glasses. The Clark Kent type. I get it.'

'What did . . .' I stammered. 'What did he say?'

'He came in like an hour ago, as soon as my shift started, waving a photo of you around. Saying his girlfriend was missing, asking if we'd seen her. What was that about? He was going into like every shop on this block.' Her eyes widened suddenly, as if remembering. 'Wait, does this have something to do with what you told your friend in the restaurant? Shit, I didn't think. He didn't seem like the type. I didn't tell him anything, don't worry.'

I shook my head in disbelief. Then I backed away so quickly, I ran into someone behind me. Mind reeling, vision blurring, I muttered an apology, turned on my heel, and stalked off down the bluestone sidewalk, back to my car, not stopping until I was in it, fumbling for my keys.

I pulled out so quickly I almost hit a pedestrian, an older lady who flipped me off as I careened down the road. I had to get home, get to Dusty before Davis did. I could grab him and head straight to Vera's.

Find a way to keep him – to keep us – safe.

It took me a half hour to get there, road work closing one of the lanes on 212 East, but as I pulled onto Shadow Creek Road, my heart sank. Two police cars idled outside my cottage.

No no no, I wanted to scream. If McKnight had changed his mind, if he was going to arrest me now, Davis would get Dusty. I'd never see him again.

'Miss King,' McKnight said, before I'd even shut the car door. 'I told you it wouldn't be long before we saw you again. Didn't expect it to be quite so soon, though.'

I swallowed, my mouth suddenly chalky. Any semblance of safety I thought I'd created for myself was evaporating from moment to moment.

'Everything okay?' he asked.

Sometimes I wished that for one second, we could be honest with each other. Cut through the bullshit and say what we really thought. That I could look at McKnight right now and tell him the man I may have loved was dead, the man I used to love may have killed him, and that it felt like the memory of one and the presence of the other were pressing against me from both sides, like the walls of a cave, squeezing tighter and tighter, and at some point, they'd eventually meet, smashing me into oblivion. Taking away all I'd ever loved. I wished for one second I didn't have to lie.

'Okay as it can be,' I said, forcing myself to speak as calmly as possible. 'Did you have more questions?'

McKnight smiled, his concern for my well-being such an obvious charade. 'No more questions for now.' He flashed a sheet of paper in front of my face. 'But we do have a warrant to search your place. Just came through. Do we have permission to enter?'

I snatched the paper from his hand. It gave full permission for them to search my residence and car. What were they looking for? Surely they'd have had to tell a judge something to get a warrant . . .

'Do I have a choice?' I managed.

McKnight smiled his awful fake smile again. 'Not really.'

As I opened the door, I prayed for the sound of Dusty's paws.

My prayers were answered. He ran immediately into my arms, and I picked him up, holding him close, pressing his tiny body to mine, never wanting to let him go.

McKnight led the way, the rest of them following. A younger female officer shot me a weak smile, but then her eyes darted around the room almost as if she were checking whether McKnight could somehow sense her kindness. Once they were inside, I shut the door, peeking out from behind the drapes to see if I could spot Davis, knowing it was no longer a matter of if, but when.

Twenty-Nine

They took over an hour. They looked through my car. They rifled through drawers, searching methodically for anything that could incriminate me. They filled evidence bags with pieces of my life: My laptop. My composition notebook. A book of hikes in the Catskills, pages dog-eared, but not by me.

And the whole time, I sat there, throat parched and stomach cemented.

The whole time I sat there, I wondered when Davis was going to show up.

I knew there was still a chance he hadn't done it. That it had been Sam Alby – or maybe even someone else. It would make more sense, in a way. Davis had never been to John's studio, and he'd have had to find it by following John off the trail or discovering it some other way.

But if Davis hadn't killed John, how could I explain the rest of it? My mother's missing scarf. The photos and note stolen, too. The faucet running just so. The dirt dug from beneath the fence so Dusty could get out.

And more than that, the sinking feeling that Davis wouldn't rest until he'd punished me; that Ellie had given him the perfect way to do it.

'Have a second to chat, Miss King?' McKnight's voice was

familiar to me now, gruff and accusatory, scratchy like he once smoked but didn't anymore. In front of me, the woman lengthened the legs of a tripod and put a camera on top, training it on me. He gestured toward it as he took the seat opposite. 'We have to record this, like I mentioned before.'

I bristled. How could I explain it to them: fear and guilt look the same way on film. Catch me now – hair matted, pallor like bone china, beads of sweat in all the right places – and anyone would think I did it.

Catch me now, like this, when I just know that Davis is going to catch me at any minute.

The officer pressed a button, and a blinking light flashed a warning, then kept its eye trained on me, watching.

McKnight reached into his jacket, and I found my eyes landing on the drapes, on the inch or so of exposed window, wishing I had opened them so I could see the road, confirm it was empty, free of Davis.

Dusty jumped onto my lap, but I shooed him off; he whined as he slunk away. From the kitchen, the sound of water being lapped from his bowl. Dusty knew how to self-soothe; I had never learned properly.

McKnight retrieved an evidence bag, marked with words I couldn't read, then used tongs to pull out its contents, a bra and underwear. 'Do these look familiar?' he asked, holding them in front of me.

It was hard to tell for sure, but, yes, they looked like mine. Black satin, pink lace. From the shop in Williamsburg, if I wasn't mistaken, where the drawers made no sound when you tugged them open. Ninety dollars of sex appeal, purchased for our first Valentine's Day together. I'd always been the girl who lived in clean-edged cotton, and I'd wanted to surprise Davis, reach into my dresser and not grab something from Uniqlo. He'd gotten them off before he'd had a chance to take them in. My secret weapon, he'd joked afterward, fingers laced with mine on the sofa in his living room – stops men in their tracks. He'd bought me plenty in our years together, but the others had felt tainted, part of a story I no longer wanted to be part of. These were the only ones I'd brought with me, a memento of a different time, when it had just been Davis and me. And then Davis and me and Dusty. But never Davis and me and things that we didn't talk about but that left me raw.

The tips of my fingers went cold and tingly as I realized they were now evidence against me.

'Miss King?'

'Sorry,' I said. 'What are you asking?'

He sighed. 'Are these yours?'

'I don't know,' I said, hedging my words until I knew *why* he was asking. 'Maybe. I mean, a lot of those sets look alike.'

He let them drop back into the evidence bag, then motioned to the officer. 'Can you get a DNA swab from Miss King?'

She nodded, and then retrieved cotton swabs, plastic, out of a silver case. 'It will only take a second,' she said, her voice kind. 'Open your mouth, if you don't mind.'

It felt so violating. Pieces of me on fuzzy cotton.

'I have an inkling they're yours,' McKnight said. 'But we do need to check.'

'Why does it even matter?' I asked as she tucked the swab into another container.

'Because today, while you were speaking to me at the station, our team found these buried pretty deep in a corner of Mr Nolan's cabin,' McKnight said, matter-of-fact. 'We'll be checking them against Ms Abernathy's and Rachel Dry's DNA as well.' He cleared his throat. 'And Claire Alby's,' he said, turning red. 'If they do match yours, we'll have hard evidence that puts you in there, adds to your motive.'

'I wasn't in there,' I said, shaking my head. 'I *told* you. If those are mine' – my voice rasped – 'it's because someone took them. Or John did, I don't know.'

It didn't make sense, it didn't align with who I thought John was, but the half-naked photo of me didn't, either. Perhaps I hadn't really known him at all.

The woman officer shot me a cutting look. *Homewrecker*, it said. *Just like the rest of them.*

'What are you saying?' McKnight asked, hands to knees. 'That someone broke in?'

'I don't know,' I said. 'Maybe.'

'Okay, so someone stole your underwear. How? There are no signs of forced entry. Do you not lock your doors?'

I pictured the unlocked door the morning I'd woken to find John in my bed. We had been so drunk the night he'd stayed over, so stupid. It wasn't beyond reason to imagine Davis coming in, seeing us, grabbing my key, finding a place to make a copy – Walmart was open twenty-four hours, and it was only a few miles away in Kingston – then slipping my key back onto its hook.

'I do, but I might have forgotten once or twice. If those are mine, and if they weren't taken by John, someone else took them.'

McKnight cut me off. 'So you're reaffirming you've never been in that cabin?'

'Yes,' I said. 'Like I said earlier, I swear.'

He made a show of checking his notes. 'Yes, you did. The thing is, we have witnesses in the area who say they saw a woman of your description around the cabin at night.'

I wrapped my arms around my body, digging my hands into my sides as my blood ran hot and my pulse sped up. 'What do you mean *of my description*?'

'Dark hair,' he said. 'Medium height. Slim build. Black coat.' He nodded to my wool winter coat, hanging on a peg near the door.

I released my grasp on myself, and for a second, the hatch had opened, and all I could do was burst through. 'That's me, all right. And half the women in this fucking town. And if it was dark, light hair might look brown. So might as well be Vera, too. Or Claire. Or Rachel. Jesus.'

McKnight's eyebrows shot up. Then his head twisted, slowly, toward the camera, reminding me.

I didn't need his admonishment. I knew. We women weren't supposed to let our anger slip, lest we seem hysterical, unhinged. It was half of why I loved Vera. She wore her anger like a designer cardigan – right there on the outside for anyone to see.

I took a deep breath, closing the hatch again.

McKnight shrugged. 'So maybe it is a common description. But we have to pursue all leads, I'm sure you understand.'

He paused, and then a smile crept to the corners of his mouth, the smile he always got when he had another card up his sleeve.

I grabbed at coils of hair, pushing them out of my face and then tugging, just enough so it hurt. 'I swear to god, I never even got out of the car.'

McKnight glared at me. 'I didn't tell you earlier, because I was hoping you'd come clean on your own, but your prints are there,' he said. 'On two different bottles of wine.'

'Because it's *John and Vera's cabin*,' I said, my voice choking at the words, anger churning once again. 'We drank a lot, okay?'

He glanced at an errant bottle of wine on my coffee table. He didn't say another word, but his eyes fixed on me, judging. It was easy to see myself as he did: a high-strung, alcoholic Brooklyn bitch. Someone who'd fucked her friend's husband and then killed him when things didn't go her way, attempted to hightail it out of town as soon as the memorial service was over. The narrative was infuriating, story after story of unhinged woman, of girl gone mad, told and whispered and reported, laying the foundation for his beliefs about me.

'If John had taken half a bottle out to the cabin when he was working, one I'd helped him drink, of *course* my prints would be on it.'

'Of course,' McKnight said. 'I suppose that's why identifying the owner of that underwear will help. As well as seeing what turns up on your laptop and from our search here.'

My gaze darted around the room – I wanted him out, I wanted all of them gone – now. I needed to know if they'd found my hiding spot, if they'd taken those parts of me, too. I needed a second to *think*. 'You've got it wrong,' I said, drawing in staccato breaths. 'I don't care how it looks, you're still wrong. And every moment you spend on me is time wasted.'

McKnight leaned forward, placing his hands on his knees. 'Is it, Miss King? Because no one else in this investigation has lied to us from the start – and in official reports, too. We have to dig deeper into someone who's made false statements on record.'

The woman took a few steps back, giving us space, as McKnight drummed his fingers on his knees. 'Here's the thing: Maybe you're innocent. Maybe you got caught in the wrong place at the wrong time. But there are things you aren't telling me. And when you're not frank with me, about your relationship with Mr Nolan, about what happened that day on the hike, what am I supposed to believe? Now, is there *anything* else you want to tell me?'

I wished I could tell him about Davis, ask McKnight to investigate him, but I couldn't. If they spoke to him, he would twist it all – it would only serve to make me look more suspicious. Instead, I jerked my head toward McKnight. 'Are you arresting me?'

He sighed, disappointed, like my dad after I lost it on my piano teacher, leaving me no choice but to quit my lessons. Like my dad, so many times.

I expected better of you.

'We're still exploring all avenues,' McKnight said.

Then, without another word, he grabbed his bags, the woman stopped the camera, and they walked out of my house.

Thirty

Heart racing, I stared at the floorboard beneath my bed. It remained hammered down, just as I'd left it. I momentarily considered reopening it, just to make sure, but before I could, I heard three quick raps at my door.

Through the drapes, I saw Vera, standing on my porch.

I opened the door and ushered her in, a burst of cold following behind her.

Her coat hung open, and she was in the same dress she'd worn at the memorial, but a run in one knee of her tights exposed pale flesh. Her topknot had come undone, and her hair bent every which way from the hair spray – contortionist hair. 'What happened?' she asked, her lips pressing into a thin line. 'You just . . . disappeared.'

'I'm sorry,' I said. The memorial felt a million miles away, but I tried to stay calm, act normal. I needed her on my side now more than ever. 'It was too much, being there, with my parents and everything. It was overwhelming.'

'I know,' Vera said. 'But why did you run out after Claire Alby, of all people? Did you really think I wouldn't notice?'

Dusty reached for Vera's legs, pawing at her tights, but she ignored him, and he hopped onto the sofa instead.

I swallowed, my throat tightening. 'I know her from School-house; I go there for brunch sometimes. She said she wanted to be a writer. We would talk.'

Vera's eyebrows arched. 'What are you, her mentor? That didn't work out too well for John.'

'No,' I said. I had to get us back on solid ground. There was so much that threatened to tear us apart now – and I knew the police could show her that photo of me in bed at any time.

I took a deep breath. 'I didn't even know she was Claire until today. She told me her name was Al, which I should have put together, but I didn't. You have to believe me, Vera. I promise.'

She opened her mouth to argue, then shut it tight, as if she no longer had the energy. Her eyes darted around the room. 'So the police searched your house?'

I nodded.

'Mine too,' she said, tugging at the hem of her dress. 'On the day of the goddamn memorial.'

'Jesus,' I said. 'Really?'

'"We only want to find out what happened."' She mimicked an officer's voice, dripping with fake compassion. 'That's what they say to make themselves feel better. They couldn't show some respect. Not at the expense of the *investigation*.'

Vera situated herself on the sofa, spine rigid. She looked like a figurine on display: *Grieving Woman, Mid-Investigation*. 'I really don't know why they're bothering with me when Sam Alby is probably gloating about what he did to John all over town. But *he* has an alibi. They think the time of death was sometime between eleven p.m. and one a.m., and Sam was supposedly at Platform all damn night.'

My eyebrows scrunched up. 'Platform? The bar?'

She nodded. 'Sam's always there, like every night – that's why we had to stop going. And because his bar buddies are vouching for him, that's it, apparently – McKnight just believes him. No need to look into it further. Go for the wife instead. Or you,' she said, letting the words pierce the air.

For a moment, I wondered again if she believed it, that I could have done this to John. If she could really think it of me, maybe the one person in this whole town besides her who believed that John was good.

Cautiously, I approached the sofa. I wanted to sit next to her, feel her warm skin, pull her close to me and never, ever let go. I wanted to beg her to keep me safe, like she'd promised she would, only I knew she couldn't; not now. I sat, leaving a foot or so of space between us, almost afraid to break her. 'Vera,' I said, my voice wavering. 'You know I would never hurt John. No matter what the police think. I swear to you, Vera. I swear to god.'

She scooted over, closing the space between us. 'I know that,' she said. 'I really do.'

Relief, like stepping into a warm bath, like getting a goodnight kiss from my mother. She still believed me. No matter what the police had told her, she still believed me.

She won't, though. Not after she sees that photo.

My eyes darted to the window, then back to her. 'I need to tell you something, though, so you understand what's going on.'

'What is it?' she asked, her voice wavering.

I cleared my throat, as if to force the words out. 'Part of me worries that it was Davis.'

'Davis?' Vera asked. 'Your ex? That's crazy.'

I nodded. 'I know it sounds that way, but Ellie told Davis where I was, and in town . . .' I hesitated. 'I saw Claire in town, and she told me that he'd been around the shops in Woodstock, asking for me, saying I was missing.'

'Oh my god,' Vera said.

'But then McKnight told me I can't leave, not while they're still investigating, and so I'm trapped here, just waiting for him, and I don't know what he's going to do – I don't know what he's already done.' I sucked in a breath. 'And now they're saying I've been to the cabin, which I've *never* even been inside. You didn't tell them I'd been there, did you?'

'God, no,' Vera said. 'Why would I? They asked me about you and John, and I told them you were friends. I told them the truth.'

'That's all they said?' I asked.

'Yes,' she said. 'Why?'

I licked my lips. Fear pumped through my veins because, so badly, I didn't want her to know. But at the same time, she was all I had left, and now I might lose her, too. I didn't know how long I had before they told her about that photo. I didn't know how long I had until the questions in her head turned into facts, presented before her, laid out on the unforgiving Formica table in the police station.

'What is it?' Vera asked. 'You're not making sense. Why would your ex want to hurt John?'

I shook my head.

'Lucy,' Vera said. 'You have to tell me. Please.'

My lips quivered. 'The police took my DNA.'

'It's okay,' she said hesitantly. 'They took mine, too. It's routine.'

'No,' I said, my face going hot. 'It's more than that. They found a pair of underwear in the cabin. I don't think they're mine, but . . .'

'But what?'

'The police think,' I said shakily, 'they think that I, that me and John . . .'

Vera took a deep breath. 'They think that about practically every woman in town, Lucy. That doesn't mean that your ex – It still doesn't make sense.'

I tugged at the neckline of my top, half wishing I could just disappear. Vera was my friend, my best friend – my *only* friend. I had to try to get ahead of this.

I had to play it right. I had to try.

'They have a reason.' I managed. 'That night. That night that you were out of town, getting the car . . . The next morning, I woke up, and John was right there in my bed. Nothing happened, he was fully clothed, only I feel so sick about it every time I see you. I feel so guilty. I'm a horrible friend. I'm not who you thought I was, and I worry that Davis somehow saw that, and he got angry, and – and – and that all of this is my fault.'

I picked at the skin around my fingers, and I imagined rage, good and pure, exploding through the tips of Vera's fingers. I saw her grabbing me, hitting me, smashing my head against the corner of the coffee table. I would deserve it.

Words flashed in my head – *whore*, *slut*, *cunt*. Awful words, ones you were told to never say about another woman. And yet, I was all of them, everything bad I had ever feared. With my best friend's husband. I was disgusting. I chanced a look up, but her face was blank, unreadable.

'Lucy,' she said finally, voice smooth.

'I'm so sorry,' I interrupted, words pouring out like jumbled blocks. 'Say you'll forgive me. I know I don't deserve it. Just say you will. Please.'

She pressed at her thighs, straightening the bottom of her dress. 'Lucy, John told me about that night.'

'What?' The shock in my voice was palpable. 'What do you mean, he told you?'

'You think we were married as long as we were and nothing inappropriate ever happened? He told me you guys had too much to drink, and he was worried about leaving you on your own, especially since you were so scared about Davis, so he crashed in your bed. He said his clothes were on, and nothing happened.'

'Really?' My mind raced, trying to understand. He'd left me that note, practically begging. *Please don't tell Vera.* But he already had.

'Is there something else I should know?' she asked, biting her lip.

He'd told her enough, enough so she wouldn't ask too many questions. He'd made an excuse, and he didn't want me to tell her the *actual* truth, the true betrayal. He'd set it up nicely so our lies would be believable. Twisted truths are better than flat-out lies – Vera herself had taught us as much. I shook my head, understanding now exactly what I had to do. If I didn't screw it up, she'd never know the whole of it. She'd never know we kissed. Even the police had no proof of that. If they showed her the photo, I'd say I had no memory of it – that was true, after all. 'No, I just –'

'The police, everyone in town, even some of the people who were at the memorial this morning, they like to think that John and I had this awful marriage, but you saw us, Lucy. You *knew* us. Do you really think we didn't love each other?' Her voice cracked. She was crying now, too. 'We loved each other enough to share *everything*. Including this.'

My body broke into sobs, and she leaned in, wrapping me in her arms, our tears mixing, salty stains on our clothing.

'We're in this together, Lucy,' she said. 'I'll still do anything to protect you.'

She pulled back, looking at me. 'And I can see why you'd have those fears, about Davis and everything, but they're just that – fears. You didn't cause this, Lucy. And neither did I. It isn't your fault or mine – it's Sam's. Remember that, okay? I still love you just as much as I loved you before.'

'Thank you,' I said, choking back a sob. 'I love you, too.'

Vera was, as always, my rock.

I followed her back to her place and huddled beside her in bed, Dusty at our feet.

But after she was asleep, I kept getting up, pulling the drapes back every other second to check for Davis.

I was still on high alert, sensitive as Dusty to every tiny sound – cracking twigs, shuffling critters, and hooting owls.

It was after midnight, 12:05, and I'd just looked out the window for what felt like the millionth time, when I heard the ding of a text message.

The sender read as an email address, not a phone number: thetruthshallsetyoufree999@gmail.com.

My throat tightened as I stared at the message, just one sentence:

i know you didn't do it

Thirty-One

Can I speak to McKnight?'

It was just after nine a.m. I'd gone straight from Vera's to the station, taking Dusty with me, too scared to leave him in my cottage alone. The receptionist, the same lady from before, looked at me with narrowed eyes, eyeliner drawn on not quite straight. She glanced at Dusty but didn't say I couldn't bring him in. 'Detective McKnight's not in yet.'

'I'll wait.'

'Go right ahead,' she said, nodding to the chairs.

The wait seemed interminable, but after twenty minutes, he appeared, wearing a faded nylon puffer, a bulging briefcase in one hand and a large Dunkin' Donuts cup in the other, the smell instantly cueing memories of crowded hallways and sweating bodies, of Penn Station. 'Can I help you, Miss King?' He nodded at Dusty. 'Hey, little buddy.'

'I got a text last night,' I said. I let Dusty down and gripped the leash tightly so he wouldn't jump on McKnight's legs, then held out my phone with my free hand.

McKnight shrugged, his hands full. 'You want to go to my office?'

I nodded and followed him down the hall. I still didn't trust him, but from the masses of papers on his desk and coffee cups littered about, it was clear he was logging hours and working diligently, if nothing else. He tossed some of the detritus into the trash, then gestured toward my phone. 'Can I see it?'

A chair sat facing his desk, its seat cushion slashed, murky yellow foam spilling out. I took a seat and pulled Dusty into my lap, then handed McKnight the phone. He stared at it for what must have been ten full seconds, his eyes blank as a freshly cleaned whiteboard, then handed it back to me.

I adjusted in the chair. 'So?'

He shrugged. 'So what?'

'So *obviously* someone knows something. Maybe you should be looking for the person who sent this, who knows you're chasing after the wrong person.'

A gulp of coffee. 'Shoot it over to me. I'll pass it on to forensics.'

'That's it?' I asked.

'Pardon me if I'm not jumping up and down, Miss King, but we see things of this sort all the time. Email addresses can be created in an instant. Those can be used to send texts. Anyone with your phone number could have done it. Or anyone who found a way to look up your number, which isn't that hard, either. *You* could have created it, for all I know, and sent that to yourself.'

'I didn't.'

'I'm sure you didn't,' he said. 'Just like I'm sure a person as smart as yourself sees people falling in the rain when they haven't.'

I pressed my lips into a thin, tight line, but he only shrugged. 'Look, it's just a text, like all the texts and emails of this nature you'd find on any tip line. It's an active investigation. People like to find a way to get involved. Like I said, send it to me, and I'll shoot it over to my guys.'

I pushed the chair back, its legs screeching against the floor, and Dusty hopped off my lap. 'Thanks for doing your job.'

'Oh, and Miss King?'

'Yeah?'

'Funny thing. We couldn't find a record of you having ever lived in Brooklyn at all. Most recent address we found is closer to here, down in Poughkeepsie.'

My chest felt suddenly raw. Sensing my sudden change in demeanor, Dusty's tail went limp.

'Care to explain?'

I swallowed, buying myself time, then concentrated on keeping my mind clear, my voice still, as I said what I knew I had to say, should it ever come up: 'You ever lived in Brooklyn?'

He raised an eyebrow. 'Excuse me?'

I kept my eyes focused on the tip of his nose. 'Well, if you had, you'd know that half of the buildings, the ones that aren't new luxury condos, are run by slumlords, or at least people who are really, really shady. In my first apartment, I never even had a lease. I took it over from a friend and paid the guy cash month to month. They don't want a record of anything, you know, so they don't have to pay taxes. Then I moved in with my boyfriend.' I shrugged, gripping Dusty's leash tighter. 'The lease was in his name. You didn't ask for my whole residential history.'

He hesitated. 'No, indeed I didn't.' He stared at me, as if trying to decide whether to believe my story. He pressed his lips together, then delivered a smile, far too sweet. 'Those DNA results should be in soon, Miss King.'

Back in my cottage, holding Dusty tight, I walked through every room, looking for a sign of Davis, but found nothing. I let Dusty down and locked every door twice, then tried to put the cottage back together.

I remade the bed, shut open drawers, returned books where

they belonged. I tossed dirty underwear, personal things that had been picked over by the team of prying cops, into the hamper. When I was done, I once again pushed the bed aside, staring at my hammered-down floorboard.

I had a terrifying thought. What if they'd found everything I'd stashed there, then hammered it down so I wouldn't know? What if McKnight was just waiting to show me what he'd discovered, another trump card up his sleeve? What if that's why he'd suddenly been digging around in my address history?

The board was wedged down too tight to pry up with the claw of the hammer, so I headed to the kitchen, sliding open the knife drawer. I reached for the butcher knife, the only thing thin enough to wedge into the crack, then stopped, forgetting about all I had hidden away under the floorboard.

Eyes locked on the drawer, heart suddenly racing, I counted them: One, two, three, four, five. I counted again, touching the red Lucite handle of each one. One, two, three, four, *five*.

Something wasn't right.

Goose bumps rising on my arms, I walked slowly to the bedroom. In the search, the police had taken my notebook, where I had jotted down all my inventories, but I'd taken backup photos on my phone when I first moved in.

Coldness crept over my skin, and I felt suddenly foolish. Why had I grown complacent, stopped checking things like this? Since I ran into Ellie, I'd been in reaction mode, too preoccupied with everything to tally up the items in my cottage. And then, after the scarf and the photos and the note went missing, it had seemed unnecessary. Davis was lurking. That much was clear. Only, what if I'd missed something, something more than those tiny things?

What if I'd missed something big?

Fingers quivering, I swiped through the photos on my phone until I found the one of the list I'd made when I moved in.

There it was, in my familiar scribble:

knife drawer (six knives, red Lucite handles)

I counted again. Five. Only five.

No, it couldn't be. It *couldn't* be.

I searched the sink. Surely I'd cut up an apple or something and tossed it in. Nothing.

Stab wounds. John had stab wounds. And the only people, supposedly, who knew this, aside from the cops, were me, Vera, and John's killer.

I whipped open the fridge, checking Pyrex containers, a weeks-old pizza box, to see if it had been tossed in haphazardly among the leftovers. Again, nothing.

One of my knives was gone. A bright red, easily distinguishable knife was gone. John had been stabbed, I was their main suspect, and one of my knives was gone.

Had the police taken it as evidence? Wouldn't they have told me? A thought struck me, slim but hopeful, a silver lining on a storm cloud: John and I had often cooked together. Him helping me chop, me stirring a sauce he'd picked out of one of his dusty cookbooks. Had I lent it to him? I racked my brain, trying to think, and among the haze of conversation and pinot noir, one moment stood out – a week or so before John was murdered they'd brought over Vera's lasagna, and she'd used one of my knives to cut it. It could have been left in the container with the lasagna, trapped under aluminum foil. It could be at her house, still.

I texted her quickly:

This is random but is there any chance you took home one of my knives one of the times you brought over dinner?

Vera called immediately. 'A knife?'

'It's stupid,' I said. 'But I can't find it, and I thought maybe you had it. It's got a red handle.'

'Oh,' Vera said. A pause, long and stretchy.

'I'm sure it's nothing, it just got misplaced, but the way it would look, if the police realized I couldn't find it. I just thought maybe if you had it . . .' My voice trailed off, and I wondered, for another horrible moment, if she could suspect me.

'Sure,' she said, her voice even and smooth. 'Let me check.'

On the other end of the phone, squeaking, and the sound of metal on metal. A drawer shut, another opened.

Finally: 'Sorry, but I don't see anything.'

'You're sure?' I asked. 'Did you check in the fridge? In a pan of leftovers or something?'

I heard a shuffle, another door opening. 'Yes,' she said after a moment. 'I'm sure.'

'Okay,' I said. 'Thanks. Maybe I could come over?'

'Now?' she asked, her voice suddenly higher pitched.

'Yes,' I said. 'Now.'

A sharp intake of breath. 'I'm going out now. Er, I have to run some errands, but . . . you'll come over tonight?'

'I was planning on it.'

'Okay,' Vera said. 'I should be back around, I don't know, eight? We can have dinner.'

'Sure,' I said. 'And –'

The line went dead. She'd already hung up.

Taking deep breaths, I returned to my bedroom, used one of the five knives in my possession to check my hiding spot – everything was there. Then I tore apart the kitchen, searching beneath the refrigerator, in the space between the cabinets and the oven, at the bottom of the recycle bin – anywhere the missing knife could have possibly fallen.

Crumbs stuck on my jeans, dust coated my hands, drops of

stale wine were spilled across the floor, and my kitchen was in worse shape than even the cops had left it.

The knife was nowhere to be found.

My heart beat wildly as it sunk in, how incredibly stupid I'd been. John, he wasn't my punishment. That was only step one. How could grief be punishment enough when I'd already lost my parents? No, the punishment was much more insidious than that, much more true to Davis.

I pictured the missing lingerie, the photos, the note, the now missing knife.

John wasn't the end goal here: I was.

If Davis had seen us that night, if a plan had started to form, if he had grabbed one of my knives . . . of course he wouldn't have been stupid enough to use his own pocketknife; of course he'd much prefer one of mine . . .

Only why go around town, asking about me?

To make you squirm. To make you fucking squirm. To let you know, without a doubt, that he's here. In case the missing items and the faucet and Dusty getting out weren't enough. To make you sure.

It would be easy, I realized, to use a glove, kill John, leave behind a knife with my prints and DNA all over it. It sounded crazy, it sounded insane, only I knew as well as anyone that crazy was very much possible, that there was plenty you could do if you only put your mind to it . . .

And if it did work out how Davis wanted it to, there was another benefit for him as well.

If he actually pulled it off – if I were actually, god, convicted – Davis would always, *always* know where I was.

I would be preserved, a precious collectible beneath a bell jar.

Trapped where no one could ever have me but him.

Thirty-Two

What do you do when you can't run anymore?

That's what I thought about, all day, at home in my cottage like a sitting duck. What was I supposed to do: Go out, buy myself a gun? Booby-trap the place like Kevin Fucking McCallister? Simply wait?

I googled lawyers, wondering how in the world I'd be able to pay one. I checked the locks multiple times. I checked my email, too – and Davis's social accounts – but there was nothing. Not surprising, since every cog and gear had already been put into place. The knife stolen, used to kill John. I wasn't sure of his next strategic move, but it wouldn't come in the form of threats. It would come in person. Him, at my door. I was as sure of this as I had ever been of anything.

Maggie came at four o'clock, T-minus four hours until I'd be once again in the safety of Vera's company. She chanced a smile as I opened the door, Pepper heeling easily by her side. 'I think you could use a walk,' she said.

'Oh, I don't –'

She held up a thickly veined hand. 'Fresh air is good for you in a time like this. Otherwise you'll go crazy. Come on,' she said, when I didn't move. 'We'll make it a long one.'

We walked up Shadow Creek Road, past Vera's, past the house

on the corner that had once been a church and was now some-one's beautifully renovated home, the stained-glass windows a reminder of what once was.

Maggie was surprisingly agile for a woman her age, her feet shuffling quicker than mine did. Dusty sniffed eagerly along the edge of the road, every pinecone a new point of interest.

As we walked, I imagined Davis on this street, watching me, making plans. I wondered, again, how he'd found John's studio. Could he really have tracked John four miles through the woods? I couldn't imagine it – not Davis. There had to be another way. Perhaps he'd followed Vera, after she'd come back that afternoon with the car. Or – more likely – John had gone there after he left my cottage, and Davis had followed him, discovered his studio, made his plan.

Davis was many things, but impulsive wasn't one of them. He'd want to make sure to check every box – a guy like him would be destroyed in prison. Perhaps he'd laid low for another day and then gone to the studio, let himself in – the place was never locked, for fuck's sake – and waited there, ready to kill him, no clue that it was the very night that Vera and I had claimed John had fallen . . .

'My husband died, you know,' Maggie said abruptly as we turned the corner.

My shoulders jolted – and I momentarily pushed theories about Davis aside. 'I didn't know. I didn't even know you were married, actually.'

'It was a long time ago, so I don't talk about it much,' she said. 'Doesn't seem to be much of a point to dwell on the past like that. It was when I was in my forties. My daughter was in high school. It was awful for us both. I don't know what's harder: to lose a parent or to lose a partner. Both, probably. In their own ways.'

I blinked a couple of times.

'You don't have your parents in your life, do you?'

I halted, turning, and my chest seemed to constrict. Suddenly, I imagined Maggie, poking around my place, looking for my secrets. Somehow finding a way to listen in on my conversations, asking around town for gossip about me.

'How did you know that?'

'You can see loneliness in others,' Maggie said, lips pressing tightly together. Then she smiled, going on. 'I mean, you can see in others what you've experienced yourself. You've never mentioned your parents,' she said. 'I got the sense that you'd lost them, that you and I were united in grief.'

It was funny, grief, the way it could hook you, keep you in its grasp, no matter how complicated it was. I wondered if Maggie knew it like that, if amid the nostalgia, the desire she felt for her husband, there was more there, too. Memories of the bad along with the good. Memories you weren't supposed to talk about – were supposed to put behind you.

I sighed, knowing it didn't matter, not really – grief was the same either way. I felt guilty, suddenly, for pitying her the way I had. Between her ugly maroon sweaters and her eagerness to accompany me on walks, I'd pegged her as some sort of sad spinster. But who was I to judge? I was just as lost as she was, probably a whole lot more. Surrounded by Vera and John, I'd thought I could cover my loneliness up, a nice slipcover over a ratty Craigslist couch. But Maggie could see it still. Perhaps everyone could, I thought, as moisture coated my eyes.

'I'm sorry,' Maggie said, reaching for my arm to console me. 'I didn't mean to upset you. Shall we take another turn?' she asked, as if she were a character in an Austen novel, her hand dropping again to her side. 'If Dusty's up for it?'

I nodded eagerly, desperate to fill the next few hours, to make it to eight, when I'd have Vera, once again. These women, the women of Shadow Creek Road, were like buoys, bobbing along, the only things breaking up a stretched-out sea of loneliness and fear.

'Yes, I think we should.'

It was nearly dark by the time I returned to my cottage, the sky velvet, the light fading quickly away. Maggie had turned off with Pepper at her house, and Dusty had dragged me home, eager for rest.

Beneath my feet, gravel crunched, and as I approached the porch, I realized I hadn't turned the light on – our walk had gone on so long, I hadn't thought I'd need to. I looked at my watch. It was five thirty. Only another two and a half hours, I thought. One hundred fifty more minutes until I was with Vera again, until, together, she and I could formulate some sort of plan.

I took off my gloves, fumbling for the keys in the dark of the porch, the cold shocking my skin, Dusty scratching at the door. Finally, I sank the right key into the lock, twisting just so. Inside, I unhooked Dusty's leash, shrugged out of my coat, tossed my bag on the ground, and reached for the light switch, then stopped short.

There was a shadow on the sofa, impossible to ignore. And at the bottom of the shadow, the outline of a shoe. Dusty ran right toward it, his tail wagging, back and forth, back and forth.

I blinked twice, trying to adjust my eyes in the dark, trying to think amid the feeling of my racing heart, the nausea swimming in my stomach, frozen between fight and flight, a scream and a run.

The shadow took a breath. The shadow stood up.

In the dim remnants of light coming through the edges of the drapes, I recognized the outline of his face, an outline I knew too well.

'Hey, babe.'

Thirty-Three

Frantically, I flipped on the light.

My heart beat mercilessly as I took him in. He looked exactly the same as when I'd left him – clean-shaven, thick glasses perched on his nose, blond hair sweeping across his forehead just so. It was like not even a day had passed, as if I were back to exactly what I'd run away from. A hollow feeling rippled through my body, and I felt fragile as an eggshell, easy to break.

'Found you,' he said, an awful smile creeping across his face. 'Didn't think I would, huh?'

'No,' I said, voice weak, as my eyes darted around. The drapes were pulled shut so I couldn't see out – and worse, no one could see in. 'No, no, no.'

He frowned. 'So you *don't* want to talk, I see.'

I struggled to catch my breath. 'What do you want?'

'What do I want?' He laughed. 'You're the one who was always going on about relationships needing an open line of communication. I'd hardly call this open, babe.'

I stared at him, and I could see it, beneath his pseudo-calm demeanor: his anger, simmering, just about ready to boil. He was trying to hold it in, trying to keep it from exploding, but I worried that this time, he couldn't.

'We haven't had a relationship in a long time,' I said.

He pressed his lips together. 'Hard to, when you disappear without so much as saying goodbye,' he said, his voice rising. 'When you abandon me, leave me like that – without even checking to see if I was okay or not.'

He glared at me, still trying to hold it together, and my eyes flitted, instinctively, to the door.

I shouldn't have done it. As if making a decision, pulling the long-sought-after trigger, Davis rushed.

I stepped aside, but in seconds, he had blocked the front door and grabbed my bag from the ground.

Dusty whimpered, tail down and terrified, and I knew it clear as day, knew what I had to do, what I'd been training myself to do for so long.

I ran.

For the sofa, my knee smashing into the hard edge of the coffee table, Dusty quivering as I grabbed him and held his warm body tight.

Then to the kitchen, toward the back door, but Davis was too fast. He blocked the exit, trapping me in the hallway, and in the dim light of the bedroom, I saw it – my dad's hammer on the nightstand.

I bolted through the doorway, my breath already coming in gasps. Dusty leapt from my grasp, scurrying beneath the bed, and my vision blurred as I flipped around, tried to shut the door.

Davis's arm stopped me. He shoved the door open, and I backed away, reaching for the hammer, only he was too fast. In seconds, he'd pushed me onto the bed, taken it himself.

Beneath us, Dusty howled.

'What do you want?' I asked, my chest tight and painful, my stomach like a rock, my eyes darting around the room, searching for exits I knew weren't there. 'Whatever you want, I'll do it if you'll just leave me alone.'

He ignored me. My bag still in his other hand, he backed away, tipping it over – everything clattering against the hardwood floor – my wallet, loose change, a couple of Dusty's treats. My phone. In another world, the mess, the chaos, would have driven him nuts. But not in this one.

'You know what I want,' Davis said, desperately trying to return his tone to normal, but I could see it in his fingers, clenching the hammer so hard they'd turned white: The anger was there; soon, it would be more than he could control.

Davis knelt down, carefully plucked my phone from the paraphernalia.

He pressed the button on the bottom, then walked forward, hovered over me again. I could practically taste him as he shoved the phone in my face, he was so close. 'Unlock it,' he said.

'Why?' I asked, shoulders hunching. I wanted to become miniature, like Alice in Wonderland, so small I could crawl under the bed, snuggle into Dusty's fur. Disappear.

'Just do it,' he said again, shoving the phone even closer to my face.

Hands trembling, I took it, holding it out so I could see it, so my eyes could focus through the tears that twisted my vision. I keyed in my passcode, but typed it wrong.

'Don't mess with me,' Davis said. 'I know what you're trying to do.'

'I'm not,' I said, the words difficult to form as my breathing became rapid, shallow. 'I promise.' Hands still shaking, I tried again, and like that, my apps appeared against a background photo of Dusty.

He took the phone, his fingers working quickly.

'I know you've got it on here. Ellie told me.'

I stared at him, holding my dad's hammer, his fingers clenching even tighter. I imagined him lifting it over my head, letting it fall, my skull his nail, smashing me into Maggie's god-awful quilt, turning me to mush.

It's all in the wrist, my dad used to say. *Gravity does the work.*

I held my breath as Davis's expression changed, as he turned the phone around. It was too close, too blurry. I scooted back, desperate to create space between us, and then, breath still tight in my throat, I saw it.

I saw me.

My face. Turned purple and blue. My bruise, captured in high definition.

Again, I imagined the hammer coming down. A flowering blossom, a spray of red. Dusty crawling out from beneath the bed, lured by the sight of blood . . .

'Delete it,' Davis said.

I swallowed, shaking my head. 'Davis –'

For once, his calm tenor escaped him. 'Delete it!'

My palms were wet as I took the phone. My fingers felt thick, as if they were drunk, as I clumsily tapped at the trash can icon, playing along with his futile exercise. Finally, the option popped up: Delete Photo.

I tapped it, and Davis took the phone eagerly from my hands. 'Are there any more?'

I shook my head.

'You promise? You swear on your mother's grave?'

'I swear,' I said instinctively, finding my words, then covering my face, my chin, with my hands. He tossed the phone onto the bed.

'You didn't have to do this,' I said. 'I was never going to show anyone else.'

His head tilted to the side, like Dusty's did when he didn't understand something I was saying, and the sudden calm, the stillness of his body, scared me more than anything else.

Beneath the bed, Dusty whimpered again.

'You thought because you lost your family, you could destroy mine, too?' he said, his voice wavering. 'She was your best friend.

You *knew* what that would do to her, how it would destroy her, and you did it anyway.'

I shook my head, cowering. 'I had no choice.'

His hand found my hair, and I thought, for a moment, that he was going to lean in, kiss me, but it tightened, so much that I gasped. Then he pulled down, hard, and I squeezed my eyes shut as he pinned me, his legs rigid on either side, his hand on my neck now, pressing, the other hand still gripping the hammer. 'You always have a choice. *We* always had a choice, until you destroyed us.'

His eyes were cold, ready to bend reality to suit his needs, manipulate the world around him, take the control he desired like a power-drunk kid in a game of Monopoly.

My mouth begged for air, but his hand pressed me down, tightening on my throat, cutting off my oxygen.

Davis came closer, his face suspended over mine. Sweat pricked his forehead. His glasses were about to become fogged. Up close, his lips were ugly, thin, and dry – flaking. His breath was hot. A faint smell of blood.

He killed John, I told myself as my own anger surged. *He killed John.*

'No matter what you told her, Ellie will always know who you are now,' I said, struggling to get the words out.

His hand whipped away as if I'd turned hot.

Oxygen invaded my lungs, and my hand shot to my throat.

I should've stopped, I knew it, but for a minute, I didn't even care.

'And I'm glad she does.'

Davis reared back, lifting the hammer over his head.

Gravity does the work, I thought as the hammer hung, waiting. *Gravity does the work.*

Thirty-Four

There are moments when time stands still, when you know that there's no stopping what's about to happen. The connection of fist to face. The blow to the back of the head. The feeling of a car's wheels losing their grip on the road beneath you. The hollow emptiness of impending loss.

The moments when, finally, you admit it – everything you've ever told yourself about your role in the world is wrong. All the calendars, all the classes, all the interviews and jobs, all the hours spent trying to arrange a life for yourself, carefully stacking jacks and queens and aces into a house of cards – it was all an illusion.

It was never real.

You never, ever had any control.

You know, suddenly, that you aren't immune to darkness, to impulse, to the sheer animal nature, the biological violence, the brutal randomness, of humanity – of life. You know that nothing really matters, when it comes right down to it. That there's no real way to protect yourself from pain.

That's how I felt as my ex-boyfriend hovered over me, holding my long-lost dad's hammer over my head like the blade of a guillotine. For one terrifying, beautiful millisecond, I was high on the insanity of it all.

I knew it would finally be over. I wouldn't have to hurt, to pretend to build a life for myself, anymore.

I was a product of fate, of circumstance, like we all were.

The hammer swooped down, and I shrieked as in midair it seemed to change course, missing me only by inches, crunching against my phone where it lay on the bed next to me.

I rolled away, sitting up and scooting backward.

My body stayed tense as I watched his hand, still gripped around the hammer, but it didn't lift again.

'You deserve much worse,' Davis said, as if answering a question I hadn't been brave enough to ask. 'But I won't become the person you think I am.'

Was it possible? Was it possible he wasn't here to hurt me, not like that?

I took deep breaths, trying to find my voice.

'The knife,' I said finally, suddenly aware that he didn't have to touch me to destroy me. 'Do you still have it? You don't have to do what you're going to. You don't have to give it to the police.'

Davis stared at me, eyes narrowed. 'What knife? What are you even talking about?'

'I know you killed John,' I said, forcing out the words. 'I figured it out.'

'Wow, you're in worse shape than I thought,' Davis said. 'I didn't kill anyone. You really think I could do that?' He knelt, hammer still in his hand, and scooped Dusty from beneath the bed. My dog – our dog, once – his tiny little body quivering.

My heart raced, and I momentarily forgot about the knife, about John, about everything else. 'Don't,' I begged. 'Don't hurt Dusty. *Please*.' I deplored the weakness, the desperation, in my voice. 'God, he's all I have.'

'You always assume the worst of me,' Davis said. 'I'm not *hurting* him, I'm taking him, just like I said I would.'

In Davis's arms, Dusty's tail fell; he began to whimper as tears pricked my eyes.

'No,' I said. 'No, please. You're squeezing him. You'll crush him.'

Davis gripped Dusty tighter. 'I would have forgiven you, you know. For leaving, even for taking that photo. I would have taken you back. I *loved* you. I still do. *You're* the one who always thought the worst of me. I knew we were perfect, you and me. I knew if we could only work out the kinks in our relationship, we would be everything either of us ever needed. It's *you* who always painted me as some kind of monster, when I was only trying to help you, to help us. To make sure we didn't just dissolve into resentment like every other couple. We had chemistry, we had similar interests, we made each other laugh, we were crazy about each other – do you know how rare that is? It would have all been *fine*, if only you'd just trusted me, if only you'd just listened.' He sighed, mourning all that could have been. 'We could have gotten married and had kids like you wanted – been a family – if only you'd learned. If you'd tried as hard as I did to improve our relationship. But you didn't care, did you? You blew it all up. You did this.'

Dusty yelped, but Davis didn't let him go. 'Even if I wanted to, I can't be with you after that,' he said. 'So I'm taking what matters most to you. I'm taking him. Maybe you'll finally learn not to ruin every good thing that comes your way.'

Dusty cried out again, and I pressed myself upright on the bed. 'You can't,' I said, begging. 'I'm the one who's been taking care of him. I'm the one he knows. Please.' I reached out my hands, but Davis gripped him tighter. 'Please, just give him to me.'

'Why should I?'

Tears ran down my cheeks, and between the way Davis was holding Dusty and the hammer still gripped in his hand, I was terrified something awful was going to happen. Like a flash, I saw Dusty sprinting across the road after his leash had snapped.

Davis wasn't above hurting our dog if it meant he could hurt me. If it fell into his grand idea of 'working out the kinks' in our relationship.

I had to do something. I had to stop this.

'If you don't let him go, right now, I'll show everyone that photo,' I said, desperately forcing confidence into my voice. 'I'll blast it across the internet. You'll be a viral fucking sensation. You'll have to kill me to stop me from doing that, I swear to god. And if you do kill me, what's your sister going to think? Whatever story you fed her, it won't mean much if I turn up dead a week after I told her myself I was afraid of you.'

Davis's grip on Dusty loosened, just the tiniest bit. 'You deleted it,' he said, as if trying to convince himself.

I half wanted to laugh. 'It's saved in the cloud, in case I lost my phone. I'm not stupid, and you're not, either.'

His eyebrows knitted together. 'You wouldn't post it. You'd be too embarrassed.'

'I have no shame,' I snapped. 'Not anymore. I would. And I will. Let Dusty go, leave him with me, and I'll never tell another person, I swear. I won't tell the police what you've done here. I won't tell anyone you killed John.'

'I don't even know who John is,' Davis said, an awful bitter laughter creeping into his voice. 'You're delusional. You always were.'

As if seeing his chance, quick as anything, Dusty turned his sweet little head and sank his teeth into Davis's arm, hard enough to break the skin.

'Christ,' he said, tossing my baby across the room so violently that his body thunked into the nightstand.

Dusty yelped once more, and I pounced, scooping him into my arms, holding him gently, protecting him.

'He's yours,' Davis said, his expression turning quickly to disgust. 'He's just as crazy as you. Stay away from me – and my sister. Or I *will* take him – I'll take away everything you love, I swear to god.'

Then he turned around, walked out of the room. Leaving us there, saved and spared.

Only somehow more broken than we had been before.

I heard my name like an echo, bouncing around as if someone was yelling it from the end of a tunnel. Bright lights flooded the room, pressing against my eyelids.

Exhausted and weak, I opened my eyes to see Vera hovering over me.

'Lucy. Oh my god, what happened?'

I blinked back sleep. I was still on the bed, in the fetal position, exactly where Davis had left me, where, at some point, half-drunk from the spike and fall of adrenaline, I'd drifted off. 'What time is it?'

'Almost eleven,' she said. 'You didn't show up for dinner, and at first I didn't worry, but then I tried calling and texting, and I couldn't get an answer. I came over here, and I knocked a bunch of times, and the door was unlocked, so I let myself in. God, I thought . . . I don't know what I thought.'

Her eyes froze, locked on my neck. 'Lucy,' she said. 'Your neck is red.'

I nodded. 'I know.'

'Davis?' she asked.

Tears dripped down my cheeks – the only answer she needed.

'What did he do? You have to tell me what happened. You have to tell me right now.'

Vera listened, eyes welling as I detailed everything. When I was done, she made me tea and brought me crackers, but I was too weak, too spent, to get anything down. She begged me to call the police, but I told her I wouldn't, and when the tea had gone cold, she took it back to the kitchen, then returned to the bedroom. She crawled into bed with me and snuggled up behind me, holding me like Davis used to, and in the safety of her arms, I let my eyes go heavy once again, knowing this nightmare was far from over, knowing any respite would be brief.

Thirty-Five

Vera was gone when I woke the next morning. I felt hazy, hungover, even though I hadn't had so much as a drop to drink. The bed was empty, not even Dusty beside me, and layers of covers had been laid, heavy, over me. She'd tucked me in like she would a child.

I pushed the covers back and reached for my phone. The screen was black – dead– and shattered nearly beyond recognition. It was cold in my room, icily so, and I needed to know the time – the only clock in the cottage was in the kitchen. Forcing myself out of bed, I padded down the hall, treading carefully, my head swiveling side to side, in case Davis had decided to come back.

There was no one in the main room – only Dusty, who hopped off the sofa and followed me.

The sight in the kitchen was awful. The window above Dusty's doggie door was broken, a spiderweb of cracks radiating outward.

'Back, Dusty,' I said as glass shards glimmered, scattered across the floor, catching the light like snowfall.

Had Davis returned, smashed my window, intent on scaring me again?

Had his words last night only been lies? Had he never intended to leave me alone at all?

Dusty retreated and I stepped forward. It was noon – I'd slept for ages – and on the counter by the stove sat a note from Vera.

I didn't want to clean this up in case you decided to tell the police (which I really think you should). I'm so sorry this happened to you. I'll check in later. V

Pushing the note aside, I stepped forward and ran my finger along an edge of the crack in the glass. Shit. I sucked on the blood from my finger and headed to the bathroom, wrapping it in a Band-Aid.

In the mirror, I saw fingerprints of blood on my neck. It was where Davis had grabbed me, stamping my skin, irritated and soon to bruise. In the bedroom, I found the hammer. There were bloody fingerprints on its handle, too. No question, Davis's hand had been bleeding when he attacked me. It had happened so quickly, I hadn't even noticed it.

I returned to the kitchen, examining the glass. Blood. Not fresh, but dry, caked.

I took a quick step back, the room beginning to spin as my mind struggled to play catch-up: Between Vera's note and the prints on my neck, it was clear that Davis had broken the window last night, probably before I even came home . . . but why?

A chill ran through me, and not from the air spilling in through the cracked glass. Dusty seemed to sense it; he began to whine.

I'd been so sure. It had been like a movie playing on repeat . . .

After learning my whereabouts from Ellie, Davis had come to my cottage that night, had seen me with John. The door had accidentally been left unlocked, and he'd stolen my key, made a copy, and returned it. He'd taken one of my knives, and he'd used it to kill John. He'd planted my underwear at the crime scene. He'd deposited the knife . . . somewhere. He'd returned in the days since, to let Dusty out, to take the photos and the note and my mother's scarf. To screw with me.

He'd gone around town, asking about his 'missing girlfriend,' just so I would know he was up here, just in case I hadn't yet figured it out, and then he sat back and watched as I quaked with fear.

Then he'd come here to confront me. He'd come here to . . . smash my phone . . . to threaten to take Dusty?

I shook my head, swallowing back a thick feeling in my throat. Davis had seemed genuinely confused when I'd asked him about the knife, about John. I thought it was all an act, but what if, what if . . .

I tossed Vera's note in the trash and then, digging through the junk drawer until I found my roll of duct tape, I added swath after swath, covering the hole in the glass. With a broom and a dust-pan, I swept up the glass and dumped it into the trash. Back in the living room, with all the drapes pulled shut, every lock twisted and retwisted, I began to pace. Dusty watched me as I moved about the room.

Could it be possible?

Could I have gotten it all wrong?

That night with John was little more than twenty-four hours after I ran into Ellie. Unless she'd lied and Davis had been here with her, he would have had to come up almost immediately, somehow find my exact address, and happen upon us. I grabbed a scrap of paper, since the police had taken my notebook, and began to write, detailing every strange thing that had happened since I'd moved in.

- *Door ajar*
- *Faucet running*
- *Dusty getting out*

- *Scarf gone*
- *Photos gone*
- *Note gone*
- *Knife gone*
- *Underwear in the cabin*

As my eyes ran down the list, I heard a crack outside, a rustle of leaves, and jumped. I ran to the front window, peeking out. Nothing more than the beginnings of snow. I ran over the list again.

Someone had been in here, there was no denying it – even if everything else could be explained, objects didn't disappear on their own, didn't simply vanish into thin air.

Until this morning, I'd never seen a single sign of forced entry. The person who'd taken these things *had* to have a key. The person who'd taken my knife, who'd stabbed John, that person had to have a way in here that did not require breaking windows.

Davis had denied even knowing who John was.

What if it hadn't been him after all?

I rushed to the bedroom, grabbed my phone. I plugged it in, praying it still worked, and after five minutes of charging, miraculously, it did. Shards catching beneath my fingers, I dialed Ellie.

It went to voice mail. I dialed her again. Another voice mail. I hung up, dialed her again. And again. And again.

Finally, she answered. 'I don't want to talk to you,' she said in lieu of a greeting, her voice icy. 'Davis told me everything after the last time you called. I never want to talk to you – or see you – again.'

'You won't have to,' I said. 'I promise. Just tell me one thing.'

'Oh my god, you just won't stop, will you? I'm hanging up –'

'Ellie, please. Just tell me this, I'm begging you. When did you tell Davis you ran into me?'

'What?' she snapped.

'Was it right away? Like, did you call him as soon as you left the restaurant where you saw me?'

'No,' she said. 'I told him a couple of days after I got home. I was still trying to figure out *what* to do with your story.'

'When was that?' I asked.

'What the hell is wrong with you?'

'It's important,' I said, my voice desperate. 'When?'

'I got back on Monday,' she said. 'I think I told him on Wednesday. Yeah, it was Wednesday night, after we did yoga together.'

'You're sure?' I asked.

'Jesus, yes, I'm sure. Not that it changes any –'

'Thank you,' I interrupted her. 'And I'm sorry for everything.'

I hung up. Then I opened my calendar app. Monday was the day of the hike. Wednesday was two full days after John disappeared.

Unless Ellie was lying to me, and I'd known her long enough to know she was a shit liar, Davis couldn't have killed John.

I shook my head. I'd been so sure, so goddamn sure, but it wasn't possible. It hadn't been him at all.

So how had someone gotten into the cottage?

And why had they taken my things?

If it wasn't Davis, why try to frame me and not Vera – she was his wife, the obvious choice. It didn't make sense.

With trembling fingers, I opened my email, scrolling until I found the last one I had from Jennifer Moon, the real estate agent who'd gotten me the cottage.

I sent her an email, and then, after refreshing my inbox too many times to count, I called her.

The office number went to voice mail, so I dialed her cell instead.

She answered after five rings: 'Hello?' Her voice was raspy, and she sounded like she'd smoked every day for ages, nothing like the voice I'd imagined from her cheerful email font. I realized, at once, that I'd never even spoken to her before; I had made every single arrangement over email. The idea made me feel suddenly unsafe – I had no idea who I was really dealing with. My dad would have been rightly horrified.

'Jennifer Moon?' I started. 'I'm sorry to bother you like this, but this is Lucy King. I'm renting the cottage that you handled, on Shadow Creek Road? Number sixty-three?'

A hesitation, and then: 'Yes?'

'Does anyone besides me have a key to the cottage? I don't know, someone in maintenance, or –'

'No,' she said, cutting me off. 'There are only two copies. The one you have and the one I have. I share an office with another company, so I keep the spare keys in my home, just to be safe.' A creaking of floorboards and then a metal clacking sound. 'I'm looking at your key – Sixty-Three Shadow Creek Road – right now, in fact. So the answer to your question is no. Just you and me. If anyone needs to do a repair, they have to sign the key out from me – and that's only if you've granted access to the space. That's the law. My company takes safety *very* seriously. You'll see I have a plethora of five-star reviews on Yelp. Top rental management and realty company in the area, I'll have you know.'

I would have laughed if I didn't want to cry. 'Okay,' I said, thoughts twisting around themselves like pretzels. 'What about prior tenants? Do you change the locks between?'

'Why? Did something happen?'

'I just – only because of my neighbor – John Nolan. The police are still investigating his death. I want to make doubly sure.'

A pause stretched across the line, and I found myself wondering if she was smoking a cigarette. She cleared her throat twice before she spoke. 'Yes,' she said, her voice deepening. 'Yes, how awful. The locks were changed, I can assure you. Now, is there anything else? I do have to get going. I have a showing this after-noon.'

'You're sure no one has access to that key besides you?'

'No one but me, my husband, and my daughter, and I'm sure you're not implying that either of them would . . .'

'No,' I said. 'No, of course not. Thank you.'

My eyes darted around the room as I hung up. Someone had to have found a way in here. Maybe she was bullshitting me. Maybe she hadn't changed the locks at all. Opening a new page on my phone, I googled her company, Jennifer Moon Real Estate. As promised, a Yelp page turned up. She wasn't lying. There were loads of five-star reviews. It was difficult to read through the cracks in my screen, but, squinting, I did.

> Incredibly professional!
> A pleasure to work with.
> Takes safety very seriously.
> Jennifer has the best rentals in the area.

And then, a longer one.

> We worked with Jennifer Moon to get our cabin in tip-top shape before renting it. Her husband is an amazing local contractor, and she got us a great deal on all the necessary repairs to bring things up to snuff. We ended up getting a far higher monthly rental rate than we'd anticipated. Can't recommend enough!

I paused. Something wasn't right. Something wasn't right at all. Heart pounding, I found the field that would let me search within the reviews as I remembered what Vera had said, early on.

He's a top contractor in the area – through his business, he's become friends with a bunch of lawyers, even a judge. . . .

Fingers shaking, I typed in *contractor*. Like that, three reviews appeared, relevant text highlighted and bolded.

> She's married to a great **contractor** in the area
> Her **contractor** husband was a life-saver before we sold

The last one on the list was the one that made my heart stop, that turned everything I thought I believed – about Davis, about John, about all of this – upside down.

The one that made me realize I had gotten it all terribly, horribly wrong.

> Jennifer set us up with her husband, **contractor** Sam Alby
> of Alby Construction

Thirty-Six

I headed to Vera's immediately, snowflakes catching in my hair. I walked as quickly as I could manage, careful not to slip on the slick road. I told myself the threat of exposing that photo was enough to hold Davis off, but how could I really be sure? I had spent so many years under his control – it was hard to believe it would end just like that. Davis could have changed his mind, or this could all be part of his plan. Perhaps he wanted to watch me squirm a little more before hurting me again.

As soon as I reached the farmhouse, I banged on the front door like my life depended on it. And, fuck it, maybe it did.

Vera opened the door after twenty seconds or so. 'Are you okay?' she asked frantically. 'God, did Davis come back? Did you finally contact the police?'

I pushed past her, traipsing into her living room, the heat of her woodstove hitting me all at once.

'You should sit down,' she said, gesturing to the sofa. 'You're still in shock.'

'I was wrong,' I said. 'I was completely wrong.'

'What do you mean?' Vera asked, voice sharp. 'What do you mean, you were wrong?'

'Davis didn't have a key.'

'I know,' she said, tugging at the bottom of her shirt. 'Didn't you see your window? That's why I wanted you to report it. You need to get it on record.'

I walked away from her, began to pace her living room. It was messier, more cluttered, than I'd ever seen it before, as if she hadn't so much as tried to put things back together after the police searched her house. 'Listen to me,' I said. 'That doesn't matter.'

Vera's eyes widened. 'Of course it matters.'

I shook my head. 'No, I told you last night. I won't. I can't.'

'But, Lucy –'

'I know it's my responsibility. I know I'm supposed to – believe me, I've told myself this a million times – but I won't tell them this, I won't have them put it down in writing. I won't have my entire past combed through just to make a point.'

'It's not just to –'

'It is, though. Listen. I thought somehow, some way, Davis got a key, made a copy of mine or something.'

She reached for the corner of an armchair, almost as if for balance. 'I don't understand. Why would you even think that?'

I sighed. 'Things have been happening. My faucet was running. Dusty got out. And things are gone. That knife. My mom's scarf. This –' I paused, knowing I couldn't tell her about the note. 'It doesn't matter. Someone's been in there, I'm completely sure of that, and I thought it was Davis. I thought he'd killed John and wanted to frame me for the murder, but it wasn't him.'

'You're in shock,' Vera said. 'You're not thinking straight. Why would –'

'*Please*, just listen. I called the real estate agent who'd set me up with this place, to see if anyone else had access.'

Her hands fell to her sides. 'Jennifer Moon?'

Heat rose to my face, and a sudden anger bubbled within me, in a way it never had toward her. 'You knew she was Sam's wife? And Claire's mom? Why didn't you tell me?'

'I did,' Vera said, placing a hand on her hip.

'No, you didn't,' I said firmly. 'Your archnemesis has access to my house – his wife keeps the keys in their home, she just told me – and you don't think that's information I should know?'

Vera bit her lip. 'I swear I did. When you first moved in. Or when I told you about Sam and Claire and all that. That's his excuse for being on this block – he has to check on his wife's properties. I know I told you. I even asked you if you'd ever met her, his wife.'

I stared at her. Was she lying? I remembered, vaguely, her mentioning something about Sam's wife, but never a name, never a clear warning. It was almost like she'd purposefully omitted it.

'Could you have been any more cryptic about it? You don't even think it's relevant information, something you might want to mention more than in passing?'

'Don't, Lucy,' Vera said.

'Seriously,' I said, walking closer now. An awful part of me almost wanted to push her, I was so mad. 'You know Sam's dangerous; you know he's angry, he's threatening you, and you can't even give me a fucking heads-up.'

Her lips pressed into a thin, tight line, but she didn't back away from me, only crossed her arms. 'Are you serious?'

'Yes, I'm serious,' I said. 'You should have told me!'

Her eyes went completely still. There was a pause, long and heartbreaking, before she spoke. 'I'm sorry, Lucy. I guess I've been a little busy mourning my husband. And before that, planning this whole thing so *you* could get away from your ex. Rushing everything and setting up John to be *murdered* to save you.'

I took a step back as she glared at me, her eyes narrowed to slits.

It's not my fault it's not my fault it's not my fault.

Her cheeks flushed, she kept going: 'And now Davis has found you, and I'm trying to take care of you, I'm trying to hold you together even though I'm coming undone myself, and you won't even tell the police? Do you know how crazy that is? Do you know how dangerous? Instead of protecting yourself, you're over here, grilling me about things I may or may not have told you. Coming up with these bullshit theories about people breaking into your house, which doesn't even make sense. Why the hell would Sam want to frame *you* and not me, the person he actively hates? You're the one who first pointed it out – it's *always* the wife. You're not the center of the universe, you know.'

My eyes welled as I walked toward the door. I prayed that she would stop me, pull me close, but she didn't even look at me as I pushed the door open and rushed outside, into the snow.

Back at my cottage, desperate to speak to someone about all I'd discovered, needing to understand how Vera could turn on me so quickly, still shocked and scared from my confrontation with Davis, I typed the message with shaking hands.

> It's Lucy. Any way you can meet me today? I don't know who else to talk to.

Thirty-Seven

Woodstock was eerily different at night – a still scene, empty and frozen, like a David Lynch film or an Edward Hopper painting gone wrong.

Every light was off as I drove down Tinker Street, passing Schoolhouse, a hippie candle shop, and a cluster of overpriced clothing stores.

Another block, and I spotted Platform, the only place still lit up. I slowed as I approached it. Half-covered with a dusting of snow, it looked almost like a postcard, or one of those overpriced paintings they sold in galleries at the mall. A shiver ran up my spine as I remembered what Vera had said. Sam apparently spent every night there. I wondered if he was there now.

I pressed the gas, passing Vera and John's gallery, and two blocks down, I turned onto a quiet, winding street. I pulled up in front of the address I'd typed into my GPS, a small brick Colonial with white trim and a tidy red mailbox. Careful not to slip, I made my way up the stone walkway, already coated in a light sheen of ice. Above me, the moon was like a silver dollar. Nearly full.

On the porch, I glanced around me, behind me – it was hard to shake the feeling of being followed, being watched. I rang the bell, and while I waited, took in the odds and ends: Clay flowerpots arched with snow. A hummingbird feeder, sugar-water frozen. Remnants of summer past.

The front door opened, and she smiled, ushering me in.

Rachel was draped in a burgundy poncho, one she might have crocheted herself, from the looks of it. Without saying a word, she wrapped me in a hug, holding me so close I could smell her shampoo – something with apples or cinnamon, something warm.

She pulled back. 'Tell me you like pinot noir.'

I nodded, my pulse slowing. 'I do.'

'Good,' she said.

She gestured to a pale gray midcentury-style sofa and told me she'd be right back. I shrugged out of my coat, setting it on the rigid arm of the sofa, and took the room in. It was minimal to the extreme, just as she'd said, done in shades of gray and white, an unexpected contrast to the colorful sorts of clothes she always wore. The coffee table was all glass, with edges that looked almost sharp, topped only with a Diane Arbus photography book. Beside it sat the pristine Eames chair she and her ex-husband had argued about. The only points of departure from the absence of visual stimuli were the walls, which were covered in photographs.

I stood, approaching the opposite wall. The photos were all portraits – men and women, children and couples – but in almost every one, something was off. One side of a face just out of focus. The lighting harsh enough so the person's eyes became black holes. A perspective so skewed, it made you dizzy.

What's more, I could see, in all of them, the same intimacy, the same closeness, I'd seen in those photos of John – only these were even more arresting, more haunting, like the John set had been nothing more than a trial run.

I took a step back, taking them all in, then inhaled sharply.

There, on the bottom right corner, was a face I recognized. Vera.

She was staring into the camera, her lips pressed together and her eyes preternaturally wide, almost as if she were frozen in a state of blank stoicism. It wasn't the smiling Vera I'd come to love or the angry Vera I'd seen on occasion, but instead it was my friend, stripped of all emotion. My friend, pared back to her rawest self. Beautiful.

'What do you think?'

I jumped, spinning around. 'Sorry, I –'

'Don't be,' Rachel said, handing me a glass of wine. 'That's what they're there for. Looking. And buying, if you're in the market.'

I glanced back again, eyes locked on Vera's. 'They're gorgeous.'

Rachel smiled. 'Thank you.' She sat down in the Eames chair, and I resumed my place on the sofa.

'I'm really glad you texted me,' she said. She took a sip of her wine, then put it down, her berry lipstick leaving a print on the glass. 'I wanted to see how you were doing, since I didn't even get to say bye at the memorial. I wanted to see how Vera was doing, too, but I didn't want to upset her. How are you? Shit, that's a stupid thing to say. I mean, how are you, all things considered?'

I tugged at the scarf I'd wrapped around my neck, the one I'd used to cover up the bruises left behind from my encounter with Davis, as I attempted to push last night out of my mind. No matter how difficult it was to shake the fear I'd been living with for so long, I had come to believe that what had happened to John wasn't about Davis. Apparently, it never had been.

'Fine. I mean, awful. But fine.' I took a sip of wine. Then I stole another look at Vera's photo.

'It must be so difficult,' Rachel said. 'And now with an ongoing investigation and everything. I hope they find the bastard. I hope they get him.'

Rachel paused, giving me some space to tell her why I was really here. From the opposite wall, Vera's photo continued to stare, but I tried my best to ignore her. She hadn't wanted to hear what I had to say, so now I was telling someone else, simple as that.

I took a large sip of wine for courage. 'I know this is strange, me showing up out of the blue, but I tried to talk to Vera, and she won't listen, and now I'm afraid she's mad at me . . .' I picked at the skin beneath my thumbnail. 'I just needed to talk to someone, and I know you get it.'

'Get what?' Rachel asked.

'What it feels like to try Vera's patience.'

She laughed, but it was bitter, and if I wasn't mistaken, it looked like she wanted to cry. 'Yes, I do,' she said, eyes flicking briefly to the photo of Vera on the wall. 'Unfortunately.'

I took another sip, feeling like Rachel and I could understand each other, like the two of us weren't all that different, when it came right down to it. Each of us a different but similarly positioned complement to Vera's radiance. Imperfect women who made her shine all the brighter.

'How well do you know Claire's dad – er, Sam Alby?'

Rachel raised an eyebrow. 'Not well. But enough to know he hates John and Vera, to know he threatened them, all that.'

'That's it?'

'Yeah, that's it,' she said. 'And his wife set me up with the cottage, but you know that already. Why?'

I gulped down more wine. 'I didn't know Jennifer was Sam's wife – or Claire's mom – actually. Not until today.'

'Really?' Rachel asked.

'Vera says she told me, but I swear she didn't.'

Her eyebrows furrowed. 'Maybe she mentioned it in passing.'

'It doesn't matter.' I gazed down at my hands, then up again. 'Someone's been coming into my house.'

Rachel leaned forward. 'What do you mean? Breaking in?'

'Yes,' I said, nodding. 'There's no other way to explain it. I thought it was my ex-boyfriend.' I adjusted my scarf. 'He was controlling,' I said. 'He hurt me.'

'Oh. Oh, Lucy, I'm so –'

I shook my head vehemently. 'That doesn't matter now. The point is, it wasn't my ex, I learned that last night, because the person who was coming in had to have a key, and he didn't – he broke the window in the kitchen door. I called Jennifer, and she said that no one else had a key besides her, that the locks were changed between you and me and everything, and that her copy of my key was stored in her house, that no one but her husband and daughter could possibly ever touch it . . .'

Rachel's mouth formed a circle of understanding. 'But you don't really think – why would Sam even want to come into your place?'

I took a sip of wine: 'A knife of mine is missing. I only realized it recently. It's just a kitchen knife, but . . . I think he killed John, and he's trying to make it look like I did it. I know it sounds absolutely crazy – like, why try and frame me and not Vera? She's the obvious target. But I think it was just convenience. Sam knew he'd be a suspect, and so he had to blame someone, and he knew I was close with them, and most important, he had access to my belongings. I've been going over and over it in my head, and it's the only explanation that makes sense.'

I didn't tell her about the photos or the note – or my mother's scarf – I still hadn't put that together myself. Why in the world would Sam take those things? But it didn't matter. The knife alone was enough.

'Have you gone to the police?' Rachel asked.

'Not yet,' I said. 'I only just figured all this out. They're all over me, the police, and I worried if I told them a knife was missing . . .'

'You're afraid it will only make them suspect you.'

'Yes.'

Rachel shook her head slowly, wheels turning.

'What is it?' I asked.

She tucked a lock of hair behind her ear. 'Of course Sam would be angry, after everything.'

I held her gaze. 'You still never told me what changed your mind about John and Claire.'

She looped one finger through a hole in her pashmina. 'I shouldn't speak ill of the –'

'Dead. I know. But if it's something that could help the investigation, that could help *me* make sense of what's happening, you have to tell me. Please.'

Rachel's eyes caught mine. *Don't make me say it,* she seemed to beg.

'Tell me the truth,' I pleaded. 'I need to hear it.'

'You'll hate John if I do.'

'I don't care,' I said. 'I have to know.'

She swallowed, pressing her hands to her thighs. Then she opened her mouth, shut it again. She took another sip, and I did, too, and I had a feeling, clear as day, that it was the last sip I'd take when the world was a certain way, a way I very much wanted it to be.

I had a feeling that everything I believed in was about to change, that my reality was about to be ripped from beneath me – again.

Rachel cleared her throat and looked, once more, to the photo of Vera, before turning her gaze on me.

'Claire was pregnant.'

Thirty-Eight

No,' I said, her words crashing into me, smashing me to pieces. 'No,' I said it again, as if the word could undo it all. 'No.'

Rachel licked a bit of wine off her lips. 'She was. And she and John took care of it. I had heard some of the art students saying things about Claire and John, but I'd always chalked it up to teenage gossip – a stupid crush. The classes ended, and I stood by John, but then, one day, something he said about Claire, about the way he missed her, what a great student she was, it made the hairs on the back of my neck stand straight up. When he was out getting supplies one afternoon – we were working on a project together, like I said, and I was in his cabin a lot – I checked his search history. He'd been too stupid to delete it. It was from about a month before, right when the talk about the two of them had really kicked into gear. John had searched for Planned Parenthoods in the area. Then he'd looked up one nearby on Google Maps. That's when I knew.'

I shook my head, not able to process this. 'Maybe he was searching for Vera.'

Rachel took another sip of wine. 'Believe me. He wasn't.'

I swallowed back the acid in my throat. 'You told her?'

'Vera? God, no. I couldn't do that to her. I don't know if she told you, but she'd had a miscarriage herself, before she and John moved here. I couldn't tell her that a kid, a child, had been carrying John's baby. But I did tell her that I had reasons to think the rumors were true. I didn't tell her exactly why – I couldn't bear to – but I tried to convince her that John wasn't as honest as she thought he was.'

'And that's what tore you guys apart?'

Rachel raised her eyebrows. 'I can't blame her. It breaks my heart, but I can't.'

I shook my head, trying to wrap my mind around all that Rachel had said. It couldn't be true. I pictured John loading canvas and two-by-fours into his pickup, chopping wood in the backyard. He was good. He had to be. Apart from that one stupid night with me, he was.

'You should have told her,' I said finally. 'If you actually thought it was true. Wouldn't she deserve to know?'

'No,' Rachel said. 'I love her too much to do that to her.'

I loved Vera, too. Only this, if this was true, it was huge. This was life-altering. Awful. This changed everything. If Sam had known – or even suspected – of course he'd be angry. Irate. He'd want to kill the guy. Who wouldn't?

'Have you told this to the police?'

Rachel hesitated.

'You have to,' I said.

She nodded. 'I know, I know I have to. I didn't want to start anything, bring even more attention to Claire. She's been through enough, and if it was her dad that killed John. God, I can't even think about it.'

'You need to tell them. Even if you're wrong, and there was some sort of explanation, if Sam got the same idea you did, they have to know.'

'There's not another explanation, Lucy.' She lowered her eyes before meeting mine again. 'But I will. I'll call McKnight tomorrow.' She drained her wine. 'Do you want another?'

All I wanted was to be home with Dusty, to have a moment to process what she'd told me: Could it really be true? Could John have been that far from the person I thought he was? Could everything I'd believed about him be a lie?

'I should get home,' I said, standing up. 'While I can still drive.'

'Okay,' Rachel said. 'I'm sorry. I'm sorry for all of this.'

'Promise me you'll tell the police, though,' I said.

'I swear.'

I shrugged into my coat and grabbed my car keys.

She stood, too, and followed me to the door.

'Lucy,' she said, once I was outside.

'Yeah?'

'Be careful, okay?'

'What do you mean?'

She leaned against the doorjamb. 'If you're right about all of this – and the more you tell me, the more it sounds like you are – Sam can be a very angry guy. You called his wife asking about keys. You followed his daughter out of John's memorial.' Her eyes caught mine. 'Yes, I saw. Just, be as safe as you can. Stay the night with Vera, if you have to.'

I paused. 'With Vera?'

'She has a guest bedroom, doesn't she?'

'Yeah,' I said slowly. 'It's full of John's things, but yeah.'

Rachel nodded. 'All I mean is, you don't want that man trying to take anything into his own hands, especially if you haven't reported this to the cops. Keep yourself safe, above everything else.'

Thirty-Nine

I woke to Dusty barking.

My heart raced as my eyes struggled to adjust to the dark. The drapes were drawn tight, and my mouth was sticky with the wine I'd had at Rachel's – plus the two glasses I'd had upon returning home, too shaken from what she'd told me to do much more than drink.

Dusty's bark turned to a growl, and I flinched, muscles tensing, then tapped at my broken phone. It was just after three a.m. He growled again, then jumped off the bed, barking viciously at my shut bedroom door.

Between the punctuation of Dusty's defensive howls, I strained to hear a muffled noise coming from the other room, a shuffling, almost like *footsteps*.

My throat seemed to close as my hands grasped at the crumpled sheets, desperate to hold on to anything for protection. There was someone in my house.

The shuffling stopped, and so did Dusty's barks, as if we were both listening for what would happen next. I still couldn't see a thing, and as I gasped for breath, I felt for the hammer on the nightstand, only it wasn't there. My hand swept into a water glass instead, knocking it off the table.

The glass landed on the hardwood floor with an awful clatter.

Before I could even think of moving, there was a creak and then a thunk. The sound of the front door shutting. Blood rushed to my head, sloshing around my brain. This was real. This was happening. Right now. I knew it was him, but I needed proof, I needed, for once, to see it for myself. Instinct taking over, I jumped out of bed and ran to the window.

I couldn't make out a thing. The front lights had been turned off. I ran out of my bedroom and into the living room, toward the front door. It was unlocked, the dead bolt turned so I didn't even have to twist it to know. I hadn't imagined it. I hadn't dreamed it.

Dusty whimpered as my heart beat mercilessly. I reached for the door. I knew what I needed to do, but as my hand touched the doorknob, I couldn't do it.

Locking the door, I checked the dead bolt multiple times. Then I made sure every drape was shut, and I flicked on the lights. At first, I didn't see anything, and I grabbed Dusty, pulling him to my body, trying to calm his little heartbeats – and my big ones.

Then there it was, as if waiting for me. A blight in the middle of the coffee table. A single sheet of paper, printed with that awful font.

The proof I craved and feared at the same time.

STOP DIGGING AND GO BACK TO BROOKLYN

It was thirty minutes between calling 911 and an officer arriving. Thirty minutes in which I sat in my bedroom closet with Dusty, back against the door, blocking anyone who dared try to come in.

Finally, the sound of a car pulling up, of wheels on gravel. A swift banging on the door. After peeking through the drapes to confirm, I let in the officer, a baby-faced guy in a uniform who didn't look older than twenty-two. He tried unsuccessfully to calm me down as I talked him through what had happened.

McKnight got there fifteen minutes later, just after four a.m. He was bleary-eyed, his hair rumpled; I'd never seen him so off-kilter. 'I'm sorry for waking you up,' I said.

'It's my job,' he said groggily. 'Now, show me this threat you've received.'

I pointed at the coffee table, where it still sat, black-and-white – proof, finally, solid and tangible, that someone else was running the show, someone who wasn't me. McKnight would have to believe me now.

'And you heard someone?' he asked.

I nodded, chin quivering as I thought, again, of him here inside. 'Dusty was barking, and that's what woke me up. He doesn't just bark at anything, okay? I heard the door shut, and when I looked out the window, the porch light had been turned off. I wanted to run after him, but –' I paused. 'I couldn't.'

For once, McKnight looked at me like I wasn't the enemy. 'You should never chase after an intruder,' he said. 'You did the right thing. Did you touch it?'

I shook my head.

He fished an evidence bag from inside his jacket and, with tweezers, he picked up the letter and dropped it in.

'It was Sam Alby,' I said.

McKnight's eyes narrowed. 'I thought you said you didn't see the intruder.'

'You don't understand,' I said, my words tumbling out. 'This is exactly like the letters he used to send Vera and John. I called his wife yesterday, asking about the spare keys to this place. He must have found out, and –'

McKnight cut me off. 'Slow down, Miss King. What keys?'

I forced myself to take a breath. 'Sam has a key here.'

McKnight narrowed his eyebrows. 'What do you mean?'

I explained my call to Jennifer Moon, how she'd said she kept the keys to all her properties in her home, how I'd discovered that her husband was Sam Alby, that she was far more tied up in this than I had ever expected. When I was done, McKnight nodded, slowly, then pointed toward the kitchen. 'If Mr Alby had a key, why are there signs of a break-in?'

I shook my head. 'He didn't do that.'

His eyebrows furrowed. 'Who did?'

I fought to hold back tears. I wanted Vera. No, I wanted my mother, for this to all go away. I hadn't wanted to tell them about Davis, to open that can of worms, but now I had no choice. 'It was my ex-boyfriend.'

'When did your ex break into your home, Miss King?'

'Saturday night.'

McKnight scratched beneath his lip. 'You're sure of this?'

'Yes,' I said. 'Yes, he confronted me.'

'Why didn't you report it?'

Because you never help women like us.

As if on cue, the baby-faced officer walked out my front door, waiting outside.

'Miss King,' McKnight said, his voice quieter than I'd ever heard it. 'Did your ex give you those marks on your neck?'

'You don't understand –'

'Did he threaten to hurt you if you talked to the police?'

'It's not about him!' I cried. It was so strange. It felt, in that moment, as if it had *always always always* been about Davis. And yet this was bigger, even, than Davis or me. This was something altogether out of our wheelhouse. 'Please,' I said. 'You have to believe me. It was Sam.'

'Are you able to file a report?' McKnight asked. 'About your ex?'

'It doesn't matter,' I argued. 'Sam killed John, and he wants you to think it was me.'

'But why do you think he's trying to frame you, Miss King? From the looks of this note, whoever wrote it is trying to get you to leave town.'

My breath caught in my throat, because in a way, McKnight was right. Of course that's how it would appear, but he didn't get it – he didn't have all the information.

Could I tell him about the knife? What if, somehow, I was wrong? It would only make me look more suspicious. Standing here, waving my hand back and forth – *Hey, one of my knives is gone, in case you didn't notice!* – I had to stay in control of this. I had to *think*.

I took a deep breath. 'I think Sam wanted to frame me, and I think he had the ability to because he had access to my house, but after I called his wife and talked to his daughter at the memorial, I think he knows I'm getting too close to the truth of what actually happened, and so now he's trying to scare me away from looking into anything further. In case I figure it all out and tell you.'

McKnight's eyes narrowed – disbelief.

'You think I'm paranoid,' I said. 'I know it's sounds wild, but –'

'Look, Miss King,' he said, interrupting me. 'I want to protect you, but here's what I know: You have an ex-boyfriend, and it looks like he's been violent. You have a broken window and a threatening note. Now, I understand, given the notes Mr Nolan and Ms Abernathy received that they *alleged* came from Mr Alby, why you would see this language and believe it was tied to him – and trust me, I will absolutely run forensics on this and log it into evidence for our investigation. However, and this is a big one, I'm going to have a hard time convincing anyone on my team of this theory when we can't rule out your ex-boyfriend, who you said yourself has broken in very recently. Until you tell us who this man is, this man who's been hurting you, it's very hard for us to move forward here. Now, would you like to file a report about the break-in?'

'You don't get it,' I said. 'You never do.'

McKnight waited a moment longer for me to change my mind,

then sighed. 'I can see you're quite shaken up, Miss King. It's only natural to be scared and try to make sense of things when something like this happens. Just try and get some rest. We can have an officer drive by and check on you once an hour for the next twenty-four hours. We'll make sure you're safe.'

But he wouldn't, I knew that.

Guys like him, they never did.

Forty

It was impossible to rest, of course it was.

My thoughts spun. It wasn't just the break-in, the note; it was more than that.

What if what Rachel had told me really *was* true?

Last night, in the shock of it all, it had been hard to believe, but in the cold light of morning, it was becoming more and more difficult to defend John. McKnight was right, in a way – stories didn't just bloom out of nowhere.

Had I let my feelings get in the way of seeing John for who he really was? Had my relationship with Davis fucked up my judgment even worse than I'd thought?

John was wonderful, he was kind – he was a man's man in a way that Davis never was. He had seemed to love Vera, but at the same time, he had kissed me. He'd inexplicably taken that photo of me in bed. He'd lied to Vera, making our night together sound far more innocent than it had been. He had protested his innocence about Claire, and yet rumors seemed to follow him wherever he went, even after his death.

Perhaps my crush, my love – for him, for them, for the safety I thought they provided – had gotten in the way of seeing it all.

It broke my heart, but it was impossible to get past: John wasn't who I thought he was. He never had been.

. . .

I didn't remember drifting off, but when I woke again, it was early evening, half past five. I pulled the drapes back, looking for any sign of a police car. After fifteen minutes or so, I saw one drive by, just as McKnight had said it would. Watching me or protecting me? At this point, it was hard to know.

I texted Vera.

Sam broke into my house last night

She started typing immediately.

Oh my god, did you tell the cops? I'm coming over.

She was there in minutes, a black wool poncho tossed over a long black dress, a drawn look to her face, like she hadn't slept in ages. She opened her arms, quickly pulling me in for a hug. 'My god, what is going on, Lucy? Did you actually – Jesus. Did you see him?'

'No,' I said, ushering her in. 'But he left a note inside. I know it's hard for you to talk about this, and I know you want me to focus on what happened between Davis and me, but –'

Vera shook her head almost viciously. 'No,' she said. 'No, I wanted to apologize about that. You were in shock, and I'm coming undone, and I just want to forget it, everything I said. It was awful. It's like part of me wanted to hurt you, so you could feel as much pain as I do.' She paused, swallowing. 'I'm sorry.'

'It's not your fault,' I said. 'None of this is your fault.'

'How do you know it's Sam, though,' she asked, gaze darting around the room, 'and not Davis? Since he was just here.'

Her jaw dropped when I told her what the note had said. 'You're lucky Sam didn't do anything worse. You're lucky . . .' She

277

cleared her throat. 'And the police know now? About him being here?'

'Yes,' I said. 'But I'm afraid they don't believe me. McKnight said they can't make any real progress unless I file an official report about Davis. He doesn't seem to understand –'

'But why target you?' Vera asked. 'Why not me?'

'I think Sam needed to pin it on someone, and if there was a way to make it you, he probably would have. But he had access to my place, not yours. And now, here I am, calling his wife, questioning his daughter, putting it all together. I don't think he's thinking straight – he's just reacting, trying to get me to stop.'

'That sounds like Sam,' she said, looking down at her hands. When her eyes met mine, I was shocked to see tears in them, dripping silently down her cheeks.

'What is it?' I asked.

'It's just –' More tears came, silent sobs rocking her body.

'What?' I asked desperately, pulling her onto the couch, next to me, knowing we were the only ones who could protect each other now. 'What is it?'

'If it really was him, if he really left a note like that, that means he won,' she said.

'What do you mean?'

'I mean Sam wanted to hurt us, he wanted to make us pay, and he did, worse than even I could have imagined.' Vera grabbed a cushion and held it to her chest like a shield. 'I knew he was dangerous, and of course I suspected him, but this is more than just leaving notes in a mailbox. I don't think he would have broken into your place unless . . .' Her voice cracked. 'Unless he killed John, and he isn't thinking straight, just like you said. This is *proof*, Lucy.'

She took a deep breath. 'It's terrible, but in a way, this is exactly what we've been waiting for.'

We agreed not to leave each other's sides, not until this was over, and we opened a bottle of wine, the last one I had in the house, and heated up a frozen pizza, trying to act as normal as possible, to get back to the way we had once been.

I prayed that forensics would turn up something on the note that linked it to Sam. A fingerprint, maybe? *Something* to tie it back to him. If not, I knew what I would have to do: I'd have to come clean about Davis to McKnight, no matter the consequences. But I wasn't ready for that yet. I still had hope that Sam would make a mistake, show his hand before I had to show mine.

The wine tasted bitter and acidic, and though Vera refilled my glass as she always did, I forced myself to slow down – after everything that had happened, drinking would only make it worse.

Of course, that didn't stop Vera. She was deep into her second glass when she drained the remains of the bottle, then lifted her drink to mine. 'You know, you're the only one, out of everyone, that's truly been here for me. You're the only one besides me who still believes John was good.'

I froze, the weight of all I knew now suddenly heavier than ever before.

'What?' Vera asked. 'Why are you looking at me like that? What's wrong?'

'Nothing,' I said quickly.

'What is it?' she snapped. 'You're a bad actress, you know.'

Claire was pregnant.

'Lucy, you're scaring me,' Vera said. 'God, just say it, whatever it is.'

I let my eyes find hers, my friend, my protector. Rachel said she didn't want to hurt Vera, but was that really the right choice?

Was it really fair to let Vera go on grieving him – mourning him – when he could have done the worst possible thing?

I pushed my wineglass aside. If I was going to say it, I had to rip off the Band-Aid, do it fast. 'Last night, I saw Rachel, and she told me . . . she told me that Claire was pregnant.' I swallowed. 'She told me John took care of it for her. He took her to Planned Parenthood to get an abortion.'

Vera was so still that at first, I thought she hadn't heard me.

'Vera?'

Then I saw it, the pallor of her face, as if the blood was draining out, milliliter by milliliter. Carefully, she set down her wineglass, stood up, walked to the door, and wrapped herself in her poncho.

'Vera,' I said, but she didn't stop. She slipped on her shoes and headed outside.

'Vera!'

I didn't know what she was going to do. Grabbing my coat and keys, quickly locking up behind me, I chased her.

'Vera,' I yelled, but she was already in the road, her pace brisk. 'Vera!'

I ran to catch up with her, the cold air accosting my lungs. 'Vera, stop!'

She kept on, around the bend, down the road, over remnants of melted snow, toward her place.

'I'm sorry,' I said. 'Just talk to me, please. I'm sorry.'

It was only when she was in her driveway that she swiveled her head to face me.

'Get in,' she said, pointing to her car.

'What? You're not thinking straight.'

'I need another drink, and you're out of wine. So get in.' She paused, eyes locking on mine. 'Or get out of the way.'

Forty-One

Are you sure you're okay to drive?' I asked as we cruised down the road.

'Fine,' Vera snapped, making the turn toward town.

She didn't say another word as she wound through Woodstock, past the shops, past all of it. *She's not doing this,* I kept telling myself. *She's not doing what I think she's doing.*

But by the time we reached Platform and she slowed down, by the time she pulled into the lot, I couldn't deny it anymore. She was doing it.

'Not here,' I said, voice quaking. 'You said Sam's always here. There's got to be somewhere else.'

'There's not,' she said. 'And besides, I don't care. I'm tired of *hiding*. He claimed every place in this town as his, and it still wasn't enough.'

Opening the door, she got out, sending a rush of cold into the car.

And I followed her, like I always did.

Behind the bar, a large man poured one beer after the next, sweat pooling in the creases of his neck as if oblivious to the chill outside. From the back, a song I couldn't make out blared from the jukebox, and I cast a look over my shoulder. A doorway opened up to more rooms – and more people. The place stretched back farther than I realized. Pool table. Jukebox. Old living room furniture permanently retired to the corners of the shitty dive.

Vera spotted two free chairs at the bar, the only ones left, and pounced, her movements purposeful, her long dress kissing the dusty, beer-spilled floor as she took a seat.

'Come on, Lucy.' She tugged out a chair so it made a scraping sound on the floor, and I felt like I was going to be sick. 'Sit next to me.'

I did, my eyes darting back and forth, looking for Sam, feeling fully exposed, but he wasn't there. Vera shot me a crooked smile. She looked gothic, decadent, as if she made this place different through the sheer force of her presence.

She shrugged out of her poncho and leaned forward, the neckline of her dress buckling, exposing a flash of eggplant-colored lace, the small curve of her left breast. 'What have you got for red, Joe?'

She used to come here all the time, she'd told me. How different had her life been before everything started with John? How much had this wrecked her, long before John died?

The bartender – Joe – grunted out the limited options, his accent thick but unplaceable, like someone who'd spent a long time in the woods, and Vera ordered two Malbecs.

'Generous pours,' she added. 'You can charge me extra.'

'Aren't you driving?' I asked.

She shrugged me off. 'We'll get a cab.'

'When I first moved here, you told me there weren't any car services around here.'

'God, Lucy, I know one, okay?' She scooted her chair closer to the bar, sat up straight. 'Sam's not even here, see?'

'He could be in the back.'

Vera ignored me as the bartender delivered two glasses, fat and brimming. She dug a credit card out of her bag and handed it to him.

She pushed one glass over to me, sloshing a bit of wine onto the counter, then took a sip from her own. 'Come on. Drink.'

I rested my hand on the glass but didn't bring it to my lips. 'I'm sorry I said anything. I shouldn't have, so soon.'

Vera shook her head so violently, it looked like her neck might snap. 'I don't want to talk about that.'

'I didn't mean –'

'I don't want to hear you say that *ever* again.'

I froze, staring at her. I feared I'd fucked it all up, just like Rachel had. That I really might have lost her this time. 'I'm sorry. I won't.'

Vera sat up straighter and took another sip. 'Lucy, you know me, I'm a social person. I didn't want to be some recluse. It's not my fault that people are obsessed with rumors, but they are, and I am not going to let them touch me, not anymore. I planned on coming up here, making just as many friends as I had in the city. Going to bars like this, eating out in town. Just like you. But –' She paused, taking a sip. 'They took that away from me. With their gossip and their looks and now these absurd accusations from Rachel. God.'

She twisted the glass in front of her, almost as if she were inspecting it for cracks. 'At least in the city,' Vera went on, 'if you pissed someone off, you didn't have to see them all the time. At least you could be anonymous. I played Sam's stupid game, I played along with all of them, but it didn't even matter. He *still* killed John. These people still hate me.' She took my hand in hers and lowered her voice to a whisper. 'We still had to do what we had to do, didn't we?'

I swallowed a touch of wine, my stomach flip-flopping. 'Maybe we should just tell them about that,' I said, my eyes again searching for Sam. 'They know I lied, but what we did is nothing compared to what Sam did. Maybe they'll finally believe me if I tell them.'

'Don't be stupid,' Vera said, her hand recoiling instantly from mine. 'I'm not going to throw away my life, too. I've already given up way too much.'

She was right, I knew that. I couldn't risk opening myself up to closer inquiry, either, only the way she dismissed it was so . . . callous.

'Let's forget about all that, okay? Let's pretend you never said a word.' She grabbed my hand again and squeezed it so hard it almost hurt, then quickly let it go. 'Let's just have one good night. I'm begging you.'

I did my best to give her what she wanted.

I barely touched my wine, taking only the most cautious of sips, but I didn't object when she ordered another.

She dragged me to the jukebox, and after tossing her things onto a chair in the corner, she picked out songs like it was her job.

I couldn't pretend so easily. I found myself constantly looking around, waiting for Sam Alby, hoping beyond hope that he wouldn't show up tonight, that McKnight had taken me seriously, that Rachel had told him what she knew and that the cops had properly taken Sam in this time, that all of this would be over soon. And that Davis, for his part, would do what he said he would – finally let me go.

Vera drained her next glass almost as quickly, and when she wasn't looking, I grabbed her car keys, nestled in the top of her handbag, and put them in my pocket so she wouldn't do anything stupid like try to drive home.

She was playing Dinah Washington, swaying back and forth, almost like she was dancing with the jukebox, when a guy my age sidled up to her – someone up from the city, most likely. With wide brown eyes, he took Vera in, top to bottom. 'Nice choice,' he said to her.

She flipped around, startled, and when her eyes caught him, they sharpened. 'I'm just trying to have a night with my friend,' she said tightly.

The guy smiled – he wasn't giving up yet. 'You shouldn't play such good music, then, if you don't want anyone to talk to you.'

Her lips pressed together.

'Sorry,' I said. 'We're just –'

'Mourning my dead husband,' Vera snapped.

'Jesus,' the guy said. 'I didn't mean to bother you. I was just making –'

'Well, you did. Come on, Lucy.' She grabbed my hand and dragged me away, past the pool table, toward the next room.

She had to stop drinking, I realized. She had to stop, or else she really would flip out – say something, do something she'd regret.

But as we entered the next room, my worries about Vera were momentarily pushed aside.

My heart stopped. And time, once again, stood still.

Sam was there, in the corner. He wore a denim shirt, perhaps the same one he'd had on when he'd spilled wine on us, and his gray-brown hair gleamed in the muted bar lights.

Staring at her – at me – drinking a beer like nothing in the world was the matter.

The man who had been in my house just last night.

The man who killed John.

Forty-Two

We have to go,' I said, but Vera grabbed my hand, jerking me closer to her.

'No, we don't.'

Out of the corner of my eye, I saw Sam sip his beer and walk off, disappearing into the next room.

'See?' Vera said bitterly. 'It's fine.'

'It's not fine,' I said, my pulse ratcheting up as I imagined Sam, only a room away, how his hands had been on my things, on my knife. 'He was in my house. Jesus, Vera. He *killed* John. Don't you even care?'

She took another sip, her lips purpling. They looked ravenous, a vampire's, having just sucked blood. 'You really think he's going to attack me in the middle of a crowded bar? You said you'd be here for me.'

My fear and guilt and heartache morphed into anger, raging like that river John was supposed to have drowned in. 'I *am* here for you. I'm always here for you.'

She raised an eyebrow. 'Are you? Because however much you supposedly cared about John, it wasn't enough for you to actually trust him. You're just as bad as everyone else, you know. Believing whatever people tell you.'

'Vera, stop,' I said. The world felt suddenly shaky, like a tower of blocks – pull the wrong one, and it all comes tumbling down. *Jenga!*

I could feel Sam somewhere nearby, just waiting for this moment, when all our defenses were down, to finish us off.

Vera took a gulp of wine. 'I'm not stupid, I know the truth,' she said. My heart beat faster as the corner of her mouth twisted into an awful smile. 'I know that you loved him, Lucy. You wanted him to be a bad guy, so you could have him.'

It was like my blood stopped pumping, like for a moment I was nothing more than a corpse. And in that moment, all I wanted to do was rewind and undo what she'd said. I knew I shouldn't be so surprised. Even if she didn't know what had really happened between John and me that night, she could read me like a book. She'd probably seen my crush from the beginning. But now, now it was out in the open between us, and I knew we could never get back to the way we were. Not when everything that had been brewing between us had boiled over, scalding us.

'Vera,' I said again, begging. 'Don't say that.'

'Why not?' she snapped. 'You had a crush on him – like so many people did – but you didn't actually care. Because if you had, you wouldn't give up on him so easily now. You wouldn't believe every goddamn word everyone says.'

'We need to get out of here,' I said. 'Let's just go home. Please.'

'You wanna go?' she said. 'Fucking go.'

'I can't leave without you,' I said.

'Well, sorry. Maybe I don't want to be around someone who believes what you do about my husband. I expected better of you, Lucy.'

Heart racing, I turned on my heel, rushing from the room, setting my glass, still half-full, on the edge of the pool table, pushing past the people, past the conversations, past all of it.

I didn't even stop to grab my coat. Instead, I rushed out of the bar, into the open air.

There he was. Sam, smoking a cigarette.

He'd been waiting, waiting to get me alone. To pounce. 'What's got you so scared?' Sam asked, his voice menacing.

'Leave me alone,' I said, voice half a scream.

I walked, briskly as I could, around him, tripping over a bit of gravel, steadying myself.

I reached Vera's car and felt desperately for her keys in my pocket as, out of the corner of my eye, I saw Sam walking toward me.

It took three tries to get the key into the lock, it was so dark. I got in, pulling the door shut before he could come any closer. I spotted something white on the cuff of my sweater. It had begun to snow.

Inside, the car smelled stale. I shoved the key in the ignition, twisted it, heart fluttering at the turn of the engine, the sound of the car coming to life. I fumbled until I found the headlights, didn't bother adjusting the mirrors, and backed out of the parking lot, blinding Sam.

I felt awful about taking her car, but I was too scared of what would happen if she tried to drive like this. She could call a cab, like she said. Or I could go back, get her later, once she'd calmed down, once the bar was getting ready to close.

Sam wouldn't attack her, not in front of everyone.

I blinked several times, trying to focus.

I made my way through town, past the shops, the restaurants, everything closed and dark. As I curved down the road, snow kissing the windshield, blinking every other second, I wished for New York City, for Brooklyn, for cabs and car services, for tall buildings, city lights, and people in the streets. I wished so badly I were anywhere but here.

I reached the turn for the road that would lead to mine. I was only a couple of miles from home, but the road wound mercilessly and I had to be extra careful in the snow. I could get home, call McKnight, beg him to arrest Sam, to somehow protect me. I blinked again, vision swimming. I realized I was crying.

I wound along the twisting road, and my phone dinged. It was Vera.

Damn it Lucy where did you go?

I watched as she kept typing, glancing quickly back at the road, then down again.

Your coat's here but you're not. I'm sorry. I didn't really mean it.

What the hell?

I shook my head, but before I could look up, I felt it. A shakiness beneath the tires, a rumbling that rocked everything.

I whipped my head up, but the road was no longer there.

I was speeding, careening, toward the woods. Toward the trees.

I slammed on the brakes, and there was an awful sound, an old man choking, and it was like time slowed down, crawling, struggling, dragging, as Vera's car began to spin.

Forty-Three

A beeping, persistent, like the sound of Davis's old alarm, the one I'd always been on him to change.

My eyes fluttered open, struggling to adjust.

The beeping continued, as my gaze locked on the ceiling. A grid, squares of drywall set apart with strips of plastic. I turned my head, and pain seared along the back of my neck, all the way down to my tailbone, as I did. The beeping was a monitor. Acid-green numbers. It took me a moment to realize it was my pulse, trudging along.

My god. What the fuck had happened?

I grabbed at my arm, where a needle was inserted, an IV drip. My pulse sped up, the beeping insistent. I twisted my neck back again, felt another rush of pain, hot and white.

The door opened, and a woman in kitten-printed scrubs walked in.

'Good to see you awake.'

I swallowed back the pain as I twisted my head around, following her movements. 'Where am I?'

'Kingston Hospital,' she said as she messed with the IV drip. 'How are you feeling?'

I blinked a few times. 'My neck,' I said, and she nodded, like I was a kid in kindergarten, sounding out a big word.

'You're a lucky woman, you know.'

The machine beeped even more quickly.

'Could have gotten hurt much worse. Far worse than you did.' She finished whatever she was doing with the drip and turned on her heel. 'Try to take it easy. Doctor will be in shortly.'

It came back in flashes as I scooted myself up, biting my cheeks as my neck lit on fire. Going to the bar with Vera. Sam there. The way Vera had almost dared me to leave her: *Fucking go.*

Then obeying her, abandoning her, Sam following me to the car as I did.

Then nothing. Nothing past that.

Only darkness, pervasive and black.

They fed me brothy soup and green Jell-O, and the doctor asked me questions, making sure my memory was intact, and explained that I'd been brought in the night before, just after midnight. I was out for nearly eighteen hours, and because I was unconscious for so long, they wanted to keep me for observation another night. She explained that I had no major injuries, besides contusions – a fancy word for bruises – on my collarbone and the back of my neck. She asked me about the other bruises on my neck, the ones that Davis had given me, but when I demurred, she didn't press it, only told me that for the most part I was okay. Vera's car, not so much.

It had veered off the road and into a tree, the front of it completely smashed. The memories of the crash came to me only in flashes. Snowfall and road and then nothing.

I worried about Dusty, but after a few phone calls made on my behalf, that was cleared up, too. My keys were luckily still in my purse, and Maggie had offered to watch him.

I spent the night flipping channels, numbing out, the IV drip removed, the Jell-O consumed. I watched the sort of TV I used to watch when I visited my parents over the holidays in college. Bad cable reruns. *Say Yes to the Dress. Real Housewives.* It was welcome, in its way. Lying in a hospital bed, nothing to do. My shattered phone now had a dead battery, too; they'd promised to dig me up a charger, but I was in no rush to get back to reality.

I was protected from Sam Alby, from Davis, from McKnight's accusations, from Vera's rightful anger, from everyone. Four white walls and my very own room – and nothing to worry about but bad reality TV.

It was a nice change, after worrying about everything for so long. It was nice, for once, to feel safe.

'You have a visitor,' the nurse said as she took away my cereal the next morning, a flavorless bran thing that looked far too much like Dusty's kibble for my liking.

I could barely manage a nod before I saw his face in the door.

McKnight raised his eyebrows. 'Up for company?'

My heartbeat quickened. Why had he come to the hospital? Did he finally have what he needed to arrest me? Was this it? Had he not taken what I'd said about Sam Alby seriously at all?

McKnight didn't wait for my answer. He took a seat next to my bed. 'I wanted to talk to you about what happened the night of your accident. I suppose I wanted to hear from you how everything went down.'

Went down.

My heart continued to race, but now for a different reason. Vera and I had had a fight, nothing more. What else had happened, after I left her? What if she hadn't found a cab after all? What if something horrible – god – why was he here? I hadn't even considered it, but now the thought slapped at me.

'Is Vera okay? Is she hurt?'

'Miss King,' he said, resting his hand on the bed rail. 'You can rest assured that Ms Abernathy is safe, but I still need to hear from you what happened. Fill in a few gaps for me.'

I didn't know what he was up to, what was going on, but at the same time, my body was tired, my neck ached. I didn't have any energy left to fight him. I wasn't sure it would be good for me if I did.

'What do you remember about the night of November ninth?' he asked.

I took a deep breath. That night had been terrible, but I hadn't done anything to make my situation with McKnight worse – I only had to tell the truth. 'Vera came over. I was really shaken up from what had happened the night before, and we were hanging out, having dinner, and then – then she wanted to go out.'

McKnight nodded. 'Go on.'

I swallowed. 'We got in her car and headed to Platform – the bar, you know. I really didn't want to go, because she'd told me Sam Alby was a regular there, but she said it was the only one open and she was tired of avoiding places due to the rumors. At the bar, she started ordering these extra-tall glasses of wine. I wasn't drinking much, but she was. It's like everything had finally gotten to her. She just wanted to forget it all.'

McKnight nodded.

'You know this?' I asked.

'Yes,' he said. 'Witnesses have confirmed that Ms Abernathy was inebriated. Including the woman who agreed to give her a ride home. A Woodstock resident, used to know Mr Nolan. They were the ones who found the car. Who found you.'

It hit me like a flash, the messages I'd received from her.

'*Vera* found me?'

'Wrapped around a tree,' he said. 'It's a miracle you came out as unscathed as you did.'

'I don't understand.'

McKnight pressed his palms to his knees. 'Just keep going. Please.'

'Sam Alby was there, and that made me nervous.'

'Did Mr Alby threaten you at all?'

'Not outright, no. But he could tell I was upset, and as I was leaving, he asked me what had me so scared. It freaked me out.'

'And why were you upset?'

I hesitated. How could I possibly explain to him that she'd broken my heart, saying what she had.

I know that you loved him, Lucy.

You wanted him to be a bad guy, so you could have him.

I expected better of you.

Just like my parents, Vera had seen right through me, seen all the most horrible parts of me. She was supposed to love me, but I had proven myself unlovable yet again.

'I really wanted to go home, but she was so drunk, she wouldn't agree to come with me. I just had to get out of there.'

McKnight tilted his head to the side. 'And why did you take Ms Abernathy's car? Why not call a cab?'

'I'd already taken her keys because she was drinking so much . . . I was worried that if I didn't use her car, she would.'

'Had *you* been drinking?' McKnight asked.

I shook my head vehemently. 'I mean, not really. Maybe one or two glasses total over the entire night.'

'Mr Alby said that he saw you stumble.'

Were they listening to him – taking him seriously – still? Maybe McKnight *was* here to arrest me, and this was just the next step in his plan . . .

'Miss King.'

'I wasn't intoxicated. I swear.'

McKnight raised his hand. 'Your hospital records confirm as much. But I want to know why you left, what had you so riled up that you had to go, right then. Without your coat, even. Or telling Ms Abernathy you'd gone.'

'I don't know,' I said. 'I wasn't thinking straight. I was scared.'

'Scared of?'

I blinked slowly. 'Of everything.'

McKnight made a couple of notes on his notepad, then sat up straighter in his chair. 'Miss King, there have been some developments in Mr Nolan's case.'

His words hung in the air as the blood drained from my face.

I imagined him pulling out his cuffs, arresting me right there. Reading me my Miranda rights while fastening me to this awful metal bed. Never seeing my sweet Dusty again . . .

When I didn't say anything, he shifted his weight. 'After you left, things escalated. Ms Abernathy was very concerned. She became quite agitated. At some point, and the details are a little shaky on this, bar witnesses and all, Mr Alby stepped in, told her, in his own creative language, to calm down. She didn't take to that, being worried about you and all, and he became . . . well, after saying that Mr Nolan got what was coming to him, Mr Alby threw a glass, missing Ms Abernathy's head by just a few inches. The bartender called it in, but Ms Abernathy didn't wait to file any sort of police report. Once she realized her car was gone, she insisted someone drive her home, which, I suppose, is very, very lucky. When they saw you, they called nine-one-one, and you can thank them for the fact that you're here, not frozen on the side of the road.'

I bit my lip, shame washing over me. I'd almost fucked it up, beyond fixing. I could have died.

'We held Mr Alby overnight and formally charged him in Mr Nolan's murder yesterday morning. His alibi had actually fallen apart a couple of days ago – he said he was at the bar all night, and though several of his friends confirmed his story, the bar receipts did not – and some details came to light, ones from another state, about a violent altercation with his first wife, ones we weren't aware of before. Not to mention, my team was able to track down the IP address on that text you forwarded to me. It was sent from a computer in Mr Alby's house. We're still waiting on the analysis from that note you provided, but DNA did come back on the notes that had been left in Mr Nolan and Ms Abernathy's mailbox, and we were able to match the saliva on the envelope to Mr Alby. Altogether, we felt we had enough to get the ball rolling. Mrs Alby –'

'Mrs Alby?'

McKnight nodded. 'Yes, or I suppose Ms Moon, since she uses her maiden name for her business. Anyway, she confirmed that she had a copy of the key to your place – Mr Alby could have easily gotten access. It's circumstantial, but it's a start. We're still looking for the murder weapon. I believe his motive is obvious.'

I stared at him, jaw agape, my heartbeat slowing. I could hardly believe it.

This was it. They'd actually gotten their heads out of their asses and done their jobs.

McKnight raised an eyebrow. 'What is it?'

'I'm sorry,' I said. 'I just didn't think you were taking anything I said seriously.'

'Don't look so shocked, Miss King. I told you from the very beginning I was. I might not be a big-city detective, but I'm no hack, either. There were reasons we held out on arresting you. We had other irons in the fire, always.'

A silence hung between us, broken only by shuffling in the hallway, the clatter of rolling carts – hospital sounds.

He stood. 'Your DNA came back this morning on that set of underwear, by the way. Is there anything, anything at all, that you feel the need to tell me? About the day Mr Nolan went missing –

about your relationship with him? Or about your ex, who you say broke into your house? The truth is for the good of all of us, Miss King.'

McKnight stared, and for a second, I swore he thought he'd finally cracked me, that, perhaps, coming so close to death had opened me right up. But he was wrong about the truth – it wasn't for the good of all of us, not in the slightest. The only people who believed that were motherfucking choirboys.

I held his gaze. 'I've already told you everything I know.'

Vera was in the waiting room when they released me that day, wearing a black sweater and black leggings, hair secured away from her face haphazardly. She pulled me into a hug. 'Thank god,' she said. 'Let's get you home.'

We rode in John's truck, her beautiful Mercedes smashed beyond repair. 'I'm sorry about your car,' I said as she took the exit for the highway that went to Woodstock. 'I know you loved it.'

'Stop, Lucy,' she said. 'It's only a goddamn car. I'm just glad' – her voice broke – 'I'm glad you're okay. After your parents' accident – god – I can't bear to think what would have happened if I hadn't found you.' She sped up, the truck's engine revving beneath the weight of her foot. 'I'm the one who should be apologizing, anyway. I was drunk, I was being stupid, lashing out at you even though you didn't deserve it; I'm embarrassed at everything that happened that night. I should have agreed to go home when you wanted to. I was in shock from what you said about John. I'd never heard that, and I wasn't in a place to take it in. I still don't believe that about him, but in the moment, hearing you say it, knowing that even a part of you believed it when you've been the only one through all of this who seemed to care about us, it was too awful. I like to act like I don't care about what anyone thinks, but I do, especially you. If things had been worse, I don't know how I'd have been able to live with myself.'

'They weren't, though,' I said.

Vera's voice cracked again. 'You're all I have left, Lucy.'

'You too,' I said. And I meant it.

Forty-Four

Back at my house, Vera got me settled, made sure the heat was on, the milk in my fridge was still good, before leaving me alone. I went straight to bed, though I knew I needed to get Dusty, but I hardly had the energy to move; I was exhausted from two nights in a hospital, from the accident, from the pain still searing my neck.

My phone was finally charging properly – the hospital chargers had been shit – and I allowed myself one check before attempting to sleep. On Instagram, I found Davis's page. There it was, another photo. Him in Brooklyn. He'd posted one yesterday – as well as the day before – after more than two months of silence on the platform.

He's finally given up, I told myself again. *You're okay.*

Still, I slept fitfully. Between dreams I couldn't quite remember but that were unsettling all the same, my mind turned to the photos of John, the note he'd left me, the scarf of my mother's. Why had Sam taken them, and what did he plan to do with them? *Could* he do anything, now that he'd been arrested? Was I, for once, actually safe?

Around two, a knock on the door jostled me out of sleep. Through the window, I saw Maggie, and at her feet –

'Dusty,' I called as I whipped the door open.

He bounded toward me, his leash trailing against the floor, jumping onto my knees and covering my face with kisses. He was so warm, so fuzzy, he reminded me that not everything in the world was bad. I scooped him into my arms and stood. 'Thank you so much for taking care of him. You want to come in?'

Maggie nodded. 'Only if you don't mind.'

I made her tea as Dusty circled my feet, begging for more scratches. When it was done, I set the cups on the coffee table, and Dusty hopped into my lap.

'Was he good, I hope?'

She smiled crookedly. 'He's a quick learner,' she said. 'And I've always been good with dogs.'

'I'm sure.'

I sipped my tea the liquid warm, bolstering.

'Are you in pain?' Maggie asked. 'My daughter – she was actually in a bad accident a few years ago.'

'Oh god,' I said. 'Really? And after your husband, too. I'm so sorry.'

Maggie shook her head. 'I didn't mean it like that. She's okay now. It just took a lot of rehabilitation and physical therapy to manage the pain. She lives in L.A. with her husband. She's your age, actually, or maybe a little older. I don't see her as much as I'd like, but who does, when we all live so far apart?'

I smiled. 'I'm glad you have her. And my pain isn't too bad,' I said. 'It's manageable, at least. I have a prescription for some hard-core painkillers if I really need them, but I'm trying to hold off.'

Maggie's eyes flitted around the room. She wanted to talk about it, only didn't know how.

'You heard what happened?' I asked.

'Well . . .'

'It's okay,' I said. 'I figured you had. About Sam.'

'I'm glad he's caught,' she said. 'No one deserves to be murdered, no matter what they've done.'

'I'm glad, too.'

Maggie dug deep in her pocket. 'By the way,' she said, tossing a silver key onto the table between us. 'I was organizing, and I found this.'

I reached for it, fingering the edges of the metal.

'It's the old spare key I had,' she said. 'Rachel gave it to me when she lived here.'

'Oh,' I said, pausing. 'I don't think it works anymore. Ms Moon' – I raised my eyebrows – 'or Mrs Alby, I guess, said the locks were changed when Rachel moved.'

'Yes, I'm sure they were,' Maggie said matter-of-factly. 'You can get rid of it if you want, but I felt weird having it. I used to water her plants and things when Vera wasn't able to.'

'Vera had a key, too?' I don't know why I hadn't thought of it before, that Rachel's neighbors might have a spare. Ellie had had one of mine in Brooklyn. So did the lady upstairs, just in case Davis or I ever got locked out.

Maggie folded her hands in her lap. 'Oh, of course Vera had a spare key, same as me. Those two were thick as thieves, popping back and forth between each other's places constantly – until things went sour.'

Claire was pregnant.

'Right,' I said. 'Because of everything with Claire.'

'Yes,' Maggie said. 'It's a shame how Vera handled everything. She took it all out on Rachel, who didn't deserve it. It's not Rachel's fault John got the girl pregnant.'

'You knew about that?' I asked, my cup nearly slipping from my hand.

'Course I did. Rachel told me as soon as she found out. She was torn up about it, didn't know what to do, what to tell Vera.'

I raised the cup to my lips, took another sip of tea. 'I wish Rachel had told Vera the truth about Claire being pregnant. Then maybe Vera wouldn't have cut Rachel out like she did. I know Rachel didn't want to hurt her, but –'

Maggie's eyebrows furrowed. 'Vera knew Claire was pregnant.'

I froze, the cup hovering in front of my face. I set it down, trying to stop my hands from shaking. 'What are you talking about? Vera only just found out, when I told her.'

'No,' Maggie said. 'That's not true.'

Heat rose to my face. 'How do you know?'

Her eyes fixed on her teacup, fingers tracing the edge, before catching mine.

'When Rachel refused to tell her, I told Vera myself.'

Forty-Five

Why would Vera lie?

I was still trying to make sense of it when Maggie left my cottage a few minutes later.

Vera had been so shaken when I'd told her Claire was pregnant, so much so that it had sent her into a spiral, careening toward that awful night.

I hadn't imagined it – Vera had told me, only this morning, that it had been a shock.

What's more, she'd told me she'd *never* doubted John's fidelity. She'd judged me when I dared to doubt him. When I had confessed to her about John waking up in my bed, her response hadn't been what I'd expected at all. She'd made it sound like their marriage wasn't perfect, but it was open and honest, strong in its way. Above the fray, above these rumors.

Her words flashed at me, sending a chill down my spine.

If they paint me as this woman scorned, that's motive, Lucy.

It's always the wife, that's what I'd told her, only I'd never truly considered it myself – not beyond a passing thought.

She was Vera, my Vera. She wasn't perfect, but she was good. She wasn't capable of something like this. She loved him.

Only . . .

Vera was the one who knew exactly where John would be, who

had never given a real explanation as to *why* she went over to the cabin the morning she found him. According to our plan, *he* was supposed to contact us. He was supposed to be deep into the Adirondacks by then.

Vera was the one who'd called me stupid when I suggested we tell the police the truth about our plan.

Vera had known that Claire was pregnant – or at least had known about the rumor – but had told me, point-blank, that she hadn't.

Looking back on that night, at the one-eighty she'd taken when I'd told her, it almost felt like she could have been overdoing it, hamming it up to show me just how shocked she was.

But Sam had been arrested. Sam's the one who did it.

Unless . . .

Unless Vera had been furious about John's infidelity, about the fact that he got a teenager pregnant. That was enough to send anyone over the edge.

Unless she'd capitalized on my neediness, my fear, to lure me into their plot. Made it look like John had disappeared and then killed him – then made it look like *I'd* killed him.

It would explain the theft of the photos of John, the note he'd left me. Another brick in the wall to prove to the police that I was obsessed with him, a jealous lover. All of this a tryst gone wrong.

No, Vera would never. She loved me, and I her.

You wanted him to be a bad guy, so you could have him.

Besides, it *had* to be Sam, because Sam had access to my key. Whoever had stolen the knife had had to have access to my place. There was no way around it.

It caught my eye then – the silver gleam of the spare key Maggie had brought over.

Of course Vera had a spare key, same as me.

It was nothing; it didn't even work. The locks had been changed. Everyone said so.

Still, I picked it up, felt its ridges, its peaks and valleys. Examining it closer, it didn't look all that different from the key I'd been using since I got here, but so many of them looked alike.

I closed my fist around it, feeling it in my hand.

There was no way. Vera was my friend. She was my family. She could never. She adored John. Loved him more than any of us.

But Davis had loved me, too, in his way. Sometimes love drove us to do the worst possible thing.

Sometimes loyalty went too far.

It couldn't hurt to check – could it? I walked to the front door, twisting the handle, stepping onto the porch. The cold snapped at me again, and I pulled the door slowly shut. Hands shaking, I slid the key Maggie had given me, the one Vera had a copy of, into the lock of the dead bolt. It sank in, but that didn't mean a thing. Most keys went into just about any lock. The trick was whether they turned.

Taking a deep breath, I tried to turn it.

Instant relief. It didn't budge.

Only there, a niggling in the back of my brain, a teensy objection.

Sometimes the lock was sticky. I knew this from turning it so many times myself.

I pulled the door closer to me, a matter of millimeters, but millimeters, I knew, could make a difference, and I attempted to turn the key again.

It was like my timeline split into before and after. Trust and deceit. Love and violence. Vera and a woman maybe I didn't know at all.

Because the key turned.

It worked.

Forty-Six

I was ready when I saw Vera pull out of her driveway and continue down the road, at the helm of her murdered husband's truck.

I headed for the farmhouse immediately – I didn't know where she was going, or how long she'd be gone – cutting across the frosted grass as soon as it came into view, making for the back door.

I'd seen Vera do it a couple of times when we'd had too much to drink and had locked ourselves out of the back. A multicolored ceramic owl perched along one of the flower beds. I knelt down and lifted it, praying she hadn't changed her hiding place. A glint of metal and a rush of relief. A key ring with two keys, marked clearly with circular tabs labeled in John's chicken scratch. One for the farmhouse. One for the cabin.

The key turned easily, and I stepped into her kitchen, quickly looking around. It was even more of a wreck than normal. Piles of dishes sat, unrinsed, in the sink. No fewer than three pots rested on the stove, old pasta and grime caked onto the bottoms. On the small kitchen island, a mostly drunk bottle of pinot noir sat next to dirty wineglasses and a thick stack of junk mail. I heard the creak of a floorboard, like someone was in the hallway, and my heart raced as I spun around, but no one was there. It was just the farmhouse, settling. Telling me it knew I was here even if she didn't.

My eyes darted around the room. At the tile, cracked in places. At the molding, beautiful but dusty. I had been here so many times, but never before had I been here like this, prying, chasing whatever secrets she was keeping from me.

Maybe she hadn't even held on to Rachel's spare key. Maybe this was all just a big misunderstanding.

The junk drawer was packed to the brim, still just as full as when John had rifled through it, looking for the baggie of weed, the first night I came over for dinner. I sank a hand into its midst – the police must have had a field day with all of this – take-out menus; loose screws and nails; batteries that had to be expired covered in dust; pamphlets for microwaves, toaster ovens, a rice cooker; papers that must have held significance at one time but surely didn't anymore. And keys, multiple sets of them, but none of them looked like mine.

I searched frantically, pushing papers aside, making a mess of it all but knowing she'd never be able to tell the difference, it was such a wreck already.

I was close to giving up – I'd looked through every drawer in the kitchen and had returned again to the cluttered junk drawer – when my hand came across it, nestled in the back among unused brackets for IKEA furniture.

A single key, silver, and the same shape as mine. With a tab on it, labeled by John. *RACHEL*.

I slipped it into my pocket, but it wasn't enough. It could just be a coincidence. I needed something more.

I hunted for Vera's laptop, an old MacBook Air she used mainly for email that she kept tucked away next to her art books on the bottom shelf of the coffee table in the living room.

When I didn't find it there, I checked everywhere: her bedroom, littered with dirty clothes, unwashed sheets; the office, packed with books but free of loose papers; even the spare bed-room, filled with John's things. It was only when I was back down-stairs that I realized it: The police had taken my laptop. They might have taken hers as well.

I had to focus. Who knew how much time I had? I walked toward the armoire, opening its drawers, where she'd once tucked away those notes from Sam, that photo of her, John, and Rachel.

In the top drawer, I found it, the picture frame I'd nearly sat on that night. I grabbed the velvet backing and flipped it over.

Breath caught in my throat. The photo was marked, thick Sharpie over Rachel's face, turning Vera's once friend into nothing more than a black hole, like she'd never even existed.

I took a few steps back, my heart racing. This didn't mean anything. She didn't like Rachel; I knew that.

I put the frame away and returned to the kitchen, gazing again at the junk drawer, the key that had been stored there, ready to use whenever she wanted.

I imagined Vera, manic, blacking out Rachel's face. The anger I'd seen at Platform only a few nights ago. What if that was only the tip of the iceberg?

What if Vera hated Rachel not because she didn't believe John, but because she was the one who exposed to her who her husband really was?

What if she hated John even more?

Frantically, I began searching through her mail, picking through West Elm catalogs and credit card offers, a padded yellow envelope, until two words caught my eye. 'Mass Mutual.'

A life insurance company. A letter addressed to Vera Abernathy.

With shaking fingers, I tore it open: A collection of papers, seven or eight of them. Near the top, it read, in formal, bureau-cratic type:

This letter is to inform you that your claim is under
review.

I flipped more pages, hungry for details. On the last page, I
found it, the information about the policy. It was, indeed, a life
insurance policy, taken out on John, to the tune of three million
dollars. It was purchased six months ago, right around when the
rumors had started, and it was a large policy – unusually so.
Could this have just been one more step in her plan?

Or was I being paranoid? They were married – and in bad fi-
nancial straits. Was it so crazy she'd take out a policy on him? But
why six months ago, exactly? And why for so much?

I pushed the papers away, as if they were scalding – a burning
truth I'd never, ever wanted to uncover – but as I shoved them, a
chain reaction: The stack of junk mail and catalogs struck the
bottle of pinot noir. It clattered against the island, then rolled
onto the floor, taking a wineglass with it, crashing to the ground,
making me jump.

The bottle didn't break, but the glass did, sending shards all
over the floor, the wine surrounding it like a bloodstain.

I grabbed the Mass Mutual letter, folded it tightly, and shoved
it into my pocket. I lunged for the wine bottle next, setting it back
on the island where it had been.

I grabbed a wad of paper towels, tossing them onto the floor,
then used another wad to sop up the mess on the island.

I froze.

The padded yellow envelope, the one that had been on the bottom of the stack of mail. It was unsealed. Something was peeking
out from it.

Something familiar.

That marred corner of silk I knew so well. My mother's scarf.

There was a grumble of gravel and the truck's growling engine, a sound I would always associate with John, with a man I thought I'd known much better than I had. Fuck.

I had only moments before Vera returned, before she walked in on me in her kitchen, before she knew exactly how much I knew.

Why did she have my scarf?

With quivering fingers, I tugged at the piece of fabric, extracting it from the envelope.

The engine of the truck cut off. Only a few more seconds and she'd be walking in, catching me.

As I pulled it out farther, the scarf unfurled, and there was a sudden clatter, unexpected, as stainless steel and red Lucite smashed against ceramic tile.

Then, my heartbeat so loud, banging against my ribs.

The knife I'd been missing was caked with blood.

The knife I'd been missing had been wrapped up in my mother's scarf and stored in an envelope, ready to send to the police, ready to make my guilt complete.

Vera had used her key to get into my cottage. Vera had taken my knife. Vera had used it.

My stomach ached, and my chest seemed to constrict; I gasped for air, clawing at my throat with both hands. Only, Davis wasn't holding me down now – she was.

Vera, the woman I'd thought would take care of me. The woman I'd thought was my friend. She'd killed her own husband. She had killed John. She had put everything in motion to try to make me go down for it.

Me, her friend. Me, the woman she'd promised to protect. Whom she'd said she loved.

Then, the sound of the key turning in the lock, of Vera's steps echoing across the hardwood floors. Desperate to protect myself, I grabbed the wine bottle, still sitting on the island, and held it tightly as her face appeared, her expression riveted in shock, in the doorway of her kitchen.

Forty-Seven

Lucy?' Vera said. 'What are you . . . what are you doing in my house?'

'Don't play dumb,' I said, gripping the bottle tighter. 'I know the truth.'

Vera's eyes flitted to the bottle in my hand, then back up to me. 'What are you talking about?'

'This,' I snapped, pointing to the knife on the ground. 'You had this the whole time.'

Her eyes caught the knife, and she drew in a quick breath. 'Lucy, I –' she said. 'I'm not going to do anything with that.'

'Stop lying,' I said. I stared at this woman, this maniac. She was a sociopath, had to be. A black widow who'd spun a web that was so many steps ahead of anything John and I could even think of that we hadn't stood a chance. 'Just stop lying for one single fucking second. I'm not as stupid as you think I am.'

'I'm not,' she said. 'Just calm down. Sam's been arrested – this is all over.'

'How did you pull it off?' I asked, my voice aching with fear, with regret. 'Grab it when you found us in bed together? Hold on to it until you could use it?'

Vera shook her head, but my words were spilling freely now, unrestricted. 'Or did you get it even before that? One of the first

311

nights you came over? That's why you were so eager to be friends with me from the start, right? You needed someone to pin it on. You needed me. How could you?' I asked, my voice cracking. 'How *could* you?' My heart raced, and my hands were sweating, and yet the tears came anyway, the hurt pushing its way through all the fear and the horror.

I had loved her, in my way. I had loved her, and all along she'd been . . . It was too awful to think.

'It's not like that,' Vera said, eyes flashing to the bottle, still held tight in my hand. She pointed to the knife, her hand shaking. 'Please, just calm down, you're not thinking straight. Sam's in jail. I don't think it was you. I know you cared about him, like I did –'

'Bullshit,' I screamed. 'You're a fucking liar, and you're still pretending to be on my side! You had a key to my place. You took out a three-million-dollar life insurance policy on John. You told me John never cheated on you, but you knew the whole time, you even knew Claire was pregnant – you knew he spent the night with me! You lie, lie, lie, and then you cut people out of your life when they call you on it, when they try to tell you the truth. You made me think I was going crazy. You've been lying to me from the beginning.'

Vera's expression faltered then, her lips pressing together, her eyes narrowing. 'Did you?' she asked weakly. 'Did you *really* do it?'

'Sleep with him? Of course not. We kissed – that was all – but it was still enough for you. Enough to blame me for everything. Enough to excuse it all.'

Her eyes widened, her face reddening. 'You kissed John?'

'Don't pretend like you didn't know,' I said.

'You acted like my friend, and you . . . you kissed my husband?' Her face seethed with rage. 'You whore.'

'This is all an act,' I said. 'You knew. You –'

'First night I leave you two alone,' she said, her words coming fast, furious. 'Seriously? You pretended like you needed a family, like we would be best friends, but you never cared about me, did you? You never cared about us.' Her voice became shrill as she mocked me. '"*Please don't leave me, I don't know what to do here without you, I'm so scared.*" It was a lie, wasn't it, just like she said? The minute you get the chance, you betray me. The minute you get a moment alone with him, you try to fuck my husband!'

It all happened so fast.

My breathing quickened and I felt hot all over, all the way up to my cheeks. Rage, rage for Vera, for John, for Davis, for Ellie, for everyone who had ever betrayed me, for my parents, for abandoning me when I needed them most. Leaving me raw and unarmed, ready to be taken advantage of by anyone and everyone. Rage. Rage that had to come out. She'd hurt me, just like they all had. And I always fucking took it.

'You killed him!' I rushed at her, lifting the bottle over my head. As I brought it down, I caught the explosion of fear in her eyes, just before it connected with her cheek. She stumbled, reeling, her arms reaching out for something to hold on to, but she couldn't catch her balance – she fell to the floor, shrieking as her face hit the tile.

She turned and tried to push herself up, but already, I was on top of her, the shards of glass digging through my jeans into my knees. There was glass on the side of her face. The shock hadn't left her eyes. I hardly knew what I was doing.

'You killed him and you're going to send the police that knife. You're going to frame me, your best friend. You won't get away with it.' My face only was inches from hers.

Vera's breath came in rasps, making a clicking sound in her lungs. From somewhere beneath her, the blood had already begun to leak, sticky, crimson, against the white tile of her kitchen. 'Please,' she begged. 'Please, just stop.' Her eyes flashed with anger. 'And I won't tell anyone what you've done.'

'What *I've* done?' I asked, disbelief swimming within me as I grabbed her by the shoulders. For a second, I could see it in her eyes – she thought I was pulling her up, she thought I was still acting the friend. That I could just let this go – the murder, her deceit – because I was sick with shame over kissing him.

'What about what *you've* done?' Before I could stop myself, I slammed her shoulders against the tile with all my might, and her head snapped back, thunking against the floor.

Blood began to pool under her head. Darker, thicker, and faster than I'd expected.

Her eyes were shut. She probably had a concussion.

I scrambled up, staring at her. She wasn't moving.

'Vera?' I said. 'Vera!'

What had I done? What the fuck had I done?

'Vera!' I said again, desperate now. I knelt, tugging at her shoulders, already heavy.

As I turned her, I saw it. A shard of glass, a big one, stuck in the back of her neck. Still there. I dropped her; stepped back, my heart racing, my breaths coming frantically.

Blood was everywhere. Spilling out of her, all over the tile.

Had I killed her? Jesus Christ, had I fucking killed her?

'Vera!'

No answer. She was gone.

I shook my head, trying to make sense of what had just happened, tears welling in my eyes. Vera was my friend, my last friend left on this earth, and now she was dead.

I had killed her.

It was self-defense, I told myself, already testing the sound of it in my head.

She killed him, and she would have killed me next, and it was self-defense.

It was self-defense it was self-defense it was self-defense.

I paused, frozen, as it all clicked into place.

It couldn't be self-defense, I realized – I didn't have a single bruise.

The wine bottle stared at me from the tile, an answer.

Hands shaking, I grabbed it. I stood up straight, looked in the reflection of the door to the backyard, and bit my lip. I'd been hurt before. I could hurt again.

I screamed one more time as the bottle connected with the side of my face. The pain exploded instantly, radiating down, and immediately, I struck again.

Exactly where I'd been struck before.

Forty-Eight

I shivered, pulling on a thicker sweater as I looked out the window.

It was snowing – fifth day in a row – nearly a foot accumulated now. Much more, and I'd need to dig out my car. It was almost three. I'd told Rachel I'd come over this afternoon, but I wanted to go by the real estate office, drop off my rent, buy myself another month of indecision until I could make the right move, decide where to go next.

It had been a week since Vera died. One week that had passed in a blur of grief and heartache and procedure. And snow. Lots and lots of snow.

I'd called 911 as soon as I'd beaten myself up. The ambulance had come for her quickly, and, not long after, McKnight. He'd taken me immediately to the station, where I'd made a full statement and answered every question they had. Calm as I could bear, I told him about the discovery that Vera had a spare key to my house. That I believed it may have been her who put that note in my house, trying to point me toward Sam Alby. I explained, lying as little as I could, that I'd been visiting Vera when I discovered the seven-figure insurance policy. I became alarmed, knocking over a half-full wine bottle and a glass in the process. As I was cleaning it up, I'd spotted the package with my things in it:

my knife, covered in blood, wrapped in my scarf. Vera walked in then, realized I knew, and attacked me, grabbing the bottle and socking me across the face with it. I hit her back, attempting to push her off me, and she fell backward, her head smashing into the tile, a shard of glass in her neck. Self-defense.

Then, in an attempt to get him to really believe me, I finally told him about our plan. That John had wanted to disappear, and Vera had asked for my help. That that's why I'd told him I'd seen John fall. I was only trying to help my new friends get out of trouble. I never once thought that the entire time, Vera was working to frame me. I explained to McKnight that the murder weapon was one of my knives, one I'd noticed missing days before and had even texted Vera about. I told him that, without a doubt, my DNA and prints would be on it, but swore up and down I'd never seen it covered in blood until it tumbled out of my mother's scarf.

They held me overnight, my cheek aching, my bones heavy as I sat in the cell, wondering if I had really fucked it up this time. I used my call to phone Maggie, asked her to take care of Dusty. Praying I would get to see him again soon.

And after twenty-four hours, my prayer had come true. After twenty-four hours, they released me.

Two days ago, McKnight had, once again, come by my cottage. He returned the items they'd taken from my house, my laptop included. Then he told me that after receiving confirmation from Mass Mutual that Vera had tried to cash in an extremely large insurance policy on John, after the knife had come back with my prints, as well as hers, after they'd discovered some disturbing journal entries on Vera's laptop dating from after she heard about the rumors, they'd released Sam Alby and charged Vera, posthumously, with John's death.

They wouldn't be pressing charges against me – for the plot, or for the altercation with Vera. My story had checked out, consistent with Vera's autopsy and the forensics on the knife, and

Maggie had even spoken to McKnight on my behalf, telling him that Vera had been lashing out, threatening me, ever since John died. It wasn't exactly true, but he didn't have to know that; I had a feeling that Maggie was only protecting me from people she thought could hurt me, just like she would her own daughter.

Even so, McKnight had looked at me as if I were a teenager caught in the middle of a graduation prank gone wrong. 'Next time someone tries to involve you in something illegal like this, run. You might not find yourself so lucky again.'

All week, while the police processed the scene of our altercation, I'd been nervous, waiting for them to find the note John had left me, for Rachel's photos of him to turn up. Vera had taken them – obviously – but I didn't know what she'd done with them. Yet McKnight didn't mention them. It seemed, against all odds, that I was safe.

I walked to the bathroom and examined my bruise in the mirror. It was yellowing already, would begin to fade soon. I dabbed on a bit of Dermablend, then grabbed my purse and leashed up Dusty. When Rachel had called yesterday, inviting me and Dusty over for an afternoon glass of wine, I'd accepted without hesitation. I had no one left, and I was eager for company, eager to speak to someone who'd known Vera and John, who was, in some way, a witness to all this.

Once I was bundled up and we were outside, Dusty pulled me toward the mailbox, one of his favorite places to pee. The box was overflowing – I'd been bad about checking since Vera's death. As Dusty lifted his leg, marking the post, I grabbed the mess of mail, walked to my car, and tossed it on the passenger seat.

Secured in his crate, Dusty didn't whine quite so much as we wound toward town – he was getting used to the car, which was good. Though I hadn't figured out exactly what my next step was – go to L.A., where I still had an old friend from college, even though I hadn't talked to her in years; head back to Brooklyn, where it would be easy for me to get work, hoping and praying that Davis was finally done with me; or simply find somewhere new on the map – there would be plenty of driving ahead of us.

As I turned left, toward downtown Woodstock, I could hardly believe I was staying another month. Rachel had been the one to suggest it, when she'd called me yesterday to invite me over and I'd opened up about the fact that I didn't know what to do – where to go next. *Just give yourself time,* she'd said. *It's easier to leave than it is to come back.*

Maybe she was right – or maybe I was just afraid to go, leave Vera and John, whom I'd been so wrong about but had loved all the same, completely behind.

As I drove, I tried to focus on the afternoon sunshine, glistening against the snow, but all I could see was her face. Vera lived in my mind now. That shard of glass in the back of her neck. Red blood pooling on white tile. The way I'd broken her for good.

She was a monster, I told myself. Had told myself over and over again, every waking moment for the past week. She was a monster who had deserved to die – who'd murdered her own husband.

I hadn't killed an innocent woman. I'd killed a killer.

Dusty whined, as if sensing my misery.

I'd killed a killer, I told myself again. Some days, it was the only thought that kept me going, kept me from returning to the hike, jumping off the cliff myself, and letting the water break me, too.

Forty-Nine

I need to talk to you.'

I jumped, banging my head on the frame of the car, which I'd parked in front of Schoolhouse before dropping off my rent check. Quickly, I secured Dusty back into his crate, then turned to see Claire, her cheeks red from the cold, wearing no more than a light sweater, her half apron from the restaurant, and jeans. 'What are you doing out here?' I asked. 'You're bound to freeze.'

'I know,' she said, blinking fast. 'I'm sorry, just – can we talk? Please?'

'Of course, but I've got him.' I motioned to Dusty, who pawed at the door of his prison.

Claire smiled, briefly, at my dog. 'It's fine. It will only take a minute.' Her head swiveled up the block and back. 'Can we, uh, get in your car?'

I walked around to the driver's side and tossed my junk mail to the back so Claire would have a place to sit. I turned the ignition, getting the heat cranking. Woodstock's hippie radio station blared – with a flick, I shut it off.

'I won't keep you long,' Claire said as she shut the door behind her. 'I'm supposed to be working, anyway. I saw you, and I told them I needed five . . .' She bit her lip, then shoved her hands into the pockets of her apron. She blinked slowly.

'What is it?'

Her eyes locked ahead, as if there were an answer in my frost-kissed windshield. 'I never meant it to turn out like this,' she said. 'I should have . . . I should have . . .' she stammered.

'Claire,' I said, reaching a hand across the console, taking hers in mine. She seemed more a child than ever. Desperate. Scared. 'What is it?' I asked again. 'Whatever it is, you can tell me.'

'Vera.' Her eyes welled with tears. 'If she had known the truth . . .'

'Claire,' I said, squeezing her hand in mine as I tried to keep my voice calm. 'I believe Vera *did* know the truth.'

She pulled her hand back, and her eyes flashed at me – a brief spot of rage – but just as quickly, the look slipped away with a shake of her head. 'No. I'm saying that I *know* she didn't. She thought that John and I were, that we . . .'

I narrowed my eyes. 'Weren't you?'

'No. We were just friends.' She huffed. 'I know you're not supposed to be friends with someone that much older, but that's how it was. My dad can be a dick sometimes, and John' – she turned, her eyes catching mine – 'he would listen. Sometimes I'd stay after class for an hour just *talking* to him.'

It had taken me so long to believe the worst of John, but over the past week, the wool had finally fallen from my eyes. Vera and John weren't the people I had thought they were. They never had been. 'You don't have to protect him, Claire. It's okay. I know you were . . . I know you were pregnant.'

Tears spilled from her eyes, and I reached out to hug her, but she shook me off. 'You don't *understand*. I found out I was pregnant last spring, but we never – I never even thought of – god, he's so *old*. It was this guy I met at a party in Poughkeepsie. I didn't even know his last name. I was too afraid to tell my parents, and I didn't have the money.'

I jolted, and even Dusty, sensing my shock, began to paw at his crate again.

'What are you saying?' I asked.

'I'm saying it *wasn't* John's. That's gross.'

It was the way she said it, that teenage way of cutting straight to the point, not holding back.

'You swear?' I asked. 'You don't have to –'

'I swear,' Claire said. 'John tried to get me to talk to my parents and my friends, but he didn't get it. It was so embarrassing. The guy said he was going to call me, and he never did. I didn't even have his number to call him and tell him what happened. I'd put mine in his phone, and he never texted after – anything. And we used protection – I'm not stupid – I just, something must have gone wrong.' She took a deep breath. 'I didn't have the money, and so John paid for it, and he drove me to the clinic the day I had to go. He said, he said that someone had come to him in trouble before, and he hadn't helped her. He said he wanted to help me.'

Like a shot to the heart, I remembered. John had felt guilty about pressuring Vera to continue the pregnancy.

I should have driven Vera to the clinic, held her hand, respected what she wanted.

My god, I thought. John had been good after all. He wasn't perfect, he never should have kissed me, but he had been trying to do the right thing. He hadn't deserved to die. *Fuck*. He'd wanted to help her, this girl who looked up to him as an artist and pseudo-father figure, nothing else. He'd been stupid enough to think that people would understand.

If the truth had only come out – god, it was too awful to think. None of this would have happened. No threats from Sam Alby. No impending lawsuit. No hike, no lies to the police. Vera would never have killed him – she loved him, in her twisted way – and more than that, I would never have had to do what I did.

I would never have had to kill her. To take the life of my best friend.

My heart ached at all that had been lost, all for nothing.

'My dad found out,' Claire went on. 'I don't know if he snooped on me or if he followed us or what, but he went nuts. He said this was proof, that he had never trusted John, had always been against the classes, and it . . . it all just kind of unraveled from there. It's not that I didn't deny it to my dad – I did. We fought about it all the time, especially after he started talking about a lawsuit, but he kept demanding that I prove it wasn't true. And it was just so humiliating to tell my dad it had been some random guy, some guy who hadn't even called. I thought if I kept saying it wasn't John, they'd eventually believe me. I kept telling myself it was none of their business, and I still don't think it was, but if I could have told everyone the truth – point-blank – then maybe my dad wouldn't have done what he did, and maybe Vera wouldn't have been so mad at John.' Her words choked in her throat. 'Maybe John would still be alive . . . maybe she wouldn't have attacked you. God, maybe she'd be alive, too.'

Another tear slipped down her cheek, black with mascara and eyeliner, forming a squiggly line that seemed to split her face in two.

She was right. If she had only been able to tell everyone the truth, none of this would have happened. But how could I expect that of a child? Someone who surely knew what sort of slut-shaming would await her if she did? We were virgins or whores, the world so ready to put us into boxes, to decide what kind of girls or women we were. I knew this well. Now she did, too.

My eyes caught hers, and it was so strong, the desire to save her – from this anger, this rage, this hate, from all the things that destroyed us, turned us into monsters, salivating for vengeance.

'Claire,' I said, forcing a bit of calm into my voice, speaking to her like my mother had spoken to me, early on, when my anger sometimes got the best of me. 'Claire, this isn't your fault. None of this is your fault.'

She looked down, shaking her head.

'There's never a reason for anyone to kill anyone else,' I said. 'Vera included. You did nothing wrong. It's the rest of us – the adults – who didn't take care of you.'

Claire looked up at me, blinking through tear-soaked lashes. 'I should have told Vera myself.'

'No,' I said. 'Vera was determined to do what Vera was going to do. You couldn't have done anything to stop this. Some people are so angry, they have to destroy the people they love.'

'I never meant to hurt anyone,' she said earnestly. 'I sent you that text, you know. "The truth shall set you free." I know it's cheesy, but I needed to make a Gmail that wasn't in my name.'

Like that, a flash of recognition. Of course it was her. McKnight had said that the text was sent from Sam Alby's house.

'I felt so bad for you,' she went on. 'I knew you would never hurt him, and I felt like, because of what happened with me, you got mixed up in it.'

'Thank you, Claire,' I said. 'Thank you for telling me that. And thank you for telling me everything. I'm sorry you got so caught up in all this. I'm sorry about your dad, too.'

'Thanks for listening.' She paused, eyeing me. 'I know that . . . I know that you understand.'

I narrowed my eyes. 'Understand what?'

Her hand reached for the door but didn't open it – not yet. 'My dad, there was this one time he hit my mom – it was just once, but – you know, I heard what you said to your friend, that day in the restaurant. I'm sorry that happened to you. Was is that guy, the guy who came around asking about you?'

'Yes, it was. It's all over now, though. He's not going to hurt me again.'

'Good. Thank god.' She sighed. 'And is that why –?'

I nodded before she could finish.

'Well, I guess I should get back to work.'

'Thanks,' I said. 'I should get going, too.'

Claire leaned across the console and wrapped me in a hug. 'Thanks again for listening.' Then, with hands half shaking from all that she'd just told me, Claire opened the door and walked away.

As soon as she was gone, I took deep breaths – in and out – calming my furiously beating heart. I flicked the radio back on, and two more songs played before I felt okay to pull out of the parking spot and drive down the road.

As I made the turnoff to Rachel's place, my mind was still reeling. I couldn't believe it. After everything, this was the truth after all.

It began to snow again, and I parked in front her house, walked around the car, and opened the back door to let Dusty out of his crate.

But as I did, I stopped short. My mail was still there, and during the drive, it had separated, fanning out across the back seat.

There, in the midst of grocery store weeklies and the usual junk mail, was a sheet of white paper.

I leaned forward, Dusty whining, and plucked it from the array.

The words were printed in large, bold type.

THIS ISN'T OVER

Fifty

Get in here – it's freezing out there.'

I turned and, through lightly falling snowflakes, saw Rachel standing in her doorway, a smile on her face.

'Be right there,' I said. Mind spinning, I tucked the sheet of paper into my pocket, then let Dusty out of his crate.

He bounded up the driveway and straight into Rachel's arms.

As I walked toward her, I tried to make sense of the note in my pocket.

THIS ISN'T OVER

When was the last time I checked my mail? I tried to focus, to remember. Could this have been from Vera, trying to make me think it was from Sam, just like the other one?

Rachel turned, and I followed her inside.

'Everything okay?' she asked.

'Yes,' I said instinctively.

Still smiling, she let Dusty down, then wrapped me in a hug that felt suddenly too tight. She wore red lipstick and an eggplant wool dress, but there were bags beneath her eyes. She looked older, and her voice sounded almost robotic. 'I'm so glad you came over.'

'Me too,' I said as I sat down on her sofa, my voice cautious.

'Can I get you some wine?'

'Yes,' I said. Between what Claire had said and the note I'd just found, I needed something to take the edge off.

In minutes, she was back, two stemless glasses in her hands. 'I just got this good cabernet, and I've been meaning to open it.' I could hear it, more clearly now, in her voice, the difference. Her words weren't robotic, they were almost slurred, as if she'd been drinking even before I arrived. It hit me then, what exactly had changed – she was torn up about Vera. No matter what Vera had done, she'd still been Rachel's friend.

She handed me a glass, then situated herself on the Eames chair. Dusty hopped into her lap. 'To friendship,' she said, lifting her glass to mine.

'To friendship.'

We both drank, and my eyes flitted to her wall, seeking out the photo of Vera, but it was no longer there.

'Well,' Rachel asked. 'How have you been, all things considered?'

'Fine,' I managed. 'I mean, okay as I can be. You?'

She opened her mouth to speak, then closed it again.

Briefly, I wondered if I should tell her what Claire had just told me, but something stopped me. Rachel had lost her best friend because of a rumor, something that hadn't even been true. A story that had been so damaging, it had led Vera to kill her own husband. The irony was too cruel to share.

'You're staying another month?' Rachel asked.

'Yes, I just paid my rent today.'

Her hand sank into Dusty's fur, scratching him just where he liked. 'It's good, I think. So much has happened – it's a lot to think about, just up and moving in the midst of it all. You'll have to deal with our winter, though.'

'I can handle it,' I said. It was hard to imagine another month of sitting in my cottage, alone, but I didn't know where else to go. Perhaps the absence of Vera and John, the hole they'd left in this place, and in me, was tether enough for now.

'Do you miss her?' Rachel asked, her lips pressing together.

'Desperately,' I confessed. 'You?'

Rachel took another sip of wine – a gulp, almost – before answering. 'I've been missing her a long time. I don't think I'll ever stop, actually. It's just horrible, that it all had to happen like it did.'

For a moment, I wondered if Rachel blamed me, just like I blamed myself. If I was the enemy to her now, the reason her estranged friend was dead.

But she smiled again, and I pushed the thought out of my mind. Rachel had encouraged me to stay. She had invited me over.

She took another sip – her glass was already almost drained. 'I don't think I'll ever forgive her, you know.'

I gulped. 'For killing John?'

Rachel laughed bitterly. 'God, no,' she said. 'He deserved it.'

He didn't, my mind practically screamed. *We were all so terribly wrong.*

'For attacking you,' Rachel said.

My chest seized up, and the glass felt slippery in my hand.

Her eyes narrowed. 'I mean, she *did* attack you, right? That's what Maggie said.'

'Yes,' I said weakly. 'Yes, she did.'

'Vera was never good at knowing who to trust,' Rachel said. 'If she hadn't cut me out of her life, if she hadn't turned on you . . . if she'd leaned on her friends instead of lashing out in anger, maybe none of this would have happened.'

She stood suddenly. 'I have some cheese and olives in the fridge. Should I make up a plate?'

'Yes,' I said. I needed a moment to collect myself, to push Vera's pleading eyes out of my mind, to pray that one morning, they wouldn't be the first thing I saw upon waking.

'Where's the bathroom?' I asked.

'First door on the left,' Rachel said as she turned on her heel and headed to the kitchen.

Dusty followed me as I made my way down the hall. There was a door on the right and one on the left, and one at the end of the hall – probably Rachel's bedroom, the only door that was shut.

I closed the bathroom door behind me, leaving Dusty to wait in the hall like he always did. Her bathroom was decked floor to ceiling in all-white tile. Vera's blood, crimson against white, flashed into my mind, and I shook my head forcefully, trying to get the images out of my brain.

I leaned against the sink, half-afraid I might throw up. This had all been so pointless, so awful. John hadn't even been a bad person – it had been a rumor, a miscommunication, a child who didn't want to be slut-shamed – and yet it had triggered something unfathomable, one step after the next.

Vera killing him.

Me killing her.

I flicked on the faucet, splashing cold water on my face, then looked in the mirror. My eyes were nearly as baggy as Rachel's, my hair a mess. The few sips of wine I'd taken had already stained my lips. I had to pull myself together. This wasn't my fault.

Vera had tried to frame me. Vera had believed the rumors about her husband. Vera had caused this all.

Vera had been my best friend.

Drying my skin on Rachel's clean white hand towel, I opened the door, returning to the hall in time to see Dusty scratching at the shut door at the end of the hallway.

'Dusty, no,' I said, but before I could stop him, he'd gotten it open – it must not have been shut all the way – his furry body disappearing behind the door.

I took a few steps, then checked behind me. Rachel must still be in the kitchen.

Pushing the door open, I walked into her bedroom.

It was as clean and beautiful as the rest of her house, her bed covered in a white duvet edged in black. I swiveled my head, looking for Dusty, then saw an open door – her closet.

Inside, it was a mess, a welcome change from the rest of the place, hangers packed full of colorful dresses and tops, a dresser, its drawers half-open, already-worn clothing littering the few feet of floor space.

Dusty had tipped over a beat-up leather tote and was nosing around inside. 'Dusty, no!'

I leaned down, pulling him off it. In his mouth was a plastic baggie filled with what looked like doggie beef jerky – Rachel must have brought it over when she visited Maggie and Pepper. 'Bad dog,' I said, but I almost wanted to laugh. Dusty had always been a pro at sniffing out a treat, used to lose it when Davis brought something new home.

I snatched the baggie, set Dusty down, and righted Rachel's tote so it sat upright on the floor.

Then I paused.

On the top of the dresser, among tossed-aside jewelry and a pashmina scarf, was Vera.

Vera, the photo that had once hung on Rachel's wall. And shoved into one corner of the frame, a Polaroid of the two of them – smiling, happy, maybe drunk – like Vera and I had been so many times.

My eyes trailed down, and beneath the frame I saw it:

A padded yellow envelope.

It looked *just* like the one I'd found at Vera's. Same size. Same shape.

Unsealed.

Hands nearly shaking, I looked over my shoulder, making sure Rachel wasn't there.

It's nothing, I told myself. *It's probably nothing. So many envelopes look like this.*

Carefully, I opened it.

I saw the photographs first. All extremely up close, so close they almost seemed intimate, snatches of brown hair and a salt-and-pepper beard catching the light.

Then there, in front of them, a small scrap of paper.

And the familiar handwriting of a dead man.

I'm sorry about the other night. Please don't tell Vera.
I'll call you soon.

Fifty-One

What are you doing?'

I turned, clutching the envelope in both hands.

Rachel stood in the doorway to the closet, a thin steel knife in her right hand. She followed my gaze to the knife, then looked back at me. 'I was slicing up a plate of cheese,' she said, forcing a smile. 'I couldn't find you.' Her eyes caught on the envelope. 'What have you got there?'

'Nothing,' I said.

She only smiled wider. 'You better give that to me.' When I didn't move, she reached out her hand. 'Now, Lucy.'

I handed it over. Rachel glanced inside, checking its contents.

'How did you –' I asked, hardly able to make sense of what was happening. 'How did you get those?'

Rachel cleared her throat. 'It doesn't really matter, does it?'

I swallowed, my mouth suddenly dry, and Dusty began to whine. 'I don't understand.'

Rachel rolled her eyes. 'Vera gave them to me. Now, come on –'

I shook my head. 'Why would Vera – you weren't even friends with her anymore.'

'Don't grill *me* about my friendship with Vera,' Rachel said. 'Please.'

'What do . . . what do you mean?'

She laughed bitterly. 'Let's just say one of us was a shitty, backstabbing friend to her, and it sure as hell wasn't me. John was never in my bed, I can promise you that.'

I closed my eyes, shaking my head as I remembered waking that morning, drapes opened wide. 'You saw us?'

Her eyes bored into mine. 'If you didn't want anyone to see you betraying the friend you supposedly loved so much, maybe you should have pulled the curtains shut.'

A weight, heavy in my stomach. Poison in my blood. Rachel had been there, Rachel had seen us. Not Vera, but Rachel.

'You don't understand,' I said desperately. 'We were drunk. It was a stupid mistake. It was just a kiss.'

Rachel's eyebrows knitted together. 'Funny you hang on to a note like that, tucked away in your drawer, if it's just a harmless little accidental drunken kiss.'

I stared at her, this woman I'd thought was on my side, after everything. Vera would *never* have given those things to her. 'Did you – did you come into my house?'

There was a slight upturn at the corner of Rachel's mouth, etching her laugh lines deeper, wrinkling her foundation. As if she were proud she'd gone so long without being discovered.

'You had a key, didn't you? You had a copy you never gave back.'

'Jennifer was supposed to send the guy over to change the locks the day I was meant to move out, but when he didn't show up' – she shrugged – 'I didn't tell her. Honestly, I expected her to take care of it. Maybe she just forgot. A lot was going on with her during that time. Her daughter, you know.'

'But . . . but why?'

Rachel's hand twisted, the edge of the knife catching the light. Dusty whined again. 'I missed Vera, that was all. It wasn't a crime to go by your house occasionally, to keep tabs on her new best friend, the one who conveniently comes along after I've been shut out. I didn't like you, but still, I never expected to find you and John like *that*, curtains open for everyone to see.'

'No,' I said. 'I told you, it wasn't like that.'

'That's not what it looked like to me.'

I shook my head, trying desperately to understand. If Rachel had been coming into my house, that meant, it meant that . . .

'You took my knife,' I said. 'You took that photo of me, so it would look like . . .' I gasped. 'You took everything.'

Rachel tilted her head to the side. 'Lot of fucking good it did me.'

No no no. This couldn't be.

'It would have all worked perfectly if you hadn't ruined it,' Rachel said.

I took quick breaths, trying to understand, trying to get a grasp on the truth, but it felt like it was all suddenly slipping away. I chanced a look at Dusty, huddled by my feet, his tail down. Then I looked back at Rachel. Was it possible? Had it really been her all along?

'Vera had the knife,' I said. 'It was right there, in her things. She was going to frame me. She had an insurance policy. She had, she had . . .' My voice faltered, temporarily stunned by disbelief. 'It had to be her.'

'I gave her the knife, told her I found it when Maggie and I went over to get Dusty when you were in the hospital. I wanted her to see for herself just what kind of a friend you were.' Rachel's face went red. 'But now I know that she never even believed me. She was always trusting the wrong people. John. *You.*'

'It wasn't like that,' I said again. 'I loved her. I never meant to –'

'Oh, shut up,' Rachel snapped, lifting the knife so it hovered in front of her hip. 'You can fool the police, maybe you could even fool Vera, but you can't fool me. She deserved better than either of you. She was my best friend. She pulled me out of the worst time of my life, got me through my divorce, but when I tried to comfort her about her own shitty husband, she still chose *him*, the guy screwing around with a teenager, over me. And after all that, he still couldn't stop. John had to have you, too. Neither of you gave a shit about her. I'm the only one who ever looked out for her. I'm the only one who ever loved her.'

'That's not true. I loved Vera. More than anything.'

'Way to show it,' Rachel spit, lifting the knife even higher.

Fear etched its way through me as I stared at this woman.

It had been Rachel. Always Rachel. Never Vera. Always Rachel.

My heart pounded. What had I done? What the fuck had I done?

My stomach churned. I didn't want it to be true. But I knew, all the same, that it was.

The knife glinted in the light, twisting in her hand. I had to keep her talking. I had to buy myself time. 'But how did you . . . how did you actually kill him?' I asked. 'How did you know where he'd be?'

'You think they never made their Van Gogh joke with me around?' Rachel said. 'When I saw the three of you head out together in John's truck, I had this feeling. I drove to the hike, saw his truck there, waited in the parking lot. When the police cars came, it was obvious what you were up to. I headed to their cabin, which was conveniently unlocked, and waited for him to arrive. I knew Vera would never believe me, no matter how much proof I gave her. She was lovesick for John. I knew she'd never let him go, never let me take care of her, be the friend that she needed, unless he was actually dead.'

Rachel laughed bitterly. 'You should have seen the look on his face when he walked in and found me, when I stabbed him before he could so much as ask me what I was doing there. He never expected all his lies to catch up with him. He was so surprised, so tired from hiking off the trail for however many miles, he could hardly even fight back.'

My heart ached, and grief flooded my body. So that was it – those were John's last moments. Death at the hands of a former friend.

It was gruesome. Pointless. Unthinkable.

But I couldn't break down now. I had to keep her talking. Keep her focused on anything but the knife in her hand. 'Why did you break into my cottage in the middle of the night and leave that note for me? Why make it look like Sam did it?'

Rachel bit her lip. 'Because you were about to report your break-ins to the police. If they started digging, they'd figure out that the locks were never changed. I needed to point you to Sam, at least long enough for me to get the knife to Vera. Show her that Lucy, her supposed best friend, had killed her husband. I was saving the note and the photos for after you were arrested. I knew, once she saw them, learned that they were kept preciously in your underwear drawer, she'd realize you were never a friend to her at all. That my falling-out with her was just a blip, and I was right all along. Once she could truly see who John was, who you were, once he was no longer around to twist the truth, to gaslight her, she'd come back to me. We'd be friends again. Best friends, like we used to be.' She pressed her lips together, then gripped the envelope tightly. 'I haven't figured it out yet, but I will, trust me. I'll find a way to use this, to make the police finally understand exactly who you are, what you did to her.'

'You can't,' I said. 'I won't let you.'

Rachel laughed. 'What are you going to do, attack me like you did her? They won't buy the whole self-defense song and dance twice.' She studied me. 'She loved you, she gave you everything, and you destroyed her.'

'I'll call McKnight,' I said quickly. 'I'll tell him what you did. I'll find a way to prove it. I'll tell him you showed me the note, and you still have those photos somewhere. I'll tell him it was you who planted my underwear. I'll tell him everything . . .'

'Will you? If you do, if they for some reason believe your ever-changing story, what are you going to tell them about what you did to Vera?'

'I didn't – I didn't mean to – It was an accident.'

'No, Lucy, you very much did mean to. Because I *know* Vera, better than you ever will. She never got physical. Her words could be cutting enough. No way on earth did she attack you first. It was you, your anger, your inability to control yourself, just like your inability to keep your legs shut. You meant to kill her. Just like I meant to kill John.'

'No,' I said. 'No, I didn't.'

Her voice was suddenly crazed, her grip on the knife even tighter. 'I would never have done any of this if I knew you were so unhinged. I never thought you'd find the knife and kill her. At least when my anger boiled over, it was toward someone who actually deserved it. You killed Vera. You killed the best friend either of us ever had. Don't think it's over. Don't think people won't discover what you're capable of. I'll find a way to show them.' Rachel glanced at the knife in her hand, as if remembering it was there. 'Or fuck it, maybe I'll just punish you myself.'

I swallowed, heart racing, as Dusty whined again at my feet. So much had gone wrong, so many misunderstandings, so many destroyed lives, but I wasn't ready to lose mine, too. I had to do something. Something to knock her off balance, before she killed me, too.

'You were wrong,' I said.

Her eyes narrowed.

'You were wrong about John.'

'No I wasn't,' she said. 'He was trash. He didn't deserve her.'

I forced the words out, even though my heart was pounding, my palms sweating from fear.

'He wasn't trash,' I said. 'Claire told me the baby wasn't even his. She got pregnant by some guy her age, at a party in

Poughkeepsie. She was *embarrassed*. The guy never called her, and she didn't know his last name. She was afraid to go to her parents, she was afraid everyone would slut-shame her –'

'And you believe her?' Rachel snapped.

I kept going, forcing confidence into my voice. 'She went to the only adult she could trust. She went to John. *That's* why he looked up Planned Parenthood. *That's* why he found directions to the clinic. He did the right thing. He helped her when no one else would.'

'No,' Rachel said, but already, her grip on the knife was loosening, her hand hovering lower by her side. 'No, you're lying.'

'Why would I lie?' I asked. 'Don't you think I feel sick, knowing this all happened for nothing?'

'John fucked a teenager,' she said. 'Vera adored him, and he shit all over their marriage.'

'Only, he didn't,' I said. 'And the truth is – and you must know this, deep down – that if you'd only believed him, if you'd only ignored the rumors, none of this would have happened.'

Rachel stared at me, her grip faltering even more.

'If you'd been the friend Vera needed, if you'd supported her the way she needed to be supported instead of going straight to judging her husband, *none of this* would have happened. She wouldn't have cut you out. She wouldn't have befriended me. You wouldn't have killed John, and I wouldn't have hurt her. She'd be alive today if you'd done things differently.'

Rachel's face fell, her eyes welling, and I could see it, that a part of her, even one so very slight, believed me.

I could see it, clear as day. This was my chance.

I rushed forward, checking her with my shoulder.

Rachel staggered back, dropping the knife as her hands instinctively braced to break her fall.

I pounced, grabbing it quickly, and Dusty ran toward me. I scooped him up, holding him close.

She struggled to push herself up, but I waved the knife in front of me. 'Don't you fucking move,' I said as I backed away slowly, toward the door. 'You're a murderer,' I said. 'You killed him for nothing.'

I expected her to push herself up, come after me anyway, but Rachel only lifted her eyes to mine, and I swear I'd never seen anyone so sad, so broken.

'So are you.'

Fifty-Two

I didn't let go of the knife.

I rushed to the living room, Dusty whining as I held him close, looped my bag onto my shoulder, and ran, quick as I could, out to my car.

I didn't let go of it until I had Dusty in his crate, until my key was in the ignition, until I was pulling away from Rachel's house, leaving behind the woman who'd killed John, who wanted to kill me, too.

When I was at the corner, I rolled down the window, chucked her knife out the window, onto the street.

I sped through town, hardly knowing where I was going, but eventually, we were back at my cottage. I rushed inside, letting Dusty free, then slammed the door behind me, so hard it shook the bookshelf. Dusty scrambled away, hiding beneath the sofa, only his tail sticking out.

It was then that it fully hit me:

I had killed Vera for nothing. I had killed my best friend.

She'd done nothing but love me, and I'd killed her.

Deep within me, the hatch split open, only it was directed at me this time.

Me, a monster. Me, a killer.

My nostrils flared as I gasped for breath. I took two quick

steps, and before I could think to stop myself, before I could close and lock the hatch again, my hands were on the bookshelf. I jerked it, easily, like one of those moms lifting a car to save their baby, pinned beneath it. It clattered to the floor, wood cracking, its guts, its books, spilling out as Dusty whined. But it wasn't enough. It was never fucking enough. Pushing the sofa aside, I lifted up the coffee table, letting glasses slip off it, and overturned it so it smashed into the floor. In the kitchen, I grabbed plates, chucking them against the tile, against the window Davis had broken in the back door. I tore drapes from the windows, ripped sheets from the bed. Overturned a desk, knocked framed prints off the walls, breaking their glass as I sent them crashing onto the floor.

I undid it all, everything I'd worked so carefully to keep neat and tidy.

All the work I'd done to make sure I'd know it if Davis ever came here.

Only, it wasn't him I had to worry about. It was them. All of them.

It was me.

I screamed, grabbing the lamp from my nightstand, smashing it against the wall until the drywall split, filling the room with dust, until my arms were tired, until tears coursed down my cheeks, until I felt glass shards beneath my feet, until my socks turned bloody.

I had killed Vera, the woman who said she'd protect me.

I had murdered her, just as Rachel said.

I was worse, even, than I could have ever imagined. An uglier person than I'd ever known.

I lifted the lamp over my head and brought it, once more, against the wall, and as I did, I saw him.

I saw the look on Davis's face as I'd lifted that whiskey bottle, bringing it down, crashing, over his head, as I'd fully let the hatch open for the first time in years, decided I wasn't going to take his controlling bullshit, his mind games, his emotional manipulation, the bruises he left when I was sleeping – none of it – anymore.

I saw him fall to the floor of our apartment. I saw him passed out, unmoving. I saw myself, realizing what I'd done, that the bruises he'd given me had long faded, that I'd been too stupid, too ashamed, to capture any proof.

I saw myself rushing to the bathroom and lifting the bottle, smashing it into my own cheek. Taking a photo of my bruise when it had appeared the next day. I knew I'd broken an unspoken agreement between us. He called the shots, I followed the rules. I knew he'd want to punish me, I knew he'd want to destroy anything I still cared about, destroy me, but I knew that Davis put appearances above all. I knew that if he did find me, that photo would be my only chance to stop him . . .

I let the lamp clatter to the ground, shaking my head.

I couldn't put it off any longer. I had to leave now, before Rachel made her next move.

I rushed back into the living room, making my way through the destruction until I found my purse, tossed aside near the front door. Dusty was still whimpering, cowering beneath the sofa.

'I'm sorry, baby,' I said. 'We'll go soon.'

There was a knock at the door, jolting me.

Digging in my purse, I pulled out my phone, keyed in 911, ready to dial it if needed. Then I went to the bedroom, grabbed my dad's hammer, the only thing I had to protect myself.

Pulse pounding, mucus thick in my throat, I crept to the window, nudged back the drapes, expecting to see Rachel, to lift the hammer overhead if I had to . . .

But the phone, the hammer, clattered to the ground.

It wasn't Rachel.

It was Detective McKnight.

Fifty-Three

The cold air snapped at me as I stepped onto the porch and quickly shut the door behind me.

My heart beat furiously – had Rachel called McKnight so quickly, told him what she knew? That I'd killed Vera? That self-defense was a tenuous excuse, that Vera wasn't the type to attack? Not physically, at least.

McKnight nodded to the door.

'It's a wreck in there,' I said, spitballing. 'Dusty's been sick and, well, grief, you know.'

He shrugged. 'You're not cold?'

I finished buttoning my coat, which I'd slipped on quickly before opening the door. 'I'm fine. How can I help you?'

He cleared his throat and leaned against the side of my cottage, taking me in. It had stopped snowing, but the sun was on its way to setting soon, the air getting even cooler.

Finally, he stood up straight, pulled a folder out from beneath his arm. 'I hate to have to do this . . .'

My mouth went dry, any security I'd had quickly slipping away. *This isn't over.*

I swallowed, knowing that these were the last moments of freedom I'd have. I thought of Dusty, inside, probably still hiding beneath the sofa. Who would take care of him when I was gone? Who would love him like I did?

McKnight sighed, sending a plume of steam into the air, before shifting the folder to his other hand. 'See, the thing is, it always bothered me, when it turned out there was no record of you having ever lived in Brooklyn. Your reasoning made sense, but it was one of those things that stuck out to me. Like a rock in your shoe. Drives you nuts.'

I swallowed, hardly knowing what to say, how to defend myself now. It was too late. He knew too much. Knew I was a liar. Knew it all.

When I didn't speak, McKnight went on. 'Believe me, it took some time to figure it out. I thought I was being paranoid, but a lead came through, clearing up a lot of the questions I had. The truth always comes out eventually. Doesn't it?'

I licked my lips, waiting for the rest of it. *Get it over with,* I wanted to tell him. *Just put me out of this misery. Take me away.*

McKnight nodded to the folder. 'Before I give you this, I want to tell you that I understand why you did what you did. I've been on the force going on twenty years. I know that there are some things – some people – who are impossible to put behind you.'

My eyes narrowed, because I didn't understand. Why was he being kind, empathetic, even? Was it all just an act?

Just do it, I begged again. *Finish me.*

He shifted his weight. 'I really don't think anyone would blame you, if they knew the whole story.'

I looked down at my feet. I didn't understand him. I didn't understand any of this.

'Miss Williams,' McKnight said, only the tiniest hint of a question in his voice. 'Olivia Williams.'

I looked up at him, then blinked slowly, confirming. I took a deep breath, waiting for the rest, for him to slide all the pieces together . . .

'I know your ex was abusive,' McKnight said. 'And I know that's why you didn't want to give me your real name.' He squeezed tighter at the folder in his hands. 'And look, I'm going to edit the official reports, but I'm not going to make a thing of this in the press. My supervisor is already breathing down my neck after we bungled it with Mr Alby. But even so, the law is the law, and I wouldn't be doing my job if I didn't give you this.'

He pressed the folder into my hands and I slowly opened it, my eyes flitting over the paper, trying to make it make sense.

'Legally, you can't give a false name to an officer, but you're lucky. "False personation"' – he pointed to the official charge, printed in blackest ink – 'it's only a misdemeanor. Class B, which means it's up to my discretion whether to arrest you or allow you to wait out your court date at home. I spoke with Jennifer Moon – she says you've elected to extend your rental agreement another month, so I don't believe you're a flight risk. But it *is* a criminal charge. You'll want to procure a lawyer. The court date is printed there at the bottom.'

I nodded. 'Okay.'

'My best advice? Plead out. Explain your situation. Collect any evidence you have of the abuse. Come down to the station when you're ready, and report the break-in by your ex. With all the extenuating circumstances, most likely scenario is going to be a fine and community service.'

I looked back up at him, searching his face, waiting to see if there was anything more. I could hardly believe that, after everything, there wasn't.

McKnight offered me a weak smile. 'And don't ever do it again. If you're in danger, if you're afraid to give your real name, tell an officer that. We'll do everything we can to protect you.'

'Okay,' I said. 'Thank you.'

He nodded. 'Goodbye, Miss Williams.'

I lifted my chin. 'Goodbye.'

Calm as I could, I went back into my cottage, shutting the door behind me. 'Dusty,' I called, and after a minute, he came out from under the sofa.

I looked around at my destroyed home. 'I'm sorry about that,' I said to him. 'I'm sorry about everything.'

I lifted up my purse and retrieved my wallet.

Stilling my hands, I pulled out my New York State ID. Lucy King. Born October 12, 1992. Brown hair, brown eyes. Five foot six. Organ donor. Address not all that far from here, in Poughkeepsie.

I fingered the ID, then shoved it into my back pocket, zippered the wallet shut, and headed to the bedroom. Kicking shards of glass out of the way, I pushed the bed aside and, using a piece of wood split from the remnants of my dresser, worked to pry up the floorboard.

Splinters had pierced my fingers by the time I got it open.

I retrieved my passport and my credit cards, and then, there it was.

It was faded from years of use. Years of going to dive bars with Ellie. Of flights to Miami with Davis. Of opening my first New York City bank account and getting my apartment in Bushwick.

For eight years, it had been well used, well loved.

Olivia Williams. Born April 16, 1991. Brown hair. Brown eyes. Five foot seven. Of course, everyone always called me Liv, or even Livvie – or occasionally just L. Olivia had served me well, until she hadn't. Until all had changed. I lifted up the license, setting it carefully aside.

McKnight had done his research – he was right about that – and he'd uncovered one piece of my story, but what I could hardly believe – it surprised me so much, it made my hands shake just thinking about it – was that he'd stopped there.

He hadn't pushed further. He hadn't uncovered the whole truth.

My heart surged as I reached for the last piece of plastic, the original.

Lucy King was blown, Olivia Williams had a court date, but this one – she was still free.

From Washington State: Stephanie Ostlund, the name I was born with.

I opened my wallet, and for the first time in years, I slipped Stephanie back in.

Fifty-Four

The evergreens must have stood fifty feet tall, guarding the sides of Snoqualmie Pass like Tolkien's Ents. Dusty whined mercilessly. Five days – and nearly three thousand miles – of driving had done little to get him used to the car. I tapped my phone to life, a new one I'd picked up at an Apple Store in Minneapolis, after retrieving the cash from my bank account. Glossy black and not cracked for the first time in what felt like ages. Fuck you, too, Davis.

Google Maps told me I was less than an hour away from Seattle, but I knew that already. Once you reached the pass, once you smelled pine trees sweet like Christmas, followed the winding bend of road, you were nearly there.

A pickup tailgated me. I got into the right lane, merging carefully. Reminding myself that even if I did get stopped, the plates wouldn't be linked to me. I'd made a quick pit stop before leaving town to switch my plates with the ones on the car Vera had procured during her trip to the city, the one that still sat, undiscovered by the police, a mile from the cabin – turns out, it had come into play after all.

The pickup sped past, and I changed lanes again.

It's not like I'd ever stopped wanting to be Stephanie, not like one day I woke up and said, *Let me change who I am,* like trying on a new outfit. Snap.

And trust me, it wasn't the slut-shaming that did it, either, that damn video taken and blasted across all the social networks. Even though it had circulated like wildfire all over campus, I could handle that. As well as the taunts. And the wolf whistles. And the announcements, from seemingly every guy at school – that their laps were cold and could I please warm them up if I had a minute? The awful sounds as they pretended to suck. Those things I could handle.

It was him I couldn't. Him, with his graphic T-shirt and his rosy cheeks and the earnest look in his eyes, every fucking day at the coffee shop on campus. Jordan Exley, telling me he was *so sorry* this had happened to me, that it was awful what everyone was saying, that if I ever needed someone to listen, he was there. That we should really go get coffee or tea sometime. Talk.

He came every day, and each time he politely asked me out, and I politely said no, because if I snapped, I'd lose my job, my work-study. I'd be fucked.

Every day he looked at me with such pity as I made his extra-hot almond milk latte. Every day he told me that he was a good listener and I should give him a chance.

Every day, until I couldn't listen to him anymore.

Every day, until that one day I let myself fully open the hatch. I reached out to hand him the latte, and he tilted his head to the side, said: 'Really? *You're* going to reject *me?*'

Without even realizing it, my hand was crunching up, popping the plastic lid off. I was throwing the drink – almond milk burned to one hundred eighty degrees – toward his smug little latte-loving face.

His scream was instant, and so was the sweet charred smell of burning skin, and it was only due to some extremely quick thinking on my manager's part, immediately dousing him with water from the sink, that the burns weren't worse than they were. It was only due to my awful aim that his whole face wasn't marred – only his neck and about two inches of his chin.

It was only because he prided himself on being spiritual that he, against his parents' strongest wishes, didn't press charges against me.

It didn't matter to the school – or my reputation. I was expelled almost instantly, three-quarters into completing my degree. What's more, articles were written. In the school newspaper, but other places, too. Blogs. Shitty news sites. Anyone who could gain a click or two from gossip, from a story of a skanky college girl who'd come unhinged. My name was fairly uncommon, something I'd been pleased with, when I'd decided to be a journalist, but after that day, it only made it easier to google me, instantly learn my whole sordid story.

My parents, they should have been on my side. They should have at least cared about the harassment or the video – or any of the extenuating circumstances. But they didn't. I had done what they'd always feared. I'd let my anger get the best of me.

It had been a problem since I could remember. A push on the playground. A fight with my piano teacher. A tirade in middle school. Anger there, beneath the surface, always. Therapy had kept it at bay all through high school, and a counselor had taught me to do the visualizations, imagining a hatch, shutting it tight, locking it with a key, and only opening it under the proper circumstances. Boxing classes. An invigorating run around the high school track. An occasional scream into my pillow.

But to my parents, it didn't matter that I'd held it all back for so long, that I'd learned to adapt to a world where anger – or female anger, at least – wasn't allowed. Every day that I'd kept the hatch closed no longer counted once I'd gone and done this. All my mom could say, over and over again, was: *Why'd you have to go and ruin your future? After all we tried to do for you.* And my dad's version, a bit more succinct: *Somehow, after everything, you found a way to fuck it all up.* Then he'd reminded me that I should have been happy that someone wanted to date me at all, with that video circling around.

It's not that my parents weren't loving. They were, in their way. They'd made me soup when I was sick, taken me to the park, enrolled me in art classes, found a therapist for my issues – all of it.

Only, I was sure, after that day, that it had all been conditional. They'd wanted me to be their perfect daughter, and they'd spent loads of money trying to contain the monster inside me.

Once it was out, for everyone to see, they were as disgusted with me as I was with myself.

I shook my head, pushing Stephanie aside for a moment as I made another turn, deeper into the pass, the trees even thicker now as Dusty whined on.

My parents had seen the worst of me, they had judged me, and their love for me, it had seemed to dissipate completely – I could see it in their eyes – so I left.

I emptied the trust my grandmother had set up for me before she died, the one I'd been saving for moving after college – twenty thousand bucks – and went to New York. I knew it would be impossible to get a job in my state, especially in a competitive field like journalism – any potential employer who googled me would see that I'd been expelled, be able to read article after article about me – I knew, more than anything, that I needed a fresh start. I was a computer science minor. It wasn't difficult to purchase a new identity on the dark web if you knew where to look. The full package: ID, health insurance info, Social Security number and everything, it only cost a couple thousand bucks, less than the price of a used car. It wasn't foolproof, but if you were careful, if you didn't try to steal money or open a ton of credit cards, it was easy enough to get by on someone else's name.

In the city, in a roach-infested room-share in Williamsburg that cost nine hundred a month and was presented to me as a very good deal, I started my new life.

I hadn't intended to lie about my parents, only my roommate, she couldn't stop going on and on about hers, how they were so supportive of her move to New York, how their dream was for her to be an artist, how they were coming to visit from Kansas in just another month.

When she'd asked me about mine, I'd blurted it out quickly: 'They're gone.'

'Oh my god,' she'd said, her bottom lip jutting into a pout. 'You're all alone?'

I nodded, understanding exactly what she'd assumed, not daring to correct her. It was a better story, I realized, than what I knew was true – that they didn't love me, wouldn't look at me the same way anymore.

Eventually, questions were asked, and a story bloomed from nothing. They'd died in an accident, during college. In a way, it hadn't been entirely untrue. They *had* died a little that day I tossed almond milk in Jordan Exley's face. I had, too. What we'd had as a family had died, at least.

In Brooklyn, I carried on as I would have if I'd graduated. I made up a résumé for the delightfully common and difficult-to-google Olivia Williams, including a journalism degree from my would-be alma mater, University of Washington, and an internship at the indie newspaper there, the *Stranger*.

Most editors – so busy worrying about the death of journalism and the impending loss of their jobs – didn't even check. They believed what I had printed on eggshell paper from the copy shop on Bedford Avenue. I'd taken most of the courses, I told them I always traveled with my pocket copy of *The Elements of Style*, and they bought it.

There was one woman who didn't believe me, that bitch at

Vogue – it had taken every bone in my body to keep the hatch shut during that interview – but she was only one editor. There were others. There would always be more people to lie to, to fool. Honestly, I would have stayed Liv my whole life if I could have.

Only then, there was Davis.

Davis, who turned my fresh start into a veritable living hell. Who punished me, physically, mentally, and emotionally. It was no wonder it eventually got to me in a way I couldn't control.

It was after he showed up at my hotel in May, Ellie in tow, that I realized I might need to get creative. After he told me he'd never, ever let me leave, that if I did, he'd find a way to take away everything I ever cared about, including Dusty, that I began to realize I might have to start over . . . again.

I was all set to leave, quietly in the night, Lucy King's brand-new ID tucked into my wallet. But then, just a couple of days before I'd planned to go, Davis had come at me, after a dinner out, going on and on, berating me about all the guys I'd flirted with at the bar we'd gone to after, guys I hadn't so much as looked at, that paranoid prick.

And like that, the hatch opened again.

I grabbed the bottle of good whiskey we always kept on our counter and . . .

Smash.

My first instinct had been to dial 911, but I ended the call quickly, tossing my phone against the brick wall. Then I'd used the bottle of whiskey to give myself the bruise, and I'd left him passed out on the hardwood floor of our apartment. I'd taken Dusty, taken my bags, and gone.

I'd spent those first few weeks half-afraid he'd find me and half-afraid of something even worse.

That the police would find me. That I just might have left him for dead.

That's why the bruise was necessary. Self-defense, if anyone ever asked, since I'd been too stupid to capture any of the bruises before. Blackmail, if he insisted on trying to control me still – that was, if he didn't kill me first.

I took another turn, leaving the pass, and the trees, behind. I was getting closer to the city, and the sky was bluer than it should be in Seattle and speckled with clouds.

I knew it now, clear as the sky above me. I never should have offered to help Vera and John. Only, I'd still been afraid Davis would come after me. I was afraid my haphazard attempt at blackmail had only made him madder. And more than anything, I couldn't bear the thought of starting over again. Of losing the people I loved so dearly. The people who I'd naively trusted to love me more unconditionally than my parents.

Of course, I'd managed to lose them both anyway.

Like my dad said, I somehow found a way to fuck it up.

It was another fifteen minutes before I pulled up to the street on the edge of North Seattle, before I found myself staring at the yellow siding, only lightly weathered, and the white trim, which looked recently painted.

I pulled the car into the driveway, behind a newer-model Subaru than they'd had before.

Leaving Dusty in the car, I climbed the stone steps with heavy feet.

I took a deep breath. I was done with all that now.

Lucy's friends were dead. Olivia's friends were well behind her. And that wasn't even taking into account the legal obligations, the court date I would never, ever, *ever* show up for.

In some ways, I had been pummeling toward rock bottom for years, but now I had finally, indisputably, hit it.

I didn't want to lie anymore. I didn't want to be that person. I wanted to find a way not to think about all the awful things I'd already done.

In the aftermath of all that had happened in college, I'd believed my parents didn't love me anymore – that they never would again. But I knew how much I'd missed them over the years, in spite of myself. I knew how much I craved my family even if I hated them for how they'd reacted. It had been impossible not to wonder if I had blown up my life too quickly, too easily. If they would have come around had I given them a chance.

So now I was giving them another chance, and I prayed, against all odds, that they'd take it. I prayed that I'd been wrong, that their love hadn't been conditional after all.

I rapped on the door three times.

After a moment, it swung open, and it smelled, suddenly, of turkey tetrazzini, the same recipe I'd made for Vera and John one night, the one Davis had loved, too.

Her hair was all gray now, her lips coated in pale pink, her earrings pearlescent and heart-wrenchingly familiar.

Behind her, he appeared, his eyes widening at the sight of me. His hair was whiter, his wrinkles deeper – a map across his face of the years I'd missed.

'Stephanie?' he asked.

'My god,' she said. 'It's you.'

I swallowed back my pride, my lies, and the anger I knew was always lying in wait, bubbling steadily and eager to come out if I let it, and I stared at this woman, fifty-six years old now and beautiful as ever. At this man, looking at me like I was no more than a child.

'Hi, Mom,' I said. 'Dad. It's me.'

Acknowledgments

A huge thanks to all the people who made this book possible.

To my incredible agent, Elisabeth Weed, thank you for believing in this story through every twist and turn. Your storytelling know-how and wild, spur-of-the-moment brainstorming sessions made the book what it is today. You are the absolute best person to have in my corner, and you've given me the perfect gift, the ability to do what I love full-time. And thanks so much to all of your team who gave me additional reads, especially Hallie Schaeffer, whose early notes were spot-on.

To Margo Lipschultz, Sally Kim, and the entire Putnam team, I can't thank you all enough for falling in love with this story and fighting for it. Margo, from our very first phone call, I knew we were a perfect editorial match. Your notes and guidance helped me uncover Lucy's voice and her purpose in this story – you got exactly what I was going for and helped me bring it all to life. And enormous thanks for reading this book again and again (and again!) as I tried to find a way to balance the production schedule with a new baby.

To Joel Richardson and everyone at Michael Joseph, I am so thankful for all the editorial and marketing work across the pond. Joel, you helped me set the pace of this novel and were instrumental in seeding twist after twist. After personally loving so many British thriller writers, it's such an honor to know this book has a home on your shelves.

To Jenny Meyer and your rock-star team, I am beyond thankful for the care you've taken in pitching this book around the globe – each sale has been such a thrill. Thank you so much for helping get it into the hands of as many readers as possible.

To Michelle Weiner and everyone at CAA, all I can say is our phone calls have been some of the craziest pinch-me moments of my writing career. Thank you so much for working so hard to find this book a great TV home. And to Marc Webb, CBS Television, Mark Martin, and the entire team at Black Lamb, I am so happy that the book has landed in your very capable hands.

No one writes in a vacuum, and I am forever grateful to my two superstar beta readers, Andrea Bartz and Danielle Rollins. Andi, thanks for all the many, many park walks and frantic phone calls it took to make this story what it is today. Danielle, your eye for plot and pacing is unmatched. And to everyone else who read the book in an early form, including Robin Bruns Worona, Kate Lord, and Julia Bartz, I am so thankful.

I've been lucky to have been surrounded by people who encouraged me to write all my life. A very special thank you to my parents, who never tried to get me to pursue a more practical career and have been my biggest cheerleaders with each new development. And an extra special thank you to my sister, Kimberly, whose guidance and notes have been instrumental in nearly every one of my books.

Finally, to Thomas, for all your support and believing in me all these years, and for taking the leap of buying a house with me in beautiful upstate New York – there is no way I could have written this book without you. To my number-one coworker, my dog, Farley, you are the best emotional support a writer could ever have. And to Eleanor, thank you for coming into our lives exactly when you did.